I0606633

# ON A CROOKED TRACK

Karen Myers

# ON A CROOKED TRACK

## The Chained Adept: 4

# Karen Myers

PERKUNAS PRESS • Tyrone, Pennsylvania

# On a Crooked Track

The Chained Adept: 4

Perkunas Press
2635 Baughman Cemetery Road
Tyrone, Pennsylvania 16686
USA

PerkunasPress.com

Author contact: KarenMyers@KarenMyersAuthor.com
KarenMyersAuthor.com

Cover and Illustrations: Jake Bullock, http://ohbullocks.com
The Kigali, Zannib, Rasesni, Ellech, Ndant, and Aitzikoa
    languages: Damátir Ando,
    http://damatir-ando.tripod.com/conlangs.html



Trade Paperback
ISBN-13: 978-1-62962-045-9
ISBN-10: 1-6296204-5-9

Library of Congress Control Number: 2017930027

# ALSO BY KAREN MYERS

## The Hounds of Annwn

To Carry the Horn
The Ways of Winter
King of the May
Bound into the Blood

*Story Collections*
Tales of Annwn

*Short Stories*
The Call
Under the Bough
Night Hunt
Cariad
The Empty Hills

## The Chained Adept

The Chained Adept
Mistress of Animals
Broken Devices
On a Crooked Track

## Science Fiction Short Stories

Second Sight
Monsters, And More
The Visitor, And More

See <u>KarenMyersAuthor.com</u> for the latest information.

# CONTENTS

# CHAPTER 1

Wood everywhere—the solid pier on which Penrys was trying to find her land legs, the ship moving gently beside it in the harbor at Ellech after almost two months at sea, and the entire forest of a city spread out before her, topped by the clusters of signals towers like groves of mountain spruce trees.

It smelled like home, all that wood—weathering away in the buildings, or freshly cut in the long arm of the hoist that was even now swinging cargo off the ship, or burning as firewood and flavoring the crisp spring breeze.

Home was in the woolens everyone wore, retentive of the odor of hard work and dinners long past. It was in the hair and beard dressings of the dock workers, leavened by the exotic aromas of some of the southern cargo, destined for the perfume manufactories.

Penrys inhaled deeply, feeling the rightness of the environment deep inside her. She hoped they'd have a few days to spend in the harbor cities at the base of the two rivers before moving upriver to Tavnastok so she could get started doing her research at the Collegium, but that would depend on her mentor, Vylkar, visible on the wharf at the end of the pier making arrangements for their cargo.

Najud and Munraz were having troubles of their own adjusting to an unmoving surface. "Come on," she said, picking up her pack. "The sooner you start walking, the easier it will get."

"Does it work that way for you?" Munraz asked, gamely lifting his own gear.

"Don't know—I've only read about it." She chuckled at his outraged expression. "I've never been on a ship before, not at sea. Never been in Stokemmi, either."

Striding off down the pier, she called over her shoulder, "Let's go explore."

She made a game of anticipating exactly where her feet would meet the planks until her body adjusted to the change of terrain and she stopped stumbling. Her footing wasn't improved by her hard-soled boots, donned for the first time in a while after the bare feet or soft shoes of shipboard life.

The three of them clattered to a stop behind Vylkar. Two piles were accumulating before him as they came off of the hoists. The larger one, goods destined for trade here in the city, were to be stored in the warehouse used by the Collegium for its own supplies. Cargo handlers were stowing the horse packs onto two wagons to move them there, and the draft horses waited patiently, their breath visible in the chilled air.

The laborers joked with each other as they worked, swapping insults that would bring a blush to a hardened campaigner. Many ships were in harbor, and this wharf, one of several, was busy, filled with people earning a living and working up a sweat doing it.

It was noisier, smellier, and far more vivid than the river harbor at Yenit Ping, and Penrys wondered what Najud and Munraz made of it. Except for the sea at their back and the size of the city, it could almost be Tavnastok, two hundred and fifty miles upstream from the mouth of the Lodentaf, just visible as a gap in the wharves far to the west along the shoreline. She'd seen sights like these there, running errands for the Collegium.

Their personal bags went into a hired two-wheeled pony cart. They would walk alongside it toward the center of Stokemmi to wherever they took rooms.

"We've fallen into the hands of talking bears," Najud muttered. "Loud, smelly bears. Great big tall ones."

"I warned you about the beards." Penrys surveyed the wharves with a stranger's eye and noted how many people were clearly natives (most of them), male (most of those), and bearded (all but the children). The few men of other nations, mostly officers from some of the ships in harbor, looked astonishingly youthful with their shaven faces.

"You'll find plenty of foreigners here, and they shave," she told them. "I was never sure if that was out of fastidiousness, or because they couldn't raise a competitive beard and were afraid to try."

Some wore their beards in braids, or loose down their chest. Others had neatly trimmed, no-nonsense specimens. And here and there, especially for the citizens who'd come down from the city on business, elaborate grooming and stiffening fashions were on display.

"Do they breed for it?" Munraz asked, in a hushed tone that said he wouldn't be surprised by an affirmative answer.

"Hard to say. The boys compete with pride to see who can sprout first, and survey their fathers and older brothers with envy. Maybe the less hairy ones have had a harder time finding a bride, and so they're all bearded now."

She smiled at the open alarm on his face. "Don't worry, you can keep a beardless face and foreign clothing—no one will think it strange. Foreigners mean money, here—trade and business and interesting foods."

Najud looked unconvinced. She wondered if he thought he had to cultivate a beard to measure up, and then she wondered if he could. She'd seen him in stubble, but she'd never seen a bearded Zan, just the somewhat patchy results of a couple of months of neglect. That would never work here, in Ellech, and they didn't expect to be here any longer than that. Better to choose a different display of manhood.

*Ah, but how do you tell a man that?* She suppressed a smile.

"What will you wear?" Najud asked her. "Ellech or Zannib clothes?'

And then it hit her. When Najud met her, she wore Ellech clothing, the same sort of work clothes she'd worn for the three years since Vylkar found her. The only years she had memory of— all her life, as it were. She'd adopted local clothing in *sarq*-Zannib, and her life was with Najud now. She'd never expected to return to Ellech, so the matter had never come up.

"Zannib," she said, firmly.

Najud eyed her skeptically. "You should use Ellech styles if you like, might be a nice change for you. Might make it easier to work with the Collegium."

She wavered. "Well, maybe—I'll find something I can wear at need. But with my foreign face, I'll never pass for Ellech anyway." Unlike the tall, fair Ellechen people, Penrys was brown of hair and eyes, round of face, and below middle height. The two men with her had the olive skin and loose curly black hair of a typical Zan.

Only Vylkar, just concluding the cargo assignments, looked at home with his tidy graying scholar's beard. He turned now to survey his companions.

"Ready?" he asked.

They added their packs to the cart so they could walk un-encumbered beside it. The small piebald cob leaned his shoulders into the load, and the carter clucked encouragingly from his well worn perch behind him.

"Is it far?" Munraz asked. He was tall, for a Zan, and not quite at his full growth yet, but Vylkar topped him by almost a head.

"We'll stop at the trade hall in the central square, up near the bridge, and take rooms nearby for the night. You'll want to see the trade goods properly stowed, too, before looking at what's left of the day's markets."

Vylkar glanced over at Penrys, and added, "You'll find it not too different from Tavnastok, I think."

She shook her head. "In Stokemmi, with no deadline, no errands for others, and my own money in my pocket—I think I'll find it very different indeed." She could feel Najud's amusement through the light link she held with him.

The cartwheels rumbled up the wooden road, adding their bit to the resonant din of all the traffic to and from the wharves. Their own footsteps were drowned out.

The harborside warehouses and trade offices along their route gave way to a sort of seamen's district of rooming houses, taverns, and shops, with open street markets visible down some of the cross streets. The faces on the streets there were of many nations, including the bearded Ellech, but she looked in vain for anyone resembling herself or the Zannib beside her. The smells of the food were of as many nations as the men, and her own stomach made its presence known as she inhaled sharply.

They saved their breath as the street continued to climb, not very steeply, away from the harbor, and gradually the main core of the city began to grow around them like a maturing forest—first the many craft shops, most of them integrated into the first floor of the dwellings they passed, and then some of the craft halls and larger markets. Up ahead, the street opened up even as the buildings gained in height, rising to three and four stories, or even higher. The decorative flourishes carved into the doors were matched by touches of wooden inlay for variety, or even painted color and gilt.

Traffic in both directions was brisk, but no one gave their party much of a look, even with the exotic Zannib robes they wore.

Penrys displayed her chain openly. When she'd left Ellech a year and a half ago, she was the only chained wizard anyone knew of—a seemingly unique and local specimen.

That had all changed, drastically. Her chain meant nothing to this crowd, but it was the reason she was here—to chase down a possible lead on who might have been involved in the creation of dozens of wizards like her, chained wizards, from all nations, scattered where they didn't belong about four years ago, with no knowledge of who they'd been before.

Two months of shipboard speculation were past, and now it was time to get to work.

*There are wizards here, lots of them.*

Penrys smiled at Najud's startled thought.

*I warned you. Ellech, land of wizards, they say.*

She spoke aloud. "So many wizards, that most of them earn a living just like any other craft, and the craft is large and varied."

A shop on their left provided her with an example. "See the power-stone on the sign, there, over the door? Cradled between two hands?"

Munraz nodded, conserving his breath for the long uphill walk. They couldn't stop—the horses pulling the wagons behind them couldn't afford to lose their momentum.

"That's a power shop. The wizards there, they recharge power-stones for other people. Power-stones are embedded in all sorts of devices, and non-wizards can't renew the power in them without help. So you can either bring your device here, or someone from the shop will come to you. For regular businesses they set up a schedule."

Vylkar added, "There's a place like this every few blocks, and more in the industrial districts. But once you get out of the cities, well—not many powered devices in use outside a wizard's household. Though that's been changing, over the last several years. More wizards of a middling level getting an education, more power-stones—means more devices and wider usage. No turning back to the old days, I keep telling my colleagues."

He chuckled. "The Kigaliwen are in for a surprise once their new wizard guilds settle down and start becoming productive."

Looking down at Penrys, he said, "I overheard Najud's question. You'll get further with Ellech clothing if you want to do research and interview people. It'll reassure them about your intentions. And your rank—blues, now, mind you. No more greens. First stop," he told her, and turned back to concentrate on the climb.

*Blues!* Penrys glanced at Vylkar's robes, the dark purple of a senior council member. He'd worn them in Yenit Ping, as a representative of Ellech there, but they'd been packed away for travel until today. The sleeves stopped well short of the wrist, giving free rein to the under-layer, a lightweight wool knit tunic to turn away the spring chill.

The informal robe fell to mid-calf, and hung open for ease of movement, but she'd seen his formal robes before, the floor length belted versions he wore in his official business. Most of the staff at the Collegium wore blues, and the rest of the robes varied between visitors in borrowed greens and students in shades of yellows and reds. Reds for the youngest, the least able to control themselves.

She'd been too old to be classed as a student when Vylkar placed her there, and her mind too blank for wizardry ranking, so Vylkar had argued for greens, during her three-year stay, since she was clearly a wizard of some power, whatever the damage was that stripped her of memory.

Penrys mulled over the statement Vylkar wanted to make with the choice of color. Blues were reserved for wizards as members of their institution, which was in her case the Collegium, where they were bound in a few days. But was she a member? She was committed now to Zannib, with Najud. She was still a visitor, and green made no comment about her rank, other than declaring her beyond her student years.

*He knows what he's doing. But do I agree with it?* She bit her lip, and watched her footing as the cart creaked beside her.

## CHAPTER 2

The street leveled off for a block or so and then opened up ahead. The cob pulling the cart turned left and walked far enough along the edge of the square for the two wagons behind to do the same before all the drivers stopped to let their horses catch their breath from the long climb.

Penrys dodged around the cart to get an unobstructed view of the entire grand plaza, the Stone Square, the center of Stokemmi. It extended for a distance of four blocks on each side, on level ground, across a stone-paved surface. The road from the docks had led them to the middle of the southern side. The far side held institutional buildings she didn't recognize, but on the right, she thought one long colonnaded front might mark the exchange, and on the far left, she saw the blue pennant and second story open porch of the wizards' guild hall, familiar to her as the subject of many illustrations back in the Collegium.

The buildings around the square were of similar heights—four or even five floors high—but at ground level, many were occupied by restaurants and shops, everywhere but the side directly across from her. It was too early for dinner, but she turned her head to seek the appetizing scent of broiled meat somewhere nearby.

Stone buildings were not unknown in Ellech—the Collegium was built of stone, for the greater safety of its books—but the Stone Square and its immediate environs were the greatest concentration of stone-built structures in the country, outside of some of the factories.

*After Kigali, I shouldn't be impressed, but for Ellech, this is quite a sight.* Penrys noted the massive nature of the stonework, as if the architects hadn't trusted the strength of an unfamiliar material. Where there were arches, they suggested the shapes of tree branches, in ornamentation if not in actual curve. In fact, all the decorative carving used the vocabulary of plants—leaves, flowers, and trees. She realized, looking back, that it had been the same at the Collegium, as though the stone buildings were just forests in a different medium.

*In Kigali, they used stone as stone. Here, it's stone as trees.* How surprising she'd never noticed it before.

Najud and Munraz joined her, and Vylkar explained the sight to them all. "Across from us are the buildings of the Great Council and the Governor's Seat, the nation's leadership. In the corner, you see the Magistrate's building, for the city of Stokemmi itself."

"We're going to be staying over there"—he waved at the wizard's guild hall—"but first we have to get our goods stowed away. I suggest…" He looked them over and pointed to the left. "Najud, you go with the wagons to the guild warehouse on the west side and make sure everything is done to your liking. I'll take the cart and Munraz with me and arrange for our stay at the guild hall, then we'll come meet you at the warehouse and finish up there."

"You," he said, turning to Penrys, "should go to Redenchek's over there and get your robes. I want you in formal blues tonight for dinner, like any Ellech wizard returned home from her travels." He pointed to a shop at the near end of the left side of the Stone Square, but he hardly needed to. The sign over the door was enough—they were the legendary outfitters for the wizards in the capital. "When you're ready, and not before, you can meet us at the guild hall."

He raised a quizzical eyebrow at her, and she nodded. The gold in her pockets in the form of Kigali coins would be enough, and the exchange was just across the square if they had any reservations about it.

She stepped out of the way of the wagons, and Najud winked at her as he moved off with them. *You sure he was never your father? Acts like one. Why blue?*

She explained, and he rolled his eyes. *Too bad—I liked you in those worn out, ratty old work clothes I met you in. Of course, I like you even better without them on.*

*Stop that! You never know who might be listening.*

He winked at her anyway, and she could feel the heat rising in her cheeks as she stepped away with the cart to accompany Vylkar and Munraz partway down the left side of the Stone Square, until they abandoned her at Redenchek's shop.

"Perhaps a band for the hair in a matching blue?"

The tailor assigned to Penrys gestured to a display of ribbons, but she shook her head, with difficulty restraining her hands from rising to check that her ears remained covered by her shoulder-length hair. The last thing she needed was to expose her dark fur-covered ears, shaped like a fox's. All the chained wizards she'd met had them, and the why was as much of a mystery as the chains themselves.

She was here to follow a trail that might give her some answers, she reminded herself, not to take up some task as a wizard newly come to her blues, preening herself in her new robes.

"No, thank you." She looked over the pile of clothing that had accumulated in the course of the last hour. Both the informal and formal robes had required shortening to accommodate her less-than-Ellech height, but the fit of the layers worn under the robes was straightforward enough. The tunics for working clothes, rightly speaking, should also contain the blue, though it needn't be solid, and they would need to be shortened, as well. Shirts, undergarments, and even shoes presented no difficulties, the latter provided from the separate establishment next door.

"I require both robes and the matching items immediately—I intend to wear them tonight in place of the clothes I entered in." She eyed the discarded Zannib garments with regret. "I can return tomorrow for the rest, and for my original clothing."

"That will take just a few minutes, *rerri*. Rather than put you to the trouble of returning, shall we deliver it all to you at the guild hall?"

"Delivery would be more convenient—thank you. I'm part of Vylkar's party there."

He nodded and went off to make the arrangements. Penrys walked out of the measuring room in the shirt, sweater, and freshly-hemmed pants of the under-layers, respectably clothed if not presentable without an outer robe. She admired the materials along the walls behind the counters, sorted by the colors of rank—the minutely differentiated student fabrics in their bright yellows, oranges and reds, and the senior ranks, greens, blues, and purples, less varied and more somber.

The blue she'd chosen was dark, rich, and quiet—well within the range of accepted colors—but now her eye was caught by the greens. Most wizards who visited an institution other than their own borrowed its green robes to wear rather instead of going to the expense of buying such infrequently used garments, and so they were characteristically ill-fitting, worn, and mended. Only the traveling scholars who spent their careers visiting one wizard hall or academy after another went to the trouble of purchasing green robes of their own, and then only if they were wealthy, as few of them were. Well-fitting greens were a rare sight. Her own greens at the Collegium had been a trial for her, with temporary hems to shorten them, and plenty of evidence of previous ownership.

Adult wizards in Ellech wore blue—that's just the way it was, unless they were out of place somewhere or officials of some sort encouraged to announce their status with the purple.

It still bothered her. It proclaimed a solidarity with Ellech that she was no longer sure she felt. She agreed with Vylkar's reasoning, but…

When her tailor returned, she waved him over and pointed. "I would also like to look at fabrics for both short and long robes, in that green there, or that other one next to it. And work tunics, too."

*I can afford it. No one has to know.*

"Think she's still there?"

Najud watched Vylkar's face as they approached the shop he'd sent Penrys to. Amusement flickered over it before he settled on his usual sobriety and replied, "She is in many ways an unusual person, our Penrys, but she is certainly a woman. I will be surprised indeed if she has already left. Entire plays have been written about the donning of one's first blues."

*Ready for us, Pen-sha? We're about to pass the tailor's shop.*

He felt her doing a mental inventory of her possessions and garments. *I'll be right with you. Come on in.*

Vylkar led them in and waved aside the staff who came to assist them. "We're meeting someone," he told them.

Munraz glanced around the place wide-eyed, but Najud only had eyes for his wife, clothed in alien fashion in an informal dark blue robe, like so many of the people on the streets he'd been passing through, almost as though she had suddenly renounced *sarq*-Zannib and her family. He blinked in momentary uneasiness, until she smiled at him uncertainly.

"What do you think? You should see the long one."

"Like the ocean waves and the peaceful mountains," he said, with a mock bow.

She half-grinned at him, reassured.

Munraz glanced at Najud. "Do we have to dress like that?"

Vylkar commented, dryly, "I would not advise it. Foreign wizards have different customs, as everyone knows. Your best Zannib garments will be very suitable for formal occasions."

Penrys finalized her arrangements with the tailor while Vylkar looked over the display of awards and badges presented on top of the counter nearby. "You are entitled to some of these, you know," he told her. "Travel, scholarship, and so forth. The Collegium seal, for example. Anything we can do to help people understand how to position you is to the good."

"And misleading," she responded. "Compared to this"—she gestured discretely at the chain around her neck—"very little of that matters."

"Nonetheless," Vylkar replied. He lifted out three small badges for the left breast of her robe and fastened them on. All three were silver.

Najud realized that all the wizards they'd seen on the street had something similar on their robes, but he hadn't known how to read the code.

"I know the Kigaliwen run to wax seals and ribbons, but didn't you receive an honor from the emperor?" Vylkar asked.

Penrys snorted. "Don't be ridiculous—it's a great big thing, and gold. No one wears something like that here."

"Not so, young Penrys. You've just never seen one—how many wizards of Ellech do you know outside the Collegium?" He turned to the tailor who was following the conversation. "Whom do you recommend to produce a badge version of a foreign honor?"

"We can arrange that for you, *raer.*"

Vylkar nodded. "Send someone to our rooms at the guild hall, and we will show him the original—I assume it's in your packs, Penrys? Warn him that we may be leaving as soon as the day after tomorrow, so the sooner the better. If it could be completed before dinner this evening, impossible as that sounds…"

"Someone can be with you in an hour, if that will be convenient. With tools and materials."

"That will do very well," Vylkar said. "We'll expect someone then."

Najud marveled at witnessing Vylkar in his element. Under his imperious gaze, the transactions were concluded and the four of them back on the street almost before he could take a breath.

He shared a look with Penrys. *Impressive. Is he always like that?*

*Don't know, Naj-sha. I've rarely seen him in this mode either.*

Vylkar glanced at them both as if he'd overheard. "Money speaks, as they say. Might as well get what you want, eh?"

"True enough," Najud answered.

They strolled down the west side of the Stone Square on the way to the guild hall, taking their time and exploring the windows of the shops. After the fourth shop, Penrys noticed Munraz lagging behind, rapt by one particular display. She went back to see why, and to hasten him along. Plenty of time tomorrow for shopping.

She smiled to herself when she saw what it was—a supplier of power-stones, devices large and small, and shelves of pamphlets and books. *They may not use devices in sarq-Zannib, but that doesn't mean it isn't startling to see the things for sale out in the open, like so many lamps. It's a veritable wizard shop to him.*

Vylkar looked back to see what had detained them. "You wouldn't want to buy anything in a *rystet* like that —too expensive. I can show you better places later, outside of the main district."

Munraz shot him a look of disappointment, and Penrys was surprised to see Vylkar relent, returning with Najud so they could all enter the shop. Munraz and Najud went first, and Penrys could almost hear the proprietor size them up as foreigners and dismiss them, puzzled at their presence.

The appearance of a blue-robe and a purple-robe behind them was another matter, and Penrys saw the shopkeeper's eyes travel first to Vylkar, as the more important, and then to her. When he caught sight of her chain, his eyes widened, and he started to speak, but then he raised them to her face and stuttered to a stop, puzzled.

*What was that about? I should pin him to the spot and have it out of him.* She glanced sideways at Vylkar and he shook his head almost imperceptibly.

*But he knows something, he's seen a chain before. This isn't something from a generation ago—it's now, today!*

She seethed in frustration but consoled herself with the thought that she could always come back later to interrogate the man.

Her fingers itching to grab for the fellow, she walked past him and joined Munraz. She showed him some of the devices, explaining what they did and how they worked. The power-stones themselves were laid out under glass on the counter, sorted and graded.

When she glanced over at Najud, she saw that the posted prices were a revelation to him, his trader's mind quickly estimating the value of the pouch of power-stones still in their possession.

*I told you what they were worth, Naj-sha.* She'd share the thought with him after they were out of this place, when no one could overhear them. She could still feel the shopkeeper's eyes on her. *Did Najud even notice?*

The proprietor joined Penrys and Munraz and casually answered their questions about devices Penrys didn't recognize, as though nothing had happened when they first walked in.

Vylkar kept his thoughts to himself while they waited. "We haven't much time, Munraz. We can return tomorrow, if you wish."

"Oh. I'm sorry, *rair*— I just hadn't expected a place like this." Munraz drew back from a magnifying device reluctantly. "I didn't mean to delay us."

"No harm done."

Vylkar looked directly at the shopkeeper. "Thank you for your attention."

And try as hard as she might, Penrys couldn't decide if she heard an edge to that remark or not.

# CHAPTER 3

"I didn't think you even saw it! And how could you set Munraz on his trail? He'll stand out like a rooster in a flock of geese."

Penrys paced the common room of their suite at the guild hall, tracing a path between the backs of the chairs and the open window. Najud and Vylkar twisted their necks to follow her from their seats, and the leather creaked as their bodies moved.

Najud raised a hand to slow her down. "What did you think, you could just pry it out of him? In civilized Stokemmi?"

He glanced over at Vylkar for assistance. "He was a wizard himself, yes?"

Vylkar nodded. "He would have to be, to demonstrate his wares."

"He wore blue robes," Najud said.

"Anyone can wear the robes," Penrys said as she changed direction again. "People have been known to bluff. But Vylkar's right—he was surely a wizard."

"He recognized the chain. I'm sure of it." Najud repeated. "He started to say something about it. What I don't understand is why he stopped."

"Because he didn't recognize the wearer. In fact, I think the fact it wasn't an Ellech face is why he was puzzled." Vylkar's tone carried certainty.

"So, he knows other chained wizards, eh? And maybe they all have Ellechen faces." Penrys whirled to face Vylkar. "And are they the few you found already in Ellech, of various nations, that you reported on in Yenit Ping, or something else?"

Vylkar shook his head. "We found none alive, except you."

Najud followed her speculation. "You think they have something to do with the makers you're looking for?"

"I don't know!"

He could hear her frustration. He pictured the two of them each holding an ankle and dangling the shopkeeper from the roof of his building, then he showed it to her. *This more what you had in mind?*

She gave an involuntary chuckle. "If only we could do that, Najsha."

It worked—finally she stopped pacing and sat down in one of the padded chairs. "This is real, then. He knows something, so there's something to know. Something that's not a generation old."

"More to the point," Najud said, "we should find out what he's going to do about it, if anything. If you scare him off, you may learn nothing. If he tells someone, that gives us another name. That's why I set Munraz on him, for an hour or two—to watch what he does next."

He hadn't liked setting his *nal-jarghal* loose in a strange place where he would be noticeable, but he hoped his youth and obvious visitor status would allay any more sinister suspicions if he were noticed.

"And does this shopkeeper have any connection with Gialfinnur and his possible sect?" Vylkar's deep voice quieted them all for a moment. "I don't see how, but then we're just starting to look."

A knock on the door of the suite interrupted them, and Vylkar opened the door to a strange woman in wizard blues carrying a rectangular case in one hand. She inclined her head, exposing hair more gray than blond.

"I am seeking Vylkar. I'm Syrlyggi, sent by Redenchek to create a badge…"

At Vylkar's nod of comprehension, she walked in far enough to clear the door and set the case down as though it were heavy.

Najud nodded to himself. *The tools of her trade, and perhaps a bit of precious metal, too. No guard—but then a wizard is her own protection, I suppose. I'll have to ask Vylkar how armed robbery works in a society with so many wizards around. Or maybe those badges over her breast say something that warns others away.*

"You can set up over here, *rerri*," Najud told her, waving her over to a table near the window that seemed to be the best height for her sort of work.

Penrys reappeared from their shared room with a velvet pouch and laid it on the table while the goldsmith opened her case and took out magnifying devices and a small balance scale, as well as a soft green felt cloth.

Clearing her throat, Penrys waved at the pouch diffidently. "This was from the Emperor of Kigali."

The goldsmith's eyes widened in spite of her urbane professionalism, and she reached for it. She drew out the square gold plaque almost the size of her palm and laid it on the felt. "Are there any documents that come with it?" she asked, her eyes never moving from their examination of the piece.

This time Najud accompanied Penrys to their room and rummaged in his pack for a small scroll encased in a leather pouch while Penrys did her own document search.

When they returned, Penrys laid out a fat paper scroll, heavy with the weight of wax and gaudy with yellow ribbons and the red chop of the emperor. Syrlyggi unrolled it and looked up puzzled. "I cannot read this, *rerri*."

Vylkar recited its contents from memory, in Kigali *yat*. "To Sar Luplen, the foreigner Penrys of *sarq*-Zannib and Ellech, the thanks of the Emperor Ki Sechat for services to the Kigali Nation." He walked over to the goldsmith and repeated it in Ellechen *guma*. Then he leaned over her and pointed to the individual characters on the gold plaque that signified the key names.

"I believe this may be the first time that a foreigner has ever received this particular honor," he told her. "The Kigaliwen consider such a thing an heirloom of their house, earned by a famous ancestor, and boast of it hundreds of years later. It becomes part of their family emblems, to distinguish their house."

Penrys had retreated out of embarrassment, and Najud took her place. He laid down the small scroll he carried. "I don't know if you've seen this one, Vylkar. This was after the Voice was destroyed. It was presented by Chang Zenju, the commander of the military expedition where Penrys and I served. It's a small thing, but I wondered if you thought it should be represented."

He read the words and translated them for the goldsmith. The scroll's simple acknowledgment of assistance, made on the behalf of the emperor by one of his military officers to two foreign wizards, from a nation which did not at the time officially recognize that it had wizards of its own, presented a puzzle.

Syrlyggi recovered from her surprise and ventured an opinion. "These are both proper honors to display, foreign though they are. The first one is, of course, the more important and should be represented at the largest size appropriate to an honor not of

Ellech. The second would be more modest, but still a separate and worthy honor."

She glanced at Najud, in his Zannib robes. "I see it bears both your names. Do you wish for your own badge?"

Smiling, he shook his head. "That's no part of our Zannib traditions. Just the ones for Penrys, suitable for Ellech."

After some discussion, they settled on an appropriate design for both. The larger honor would be in the form of crossed Kigali-style swords, since the service rendered included physical battle, even if most of it was magical in nature. It would include the characters for the Kigali Emperor's name, and any decorative touches would complement the foreign style. All in gold, of course, to match the original plaque.

For the minor honor, they agreed that silver was more appropriate. At Najud's request, the design included the hand-axe used to kill the Voice, the chained wizard eliminated by Penrys at such cost.

"Too bad you've nothing to show for your defeat of the *qahulajti* in *sarq*-Zannib," he said to Penrys.

She glared at him. "Just as well. It's nothing to boast of."

Najud shook his head. "You're wrong. Think of all the lives saved."

"I'd never be able to look at it without thinking of that poor girl. The last thing I want to do is keep count…"

She broke off, conscious of the stranger in the room with them, but Najud knew how to complete the phrase—"count of the dead."

Syrlyggi followed their conversation without interruption, but when they paused, she ventured, "If I may… I see you are of foreign birth and perhaps you are not aware… When wearing your wizard's robe and Ellech honors, it is not customary to distract from them with jewelry, other than of the most discreet variety. Your necklace…"

Despite herself, Penrys stiffened, and Najud watched as she made herself relax. "It doesn't come off, I'm afraid. Would you recommend I conceal it behind a piece of cloth, or would that be just as incongruous?"

"Ah, I see… Well, in that case, please forget my words. It's always better to present yourself when in formal robes in your truest form, without concealment."

Najud wondered what she would make of the wings. He caught Penrys's eye and thought she might be considering the same thing.

The goldsmith worked on a piece of paper for a few moments and then laid down her quill. "For the design work, the materials, and the making of the badges, here is my charge. For the registration of the new honors with the heraldry guild, and for the special urgency, this additional amount."

She looked uncertainly between Vylkar and Penrys, and Vylkar took charge. "This is for me to pay. You may lay it to my account with the wizard guild—half now, and half upon delivery, if that suits you."

"If you will so indicate here, that will be satisfactory. Since I expect to stay here and deliver within two hours, I see no need to delay by taking the first payment in advance. Your name is known."

Vylkar acknowledged her courtesy. "May we offer you a place to get started, or will this arrangement do?"

"Any private room with an appropriate table will be fine."

"Munraz is still out," Najud said. "Let's put her in his room. If he comes back too soon, we'll work around it."

"How long before we have to show ourselves at dinner?" Penrys asked.

"Two hours, Pen-sha," Najud told her. "Just enough time."

"Please, *raer*, would it be possible to see how it works?"

Munraz concentrated on making his demeanor seem younger, rounding his eyes to convey guilelessness. He thought it helped to be beardless—young men his age here were all bearded, as best they could manage.

"And what does a Zannib youngster want with my signals tower?"

The middle-aged man, unremarkable except for his butter-yellow beard that was trimmed to the level of his collarbone, stood at the door of the westernmost of the four wooden towers at the top of the city's hill. A steady stream of foot traffic passed them by in the warrens surrounding the cluster of buildings, the tallest ones in the middle, five stories high, and the rest of varying heights in loose rings around them.

It looked as if the clerk who had opened the door to Munraz's knock had fetched the master of the tower, and Munraz bowed his best elaborate Zannib greeting.

"My apologies, most esteemed *raer*, but my master and I are newly arrived in Ellech, and he wanted me to study how things are done here. He's a wizard, you understand. It was my idea to begin with these magnificent structures, but I had no intention to disturb a man such as you in your daily activities. I apologize."

There. That would never work in *sarq*-Zannib, but maybe here, if he looked really young, and foreign… That shopkeeper, the one who'd stared at Penrys's chain, had come here in haste and left more calmly, as if he'd taken care of a problem, and this was the only way Munraz could think of to find out what he'd done.

"Hmmph. Off to the Collegium, I shouldn't wonder." The man fingered his beard. "Educating foreigners now, are we?" He studied Munraz's robe and the simple turban that surmounted it.

*Now would not be the time for any of the small sharp items secreted in my anah-im-ghabr to suddenly poke out from the folds.* Munraz's fingers crept surreptitiously to the pouch at his belt and felt the outline of his *lud* for what luck it might bring him. He'd stumbled upon the small stone in the tunnels under the upper city of Yenit Ping, the Kigali capital, and it had seemed meant for him, as a *lud* does, but it was chancy to rely on that.

The man pulled the door wide, and waved Munraz in. A counter stood to his left in the small anteroom with benches, and the clerk who had opened the door to him in the first place stood nervously behind it, watching them. The master yanked open the heavy door at the far end of the room and bellowed into it. "Gechendair! Spend a few minutes showing our visitor around, eh?"

Munraz followed him into a large workroom at the base of the tower. Shelves with boxes and labels filled the walls, and his eyes sorted the bustle of activity into young men and a few women working at the narrowly-spaced tables throughout the room with stacks of paper sheets, quills and ink, and long, thin strips of paper. The center of the room was blocked by some sort of complicated column, and Munraz noticed the start of a staircase at its base.

The young man who raised his head near the front of the room waved a hand in acknowledgment and unfolded himself from his work at a table. Munraz turned to the tower master and bowed again. "My thanks to you, *raer*, and I will try not to be a disruption to you."

He grunted. "It's just as well for foreigners to get an idea of how we Ellechen *taurath* manage things, I suppose. Don't take up too much of his time, now."

He stalked off and made his way to the right of the room, where Munraz saw a group of doorways with windows to view the activity in the central space. *A supervisor's room. Must be complicated, this work they do here.*

"You're a Zan, aren't you? I'm one of the signals clerks."

Munraz turned to look at his guide and then tilted his head back. *Younger than me, even with that little yellow beard he's got, but does that mean he's going to be even taller when he stops growing?*

He bowed anyway, deadpan. "I am indeed. My name's Munraz, apprentice to Najud, come to visit the Collegium. My master has told me to find out more about how things are done in Ellech, so… what do you do here? How does it work?"

"Oh! You're a wizard, then? I guess they don't wear the colors where you come from."

Munraz pictured himself in the yellow robes of a student and was grateful for his familiar clothing. He waved a hand at himself. "No, as you see."

Gechendair glanced at the closed door where his master had vanished. "What we do… we send messages, all around the country."

Munraz blinked. Could he find the shopkeeper's message? "We don't have anything like this in *sarq*-Zannib. Can you show me?"

"Sure. Follow me."

Munraz tried not to feel that he was scurrying to keep up with those long legs as the two of them headed for the central column.

"Up to the top." Gechendair grinned, and opened a door next to the stairs to reveal a small cubicle, large enough to hold four people, illuminated by a device embedded in the ceiling. He waved Munraz in to join him and shut the door, while Munraz tried not to panic in the small space. Still grinning, Gechendair yanked the top lever of four next to the door, and the tiny room jerked and began moving.

"First time in an *ossanutkenbendu*? Thought it might be."

Munraz swallowed and refused to let his reaction show on his face. *This is like the lift cages in Yenit Ping*, he told himself, *only much, much smaller.*

His dignified silence apparently abashed his guide to some degree, for a note of apology crept into his voice. "Don't worry—only the best lifters for the signals tower. The *hortkendrosi* look them over every week." At Munraz's blank look, he added, "The wizards, the ones that check and inspect all the devices and keep 'em powered."

Munraz looked for power-stones, now that his fear was subsiding. Penrys had showed him how they felt, and now he recognized them, first in the ceiling device that provided light, and then in the levers. *Floors—they must indicate what floor to lift this little room to. But they seem like small devices. How could they do all that work?*

He forced his body to relax. "Yes, my first time. What pulls this little room up?" He kept his voice friendly, the good-natured recipient of a joke.

"Oh, there's a device at the top that turns a wheel attached to a rope, and the controls here tell it how far. We're lucky to be one of the long-distance towers—the shorter ones don't have this luxury. Stair-climbing all the time for them."

The room stopped moving, and Gechendair opened the door. "Top of the tower," he announced.

When Munraz followed him out, he was confronted by a noisy clacking sound. Before he could pinpoint it, Gechendair dragged him over to one of the windows that penetrated each of the four sides of the room. "How do you like this?"

They faced west, where no other buildings restricted their view at that height, though others almost as tall ringed them. Before them, the land dropped off rapidly to the river, and Munraz could see the concentrations of structures across the water, and boat traffic, but no bridges.

He walked over to the north windows, and looked past the great tower there which partially blocked it. The city continued, and then the land rolled out beyond it, a mixture of fields and forests. "Can you see the big mountains from here?" he asked.

"What, the Dunnarfeol? Much too far away," Gechendair replied. "It's the south tower that gets most of the visitors—they want to see the harbor."

Munraz turned away and looked for the source of the noise. There were two complex machines, one above the other, and strips of paper.

"This one sends." Gechendair patted the bottom one. "And this one receives. We're getting a message now. Come see."

Munraz felt a cluster of power-stones in the two devices, both large and small ones. *These must be very expensive devices. Everything in this building must be very costly, and there are how many buildings like this, clustered on this hill?*

*This is as big an investment, in its way, as the places where they forge metal in Yenit Ping. Do we have anything like this in sarq-Zannib? I'll have to ask Najud.*

Meanwhile, his guide was explaining things. "We get the messages from the distant west—the lower buildings below us get the more local traffic. If you were already at the Collegium, your message would come in here." He grinned at Munraz.

"The scriber marks it on this double strip of paper, see? The first part is the destination tower and priority, then the person it should go to, and where, and then the person sending. The rest is the message itself, and this little bit here marks the end so you know you've gotten the whole thing."

To Munraz's eyes, these were holes punched in the paper grouped in little clusters of nine, with the center hole always punched and larger than the rest in its cluster, while some of the other eight holes were punched and some were not. He could see that each cluster was different from its neighbor. "You can read this?"

"That's what we do all day." He lifted the upper strip which was loose at the end and accumulated in an open wooden bucket—the lower strip was wound up slowly on a wheel, kept aligned by a ratchet through the large center holes. "This one is for some woman at the Stumbling Man, from some man, about a shipment of brandy being delayed."

He let the paper strip drop. "They swap buckets every few minutes, cut the *rekenponkenkiemmenbar*—we call it a *ponka*— into individual messages, sort them by priority, and send them downstairs. We use the tubes for that." He pointed at the central column, and Munraz saw the buckets of empty colored capsules and an opening they would fit into. A woman sat there and spun paper strips into tight inserts for the capsules, then dropped them through the opening.

"The daily wheels are saved for a week, in case there're any questions."

A man brushed by them and perched in front of the lower device with a punched strip of paper. He carefully fed it in, and beside him, another strip copied it and accumulated around a wheel. His beard was neatly trimmed, and Munraz realized he had seen nothing but short beards on the men in the building. *I guess you wouldn't want to catch one in the moving machines.*

"Now he's sending a message. If you walked in downstairs, you'd write your message on a piece of paper and pay the fee. The clerk would send it back to us, and we'd use a different device to transcribe it onto a *ponka*. That comes up here, and it gets sent."

"What happens if two messages are sent to you at the same time? From different towers?"

"The competing strip won't advance past the tower name, and the sending tower will just have to try again later. Sometimes they can send to another tower and relay it, if it's a long delay—a broken receiver, say. Last year there was a fire which damaged a tower and they had to route around it for weeks."

*The shopkeeper's message is around here somewhere, but how would I find it?*

"What happens to the original message?" Munraz said.

"We keep the message sheet, and a wheel for messages sent and received, so we can tell if a message was never sent. Some people pay more to get an official receipt from the other tower, when it's important."

Gechendair looked at Munraz cheerfully. "You going to study this at the Collegium?"

"I'm thinking about it. I've never seen such a complicated combination of devices before." This was no deception. There was something about the designed nature of the system that fascinated Munraz, the creation of something that had never existed before. Like Najud's planned caravan in the west… No wonder it appealed to his *jarghal*, fond as he was of organizing people. This added devices to the mix, and Najud would never do that. The Zannib with their prohibition against physical magic would never permit it. *Too bad.*

"Can I see how the original messages are stored, so I can get a clear picture of it in my head when I report back to my master?"

'Of course! Follow me."

The little lifting room was in use, so they clattered down the stairs instead. Munraz wondered what he was missing on the intermediate floors but couldn't think of a way to ask.

At the bottom, Gechendair led the way to a set of painted bins with individual sheets thrown haphazardly in. "The bins in front hold the messages from the senders, sorted by priority. One of us goes over and takes the oldest message with the highest priority— those are the ones in the red bin there— and makes a *ponka* for it. We send that upstairs, and then put the original message into the bin in back. Every time that fills up, someone swaps it out for an empty one, and we stash it over there." He pointed at shelving that held a dozen bins in four colors. "That's the traffic for a day. Someone compares it to the sent-message wheel each day to make sure they're all accounted for, then they sit over there for a week before we discard them." He waved over at bundles tied with string on a different set of shelves.

Munraz watched the process. The bins not yet sent were almost empty, so the message form he wanted was probably in the bin in back, already sent. He strode there casually and poked around the slips of paper, but nothing caught his eye until he noticed one near the top. "That doesn't make any sense."

Gechendair leaned over him to see what he was talking about. "Oh, one of those." He plucked it out of Munraz's hand. "That's in code, you see. Merchants with secrets, sometimes government stuff. They're a nuisance to transcribe—you have to be very careful to get them right. And look, see the destination? It gives the tower name and then says 'Relay 1139.' That's the big central tower for the west, and they'll look that number up and forward the message according to instructions. Even the sender's name looks like code, doesn't it?"

*A dead end.* Munraz's heart sank. He ran his eye over the room full of chattering voices and busy hands. The ingenuity that put all of this together supported even more ingenuity that obscured the information he wanted. Clever systems and devious minds.

# CHAPTER 4

"It been almost two hours. Where is he?"

Penrys sought Munraz's mind but there were hundreds of wizards in Stokemmi to wade through. She still couldn't believe that Najud had just sent him to spy on someone on his first day in a foreign city.

Vylkar glanced up. "He's resourceful, that one. I wouldn't worry yet."

Penrys and Najud had spent much of the time waiting in their own room while Vylkar entertained guests in the main room of the suite. He'd let his name be posted as "in residence" at the entrance, and colleagues who were in town had been dropping by for some time. Vylkar invited each to dinner in a special hall downstairs, and several promised to bring friends. All wanted to hear the details about the Kigali expedition from which he had just returned.

He kept his foreign guests under wraps, planning to introduce them formally tonight. In-between the knocks on the door, Penrys worked with him on their plans for the evening. She hadn't expected a reaction to her chain like that, and now she thought there was everything to gain by trolling the line out deliberately, trying to see who else might react, once they learned what she was and why she was there.

"I've talked to some of my colleagues about Gialfinnur," Vylkar said, abruptly. "One of them muttered something about *yrmkenrolek* but that was all I've heard."

At Najud's puzzled glance, he explained. "That's crooked learning, forbidden subjects—what Gialfinnur wrote about before they dismissed him from the Collegium. No one would want to admit what they know about something like that, for there could be consequences."

He pursed his lips thoughtfully. "I'm not surprised no one volunteered anything, but I am somewhat disturbed that no one had to be reminded who I was talking about."

"You think his influence is still alive, or he would have been forgotten by now?" Penrys said.

"Something like that. I've sent feelers out—I should know more in a day or two."

The opening of the door to Munraz's room startled them all. Syrlyggi came in with her case in one hand and a small velvet cushion holding two gleaming items in the other. She put the case down and handed the fabric with its two pinned badges to Vylkar, then stepped back to hear his opinion. Penrys got up from her chair to look over his shoulder. She could feel that the power-stones in the devices in the case had lost much of their charge.

The gold of the Emperor's award was subdued, almost molten in color, rather than brash and new. There were subtle touches of Kigali styling to it that would make it exotic to Ellechen eyes, beyond the crossed swords themselves. On the back were the details of dates and names.

The minor honor in silver mirrored the Kigali styling though its subject was different. Despite the differences in size and material, they went well together, fruit of the same tree.

"I am well pleased," Vylkar said. "May I offer you any refreshment for your trouble?"

The remark drew Penrys's attention to the woman's wan face. "No, I need to be going. The task was a bit more difficult than I expected, getting the engraving right for the mold." She smiled wearily.

She looked Penrys in the face. "Be cautious when you wear this—a man might be tempted to steal it to melt it down."

Najud chuckled. "The woman who won these both in personal combat will not be so easy to overwhelm."

"As you say," she said. "Is our business concluded?" she asked Vylkar.

"It is, and I will convey my satisfaction to the one who recommended you." He pressed a small pouch into her hand, which she accepted.

She paused at the outer doorway, her case heavy in her hand. "Look to find these honors registered in the archives by me tomorrow morning."

When she pulled the door open, she almost stumbled into Munraz, his hand lifted to knock. They sorted themselves out, and Munraz came in and shut the door behind him.

Najud belied his nonchalance about assigning the task to Munraz by leaping up and striding over to him, with a "where were you?" Vylkar twitched as if he meant to do the same before subsiding with dignity back into his chair.

Penrys noted that Munraz's expression combined satisfaction in having completed a difficult assignment with surprise at so much concern for his welfare. *Still not used to having a new family that cares what happens to him.*

She resumed her own seat, leaned back, and crossed her hands over her stomach. "Tell us all about it."

"I can't believe he didn't see you following him." Penrys was impressed in spite of herself.

"I gave him no reason to look back, and he was in a hurry," Munraz said. "Finding the building up on the hill wasn't hard, but deciding what to do when he left… I wasn't sure I made the right choice."

"I'm sure," Najud replied. "And I'm proud of you, *nal-jarghal*, for taking the chance and learning so much."

"But I couldn't read the message, and I can't even be sure it's the one he sent!"

Munraz had stopped pacing after he'd finished the story and was perched now on the edge of a chair, pulled away from a writing table in the central room of the suite.

Vylkar's low voice chimed in. "That was most likely his. The merchants don't use code unless it's truly important, and official messages are usually sent in batches. No, we can't be sure, but it's likely."

"But it doesn't tell us anything." Munraz lifted his hands in a half-shrug.

"On the contrary," Vylkar said. "If we're right in thinking we know who sent it, it tells us quite a lot. The timing tells us that he truly did react to the sight of Penrys's chain, that we didn't just imagine it. The relay designation makes it clear that this is a customary channel, one that he's used before, perhaps many times. That, and the code itself, tells us that the message is both important and private, that there is a need for secrecy."

"And it tells us that its destination is in the west," Najud added.

Penrys raised a finger to slow him down. "Not necessarily. The destination could be another relay that sends the message elsewhere."

"And there could be a chain of such relays," Vylkar said. "It might even come back into Stokemmi from another direction through a different tower, so that no one notices the same coded message. But it's best not to multiply unknowns. Until we have evidence to the contrary, I would take 'west' for the simple clue that it is."

"The Collegium is in the west, and not far from that destination tower," Penrys observed.

"So is a quarter or more of the nation," Vylkar replied. "Let's not jump too far ahead in our suppositions."

He paused. "So, you got a tour of a signals tower, did you? What did you think of it?"

Munraz turned to Najud. "You'd have liked it, *jarghal*. All these people were organized, each with a task, and if you think about it the right way, all the documents were organized, too. Everything moved around through the system like, like..." He searched for a comparison. "Like grain through a mill. The message goes in at one end, and comes out the other having been sent and filed away."

He watched Najud's face. "And the devices... The way they were put together—so clever! Big ones to do complicated things, little ones to control the big ones. The men who thought those up... They were organizing things, too. Just different kinds of things."

Penrys felt for Najud's reaction, behind his deadpan face. Devices and all the physical magics were frowned upon in *sarq-Zannib*. Though Najud had not seemed disturbed by her own work in that area, his apprentice was another matter. Clearly Munraz had found the tour fascinating.

Vylkar must have been concerned about Najud's possible response, too, for he spoke before Najud could. "The signals towers employ some of our most complex devices. Many techniques were pioneered there. You'll find that the Collegium has entire courses of study that concentrate in that field."

Munraz looked to Vylkar. "We Zannib must seem awfully primitive to the Kigaliwen and the Ellechen *taurath*."

"You have your own expertises and your own complexities," Vylkar said.

"But no devices. And no systems of men like that."

"Not true, Munraz," Penrys said. "Look at the *taridiqa*, the annual migration, with its tasks and roles. Everyone knows his job. Any military unit is organized the same way, and the caravans—think how complicated, and yet they run smoothly across two nations."

Munraz nodded. "I thought of your caravan, *jarghal*, when I saw all this," he told Najud. He subsided, but Penrys could almost here him repeat his "no devices" observation to himself.

Najud made no reply.

*I'm bait, that what I am. Staked out like a bleating goat for everyone to get a good look at. Well, I asked for it.*

Penrys tried to ignore the itch between her shoulder-blades where she fancied a knife might appear. No one in the guild's smaller dining hall, the Founder's Hall, Vylkar had called it, had been hostile, but they were certainly curious.

Vylkar had planted himself near the entrance, with his three guests, and greeted everyone who arrived, performing introductions before directing them to a serving area for a variety of beverages, not all of which were familiar to Penrys.

"Where do they all come from?" she muttered to Vylkar during a brief gap.

"Some live here most of the year, in this guild hall or nearby, and some just happen to be in town. We're in luck to get so many with so little notice."

They were interrupted by a deep voice. "So where's that big one from, then? Never seen that one before."

She turned to face a broad fellow with an unkempt gray beard and a mug in one hand. He was pointing his chin at the gold honor over her left breast, and she launched into a repetition of her abbreviated response. "I was able to perform a small service for the emperor in Kigali," she said, with a neutral voice.

The touch of Vylkar's hand on her arm drew her away to be introduced to the next new entrants, a redhead going bald this time, and his blond wife, both in their blues. "May I present the *hakkengenni* Penrys, back from her travels for a while?"

They bowed, and she bowed, all the time thinking, *'Adept,' is it? No one uses that title in the modern world.*

"And this is her husband, the wizard Najud, son of Ilsahr, of clan Zamjilah, and his apprentice Munraz, come all the way from *sarq*-Zannib to visit our Collegium."

The two of them were in their finest Zannib robes, with ornamented weapons on display in their sashes, and less fancy ones hidden elsewhere. Their turbans were another exotic touch that widened the eyes of the new visitors, before they wandered off for liquid refreshment.

Penrys had her own small knives stashed away, which was a comfort to her. Her robes on the other hand were a mixed blessing. She had to think carefully about her movements, for this was the first time she'd worn the formal robes, so much longer than the everyday ones, though with her lack of height, the borrowed greens at the Collegium had sometimes been almost as difficult to maneuver.

These robes were new—her first new ones—and she held herself straight in the pride of new clothing. Still, this was a lot of strangers to greet at once, to… expose herself to, and her shoulder blades continue to itch.

"I'm very pleased to meet you," she said, bowing to people whose names she forgot as soon as they passed down the line.

A clamor of well-lubricated conversation rose gradually from the corner of the room nearest to the beverages. Penrys let her eyes drift there and then over to the table that occupied most of the long wall, in sections shoved together. She longed for the food to arrive, so that they could take a place and eat in relative peace. *Such a lot of strange wizards—could I take them on in an emergency?*

Najud commented on the room-wide mural that ran behind the table. "I see the Ellechen *taurath* carry their love of trees and wood indoors."

Penrys shook her head. "That's not what that is." The painted carving depicted a grove of leafless trees with the tallest in the middle, straight as a waterfall. Their roots were exposed and intertwined.

"That's a symbol, the *drosnommystu*, the woven roots of magic. It represents all the ways that wizards intertwine, from young ones in their schools, to teachers of the craft, to practitioners in the businesses, to the researchers. All have roots that support the craft, and each leans upon the others. That tree in the center… that's supposed to be the axis upon which the world spins, the tree that connects the earth to the sky."

She cleared her throat and looked at Munraz. "It's an old belief, that one. No one much speaks of it anymore. Me, I always thought what it really meant was that no one understood quite how wizardry worked, so they threw in something even more impossible to believe in, out of embarrassment." She chuckled at his startled expression.

"Anyway, that's the path of *redenrolek*, the straight track. The orthodox teachings, what the Collegium offers."

"Is there another kind?" Munraz asked.

Vylkar overheard him. "Several, with varying beliefs. Each is an *yrmkenrolek*, a crooked track. Don't speak of this here, tonight," he added. "Not in this company." And he fixed his eyes upon Munraz until the young man nodded agreement.

*The Kigali with their gods, the Zannib with their lud—whatever those are—and the Ellech with… hard to explain, isn't it? And what the wizards think, most of them, is not necessarily what everyone else believes.*

The woman in blue robes across the narrow table from Penrys made polite conversation. Penrys had forgotten her name—there were just too many strangers to keep track of, a sea stretching down to her right on both sides with extensive pools of blues and a few purples puddled up. There was a scattering of non-wizards, but fewer than half a dozen, and she would have wagered they were all married to wizards also present. She recalled some such couples from the presentation line.

"It must be pleasant for you, returning for your studies after being away?"

"It does feel a bit like home to me," Penrys admitted. "I'm still somewhat disoriented, though. I seem to have misplaced winter somewhere."

Najud at her side explained, "We crossed the equator, you see, and all the seasons have shifted. We've come back to spring a second time this year."

The two of them and Munraz sat at Vylkar's right hand, with their backs to the *drosnommystu* mural. Penrys eyed her patron to her left, at the head of the table. She felt sure this was a deliberate maneuver, Vylkar taking advantage of the symbolism to suggest that his *byrindyrri* walked the straight path, not the crooked one.

She looked past Najud at Munraz and overheard explanations about Zannib clothing and customs. Safe topics. In fact, it had been safe topics throughout the meal, up and down the table, a pleasant rumbling of voices and clinking of glasses.

Now the guild hall's servants began clearing the plates and platters, leaving only drinks behind. When the last of them had vanished and closed the doors, the conversations subsided, as if in anticipation of the real purpose of the evening.

Vylkar pushed his chair back from the table and rose, and all eyes turned to him and granted him silence.

"You have all heard of the people we searched for, before I and the other ambassadors departed for Kigali. Dead men and women, wearing a chain like the *hakkengenni* Penrys here.

"Since then, the news will have returned ahead of us—the death of our ambassadors, and the presence of hundreds of wizards in wizardless Kigali, many of them wearing chains, and the rise of a new wizard guild there, out in the open. And dead wizards in chains scattered from Zannib to Rasesni to Ndant, as well as here in Ellech."

The attentive silence was complete.

"We know more, now, than we did. We know the chains are devices, and we know they store power like power-stones."

"Impossible!" The interruption came from a man of Vylkar's age who stood up to protest. What could only be his wife grabbed his arm to pull him back down, but to no avail. "We all know it's the nature of their crystalline structures that sets the power-stones apart from the true gems."

Heads nodded around the table.

Vylkar paused a moment until he had their attention. "I say here that I have witnessed proof." He waited a beat for them to recall his purple-robed dignity. "As any sword-smith can tell you, metals exhibit crystalline structures, too."

At that, cries of "*yrmkenrolek*" rose from several places.

Vylkar raised his hand to request silence.

"Perhaps this is crooked magic, perhaps not. We are journeying to the Collegium in a few days to see if its archives can help us understand how this might be, and Penrys will join me in the investigation. She is after all a *hakkengenni* in this area, an Adept."

*Nothing about the wiped memories, or about the extra flourishes like animal ears and wings and other appurtenances. Nothing about the discrete period of time that covered the creation of all the chained wizards she'd encountered. Nothing about the whiff of a suspicion around the old banned Ellechen wizard Gialfinnur.* Penrys shook her head faintly in admiration of Vylkar's use of limited information to maneuver his audience.

"I hope that all of you will share with us anything you might know on the topic, before we leave, or send it on to us afterward. I would be most grateful."

*And there we are. Bait, indeed. They will know where to find us, when the word spreads, as it will, and they will realize we might be dangerous in our knowledge.*

She turned her head and smiled tightly at Najud. *Good. I want to get my hands on whoever made us, stole our past lives, and scattered us randomly and indifferently about the landscape to live or die.*

# CHAPTER 5

Late the next morning, Penrys fingered her exposed chain while she waited for Najud to refill his and Munraz's packs with samples for the third time.

The movement caught Najud's eye, and he paused, with two small wooden sample boxes of *kassa* snatched up in one hand. "You could always cover it up."

She glanced down at her informal robes which so clearly declared her occupation. The fancier honors were gone from her left breast—unsuitable for everyday wear. She shook her head. "Won't help. My face is almost as obvious. Might as well make it easy for everyone to know who I am."

The three of them were gathered around the large horse packs that had been stowed in the wizard guild's warehouse, near the river docks. They weren't the only people in the gloomy building, but Najud was pleased that their goods had been so conveniently and securely stored, far from any windows and with a watchman on the entrance.

The morning had been spent visiting wholesale merchants up and down the river. Najud had already filled four of the Zannib wax tablets with names, prices, and other notes, and he would need to take them along with him to the guild hall to transcribe them onto paper and smooth the tablets back to blankness.

"I don't understand. If it's dangerous, why do it?" Munraz said.

"Ah, but she has a perfect excuse to go round with me to the merchants to do a little trading of samples and selling of goods." Najud told him.

Penrys added, "I want to be noticed, so that the word will spread and maybe someone like the man you followed will do something imprudent that gives us something useful. But it doesn't do for the staked goat to have "wizard trap" inked all along her side—tends to scare off the predators. So I need a reason to walk around all innocently like this."

A smile flickered across her face. "Not that anyone's likely to notice, when they have two exotic Zannib men to admire instead."

That provoked a grin from Najud.

"And besides," she said, "we don't know if Ellech really has anything to do with the chained wizards, anyway. That's just a long line thrown into the sea."

"But that man sent a message…" Munraz said.

"So maybe the line got a little shorter." She shrugged. "That's still quite a way from proof."

She rounded on Najud. "Explain to Munraz how you benefit from making connections with merchants you can't trade with from the west of *sarq*-Zannib. They can't reach your ports on that side of the country, without ridiculously long voyages, halfway around the world."

"True, but there's customers and then there's wholesale customers."

Najud put the sample boxes of *kassa* in his pack to free up his hands. "Ellech trades with Ndant, and Kigali at Kwattu, in the northeast. Those are the most important places for them. Now, goods that go to Ndant can be carried over the mountain spine to the west coast of the isthmus, and then back by sea down to the north coast of Rasesni, but that doesn't do us much good. Maybe we can make a connection to that later—depends on the cost." He illustrated the configuration of the lands with his hands in the air.

"But goods from Ellech reach Yenit Ping and the rest of eastern Kigali now, and that's what counts."

"Your new caravan won't be in eastern Kigali, but in the far west," Munraz objected.

Penrys told him, impatiently. "The *Biziz Rahr* will trade with Kigali, which has ports for Ellech. And the Grand Caravan will eventually send goods along to his new caravan."

She turned back to Najud. "But what I don't understand is how you can make any profit on something that has to pass through that many hands over such long distances."

Najud held up a hand and started to tick off his fingers.

"Small rare things, like spices, dyes, and gems. Right, Munraz?"

The young man nodded, remembering his lessons last winter.

"New lightweight things that can become exotic fashions. *Bunnas* and *kassa*, for example. Everyone likes beverages that wake them up and form part of the habits of civilized people."

A second finger went down.

"Unique things—small treasures from far-away places. Not expensive where they're made, but suggestive of world travel. Something you've got, but your neighbor doesn't."

That took care of a third finger.

"Knowledge," Penrys suggested, for the fourth finger. "Books, for example."

"Or people." Najud looked at her speculatively. "You're a valuable commodity yourself, Pen-sha. New ways of doing things will travel, and some of those have measurable value. What price for a master wood-worker out of Ellech for a builder in Yenit Ping? Or communication devices for their guilds? Animals and plants for breeding, too—that's a form of knowledge. You know that—look at the donkeys we brought from Kigali to breed mules in *sarq*-Zannib."

He closed his fist.

"And finally ordinary commodities that no one can do without, like all trade. Iron via Kigali to *sarq*-Zannib, for example. Who's to say something like that might not be found here in Ellech?"

Munraz murmured, "Power-stones."

Najud frowned at him. "Yes, well, perhaps to trade in Kigali."

His hand sprang open again. "So I'm looking for those things that might be useful either to the Grand Caravan, or to mine, items I can buy inexpensively here and sell for enough to make it worthwhile. And I'm showing them a few of the goods that *sarq*-Zannib has to offer, and describing what could come from western Kigali or eastern Rasesni. I'm learning prices and meeting people, setting up a network."

Penrys could hear the excitement in his voice and feel it, even without the mind-speech.

He glanced around at the twenty-odd leather horse packs he'd brought to the harbor at Kwattu for this voyage to Ellech, with goods partially from *sarq*-Zannib, and partially from Kigali. "I may never get to come this way myself again, but I want to make the most of it—sell all of this, and fill them up for the return."

"Better leave room for books, from Tavnastok," Penrys told him. She had visions of shelves going up in the as-yet-unbuilt caravan base in western *sarq*-Zannib, where a city would eventually rise with a Collegium of its own for Zannib wizards.

"I can always buy more packs," he said.

Penrys escaped Najud and Munraz's rounds with the merchants by telling them she had errands of her own to run. It was true, but it wasn't the whole truth.

She had a plan.

The recognition of her chain by that one shopkeeper still bothered her. What if he wasn't alone? What if there were others? If a chained wizard had come to Stokemmi before her, perhaps he had done business in that shop. What better place for equipment than the center of commerce in Ellech?

Though the shopkeeper acted as if he hadn't just recognized the chain, but had some understanding of what it meant, and how would that have happened?

Penrys shook her head as she reached the top of the street where it leveled off before entering the Stone Square. *Too much speculation, not enough information. I need more facts.*

She intended to walk ever-widening rings, starting with the Stone Square. The most expensive shops were there. Later, she would seek out the specialists in the other districts—anywhere she thought a chained wizard might have gone where his chain might have been recognized for what it was. She patted her throat to make sure her own chain was easily visible and began her tour.

Now if someone stared at her, it wouldn't be for the Zannib strangers at her side.

Three blocks east and south of the Stone Square, Penrys paused at the edge of a food market to sit next to a stall and sip cider from a borrowed wooden mug. Her feet needed the rest, and this walk wasn't working out the way she'd planned.

No one had apparently noticed her chain so far—no one at all. She'd kept her mind open for the general impression of the minds around her, but each time she'd felt surprise or fear, she'd been able to match it up with something that wasn't her.

Now she stuck her nose in the mug and inhaled the sweet smell of crisp cider in wood, and watched everyone else for a change instead of inviting their attention. How long had it been since she'd tasted cider? Only a year? It didn't seem possible. Three years in Ellech after Vylkar found her, and a year elsewhere.

Only a year since she'd made that stupid, clumsy mistake with her experiment, and ended up in western Kigali. A year since she'd encountered Najud in a military tent under attack. The seasons were reversed in the south, and it threw off all her sense of timing. She'd met Najud in the autumn, on the plains around the Mother of Rivers, and spent that horrible winter in *sarq*-Zannib, buried in the snow and chasing a nightmare—the second chained wizard they'd fought together to stop all the deaths that they brought with them, wherever they went. The one that Munraz executed, that haunted his mind still for all that he refused to talk about it.

She'd married Najud after that—six couples standing in the snow in the winter camp of the partially recovered Kurighdunaq clan, she in her borrowed clothing leaning on a crutch.

She lifted the hand not holding the cider to pat her right breast, where the wedding brooch should be, the silver spread-winged eagle, but her blues were bare there—only the simple honors on her left breast for informal robes and ordinary occasions. And what did that goldsmith say? That she shouldn't wear jewelry while wearing her honors, any honors, like the small ones above her left breast?

Her hand dropped. She was in Ellech now, and should adhere to the conventions.

The months after that, more than half a year crossing *sarq*-Zannib on the way to eastern Kigali and Yenit Ping and meeting Najud's family. Her lips curved upward at the recollection. So curious and lively, so casually fond of each other. So warm. Wanting the best for him, and willing to honor his exotic choice. She knew it wasn't what they'd envisioned, but no one said a word. She could feel their acceptance, and the puzzlement that went with it.

A child's shriek out in the market turned her head and she watched a group of three boys and a girl as they dodged around their elders in some sort of game.

She felt the familiar ache in her gut, the emptiness in her. *It's been how many months? I warned him, didn't I—a body that heals so quickly and completely, it might "heal" a pregnancy, too, before it could take.*

No children. Probably never. Another legacy of whoever had made the chained wizards. None of the dozens she'd met in Yenit Ping knew of any pregnancies among the women. Sterile, on top of everything else.

No children for Najud. *I wonder if he told his family what I feared. Wouldn't have been so welcoming then, would they?*

*What was I before they snatched me, emptied my mind, forged a chain around my neck? Put wings on my back and furry ears on my head? Made it easy to heal myself? Who were my people, my family?*

*I had a life, I must have had. Mpeowake's nephew had a life in Ndant before he vanished and reappeared as a chained wizard in Kigali. He'd been a wizard in Ndant, but nothing touched him from his life before, not even the face of his aunt. Wiped clean, like me.*

*Was I married? Were their children, before my body was made unwelcoming to change? Will I age, or is that just something else to heal?*

A vision of an elderly Najud struck her, watching his unchanging wife, in a round Zannib *kazr*, empty without sons or daughters or their children, empty as the *zamjilah*, the wheel-ring that held the smoke-hole open.

*This isn't what he asked for. He deserves a family. Maybe he can build one with someone else.*

And the thought raised a different ache in her.

*He's in his element as a merchant, and I'm useless to him even in that.*

She took a deep breath and finished her cider. *This is pointless. I'll find out... something in Ellech, about my makers. Or I won't. I can keep looking. None of this is Najud's fault, and there's no reason he should suffer for it, whatever happens. He'll leave Ellech eventually, with Munraz. Start his caravan, build his city.*

She smiled wistfully.

*Will I be there to see it, or can I set him free for a normal life? And heirs to follow him?*

"I must have walked for miles," Penrys said.

Najud's eyes followed his wife as she described her afternoon exploring the shopping beyond the Stone Square. She fussed around their room at the guild hall, avoiding his eyes as she put things away, and he couldn't identify what the trouble was.

Penrys hadn't purchased much except for books, most of which had been delivered directly to the warehouse—almost a hundred of them, apparently. The papers itemizing them, provided by the sellers, were scattered on the table next to his chair in their room.

He'd told her about his day in return, hoping to distract her from whatever was worrying her, but she'd been disturbed all through dinner. As if reading his concern, she paused with her hands on a still-wrapped small package and lifted her face toward the handful of books on the table.

"Thought you'd like to look at those, on the trip upriver." She pointed her chin at the two nearest to him. "They're standards for all the Collegium students, whatever their eventual specializations. Basic texts for Ellech, like the ones you got from your teacher, the ones you showed me, when we met."

*The ones I carry around in my pack for when I take on students—children, not like Munraz.*

"That was thoughtful. I'll study them, see how we might make something suitable for the kind of school I'd like to build." He added a bit of worry to the warmth in his voice, and she turned her head away.

"The others are for Munraz. You won't like them."

He smiled privately at the hint of defiance in her voice. Beginner's books on devices, he knew.

"I thought we might as well indulge him while he's here," she said. "Vylkar can provide guidance for him. It's not like he'll have the opportunity once he goes back."

He lifted a hand. "I count Munraz a man grown. If he wishes to explore other ways while in a foreign land, who am I to stop him?"

"And if he wishes to continue, in depth, and bring it to your home in *sarq*-Zannib?"

Najud almost didn't answer. *Your home? Is that where the problem lies? Not our home?*

His stomach clenched, but he kept his face bland and his voice mild. "Munraz and I will discuss that if it arises, and we will hear each other's reasons."

*I knew she was homesick for Ellech, but is it that bad? She's been three years here and one with me. I thought I'd won that balance when she married me. Three years isn't very long.*

*But for her, it's her entire life, isn't it?*

Encouraged, she continued. "We'll get some more books in Tavnastok, but I didn't think you'd want to carry today's purchases up the river and back again. That's why I sent them to the warehouse and had them make those lists, so you'd know what you already had."

She cleared her throat. "You were so busy with your merchants and their ships, and the exchange. And then it occurred to me this was something I could do for you. I know the books to buy, assuming you can't just carry away the contents of the Collegium as a whole. You should be able to lay a foundation at your new school, if not do a lot of advanced research."

*Something's very wrong. She doesn't say it, but her words are giving it away. As if I'll be there, and she won't. As if she's thinking of these books as a… a farewell gift.*

*I expected her to be eager to visit the Collegium again—I want to see it myself. It's familiar territory for her. Must feel like home.*

*Was it a mistake to encourage her to come back to Ellech, just because I wanted to see it, too? To follow up on that tenuous clue about the obscure Gialfinnur? What if her past captures her again?*

He thought of his gift to her at their wedding. A necklace was customary, but that wouldn't work with her chain, so he'd found something in Neshilik, long before he'd convinced her to actually stay with him.

*Do you still have it, Pen-sha?*

He pictured the silver brooch with the spread-winged eagle for her, and a smile lit her troubled face.

*Of course I do. Wish I could wear it here.*

He stood up then, and plucked the package out of her hands, tossing it lightly to the chair he'd just vacated. He hauled her up by her empty hands and wrapped himself around her.

"There won't be anywhere to pin it, in a moment," he murmured, as he freed her arms from the foreign wizard robes she'd taken to wearing and felt her immerse herself willingly into sensation. He kept the rest of his thought private. *Where we are is home, Pen-sha, don't you know that? But I wish we were back there now, thousands of miles away. Safe.*

"What does Vylkar think he's playing at?"

Neinnur slid his eyes to Aergon, his usual ally in the senior council at the Collegium, but Vylkar's friend refused to meet them.

Ossadaer was spouting his cutomary querulous rant, and Luveri was starting to stiffen up, in her usual reaction to the old man's quavering voice.

*I don't belong here. No one listens to me. Just one more reliable vote for Vylkar's faction, and he's been away for months leaving Aergon to hold up his end. And old Ossadaer's been relentless, like a rat gnawing on a tree. Luveri's not the woman she was a year ago—Vylkar knew how to keep her flexible, but Aergon hasn't the knack. Nor do I, if I'm being honest.*

"He knew we'd hear about that dinner," Luveri responded.

"From a dozen participants," Aergon commented, quietly.

Neinnur snorted softly. The basket full of messages from the signal tower three days ago had been the impetus for this series of debates that showed no signs of coming to a conclusion.

He had work of his own he wanted to get back to. Another afternoon wasted.

"Clearly he had no intention of hiding his actions," Luveri said, and she turned a shoulder slightly to Ossadaer's side of the table.

Neinnur couldn't see Ossadaer's reaction without leaning forward to look up his side of the council table and being obvious, but he watched Feolderri taking notes across from him at the far end of the table and wondered what made a woman in her thirties spend so much time with the old steward. Ossadaer had been irritating chancellors at the Collegium since long before Neinnur's time. Four chancellors he'd served, and no sign of stopping now. And Feolderri was the newest member of the council, and by far the youngest. Seemed a pity that she wanted to spend all her time with the records, but then the council always needed an archivist.

"Penrys is one of ours," Neinnur ventured. "Surely we know her well enough to sift the truth from all of this… gossip. We sent Vylkar to Yenit Ping because of his experience—he knows the situation best and we should wait for him. They'll be here soon enough."

Istacher, next to Luveri, nodded at his words, but said nothing. *A chancy ally—she won't interfere with Luveri's actions unless they become truly outrageous.* He could hear her in his head, saying "Not my business," the way she did when the topic wandered from her duties with the council's physical arm. *At least she was good at what she did, though the days of us sallying forth to control some rogue wizard are long past. It's all play-acting now. And tradition.*

Luveri said, "Vylkar has once again tried to force my hand by lining up this public… support before speaking with me. He presumes an authority he doesn't have."

*That's torn it. She's got the bit between her teeth now.* Neinnur wished Vylkar would finally make an effort to push her out of her position. Aergon looked uncomfortable but said nothing to support Neinnur's attempt at deflecting her wounded pride. He'd tried before, at earlier meetings, but Ossadaer's relentless antagonism was taking its toll.

"I'm sure he was just taking an opportunity to defuse the rumors while he was in Stokemmi," he ventured. "We've seen his reports all along—he must have thought we'd agree with his actions."

"It's not his place to usurp the council's decision about this Penrys. The picture he paints of these chained wizards is very disturbing. It reeks of *yrmkenrolek*, and I suspect he's been seduced by it, like many another. I thought he knew better."

Istacher nodded at Luveri's words, and straightened up in her seat as though she could hear a distant horn, calling her to battle.

Luveri's gaze took in all the wizards in purples at the council table. "It's not just us. There are plenty of senior wizards here in their greens watching, waiting to see what we'll do. Whether we'll hold to our ancient responsibilities, or be driven by one lone council member. If he thinks to tie my hands, he's mistaken."

# CHAPTER 6

A week later, Penrys strolled with Najud around the deck of the riverboat. They nodded casually to the other passengers and crewmen as they passed each other, familiar with their faces and sometimes their names after five days together on board.

Neither Najud or Munraz had ever seen a powered riverboat before, so they had thoroughly explored the workings, especially Munraz who had dozens of questions about how the devices worked that spun a bladed steel wheel underwater to give the boat its propulsion to travel upstream.

Penrys had explained. "They need wizards to keep those power-stones charged, so they can't use them all the time. That's what the sail is for, when the winds are right. And coming downstream, they let the current do most of the work, using just enough power for steerage way."

She'd felt the recharging of the power-stones after they moored each evening, sometimes at a dock near a town, and sometimes wherever they could, if they were caught between landings.

Just now, they were waiting in the middle of three locks in a canal that bypassed the Meirgas rapids, the last navigational barrier below Tavnastok at the forks, still a day away if nothing delayed them. The holding pen upstream had discharged its vessels back into the upper canal to re-enter the river, and the extra water was now flowing in and raising their own boat to the level of the top lock, so that they could power through the lock gate into the final pen.

All but the most jaded passengers had come on deck to watch. Munraz was hanging over the railings at the rounded bow, trying to get a good view of the lock works, while Vylkar explained what he was looking at. Penrys and Najud settled nearby.

She watched them with a bit of an ache round her heart. *Look how well they get along, Naj-sha. Like master and apprentice. You can hear the back-and-forth.*

Najud glance at her. *They shared a cabin at sea for two months. Must have shared stories, too, despite their differences.*

Penrys, remembering some of the pastimes in the close quarters of her own cabin with Najud, felt her cheeks redden. Najud's understanding grin drew an embarrassed smile.

Najud cocked his head to catch their conversation. *He must've told Vylkar about his family. Their... breeding practices.*

Penrys concentrated on listening to Vylkar. "There were famous wizards in Ellech's past who did things like your family—they bred for power," he said.

Munraz asked, "What happened to them?"

"It was a long time ago. They tended to gain power but lose vigor and sanity with each generation.There was a line of them from the northern stretch of the Baegyl Gaer which culminated with Asuthrys, notorious for just how bad an end he came to. The annals tell us it took several dozen wizards to overpower him in the pool of the Drosentaech. After they stunned and captured him, they hung him with weights below the falls and engaged in a silent battle from both shores for a day and a night, while he fought to pull down air to breathe underwater, until he was finally exhausted. 'Drowned like Asuthrys' became a byword for well and truly dead."

Munraz grimaced. "How can I break away from that past myself? Everywhere I go in *sarq*-Zannib, every time I meet *bikrajab*... the wizards know about my family, my... line. The very name of my clan, my ex-clan, is enough to tell them my story. They don't want to share a meal with me in their *kazrab*. Who would want my blood mixed with theirs?"

"Surely it's not that way with Najud or Penrys?" Vylkar's voice was deep and calm.

"No, no. But I can't live with them all my life."

Munraz was quiet for a time while the boat slowly lifted on the rising water in the lock pen.

"I miss the annual loop of the migrations, all organized, the way my *jarghal* likes things. Everyone in his place. Maybe his new caravan will be like that. But what's *my* place?"

Penrys glanced at Najud. *Did you know it was this bad?*

He shook his head slightly. *He never speaks of it to me. It would imply ingratitude to his master, I suppose.*

*But he's not wrong, is he, Naj-sha? What will his life be like in sarq-Zannib, when he returns?*

"The caravan," he murmured. "Building the new city."

Keeping her voice down, Penrys said, "But that's in the same general region where his clan is well-known. There's no escape for him that way."

As the lock gates ahead of them swung open, the thrum of the propeller rose as it pushed the vessel forward, and then it stopped abruptly and the boat drifted slowly in the enclosed space.

She laid her hand on Najud's sleeve as though to quiet him so she could listen better, and cocked her head. The power-stones for the devices in the stern were disturbed—broken or drained.

While the passengers speculated among themselves, the captain engaged in a hurried conference with the ship's wizard who had emerged from below decks, his blue robes in some disarray. The captain raised his head and glanced over his passengers, and his eyes settled on Vylkar and his party. He strode in their direction.

With a curt nod, he said, "*Raerra, rerri*, we have an unfortunate situation and could use the assistance of any of our passengers who could help with our propellers. Do you think...?"

Penrys already knew they were the only wizards among the passengers. Even without the robes, she'd scanned the minds while they traveled to assess their occupations—so little else to do in this small enclosed space. They were just the normal batch of travelers you would expect for Tavnastok. Being the middle of the spring session, there were no students, and it was relatively unusual for any of the faculty or staff to absent themselves. The Collegium tended to operate as a little, closed world most of the time, with release sought no further away than just across the bridge.

"We would be happy to see what we can do, Captain," Vylkar said.

All of them clambered down the steps after the captain and walked astern into the room that occupied a third of the length of the boat below decks.

The ship's wizard waited until everyone was assembled before him before brushing the hair out of his face to give them a summary of the problem.

"It's like this, see. This is the very latest model of propeller system. Four power-stones on each side, to keep them in balance.

Can't do more with just the one wizard, at least not going upstream, 'cause they have to be refilled each night, y'understand?"

Heads nodded.

"Now sometimes there's a problem. Power-stones break, or we have to use more than normal for the day's journey for some reason. So that's why there's a second array of eight power-stones to slip into place instead, if need be."

He took a deep breath. "So, there was some slippage on the rotating blade earlier, while we were waiting on station in the pen, and before we could stop it, it drained the power-stones. Then we fixed it, and hooked up the new array—just a normal repair."

He glanced sideways at his captain.

"Only the fix didn't work right, and it's drained the second set of power-stones. Now we're stuck. Even if we get the repair done right a second time, I can't fill the power-stones for an array, all by myself, before tomorrow morning. I'm hoping some of you folk would be willing to help. Otherwise we'll be delayed here for half a day or more."

Penrys felt all eyes in her own party turn her way, and she cleared her throat with some hesitation. "I can power them for you. It's something of a specialty for me."

The ship's wizard looked at her. "Well, and I thank you, *rerri*. How long do you think it will take you?"

"No time at all. Whenever you're ready."

He blinked at her in disbelief.

She continued, "One of them's broken, though, so maybe you'll only get one array working."

Vylkar spoke up. "If you'll let me have a look at the device, perhaps there's a way to balance an array with three on a side, so you'll still have a backup available until you can get a permanent repair."

The anxiety on the wizard's face lightened considerably. "I guess this is our lucky day, then."

The captain pulled Vylkar aside briefly for a private conversation and then left to oversee the crew poling the ship out of the way of the rest of the canal traffic.

Vylkar and Munraz followed the ship's wizard back to look at the device, already partially disassembled at the head of the propeller shaft. Penrys would have liked to inspect the details herself, but instead she kept Najud company, since he declined either to follow them or to go back on deck. Together, they cleared a couple of boxes off to perch upon while they waited.

"It's fascinating the way everything has its own specialty here," Najud said, with sparkling eyes. "Imagine a wizard like that one spending his days keeping a boat running up and down the river. He's half wizard, and half artisan."

"Well, but they pay him for it," Penrys said. "That's how he earns his living. Like a carpenter or a blacksmith."

"In *sarq*-Zannib, our carpenters and blacksmiths also have herds and families they travel with, a clan to belong to. This fellow's family must see him only rarely."

"Maybe he's not married," Penrys suggested. "If he is, the captain probably keeps a wife and family in one of the towns he visits on his route, and other married crew must do the same."

Najud wasn't satisfied. "When we crossed the sea, that captain brought his wife, and both of his little daughters."

"They sure were cute, weren't they? Climbed like monkeys." Her smile faded as the familiar ache returned. None of his children would be following Naj-sha in his caravan. She wondered if he realized that yet.

"You know what that captain was saying to Vylkar?" she said.

Najud shook his head.

"He was no doubt offering to pay for our services. Refunding our passage cost, at least. So we're no different from that ship's wizard, are we? Everyone's got to earn their way."

She saw Najud's nostrils flair in affront, and asked him, "What, trading goods is a perfectly fine way to make a living, but not being paid for wizardry?"

He sat silent for a moment, choosing his words. "The magic that makes a *bikraj*, that's not like the feel for wood in carpentry or metal in smithing. All of those are gifts, but a *bikraj* has so much more power. And responsibility. Did you ask a fee to track the stolen people of the Kurighdunaq in snow and storm at the risk of your life? You did not. Did you ask it to put an end to the Voice before he could kill more people? You did not."

She raised her hand. "Yes. But those are things I chose to do. I couldn't spend my whole life like that—I'd starve. Wizardry is also a skill with a place in society. In that capacity, why shouldn't it be a useful skill that people are willing to pay for? A wizard has to live, too."

An uneasy silence settled on Najud, and Penrys bit her lip. "I wouldn't have charged for what we're doing right now nor, I think, would Vylkar. I don't know if he accepted the offer I suspected the captain made, or not. But what if I were someone who keeps the power-stones charged for one of the signals towers? Shouldn't that be regular service with a price?"

He looked her soberly in the face. "I have to think about this, Pen-sha. It's not what I'm used to."

With that, he stood up and walked out of the room. Penrys listened to his footsteps as they receded, then the change in timbre as he ascended the wooden stairway that connected to the upper deck.

The blood had drained from her face and she felt the chill of it. *For once, Najud's found something he maybe can't live with. And something so ordinary—wizards being paid. Why? Do you suppose it's a religious objection? Wizards should come when they're called to help, else what... sacrilege?*

Irrepressibly she pictured one of those enigmatic stones the Zannib treasured. Each of them seemed to have one, a *lud*, some found object that called to them. Najud and Munraz did—she'd seen them. She had one herself, picked up a year ago, weighing down her pack with one of Najud's. There was something about it...

For a moment she envisioned the stone standing up on end and scolding her for selling her services, but it didn't make any sense to her. Even the Kigali and Rasesni priests asked for donations or fees—how else would their temples survive?

Her stomach roiled. *He acted as if the concept were some sort of desecration. But he knows how it works in Ellech—Munraz's description of the signals tower was clear enough. So what was it? Was it something he could ignore as a foreign practice, until it was me?*

She couldn't help feeling she'd somehow soiled herself in his estimation, and it hurt. She didn't agree with his position, but it hurt all the same.

When she tried to get a sense for his mood, his mind was shut against her. It couldn't keep her out if she insisted, not with the help of her chain, but it was like a closed door to a room—the intent was enough to make her veer off without making herself known.

*We think what we think and value what we value. All this time he's been easy and understanding, but I seem to have blundered into something that matters to him fundamentally. We'll work it out. Best if I give him some privacy for now.*

She drew a deep breath and tried to calm herself, then followed the noise of three men with frustration in their voices to the back of the chamber.

"Charge that, will you?"

Vylkar, seated cross-legged on the floor, casually waved his hand over at the array straddling the propeller shaft without lifting his eyes from the disassembled device in front of him. Munraz peered intently over his knee, and the ship's wizard hovered anxiously in the background.

Penrys snorted and reached out to sense the mounted power-stones. All eight were healthy but drained. They were fixed to a rectangular metal panel with a circular hole that bit in at the bottom, four power-stones on each side evenly-spaced in an arc. The panel itself was the length of her arms, and the circular cutout fit the device Vylkar was staring at. That device had its own cutout, and Penrys noted the shaft of the propeller, still in place, surrounded at the moment by empty space where the device would go.

It was the work of a moment to charge the power-stones, and she included the seven good ones on a second panel, leaning against the wall behind them. Her chain barely felt the drain.

The ship's wizard, on the other hand, straightened with surprise when he felt the change. "How'd you do that?"

She shrugged and provided no explanation.

Like Munraz, she leaned over Vylkar. "So, how does it work, exactly?"

He resurfaced from whatever thought he was chasing and noted Munraz also watching attentively on his other side. "See the shaft? The wide extension that was added to it right where the device would go, with a small gap, of course?"

Both his students looked and nodded.

"The stones in the outer array pull on that extension, in a balanced sequence, to make it spin. Depending on the order and the speed you can spin it one way or the other, and make it go faster or slower, within limits. That extension spins the actual shaft that runs through it, and the propeller blade out in the water drives the ship."

He rubbed his chin while he thought. "The problem's either in the main power transmission device, this thing here, or in the control device, over there."

He pointed over at a small device, hung in a protective slot next to the ship's wizard. "I can't find anything wrong with this, so I'm going to put it back and run a test, and then we'll take apart the control."

The ship's wizard protested. "But that's what we did, and it drained the power-stones before we could stop it."

Vylkar smiled briefly. "And if that happens, Penrys will just recharge them for you again."

Munraz glanced at her with visible respect, though he knew almost as well as she did how easy that would be for her.

*At least someone thinks I'm doing the right thing.*

Munraz swept Najud into his excited recounting of the experiments and repairs below decks.

"She had to do a complete recharge three times, before they figured it out. I thought that wizard's eyes would pop right out of his head each time. Finally Vylkar found the fault that interrupted the flow in the control device. A bit of corrosion in the metal. They're going to claim compensation for the flaw, the captain said—he thinks they'll get a replacement unit for free when they get back to Stokemmi, and a new power-stone, too."

Penrys leaned silently on the rail on the other side of Munraz and glanced at Najud for a moment before lowering her eyes again. The breeze of movement as they exited the last lock into the westering light and followed the canal back to the main river rustled her hair. Her face was somber, and her mind wide open, inviting him to speak with her without intruding on his privacy.

Najud kept his own mind closed, barriers raised. Inside his chest, his heart seemed to skip and stutter as he ran his thoughts over what had happened below, what he'd finally realized. *This is Penrys, the foreigner who risked everything, several times, to fix the balance of the world when she found it in chaos and disorder. She's saved many lives. She's taken them, too, but no more than was proper, considering the challenges.*

*To watch her in action fires my admiration. To join her in her bed warms my heart. This is my Pen-sha, my wife—against all odds I won her.*

His muscles could feel the sensation of holding her when they'd last made love, and he rubbed his hands along his forearms to chase the feeling away.

*All this, and she doesn't understand at all. To live as a bikraj… this is a calling, not a trade. The caravan, that's a trade. But a bikraj… that's a blessing, Protector of the people, teacher to the young, restorer of balance. Not an artisan tinkering with a device, or someone who sells her services for pay, like a woman in the pleasure trades of Yenit Ping.*

*How have I missed this understanding? Did I see only what I wished to see?*

*She's right—this is the way of the Ellechen taurath, and of the Kigaliwen, too, I suppose—mercantile peoples that they are. But the Zannib…*

He surreptitiously let his eyes rest on her bent head while Munraz continued to describe the repairs to their deaf ears. *And he's another one, seduced into the Ellech ways as if he's hardly noticed what that means. The way his family was, lost to all sense of evil—I suppose I shouldn't be surprised. I have to do something about that, too.*

*But what am I to do? She knows something's wrong, but she doesn't understand. Can I explain it to her? Can she change?*

He tuned out Munraz, but his voice reminded him that Penrys had spent all afternoon fixing a device. Practical knowledge. And whether or not they paid her for it, she clearly enjoyed the exercise of her skills, as any expert would.

She'd come to him in Kigali that first time, in the tent under attack, fresh from another device in that very Collegium they were approaching, at the river fork a day's journey further up the river.

His mind conjured up a vision of *bikrajab* standing in a row at a market fair, like so many sheep for sale, and his stomach revolted. He turned his head away and watched the shore go by while his thoughts spun in circles.

"It's the devices underneath it all, I think. I'm going to have to keep Munraz from that seduction, before it's too late for *him*."

Najud's hesitant voice in the dark of their cabin reached across the little space between their built-in narrow bunks.

Penrys froze to hear what he had to say. All day long he'd kept his barriers up and she'd respected that. Now she could hear the underlying phrase, "too late for him, too." Too late for her?

Dinner that evening on shipboard had been wretched. Even polite conversation had failed them and Vylkar had been quick to notice. His eyes searched each face, but he said nothing. It took a bit longer for Munraz to catch on, and the puzzled look on his face as he glanced between them tugged at her. *I wish I could explain it to you, but I don't understand it myself.*

Najud cleared his throat in the dark and tried again. "You've felt the presence of a *lud*, haven't you? I know you have."

*You were there when I showed you what I found, Naj-sha, and you matched it with yours, and they fit together.* Two different sorts of rock they were, each unbalanced on its own.

He refused to expose his mind to her in response. "The *lud* are a sort of gift of the world, something we must respect, as we respect the world itself. It's hard to explain, even to ourselves, much less to outsiders."

Penrys's heart sank. *Outsiders like me.* She swallowed.

"So when someone comes to a *bikraj* for help, he is obliged to listen and to render whatever aid he can. Now I will not say that he goes unrewarded. The family of a student or *nal-jarghal* will make a gift, if they can afford it, for the student must be fed, and even an apprentice cannot be expected to support himself completely. Gifts are customary. But they are not required, and no *bikraj* would turn someone away on those grounds.

"If he had no time, or other commitments, or was too old or frail, or the student was inappropriate… everyone would understand. But not for lack of payment."

Penrys listened carefully, but she dreaded what was coming. At least he was speaking to her.

His bedclothes rustled as he shifted position. "As you said, even a *bikraj* must earn a living. They earn it from their other work. They tend their herds and raise their food like anyone else. They teach young ones their letters. Their families, if they live with them, make room for them around the fire and they set their hand to whatever work they find. Sometime they even become masters of it, as I seek to do with my caravan.

"But no one, coming to seek help in finding a lost horse, expects to be charged for it, as if he were buying a knife from a smith. A gift of gratitude is suitable, whatever can be afforded, but not a fee."

Penrys ventured, "But I have never done differently, Naj-sha, nor refused anyone who asked."

"No, no—I know you haven't, Pen-sha."

She could hear the strain in his voice, and even sense some of it behind his mind's barriers.

"But the devices, now… The reasons we Zannib don't use them have always seemed dry and dusty to me. Now they're beginning to make sense.

"I've traveled in foreign lands a great deal for a Zan. People at home find me rather strange in that. We like to travel, we nomads, but only in our customary annual migrations, where we recognize all the country, all of its secrets and customs. It's been simple for me to put the foreign ways I encounter into the same pack in my mind—how they greet each other, the work they turn their hands to, how the crops are different, or the rugs, or the guest customs, the languages and the clothing and the food.

"But foreign lands I traveled in had no *bikrajab*, or so we believed. The Kigaliwen thought they had no wizards, and the Rasesni kept theirs secret. Now, of course, all that has changed. We helped change it. Now they are like the Ellechen *taurath* to me, people with wizards and devices."

Penrys spoke, softly into the dark. "You must have known about Ellechen devices. And you saw the ones the Rasesni used, and the lamps and forges in Yenit Ping."

"Yes, that's true. But not until I came here did I fully understand. The devices that a wizard can make in Ellech are wonderful, but in the process the wizards have…"

She could feel him searching for a polite word.

"They've debased themselves. They study their craft like a young blacksmith who will eventually expect payment for his latches and arrowheads, so much a dozen."

Now Penrys made her own search for polite words. "If someone needs a latch, he expects to pay for it. If someone needs a device-powered light, he should expect to pay for it. If it were a candle, it would burn down and he would need to buy another. As a powered device, it would need to be recharged for a fee. It *is* artisan work, like any other. How can it be otherwise?"

She found other examples. "The new guild in Kigali… remember how the chained wizards decided to offer their services as wizard bodyguards, to take advantage of their strength? That doesn't even involve devices.

"A man might earn a living as a wizard-guard on a warehouse, and still decide to answer an appeal for help without expecting payment. The two things do not exclude each other."

Silence from the other bunk. Then a heavy sigh. "What you say is true, Pen-sha, I know it has merit. But I've pictured myself having that conversation with Khizuwi, a *bikraj* I respect. And it doesn't go the way you might expect. It would be as if, say, you used the Kigali emperor's sacred flame to light a kitchen fire."

"I know what the Kigaliwen would do, Naj-sha—they're a very practical people. Fire is fire."

"That's just it—fire *isn't* just fire, not all the time."

"It is if you have no gods," she whispered. "Or if you believe the gods don't mind."

She thought he wouldn't reply. Then the deep, familiar voice out of the dark spoke. "It's not what the gods think of you, Pen-sha—it's what you think of the gods. You, who have felt a *lud*."

She reached for his mind, but it was still wrapped tightly against her touch. *He must think even less of me than he's willing to say out loud.*

Her eyes filled and she blotted them with the edge of her sheet, trying to keep her ragged breathing silent. She waited for him to say something else, but all was silence.

*Well, I wanted him to have a real family, didn't I? Children he could raise, in sarq-Zannib. I expected him to protest, when I told him.*

*I should be grateful he's taken the initiative himself, for other reasons.*

*I just didn't expect it to hurt like this.*

She lay there, wide-awake with her bitter thoughts, as her pulse raced and her skin chilled, until she gave up on sleep. As quietly as she could, she sat up and groped for tunic, pants, and robe, and then she padded barefoot out of the cabin.

# CHAPTER 7

*What have I done?*

Najud watched for the glimpses of Penrys's face as she preceded him down the gangplank at the landing in Tavnastok. Her mind was closed to him now, but her demeanor was clear. Not angry—he'd expected angry—but alone and tired. Dejected. She'd never returned to her bed last night, and the bags beneath her eyes were eloquent. *I didn't mean to do that to her.*

*She'd so looked forward to this. Why did I have to confront her so quickly, while I was still upset? I should have waited.*

*But would anything be different if I had? If she doesn't understand what was wrong, no amount of talking will convince her. Can I live with someone who can feel a lud but can't respect the calling? But she's my wife, I can't let anything come between us. Not even that.*

She lifted her eyes for a moment to look at the city and brightened at what must be a familiar view. He watched her pointing out the sights to Munraz.

*She's come home now, after her long journey. They can take care of her here. Vylkar will see to that.*

It sounded hollow even to himself. *Does she want to stay here? She hasn't said so. She talks about the caravan sometimes as if she planned to see it.*

His thoughts dwelt for a moment on an image of the two of them riding together, with dozens of others leading pack animals, and children riding with them. *Ours or someone else's—it doesn't matter, not really. I've told her so, but I know she doesn't believe me. It's been almost a year—she must be worried about it.*

*How can I convince her it doesn't matter?*

He'd seen her unguarded face when a boy in a crowd bumped into her in Stokemmi.

*I can't. She has to convince herself.*

*We'll talk again tonight. I can't stand this silence between us—it's not right. It's already afternoon—we'll be at the Collegium by evening.*

"This will do well," Vylkar said, as he paid off the carter who'd carried their spare gear from the landing.

Penrys looked at the small pile—empty packs, horse gear, trade goods for the local market, but nothing like the volume of what was still waiting for them in the guild warehouse in Stokemmi— more than a dozen loaded packs, ready for transport. A separate pile contained everything Vylkar had brought back from Kigali. He'd send for it later, after he'd settled back into his rooms in the Collegium.

She still felt too raw from the night before to talk to Najud beyond the bare necessities. She concentrated instead on describing everything to Munraz, pitching her voice loud enough to travel to Najud's ears, too.

"You saw the river fork just before the landing," she told Munraz, after the gear was stowed. "That was the Virtaengi Gaer flowing in from the west. That's wild country up that way, farmland for a while, and then small, steep hollows with creeks that flow down to the Virtaengi, just big enough for a few families each. You see the people sometimes in Tavnastok, in their shaggy clothes. They keep to themselves, and paddle back upstream in small tippy boats."

"That river peters out before it ever gets far into the foothills," Vylkar added. "Not like the Lodentaf, which heads north past my home in Asuthgrata and climbs to its source high in the Dunnarfeol mountains."

"Can you see them from your home?" Munraz asked.

"Very well indeed. The foothills run down a great distance, and finger-like extensions of the high peaks, too."

He looked down at the young man, already taller than Najud and still growing. "That's where we found Penrys. Maybe you'll be able to visit us there, and see what it's like."

His eyes shifted to her face and she met them with a bland expression.

"Why isn't the Collegium here, in Tavnastok?" Munraz asked. "I thought that's where it was."

"It's across the river," Penrys said. "You just couldn't see the bridge from where we landed. Tavnastok's wedged into the fork of the rivers, on the high ground. Much of the district across the Lodentaf is owned by the Collegium, and the rest is farmland, like the hinterland northwest of the city itself—Estirmet, they call that. It's good land there, lush and fertile."

She smiled at him. "I'll find you a history of the region when we get to the library tonight." Her fingers itched to start going through the catalogues and shelves.

Then she noticed Najud listening to her explanation, and her spirits fell again, though she held her face unchanged. *Tonight. We'll have this out tonight.*

Penrys brightened when they climbed up the city's hill from the warehouse district, and then rounded the eastern heights, where the signals towers were, and got their first sight of the famous bridge.

Najud stopped in his tracks, and Munraz found a curb to stand on, to raise his elevation. The great stone piers, all seven of them, stood like buttresses in the middle of the broad surging river. Spring runoff was over, but the snow was still melting up at the mountain sources. The simple, flat bridge surface was supported by arches below, dozens of feet above the water, and the ends of the roadway were grounded on either shore well inland, at the same height as the bridge itself.

No spring floods or winter ice would impede the traffic on this bridge.

It was wide enough to support four wagons abreast, and people crossed it in both directions in a steady stream. The low parapets on each side were all that stood between the strollers and a deadly plunge, but none of them seemed to care. Instead, they leaned over and stared down at the froth, or waved at friends on the roadway.

Some were robed as students of the Collegium—the reds and yellows caught the eye from a distance, and Penrys saw the blues and greens of older wizards, though the colors didn't carry as brightly.

"However did they build it?" Najud wondered aloud.

"They diverted the river, pier by pier," Vylkar replied. Penrys heard the pride in his voice. "Once the piers were up, it took two years, when the ice was absent, to lay the supports and surface for the roadway."

He glanced at Munraz. "There are books about that, too, in the library. It took many wizards, working together, and a great many devices to do it. Well over two hundred years ago. There are pictures of the construction all over the walls of the school."

He strode out eagerly. "Let's get across—we still have almost a mile to go to reach the Collegium gates, and our packs get no lighter."

He led them all to the entrance of the bridge at Bridge Square, one of the market squares Tavnastok was famous for. The best of the town's many bookstores were clustered there, and Penrys saw Najud pause at the sight.

"There'll be plenty of time for that later," she told him. "They're just a short walk from the Collegium where we'll be staying."

The whole square seemed to cater to the needs of the school, primarily for food and drink, clothing, and academic supplies.

Wizards in blues and purples were clustered in a knot at the entrance to the bridge, as if waiting for someone, and Penrys focused on them, hoping to see someone she knew. She didn't like to just scan their minds—they would think it rude. She could wait until she could make them out more clearly.

Vylkar glanced over his shoulder to make sure everyone was still behind him, then raised his hand in greeting to a stout, graying woman in purple. She frowned severely, and he dropped his hand and halted some distance from her, and surveyed her companions.

Penrys recognized her—Luveri, the Chancellor of the Collegium. There were others there she knew—senior staff, mostly, and administrators of the Drosenrolkentham, to give the Collegium its full name. Two were in greens, and those were strangers to her, visitors from some other institution. All but those two she could put a name to, though she would have been of no importance to them while she was there, a strange and obscure researcher. An object of curiosity, never permitted to teach, to contaminate young students, and suffered to remain mostly due to Vylkar's influence.

*What is this? Not a coincidence. This is some sort of bad news.*

Now she scanned their minds, regardless of her manners. All were shut securely, and she didn't want to make a point of forcing her way in.

Her eyes narrowed. *No mind-speech here, eh?*

Najud touched her arm, and she saw the question in his eye when she turned. "What is this?" he murmured.

"Don't know. Highly unusual. Let's see what Vylkar does."

She kept her voice to a whisper, but she thought Vylkar might have heard her, and Munraz certainly did.

Vylkar bowed to the waiting wizards. "It's pleasant to see you all again. I hardly expected such a welcome, but then I've been gone a long time, in Yenit Ping. I'm eager to tell you all about it."

Penrys noted uncertainty on a couple of the faces, but not on Luveri's.

She stepped forward and lifted her hand to stop him from approaching. "You travel with someone who practices *yrmkenrolek*. There is no place for crooked magic here."

Vylkar raised a single eyebrow inquisitively. "Could you, perhaps, clarify your accusation?"

"That… thing behind you." She pointed directly at Penrys, who felt the furry ears hidden by her hair creep back along her scalp. All around them, a space was clearing. No one wanted to interfere in wizard business, though some stayed to watch.

"We let her in for three years, and who knows what damage she did before fleeing like a thief in the night. Not again."

Najud took a step toward her, protectively.

Vylkar said, mildly, "This *hakkengenni* has done nothing that would discredit the Drosenrolkentham or its teachings. She comes with her family to do research and to greet her old friends."

"No. She will not be permitted to enter."

Penrys straightened and leaned forward. *As if they could stop me.* Najud put a hand on her arm and she subsided.

She glanced at him and nodded. *Us against all others, eh? No matter what?*

She raised her voice. "And may I know of what I am accused, Luveri? No one was afraid of me when I left."

"I need not explain myself to you," she spat.

To Vylkar, she added, "We welcome *you* back, however, Vylkar. You have been missed. And these Zannib visitors may accompany you, if they wish it."

Munraz looked to Vylkar, confused, and Najud shook his head. "I'm not leaving."

"Listen to me, both of you," Penrys said softly. "You can't come all this way and not visit the Collegium. Go with Vylkar. He'll take care of you, and I'll be fine."

She pinned Najud with her eyes. "You know they can't stop me from just flying across. If it's too far for you to mind-speak, I'll just go land somewhere close enough. Meanwhile you can send messages. I'll let Vylkar know where I'm staying."

Najud looked stubborn, so she insisted. "It'll be all right. I have money and the power-stones, and think of all the bookshops. You be sure to take plenty of notes and make contacts for when you build your school. It won't be for long."

Vylkar waited impatiently for the discussion to reach its conclusion, and Najud nodded reluctantly.

"Good," Vylkar said. "I'll wait for your message, Penrys." He turned his head quizzically to the tense group barring the entry to the bridge, then looked at her again. "Don't do anything rash. I'll look after them for you."

"Thank you, *bilappa*." She stood where she was and watched with the gathered bystanders as they all walked onto the bridge and began the long crossing of the river. Munraz looked back once.

She lifted her eyes and saw, in the dim distance, the hill where the stone buildings of the Drosenrolkentham had been raised, topped by its signals tower—defensible and secure. Scarcely a mile away, and as accessible and welcoming as the moon.

Penrys refused to stand there under the public eye to watch her companions cross the bridge. She shifted the weight of the pack on her shoulders that disturbed the hang of her blues, and checked Bridge Square for changes since the last time she'd been here.

She spotted several wizards of various ranks, mostly students, scattered through the bystanders that were beginning to disperse. Gossip would report this all over the Collegium by nightfall, she knew, as it would relate whatever she did next.

Setting her expression to serious but unconcerned, she scanned the crowd lightly to see if there was anyone she knew. One of the blues… ah, Aergon—she remembered him. Neither friend nor enemy. When she met his eyes, he nodded at her, but didn't approach. *They must've all heard that accusation of yrmkenrolek. There'd be no reunion out here in public, not after that.*

Her eyes itched from lack of sleep. Things would look better with a meal and an early bed. It was time to secure the latter.

She ran her eyes over the buildings that lined the square. Many of them rented rooms out on the upper floors over the businesses. There'd never been occasion for her to stay overnight here before, but she'd heard stories about drinking bouts that got out of hand, or family members visiting for the short or long term while someone studied at the Collegium.

She didn't need much—a bed, a table and chair. Shelves. Shelves would be good. Someplace she could secure. She chuckled to herself—with all the shops supplying the needs of the Collegium, it wouldn't be hard to make a few devices that would deter thieves.

Her favorite bookshop was still there, in the middle of the western side of the square. She'd see if old Lepicher was still in charge—maybe she could give her some tips on where to stay. Settle in, send a message to Vylkar, and worry about things tomorrow. Maybe she'd be able to reach Najud, or even Vylkar, directly, but she'd wait until after dinner to try it.

It wasn't much, but it would do. At least it came with bedding.

It turned out that Lepicher wasn't just the owner of the bookshop—she owned the whole building. Penrys had chosen the fourth floor at the top of the stairs, with access to the roof. That would be handy for midnight flights, if any.

The downside was that the window faced east, with a view of the bridge across the square and the Collegium in the far distance, a reminder she didn't need. Shelves were promised for tomorrow, overflow cases from the shop that occupied the entire ground floor. She had plumbing, out in the hall, but no way to prepare food—no real hardship with the many cook-shops in the square and around it.

The old-fashioned ceramic stove in the corner gave the room its one spot of color—a warm red. The chilly spring of Ellech didn't bother Penrys, not with the heat rising in the building generally, and she'd declined the daily service that would supply wood or even coal for it. Didn't want to let strangers into the room anyway.

One bonus was the extra armchair, its leather worn but comfortable for a quiet read when she didn't need to take notes. She'd almost turned the room down when she saw the chair—it felt like bad luck to her, as though she'd be here for a long time instead of just a week or two, as she hoped.

She yawned, tempted to just skip supper and got to bed, but the message to Vylkar still had to be sent. The old book with its maroon cover lay open on the table next to her ink and paper. That was a fortunate find, at least if Vylkar still had his own copy.

Her devices were ready, too. Lock-dogs, she called them. Anything she could set another wizard powerful enough could disarm, but these were an invention of her own. If a wizard tried to drain their power-stones to disable them in the wrong order, then they would make a loud, continuous noise and, if moved, discharge all their power at once into the person that touched them. Ultimately they wouldn't stop anyone but, like a dog too small to be a danger, they could bark and bite, and that should be enough.

One for the door, and one for the window. The more power-stones they had, the more difficult it was to come up with the proper sequence, and the more power they could release when triggered. She'd refined her old design after seeing the way the propeller device on the riverboat handled the sequenced discharge of its power-stones. Whoever'd designed that had had some good ideas. And she had plenty of power-stones.

All evening, Najud hoped for word from Penrys but he feared the distance was just out of his reach. When he'd asked Vylkar if it was any different for him, the man had just shaken his head, and when Najud joined Munraz in the guest room they shared and tried it for himself, he had no better luck.

The buildings and the grounds and the gated wall around them were certainly impressive, stone throughout, as Penrys had told him. He approved the notion of a library housed in a stone building, something he'd have to emulate in his new caravan base.

The company, however… The Collegium wizards that barred his wife may have permitted Munraz and him entry, but that was all. They had dined together, wagging their beards as they chewed, but he was not included in the conversation. They were not encouraged to seek out other wizards and they were kept particularly out of the way of the curious students.

This was going to have to change. He wanted to go everywhere, see everything, especially the library. He needed to make friends here.

And he wanted to talk to Penrys, really talk.

A tap on the door brought him out of his chair and startled Munraz. He opened the door to Vylkar, who wasted no time. "Come with me," he said, and turned on his heel.

With a silent exchange of glances, the two Zannib followed him out into the corridor in the guest wing. Vylkar led them quietly through empty passages and obscure doors into a different part of the massive structure, until he reached another passage, well-lit, and opened a door halfway along it.

"My quarters, when I'm in residence," he told them, after he'd closed the door behind them.

"I have some protections." He waved his hand vaguely around the room. "If we keep our voices down, we should be perfectly safe."

He offered them chairs in the main room, a sort of book-lined study with its own corner heating-stove faced with dark red tiles. Three closed doors led further inward. More chairs testified to the room's customary use for hosting several people at once.

Warm rugs covered most of the floor, and the few spots on the wall that could not accommodate books displayed furs, or curious painted wooden objects. Najud suspected that souvenirs of Yenit Ping would soon appear to join them.

"I'm sorry it took so long for me to arrange for us to speak freely," Vylkar said, after he'd indicated a group of chairs for all of them to sit together. "I wanted to give every appearance of compliance to my colleagues."

It surprised Najud to see his host's teeth clenched. *Why, he really does care what happens to his foundling. He rarely shows it. I wonder if she knows?*

"I'd planned to return to Tavnastok tomorrow to close the distance between Penrys and us, to communicate, but she has forestalled me."

He reached inside his robe and pulled out a folded piece of paper, and handed it to Najud.

"This came from the Collegium's signals tower."

Najud looked it over. The first part was clear, but the rest was gibberish.

> To: Vylkar, Drosenrolkentham
> From: Vylkerri
>
> Remember the book you could never find because it was always borrowed? If no reply, I'll assume not.

23:8/19:4/3:9//47:23/ …

And so on, for a full page, with occasional periods and commas between the slashes, and double slashes.

*Vylkerri was the name Penrys gave the young qahulajti that Munraz finished off in western sarq-Zannib.* His spirits rose at this evidence that she was taking charge of the situation on her side. He passed it along to Munraz.

"I understand it's from Penrys, but what about the rest of it?"

Vylkar smiled. "My copy of Bendondaer's book on devices was always going missing because Penrys would borrow it to look something up after hours. She must have found another copy." He walked over to one of the shelves and pulled out a rather tattered book covered in worn maroon leather.

"This is what's known as a book code, and those numbers are the page and number of each letter. Unless you know what the book is and have the same edition, you can't read it."

Najud grinned light-heartedly for the first time in two days. "Clever!"

Munraz's eyes lit up. "That's a great idea! Did she invent that? What are the double-slashes?"

"It's not her invention, but it's well-thought of on her part," Vylkar said. "The double-slashes are spaces—not really necessary, but she always liked to keep the details clean."

He put the book back. "Anyone who sees this message will know it's a book code, but I intend to give them no clue about which book it is," he said over his shoulder as he carefully buried it in the bookcase.

As he walked back, he pulled another paper out for Najud. "Here's the transcription."

Msg 1

Use relay 12994 to reach me by signals tower, and confirm this receipt. Number every message. I'm lodged on the fourth floor front of old Lepicher's shop—she's renting me the room. I'm keeping my blues and my chain visible as bait and looking for books in the market tomorrow.

Everyone all right? Can't pick you out easily from all the other wizard minds there, but I can always fly by as needed.

What in all the names of the Kigali gods is going on?

P

Najud handed it to Munraz and looked at Vylkar. "Well, what *is* going on?"

Vylkar settled into his chair. "There hasn't been enough time to dig it all out, but it goes something like this… The business with Gialfinnur a generation ago–Penrys told you, yes?"

"She said he wrote about power-stones, and how to power devices with something else. I… didn't pay a lot of attention to the details."

"Close enough. That was declared to be *yrmkenrolek*, forbidden learning, though it was never clear to me what the danger was."

Vylkar looked over at Munraz. "Did she tell you about it? The book was supposed to be removed from the library here and cleansed from the catalogue, but she found a copy, shoved behind a shelf.

"He talked about crystal structures and what made power-stones unique as ways to store and release power. That part was good, solid work. Then he began experimenting with metallic crystals, and wrote about some of his theories. He gave a presentation to the senior masters here, the *raegrar*, and that's when all the controversy started."

Why?" Munraz asked. "What did he do?"

"It was before my time, and I don't know for sure, though I've heard rumors. No one would talk about it afterward. That's when they banished him, as if denying him workrooms here would stop him."

Najud said, slowly, "Crystals in metal, like the smiths study, to refine their products. Penrys thought that might include her chain. Is it so?"

"We'd have to ask Gialfinnur," Vylkar said, dryly. "I shared a class with his eldest daughter, Elkif, but she wouldn't discuss it, and she didn't stay long. I never met the son and the other daughter."

He sighed. "I don't know if anyone has any proof if Gialfinnur's even alive—he'd be older than me by more than twenty years, I imagine."

Najud said, "I know this is what brought Penrys to Ellech, chasing an old hint. But it may mean nothing at all."

Vylkar nodded. "Indeed. But apparently she has successfully disturbed enough of the senior council here to cause herself trouble. I've made a similar mistake—I've let my experience of foreign practices blind me to the parochialism of the local orthodoxy. I thought the reports on the chained wizards we found, when we looked for them, and Penrys's own report which I shared with the council here, were enough to widen their views."

"But instead?" Najud prompted.

"Instead they've gone from ignoring Penrys to being alarmed by her and the implication that Gialfinnur is somehow still around, involved with something monstrous."

"That dinner in the guild hall—not a good idea?" Najud's mouth quirked.

"Well, it remains to be seen if it might not bring new leads. But as far as the council here's concerned, the damage is done. The reports arrived here days ago from Stokemmi. And then the riverboat…"

"What about it?" Munraz said.

"How many times did she recharge those power-stones? Five times? Six? That ship's wizard was shocked. He reported it to one of his friends in town and the word spread faster than we could complete our business and walk to the bridge. 'Uncanny' was the word he used, I believe. That seems to have been the last straw."

Najud laughed sourly in spite of himself. *In trouble for just the sort of generous gesture I encouraged her to make.*

Vylkar shook his head. "I haven't sorted out all the politics yet—why some people are so strongly set on this course of action and others are not. But it's no laughing matter."

He pursed his lips, considering. "I can't put all this in a coded message. I'm going to have to speak with her in the morning, in town."

Najud said, "See if you can convince her to come somewhere within range tomorrow night, and tell me how to meet her. Tell her we've got to talk."

He though of her face, stonily set as she received unambiguous rejection by her own colleagues. *After my rejection.* He winced internally. *We'll settle this. It'll be all right.*

And those wizards at the bridge, maybe that wasn't a consensus opinion. Maybe she has friends here.

He bounced up and ran his hands down his Zannib robes.

"And tell me where I can get a set of greens. Munraz, too. We're visiting wizards, aren't we? Maybe if we look a little less foreign, I can make some new friends here. We could use some friends. Maybe we can persuade them that two beardless youths like us are harmless."

# CHAPTER 8

"That's the old edition of Eldendaer's book. You want the later one. I'm sure I saw a copy over here…"

Penrys looked up in surprise at the man already turning away from her to scan the shelves. The half-dozen books under her arm sagged, and she shifted their weight to a more comfortable position, laying down the book she'd been holding open in her free hand to do it.

This was the most expensive bookstore in Tavnastok, off the main Bridge Square which catered more to the budget-limited. It was well lit, and so clean it didn't smell quite real—the familiar scents of ink and decaying leather and paper were overlaid by sharp notes of something like vinegar. She hadn't sneezed once since walking inside.

She'd never been able to afford many of its books when she'd been here last, and had been forced to be content with chasing the same items down in the Collegium library instead of owning her own copy. *Whatever happened to the books I left behind? My clothes and things?*

The last time she'd wandered through here, working her way along shelves of books too pricey for her pocket, she'd been clad in ill-fitting, hand-me-down greens. Now she looked like she belonged, in her new, tailored blues. Everything but her face, and even that wasn't so out-of-place—not Ellech, clearly, but not too far from it. Even her brown hair matched a few of the locals.

Now money was no longer a problem, and she was swooping down on books she'd coveted for three years. *It's not just my own research, I have to line up more of the seminal works for Naj-sha, for him to take back for his school.*

The fellow was returning, book in hand and a smile of success on his face. He was a few years older than she was, and his blues were worn. His golden beard and mustache were neatly trimmed, not the bird's nest that you sometimes saw. Still, he didn't really look like the sort of prosperous citizen who shopped here—no boastful badges over his left breast. *Although there're plenty of lone researchers, working on stipends or backed by their families, who can afford the more esoteric works. And they're typically a shaggy lot.*

His mind was tightly wrapped, like many of the younger wizards Vylkar complained about. Said they were as vain of their perfect responses as they were of their clothes and, if they felt they couldn't live up to that, preferred to let no one in to catch their moods.

*I'm shielded myself, after all. Most of the wizards here are.*

He handed her the later edition and brazenly bent down to look over the titles of the ones under her arm.

"That's an odd assortment. Beginner's books, and oddball advanced things." He straightened up again, a head taller than she was, and hooked his thumb over at the counter near the entrance. "Is that your pile over there? I think I recognize the eclectic selection process."

She nodded reluctantly, somewhat overwhelmed by all this attention from a stranger.

He tilted his head suddenly. "I'm Baelnei, by the way. Are you part of the Collegium staff?"

"I'm just returning after a year away," she replied, unspecifically. "M'name's Penrys. Thanks for this." She waved the book in her hand at him and turned away to edge further down the shelf she'd been searching, but he didn't take the hint and tagged along.

"So, what's with your choices?" He was persistent, and she wasn't sure how best to handle him.

"Most of it's for someone else," she said.

"Ah, that explains it. A young relative?"

"No, my husband." There. That should be a clear enough message.

"He's not around to get it himself? There must be a story there. Why would he need beginner books?"

When she didn't answer, he continued unabashed. "So the unusual stuff must be for some project of your own. Can't make it out from the selection." He moved a little closer to check the spines of the books she carried again, and when he straightened up, he didn't move back this time. He was close enough that she could smell the dusty wool of his robe and something of his own scent beneath it. Her nostrils flared as she tried to identify what it reminded her of.

*I should tell him I'm looking for Gialfinnur's banned work and see how he reacts.* She snorted. *That would drive him away. If he knows who that is, anyway.*

When she didn't respond to his invitation to elaborate, he raised his head as if spotting a friend, and stepped away. "I'll see you around, perhaps. Good luck with your work."

*At last.* He walked off and headed for the counter, glanced at her book pile there, then gave a wave of the hand to the woman who owned the business. She greeted him like a familiar customer, and he walked out of the shop.

*What was that about? Just a friendly man, a little too curious? Or maybe just socially inept?*

*He stood too close, expressed too much interest. Or was it all harmless? Maybe he just thought I was unattached.* She glanced down at her new robe. *Maybe I just look better than usual.*

She smiled faintly. *Not used to the attention of men, is it? Three years of drought in Ellech, and then Najud.* Her smile faded. *And if Najud goes back to sarq-Zannib without me? What then?*

Penrys turned the corner into the Bridge Square, headed for her room. She'd sent more than half of her most recent book purchases on to the warehouse near the landing where they'd be added to their goods, but the ones remaining were bulky and heavy enough that she wanted to get rid of them before her lunch.

The square at mid-day was teeming with students who were able to escape their classes for a better meal or some other convivial activity, and a handful of older wizards. Fully a third of the people she could see wore wizard robes. A normal day, she thought, one she'd seen many times before.

She ran her mind over them automatically. Most were shielded, and only a couple were familiar, until, nearby, she recognized Vylkar. There'd been no message from him this morning—she'd checked at the signals tower.

Her stride stuttered, but she managed not to look around for him. She turned into the alley next to her own building and took the back entrance, bounding up the stairs with her books until she ran out of breath, then plodding the rest of the way while her heart pounded. She concentrated on disarming the device she'd set at the door, then dumped her books on the table and collapsed into the chair near the window.

In a moment, she stood up again and drew the curtain across to block out the square, and anyone else's view who might be using a far-seeing device to look in.

*Bilappa? I didn't see where you were.*

*Lingering over my second serving of bunnas after a nice meal. They want to throw me out to make room for a better customer, but I'm wearing my purples.*

She could hear the humor in his mind. It was unlike him to be so open with her.

*You're late.*

Now that sounded more like the Vylkar she knew. By now she'd placed him. Must be that inn on the corner—a logical spot for a good meal, too expensive for students.

*Well, I didn't know you were waiting for me. I had errands to run.*

*As did I, a good excuse for coming here that no one will believe. Even so, better you not join me so publicly. I left you some parcels down at the warehouse. Didn't want to betray that I knew where you were.* There was a pause. *I have a great deal to tell you.*

Her stomach rumbled, but she'd just have to wait. *I'm listening. I take it you found the book you needed.*

*Yes, yes, that was well done. Now attend, hakkengenni.*

He described what had occurred since they separated and the immediate causes of the Collegium's reactions.

*I've been away several months and it will take a few days to understand everyone's position and why.*

She considered his information. *I thought the senior council just ignored me when I was there. I had no idea they were actively afraid of me. What did I ever do to them?*

Memories of solitary meals, snatched at odd hours, of watching clusters of young students chattering with their friends, of eventually winning some grudging respect from others doing obscure research alone or experimenting with devices—that's what came to mind when she thought of the place. They were her oldest memories, after the first few days when Vylkar found her on the hillside in the snow. Her only memories.

Not a warm place, the Collegium, for someone like her, but she wasn't a child. For three years, it had been her home. She had shelter, resources, and a place to work. She could have picked up where she left off, now. Under other circumstances.

Still, it was quite a distance between that and downright exile. And now she needed them, the library in particular.

*You've made them uncomfortable, and for rigid minds, that's enough. And in their defense, there's more. The hints of yrmkenrolek, specifically Gialfinnur's, are greater than when I left. More than gossip, less than evidence.*

*Rumors.*

*Yes. I would have paid them no attention except that I've seen things since then.*

Things like her experiments under his eye on how a chain like hers could store and release power, how she could call upon a chain not her own to move, bind, or destroy—just like a power-stone, only much more powerful. She still had half a dozen chains in her pack, and a few bits of link fragments, wrapped up neatly next to her half-filled sack of power-stones. Gifts from Tun Jeju, of Kigali's Imperial Security, taken from the dozens of chained wizards that had been identified and killed before the panic could be stopped.

*So they're not going to let me into the library. And there are people there I'd like to talk to.*

*I don't think you should plan on it any time soon. We can do research for you…*

She interrupted him. *And draw down the same accusation of yrmkenrolek on your own behalf? I won't do that to you. By the same token, it wouldn't be wise for me to meet with others like this, either, lest it be discovered. No reason for me to drag anyone else down.*

The whole thing left a sour taste in her mouth. *I can do some research here—there are books I never got around to in the library. And I have what I need for making devices. If there are fresh rumors, as you say, get me the details. Maybe there's some truth behind them, and maybe it's what I'm looking for. Maybe I can track the smoke to the source from outside the all-knowing Collegium. If not, we'll worry about it then.*

There was no response for a moment.

*You haven't asked about Najud. Or Munraz. Najud wants to speak with you, but we thought he would be too conspicuous coming here like this.*

She tried to keep her clenching stomach from coloring her thoughts.

*I'd like to speak with him, too. At least like this if not face to face. I scanned the Collegium last night, but there are just so many wizards there, and I thought it would be out of his range.*

*He wanted to position himself someplace along the walls where he would stand out for you, but I explained he would attract attention. So I suggested the main study room of the library, for the books that are not allowed to be carried out. It never closes, and you know where it is. He'll be there every night for the hour before midnight and, if he can't, Munraz or I will try to be in his place.*

*That'll work. I can fly over there and reach him easily. Good idea. We can still use the book code for anything that can't wait.*

Another pause from Vylkar, She pictured him paying for his meal.

*What's the matter between you and Najud? It troubles me.*

*It's… private, bilappa. There are things we've discovered that we think about differently. Important things.*

*Perhaps not as important as you both think, in what passes for the wisdom of youth.*

Her mouth puckered at the tartness of the observation.

*How are they settling in?*

She felt Vylkar's astringent humor. *He was choosy, but we finally found him some greens that satisfied him, and some for Munraz, too. And the turbans have vanished. They look young and innocent, and I know them both well enough to marvel at the illusion. When I left them, your husband was setting off to make some new friends.*

A smile warmed her. She could picture it so easily.

*Tell him I'll look to speak to him tonight. And thank you, bilappa, for your help.*

*I want answers, too. Pretending there's nothing to look into is like denying the chained wizards exist. I know better, and so should they.*

Penrys took Vylkar's hint and made sure the warehouse near the landing was on her circuit for the afternoon excursion. She presented the token they'd each received when they reserved the space and followed the attendant into the stone-floored building, his boot heels and hers audible once the outer door was closed to shut out the sound of the river, just two blocks away.

The large horse packs they'd brought with them from Stokemmi, both full and empty, rested partway along one wall on a wooden platform to keep them out of the dust and any potential floodwater. In front of them new packages were beginning to accumulate.

She recognized the book parcels from several stores—all the morning's purchases had already arrived. Next to those were three crates, each covered only by a dusty cloth, and some small rolls of carpet. She freed a corner of the nearest crate and suppressed a gasp, conscious of the warehouse attendant standing behind her with his raised lamp. These were books, books she recognized from her room at the Collegium.

Penrys pawed through them briefly—most were not pertinent to her current need, but here was her copy of Varmatau, the standard for advanced device theory. She pulled that out, and a few more from the second crate, and put them aside before she laid the cloths over the top again.

*They must have emptied my room, and not recently. No doubt right after I vanished. No library books. What about my old notebooks? Anything useful there?*

She dug into the second crate again and found the bound ledgers buried at the bottom, eight of them, dinged on the edges and scarred by casual treatment in the workroom. Loose slips of paper peeked out between the pages.

*Seems like yesterday. My notes on Gialfinnur's book should be in there. D'ya suppose they never looked through them? Why would they, after all?*

She replaced the cloth over the crate and turned to the third one. There, wrapped in bits of her abandoned clothing for protection, were all the little treasures of her room. Two small carvings from Vylkar's family home in Asuthgrata, one a landscape of the mountains, quite old, and the other a portrait of a nut-tree, carved into a small panel of the tree's own wood. There were dozens more like them in the sprawling wooden lodge, and her *bilappa* had gifted her with these two for her walls in the Collegium.

There was no point going through all this under the eyes of a stranger. Penrys rearranged the contents more compactly and found room for the books and notebooks she'd pulled out of the other two.

"I'd like this crate delivered up by the Bridge Square," she told the attendant. "D'ya think you can find someone for that? I'll walk up with him. Those rugs, too."

*Imagine Vylkar thinking of this. I wonder where they were stored?*

Penrys slumped into the chair by her window after her solitary dinner and admired the room. One of the two bookcases was now half-filled. Her three old rugs did much to warm up the wooden floors, and the carvings and other small decorations hung from old nails or sat on whatever surface would hold them, bright bits of color that echoed the unlit red corner stove.

When she'd unrolled the largest rug, almost as long as she was, she'd been delighted to discover inside it the quilt she'd brought to Tavnastok from Asuthgrata, a present from Vylkar's elderly mother. It was intended for warmth and wear, pieced in random fashion from woolen remnants, and decorated along the seams with colorful coarse yarn embroidery. The backside was a single piece of blanket flannel, tacked through the padding to the decorative front at regular intervals.

It was the work of some farmer's wife, decades ago, pulled out of a chest in a spare room in the lodge in Asuthgrata and judged suitable for a student. She hadn't been a student, not exactly—too old for that, too powerful for the red robes or the yellows—but her life of study and research wasn't very different, and she remembered vividly the pleasure of slipping under its heavy warmth after hours spent in a cold room reading by an unlit fire.

On the table next to her old notebooks lay a new one, with her new pens and ink. Her *lud* was there, too, balanced on Najud's, his stone serving to uphold hers. He'd given her his to carry, since neither felt right in isolation, and her eye kept coming back to it. The palm-sized dark-gray granite, speckled with bits of black, supported her streaky orange-gray sandstone with its rough base as though they'd been carved together, though each had been picked up separately, and at different times. The leather pouches Najud had made for them were neatly stacked on an empty shelf.

Penrys didn't understand this Zannib business about a *lud*—a small rock, or bit of wood, or a spot by a tree, or an entire cliff face. Something numinous that they didn't analyze. The ones that were part of the terrain had names, sometimes. Even stories.

Even so, she wasn't immune to the sense that there was something... *more* about her stone than just what was apparent. A Zan hoped to find a few such portable... whatever-they-weres in his lifetime. *I suppose if I think it's something more than a rock, then it is, at least to me. You get out of it what you put into it. Maybe that's all it is.*

Najud had never heard of a two-part *lud*, but there it sat.

She'd be talking to him tonight. Her old workroom clothes were hanging behind the door to rid them of some of the wrinkles they'd picked up as padding. Nice and dark they were, with no betraying bits of white for her flight across the river in a couple of hours.

What were they going to say to each other? She couldn't work it out, couldn't envision how it would go.

Her eye fell on her narrow bed in the rented room, and the warmth faded out of it. *It's like the nightmare version of coming home, the ghost of my old room, only smaller, older, and emptier. And everyone I know is over there.*

She scanned across the river, the hundreds of minds in the Collegium, but she couldn't pick out the one she wanted.

It was a chilly spring night, but the distance was short, and it took only a few minutes for Penrys to identify a spot downstream of the Collegium walls with no minds nearby. There was enough starlight to make out the edge of a field, cleaned from its winter cover but not yet sown, and a border of trees to conceal her once she landed.

Her wings flared out behind her to spill the wind and brake her flight.

*How long ago was I last in the air? Not since we left Kigali. Too many Ellechen taurath on board the ship to indulge then, and after we reached Stokemmi, no opportunity. I could detour around the countryside tonight after we're done, and get some exercise.*

She glanced up at the starlight, and reconsidered. *Maybe I should wait for a darker overcast night for that.* She pulled her shoulder-length hair out of its loose ponytail and coiled up the ribbon for later before shoving it into a pocket. *Too irritating to have my hair blowing in my face every time I turn my head out of the wind.*

A few feet into the trees she found a reasonable place to sit, on a rock bordered by a tree sturdy enough to lean against. She brushed the winter leaves off and settled herself, sliding one hand into her pocket and fondling the *tennendaer*, one of two she'd recovered from her crate. The little finger toy gave her something to fidget with, and she hadn't found good substitutes since she'd been gone, something to run her fingers over while thinking. The metal one was the first that came to her hand when she scooped one off the table in her room before she shut the door behind her and sneaked up to the roof.

The ivory one she'd left behind came from Vylkar's lodge in Asuthgrata, something she'd picked up out of the same trunk that provided her bed quilt. She had to be careful with it, since sharp things in her pocket would scratch it, so it always needed a pocket of its own. She'd formed the habit of slipping that one into her night-robe when she studied in her room.

The metal one could stand up to anything. She'd found it in the corner of the old workroom they let her use, almost as far as you could get from the larger, better-equipped ones. *Took me a day just to sweep it out and clean it up, and that finger-friend was part of the sweepings.* It looked like a bit of surplus metal from a casting, maybe, rounded at the edges and melted. There was still a small forge in the room which had come in handy for her experiments—she'd "borrowed" the other things she'd needed to equip the room one by one over time.

The tree was cold against her back and the chill of the ground crept upward from the rock she sat on. *Next time a warmer undergarment.*

She snorted at herself. *Quit stalling.*

Enough vegetation grew between her and her target to render the buildings and any lighted windows invisible, but that didn't matter. To her mental scan, the wizard minds in that direction blazed like a bonfire. She worked out just where the library's main reading room was, relative to her position and elevation, and tried to narrow down her focus to just that spot, looking for the three minds of her companions, any or all of them.

*There he is. Najud. Just him.*

She composed herself. *Been waiting long?* She pictured for him her sylvan location and the flight across the river.

*Happily there's no moon out yet so I didn't have to worry much about being silhouetted. I hope.*

*Ah, Pen-sha—I wish you were here!*

She felt the warmth of his welcome, and it made her ashamed of her doubts. His mind was lightly shielded, to keep their conversation private, but enough got through to make his emotions clear.

*Vylkar told us everything, but he didn't see the place where you're staying. What's it like?*

*Like my room at the Collegium. Literally—Vylkar found my old clothes and things, and I used some of that to decorate it.* She took a moment to show him, complete with the view out her window to the Collegium buildings across the river.

*Got you some more books, too. Started a new list.*

*Books! Pen-sha, I spent most of the day wandering through part of the library, like a horse looking greedily for its next bit of tasty grass and abandoning what's already in his mouth in the process. I couldn't choose—too much abundance. Munraz eventually asked me how they're organized, and then I realized that's where I should start. You know how it works, of course.*

*I ought to. Spent most of my time there, when I wasn't in a workroom.*

She felt his hesitation. *I thought you could show us how to do that right when we got home. You'll do that for us, won't you?*

*Assuming I'll be there,* he means. Penrys took a deep breath.

*Let's talk about this, Naj-sha. Wish I could see your face. Can you do it, in public like this, and silently? I don't know when we'll be able to see each other next, and I hate the waiting.*

He took a moment to steady himself. *Pen-sha, I should never have said what I did about wizards taking a fee. I was just...surprised, and it slipped out.*

*No it didn't. Or rather, yes it did, but it's important to you, however it came out. And we should talk about it.*

He paused. *I know you were looking forward to getting here, eager to come... home like this, and I spoiled that.*

*Less eager by the moment, Naj-sha. And it wasn't you who spoiled it, but that bunch of self-appointed, closed-minded, orthodox, redenrolek, hidebound...* She lost the thread of her sentence and felt Najud's laughter.

*You just caught me in a low moment, Naj-sha. Not your fault. But...*
She felt Najud's mind sober in anticipation.

*But you know it's not right for me to take you away from children, a family of your own. And I'm not your model of what a bikrajti should be, like a real Zan. And that... that worries me.*

*And I'm not tall, and my family is boisterous, and I plan to do things no sane Zan would. I'm no perfect bikraj myself. It's you I want, not some non-existent paragon. It's you I want in my bed, and riding a horse beside me, and...*

She interrupted him. *And discovering ever more monstrous things about what this chain can do, and where I come from? I still believe that it's *slaves who wear chains, and I'm waiting for the tug of my master. I can't let that disrupt your life.*

There was a pause before he replied.

*You may never know, Pen-sha.*

She moistened her lips. *Yes, I may never know. And what kind of foundation is that? Even my people, my tribe… no one recognizes it.*

*The world is a big place, and many strange things have yet to be discovered.*

There was acceptance in his mind for whatever she found, but she couldn't just sink into that. And it wasn't fair to just leave him hanging either.

*I'll try to set a limit. I don't know if I can live with it, but I'll try. I want to stay long enough to track down the whole yrmkenrolek thing, the rumors about Gialfinnur. If that provides no answers then… well, then I'll learn to live with it. It might take a while—you might need to go back to sarq-Zannib ahead of me for the first caravan.*

Najud cut her off. *I won't leave here without you. It if takes longer, then it takes longer.*

She could feel him bracing himself. *You wouldn't want to remain here, if the whole problem were just cleared up? If they let you in?*

Suddenly she realized just how scared of that he must be. That she had "come home" and now would want to stay. She pictured it for a moment and shook her head.

*No. No, Naj-sha. You and I have things to settle, but I'd rather be with you, wherever that takes us. This place make me sad, now, not contented. It's a poor second choice.*

His obvious relief brought a smile to her own face. *Then how can I help? The sooner you run down this trail, crooked or straight, the sooner we can go home.*

He pictured for her the inside of the fancy canvas and felt-walled *kazr* gifted to them by Umzakhilin of the Kurighdunaq, the one he'd had made for his son who never returned from the disaster that had overtaken the tribe. It was packed away, supports, smoke-hole, and furnishings, in their big horse packs back in Stokemmi. That was "home" for him, now.

And for her, too, if she could get back to it. But there was a lot of work to do first.

*I don't know, Naj-sha. You can't do research in the library for me on devices—neither you nor Munraz know enough. I'll talk to Vylkar about that. What you can do… First, build your own business. Make contacts you* can call upon later from sarq-Zannib for advice on books and other things. Maybe you can find books in the library that are especially tempting—tell me about them and I'll see if I can find copies for you. Maybe I've already gotten them.*

She felt his agreement. *Then, while you're doing that, maybe you can find out why there's such a stir about yrmkenrolek just now. They know the Zannib think of devices as forbidden, an yrmkenrolek of sorts—maybe you can use that to explore the larger version of the taboo that has shut me out of there. Maybe they'll talk to you, a charming outsider not part of their world. No threat.*

*You think I'm charming?*

She could almost hear the self-satisfied chuckle.

*I hope that bed you've got is just as narrow as mine.*

Rhetorical woe colored his mental voice. *And I'm sharing the room with Munraz.*

*Serves you right, Naj-sha. Think of it as motivation.*

# CHAPTER 9

Four days later, Penrys leaned back from the table in her room and stretched her back. It seemed like hours since she'd left the room for lunch.

The first gleaning of the bookshops in Tavnastok had been completed. The books for Najud had gone straight to the warehouse near the landing to join the others, but the ones for her project were here. One bookcase was filled and the overflow had begun for the second one. She didn't have everything she needed—the notebook open before her had a growing list of books she knew that existed, many in the Collegium's library. But she'd found many of the key works, the places she would turn to for information about metal and crystals and power-stones if she'd had the full library at her disposal.

Her notes from reading Gialfinnur's work a couple of years ago were not very detailed, but they did include references to other books that she wanted especially to find, in an attempt to reconstruct what he was working on. It was time to give the bookshops a search list so they could speak to other collectors on her behalf.

She fingered the metal *tennendaer* in her pocket. *Those lists would confirm for everyone that I'm looking into yrmkenrolek, which is what they accuse me of. Doubt it can make the situation worse.*

It took her at least an hour to skim the denser books, looking for anything that might bear on her narrow topic. She glanced at the bookcases. *Halfway through. Another few days of this is about all I can take.*

Her meals forced her outside to take a break every few hours, and the evenings let her slip away to visit Najud, mind to mind, from her favorite tree and rock.

Two nights ago, his place had been taken by Vylkar. Najud was being entertained by some of the senior librarians and a few of the instructors who had decided to make his quest to build another library in the far south into a pet project they could help with.

Vylkar filled her in on his cautious inquiries into the rumors that swirled around Gialfinnur. Alive. No, not alive. People in Tavnastok that looked like him. No, they were too young. His children have left the country. No, someone saw the younger daughter, remember her? Not so young, now.

Penrys had judged them useless, and Vylkar agreed. If she didn't turn up anything else in the rest of these books, or the ones that might be found for her, what would her next step be?

Vylkar had asked for a list of the books she sought, and offered to look through them himself if they were in the library, but she was reluctant to tar him with the *yrmkenrolek* brush, and she'd evaded the issue for now.

*Maybe this will be a dead end after all. Would that be so bad? I could admit defeat and return to sarq-Zannib with Najud, and we could get on with our lives.*

*Can I live with that?*

*Well, I'd have to, wouldn't I? We can't always get what we want.*

She'd left Vylkar with one line of questioning. What happened when Gialfinnur was expelled? Was it sudden or did he take everything with him? Were there things abandoned, destroyed, or maybe even stored somewhere, forgotten, like her things had been?

And when his oldest daughter Elkif returned as a student, an age-mate to Vylkar, where had she come from?

No answers yet, and they might not be helpful when they came.

After a glance out the window to judge the angle of the sun, Penrys decided it was time for dinner. She'd sampled several of the choices in and beyond the square, and the thought of trout and spring greens inclined her to the River Home, two blocks west. When she'd lived here before, there'd been little opportunity to explore—the Collegium provided her meals, and if she was going to eat alone, she'd rather do it there, in her workroom or late at night.

She'd eaten an evening meal at the River Home twice already and there was still plenty to sample from its bill of fare. They let her sit quietly in a well-lit corner with a book and she was not above listening into conversations, both spoken and silent, trying to see if she stirred any curiosity or interest beyond the ordinary.

She shut her notebook and picked up one of the dryer foundation works on metallurgy. It would go down better with a mug or two of their excellent cider.

"D'ya want horseradish with that?"

The very notion brought a broad smile to Penrys's face. She hadn't tasted that in more than a year. "Excellent idea."

The server laid the hot trout before her, and the platter of fresh bread and a pot of butter. "Be right back with it," she said.

Penrys inhaled deeply and didn't bother waiting. She'd managed three savory bites, by the time the woman brought the dish of horseradish and set it down.

"Don'cha have no one to eat with? Seems a shame—every time I've seen you, it's a book keepin' you company, 'stead of a friend. Or a man."

Penrys blinked as she realized she'd been so well-noticed on her two previous visits. "I'm just visiting, and my husband's away for a little while. You know what we're like."

She gestured at her blue robes, and the server nodded. "No tellin' wizards anything, is there?" She softened the rueful saying with a smile. "You just let me know if you want anything else. Got a nice dried-apple tart for after, if ya want it. With honey."

After a few bites, Penrys turned away from listening in on the ordinary conversations. *Nothing useful there.* Her book may be dry, but her meal and, more importantly, her cider were not.

Two chapters went by and she was sopping up the last bits of flavor with a chunk of her bread when she was broken out of her concentration by a man looming over her, blocking her view of the other diners

*How'd he get so close without me noticing?*

She kept her face smooth as she looked up from her book. *Him again!* The persistent fellow from the bookshop a few days ago smiled down at her, like a very tall lion in his golden beard. *How did he find me?*

"I thought that was you, when I came in here," he said, with a little nod. "I hope I'm not disturbing you?"

He didn't quite snatch the book out of her hand to see what it was, but his body language made it apparent that he wanted to know.

Penrys tried to get some sense of him but he was well-shielded against her mind scan. *Well, if I'm going to be bait, I have to let him get a taste, don't I?*

"No, not at all. Are you alone? Have you eaten?"

The serving woman showed up to clear the dishes but hovered over them as if making herself available if Penrys wanted help disposing of her visitor.

Penrys, much amused, offered the man a seat. "I'm about to have dessert. May I offer you some?"

Baelnei pulled an unused chair away from a nearby table, and placed it next to Penrys, with much flapping of the sleeves of his robes. Up close, she could see the careful stitches and the tiny holes of spark burns which were the marks of a well-used garment. All this commotion did not hide from her that he'd managed to wedge her in so that she would have a hard time leaving without his cooperation.

"What was your name, again? Ah, Penrys—that's it, isn't it?"

She would have bet most of her sack of power-stones that he knew exactly what her name was.

"Still on your own, I see. Your husband not back yet?"

"No, not yet," she said.

"I must admit I'm curious about your project, the one you said you were working on."

He nodded off-handedly at the server who brought them each a plate with a warmed-up tart, and small pots of honey and cream.

Penrys ignored him for a moment to drop a dollop of honey onto her tart and a generous helping of cream. She took a bite, licked her lips, and smiled.

The man had stopped speaking.

"Sorry, you were saying?" she asked.

His face went still as he tried to decide if she was being deliberately rude or not. "I was wondering if your work had anything to do with…" He raised his hand and gestured toward his throat.

*Snap! There's a mouthful of bait gone.*

"This chain of mine?" she asked, casually. "Why, have you seen one like it before?"

"No, but I've been hearing stories. I wondered if that's what they were talking about."

She couldn't decide if he was lying or not. "Stories?"

"Well, they talked about—excuse me—dead wizards."

She let that line just sit there while she had another bite and savored the taste of cinnamon.

"*I'm* not dead. I'd like to find out more m'self."

*There. Let's see what he does with that.*

"Really? I'll check with my friends and see if they can remember anything else."

He forked up his own tart, without honey or cream, as if it were a matter of indifference what he was eating.

"That would be kind of you," she said. "Perhaps we'll run into each other again before I have to go."

She'd deliberately timed it so that she caught him with his mouth full, and kept her expression bland while he hastily swallowed.

"I'd be delighted to escort you around Tavnastok," he said, when he could.

"Thank you, but I know the town well. And, besides, I plan to show my husband the place myself, soon as I can. Now, if you'll excuse me, I need to get back to my work."

She caught the eye of the serving woman, and Baelnei was finally obliged to stand up again and take his leave.

"Not a good idea to let one of them *taunnupar* get close to you like that. They don't usually come to the east side, that far from their river—thought you might not know what he was."

Penrys looked up at the woman's remark, her hand suspended in mid-air with the coins for her meal. She knew of the Glymbeod folk, up the Virtaengi, but she didn't remember them hanging around the Bridge Square much. Not that it was easy to tell, since they looked like everyone else, except for the poorest of them—no one was as ragged as a woods-rat. "Why do you think he's one?"

"Stands too close, pushy, and the boots give it away."

"Boots?"

"Didn't you see the laces? That old-fashioned lacing across the instep's a dead giveaway—they're the only folk who still fancy it."

On her way back from dinner, Penrys searched for Baelnei. His mind may have been shielded, but she had the flavor of it, now, and he was nowhere to be found.

Half a block away from the back entrance to her building, a mechanical shrieking sound caught her attention, and she noticed people milling around outside the buildings as if trying to detect where it came from.

*Where have I heard that before? Something about a workroom...*

She ran the rest of the way and pelted up the back stairs until she reached the top floor, where she pushed her way through the people standing along the hallway.

With a sigh, she drained the power-stones of her intruder devices back into her chain, and the grating noise ceased. She looked sheepishly at Lepicher, prominent among the bystanders with her arms crossed and a pained expression on her face.

"I am sorry to have created a disturbance, *rerri*, but I set something up to deter those who would enter my room in my absence."

By then everyone had seen her blues and she could see the looks of "wizard affairs are for wizards" dismissal that put the disruption into a tidy category for them, instead of a sinister, unfamiliar experience.

One old woman said, "I hear'd some footsteps go by my door, and then all that noise. Couldn't tell where it was comin' from right off."

She nodded with a certain air of satisfaction. "Hear'd them footsteps going away a mite faster."

Before Lepicher could open her mouth to speak, Penrys's neighbor added, "Good to have a wizard around, keep the place a bit safer, eh?" With that, she retreated into her room and shut the door behind her.

Penrys's landlady took a deep breath and tried again. "I know you warned me about this but I had no idea how much noise it would make."

"I know, and I'm sorry, *rerri*, but…" Penrys unlocked the door. "Why don't you come in and I'll explain."

She let her in and offered her the armchair. Then she closed the door and shut the rest of her nosy neighbors out.

Lepicher's quick eyes took in her decorations and the books. "I thought you were joking when you asked for two book cases," she said, "but I see I was wrong. Think you'll need another one?"

Penrys laughed. "I hope not. Though there's a list of things I'm looking for you might be able to help me find."

She stooped down to pick up the device that had been shoved to the side by the opening of the door. "About the noise… Look, here's one of the devices, see? There's another one just like it at the window. I set them when I leave, and if someone tampers with them while I'm away they go off." She looked Lepicher in the face.

"If they persist and try to pick them up, they'll get a nasty shock, too."

Her landlady nodded slowly. "That's why you turned down the cleaning service, right? Well, you did warn me, and I can't see that you've let the room get dirty. But what happens if you're gone for a while?"

"The charge only lasts a few hours before it wears off. Then they're harmless."

Lepicher grunted, unconvinced. She turned her gray head and did a practiced survey of the furnishings. "Where'd you get all this nice stuff? Didn't have it with you when you came."

Penrys hooked her thumb out the window in the direction of the Collegium. "I lived over there a while, and my friends sent me my things out of storage. Glad to get them back. Memories, you know."

Lepicher smiled in understanding, then pushed herself out of the chair. "Not too bad, this," she said, looking down at it.

She turned at the door to look back at Penrys. "Will there be much more of that, do you think?" She pointed her chin at the device still in Penrys's hand.

"I don't know, *rerri*."

"Hmmph. Well, you've a right to sleep safe in your bed, I suppose, and I don't imagine whoever it was will try it again. Goodnight to you."

With that, she took her leave and Penrys sank down on the edge of her bed in relief. She hadn't thought about what might happen if the alarm was triggered, and realized she might have been evicted.

*Who was it? Not Baelnei—there hadn't been enough time for it to be him. His job must have been to follow me to the River Home and keep me there while someone else broke into my room. What do they want?*

With a sigh, she locked her door from the inside and reset the devices. *Better leave them on, now, even when I'm here.*

"Thought I might find you here."

Najud straightened up from trying to read titles along a lower shelf back in one of the dimmer parts of the research library and recognized the red-haired man in blues who'd spoken.

"Were you looking for me, Daerget?"

Of all the librarians Najud had approached, describing what he wanted to accomplish with this visit, this tall young man with the odd accent, the slightly shaggy red beard, and the eye-patch had been the friendliest, willing to spend time with him instead of just dismissing him with a list of recommended books for a new library.

Daerget glanced around to see if anyone could hear them, but the stacks in this area were deserted. "I have a couple of things I think you might find interesting. Or rather, Penrys."

Najud lifted an eyebrow.

"I knew her when she was here, did you know? We all did." He gestured vaguely to include the other absent librarians. "She was in here enough."

He shook his head. "Never did understand the things she worked on, you know, but I helped her find the books she needed."

Najud made his expression as open as possible, to encourage the conversation. "Did you two become… close?"

Daerget looked faintly shocked. "I wouldn't have dared. She didn't show off, but we all knew how strong she was. I sometimes thought she didn't realize the difference between what she could do and the rest of us. And then she kept to herself a lot."

Najud remembered Penrys's summary of her male colleagues when he'd asked her about her relationships here. "I was too scary for them," she'd said ruefully, and here was the proof. He kept his grin to himself.

"So, what happened to her?" Daerget asked. "Where did she go, and how?"

"Too long a story to tell standing up and with a dry throat, don't you think?" Najud replied.

A smile flickered on Daerget's face. "Would you care to visit my room? I can provide both a seat and refreshment, as well as those things I thought Penrys might like."

"And there we were, frozen in our places inside the Kigali command tent when this woman pops up out of nowhere."

Najud recounted Penrys's accidental appearance in western Kigali a year ago, her experimental device in her workroom at the Collegium having properly located a strong source of power, and improperly sent her there, unprepared.

"It's a long story… The Kigali went in to push out the Rasesni who had invaded their westernmost province of Neshilik, only to discover that the Rasesni were fleeing a wizard they named Surdo, that's 'The Voice' in their speech—a man with a chain around his neck, like Penrys's, who could control both wizards and others."

Daerget's one eye was wide, and the mug in his hand forgotten as Najud paused in his account. Najud lifted his own and sipped at the device-cooled ale. He'd been surprised to discover that Penrys's report of events to Vylkar was not common news among the staff.

*No wonder the council here thinks it can just declare her to be on some sort of crooked track and dismiss her out of hand. No one knows what's really going on. I don't know what Vylkar's thinking, but it's time the story got out generally.*

"Penrys trained some of the Rasesni mages and organized a stand against the Voice, before the Kigali reached them. They were successful, and a war was prevented."

"What happened to the wizard?"

Najud swallowed. *Better tell it all.* "Penrys killed him. With a hatchet. It was a bloody mess."

Daerget looked around his tidy room, the small rugs in cool blues with angular patterns, the quiet crackling of coals in his stove to ward off the spring chill, and his books tidily ranged along his many shelves. "I… I can't imagine it. A chain like Penrys's, you say? I'd heard they found some other people like that, but they were all dead."

"That's what was found in Ellech," Najud said. "In other countries, they turned up both living and dead ones, and the living were all wizards. Even in Kigali, where the wizards had been in hiding for centuries."

"What made them start looking? Was it Penrys?"

"Not exactly. You know the story of how Vylkar found her, about four years ago now? That's about when the Voice first appeared. And when we went to *sarq*-Zannib, we found a child wizard with a chain. She seems to have shown up about then, too."

*Young, so young, and unreachable. Attuned to animals instead of people, and hundreds of deaths to lay at her feet. What a waste.*

"She's dead, too," he said, to forestall Daerget's questions. "Then the Kigali government summoned us there, because their underground wizards came out of hiding to confront the dozens of chained wizards that turned up. The ones that had survived all appeared at about the same time. The Kigali asked for reports from several of their neighbors, and Ellech—that's where Vylkar went—and we heard of similar chained wizards in Rasesni and Ndant. All from about four years ago, for those that we could get good information from."

Daerget gave him a puzzled look, so he added, "Not so easy to get dates from a corpse."

His host gulped what was left of his ale and put the mug on the corner of the small table between them. Their deep leather-covered chairs were positioned to take advantage of the warmth of the stove.

"So there's a common point when all these chained wizards appear?" Daerget was chewing on the issue as a puzzle rather than an outrage, Najud was pleased to see. "Like Penrys?"

"More or less. There's some variation, but within a narrow window of about nine months, close as we could figure it. And they're from all over—different nationalities scattered around like sown barley."

"None of them knows what happened?"

"Not really. Their bodies remember some things… We found the nephew of one of the Ndant emissaries, in Kigali. He'd been a wizard before he vanished, and a wood carver. He has no memories of his aunt or his country, or anything personal. But he can still carve wood. His hands remember."

Najud cleared his throat. "His aunt says he's a stronger wizard now, much stronger. How much of that is the chain…? They were all wizards, we assume, before whatever happened."

"Is that why you're here?"

"Yes, in part. Penrys believes someone made all the chained wizards and sent them out around the world. Many died, and some of the others have caused many deaths. The ones that are left, the ones we've reached, they're trying to find a place for themselves, and to ensure that no more of them turn into monsters of destruction.

"But Penrys… she wants to find the maker, to confront him. She and Vylkar, they uncovered a clue—your wizard Gialfinnur and the old scandal, whatever it was—and that was enough to bring her back here, to find out what she could.

"And I came along, as I told you, to see the Collegium and its library, and to get help founding a new library in western *sarq-Zannib*."

Daerget glanced around his peaceful room. "It's a lot to digest. That's why the council won't let Penrys return, is it, her research?"

"What Vylkar says is, they don't think the chained wizards are a threat, and anything related to Gialfinnur is crooked learning, and forbidden. Vylkar pointed out that Gialfinnur is a generation older than he is, if he's still alive, but the chained wizards all appeared only four years ago. Doesn't seem to have changed their thinking any."

More quietly, almost to himself, Najud added, "I'm about ready to leave and join her in town. It's not right to separate man and wife."

"But your work isn't done. We're still getting the master lists together for you."

"So I can come back and pick them up. I'm not going to stay here much longer without her." He paused. "All my life I've wanted to see the grand library. Penrys was going to show me around. Now I can't wait to leave."

He heaved a sigh and turned to his companion. "So, how did you lose the eye, if I might ask?"

The man's pleasant face, with the pale skin of the typical light redhead, was marred by its brown leather eyepatch, somewhat darker than his hair and beard, but the man himself merely shrugged. "Ah, it was my own fault. They say you can tell the age of a wizard by how old his work robe is and how many little burn marks it carries, but I skipped the indirect steps and went right to inscribing my experience on my face."

In response to Najud's puzzled look, he said, "A workroom accident—what else? I was over-careless with a splash of molten silver. The damage wasn't deep, but the eye did not survive it."

He shrugged. "I wasn't used to the forge where I grew up, in the eastern uplands of the Baegyl Gaer and its valley. It was all wood, for us. How I stared when I saw Stokemmi for the first time, the stone and the metal, and the signals towers."

"Do you have friends here, from your home? I heard the Collegium takes students from all over."

"I had a few in the reds and yellows, but not many from the East stay on after their blues. The staff themselves, they're not Easterners. There's one other, from my father's generation."

"But you stayed."

"Well, not much for me at home, was there, with a face like this. Not many girls wanting to wake up to that in the morning, are there? Besides, I like the research. The library and the teaching—that's my life now. It's quieter than I expected, but life has a way of changing these things."

He smiled at Najud. "No one's written much about the Zannib and their wizard practices—I looked, when you came. Maybe I can be the first."

Penrys's evening conversation from her tree outside the Collegium was with Vylkar this time. Najud was off somewhere "making friends" as Vylkar put it, with an echo of emotions she couldn't quite identify, though they seemed approving enough.

She described her dinner encounter to him, and this time she had no trouble recognizing his alarm.

*Someone knows you're here, knows something about you.*

*Well I should hope so. That's why I'm marching around in blues with my chain exposed, eh?*

She'd wanted reactions from strangers—it's just that she didn't know what to make of this one.

*I've passed around my book lists to all the shops. I'll have quite the specialist's library when all this is done.*

*Don't tell the Council.*

That made her laugh. True—might be enough to condemn her, at that. In fact, the list of books she still wanted was probably bad enough by itself, and the thought sobered her.

*I've got something of a handle on what sparked Gialfinnur's interests, I think. I've been trying to read the same books he must have, and I'm starting to see, oh, the shape of where he might have been focused, like a shadow cast by the real thing.*

*And that's what has the Council worried. And me, too. Gialfinnur may be long gone, but there are living people taking an interest in you, and maybe he had followers.*

Penrys shrugged, in the dark, but Vylkar continued. *And they're right to call this crooked learning if our suspicions have any merit—look at the result.*

That was hard to argue with. The chain made her more powerful, by far, than other wizards, amplifying and storing power like a pile of personal power-stones, and the healing made it harder to kill her. The wings, well, each of the chained wizards seemed to have some sort of unusual *addition*, though not all had discovered what it was. She'd seen dozens of them—tails, gills, wings—no two alike. One preserved corpse had been caught in mid-change of his entire body into something like a seal.

But they all had something in common—animal ears, like a fox's, and no memory. And the chain itself.

She had a small bag of the chains, intact loops taken from the dead and fragments and links from various sources. Fragments were what you got when an unchained wizard tried to use a chain as a power source, or when you wanted to carefully cut one of the chains and avoided being killed by the resultant explosion. The unbroken circles almost felt alive, and each of them carried its own… signature.

Not like the fragments, which were dead and uninteresting.

Her fingers reached into her pocket and pulled out the *tennendaer*, the little bit of metal she liked to play with while she was thinking. The chain fragments had no more personality than this.

*I wish I could set up an actual workroom, bilappa. I need to try some things. I counted on being able to do that here, maybe in my old workroom if it was still available.*

*They're not going to let you in to do that.*

*Clearly not.*

She let Vylkar's warning sit there. She could always equip an experimental workroom somewhere else, but it would be impossible to hide it in Tavnastok—the things she would need would give it away. Maybe after they left… And it wouldn't be cheap, what with a forge, and tools. She missed her own workroom, just the other side of the walls, with all the gear she'd borrowed or stolen over the years. It would all be dissipated by now.

Vylkar's thought intruded again.

*I've been doing my own checking here. Gialfinnur abandoned things in storage that had been judged harmless and ignored, but they vanished somewhere around the time his daughter Elkif left. That alarmed the Council once it became known, that they might have overlooked something important. They searched his workroom again.*

*How did you find all this out?*

*The oldsters have all sorts of stories about it. The Council declared his tools off limits, but you know how things vanish. I've heard boasts from several people—how this one has his short hammer, that one has the longer tongs—all announced with a sort of mock horror. They stripped the place clean.*

Penrys smiled. She could picture it—both the original surreptitious taking of the abandoned gear, and the pride of the boasts, decades later. She wondered if she'd ever been in the room herself and who had it now.

*Which workroom was it?*

*Don't know. I'll find out.*

# CHAPTER 10

What Penrys needed most, she thought, was a colleague—someone to bounce ideas off of. She laid her book down on the table in her room and rubbed her eyes, ignoring the growl of her stomach that confirmed the fading light—time to break for another solitary dinner.

She thought she had a grasp on what might have interested Gialfinnur. If you heated the right metals in the right alloys to the right temperatures, all of which was no easy thing to control, you got metals with certain crystalline structures. So far, so good. More than one lattice structure was attainable.

But if you started *layering* these structures in certain way, the result was much more complicated than a power-stone, and power-stones only came in one crystalline format. These metals were an entirely different class of materials.

Physically, they were very difficult to cut. The metal alloys were stable, but not necessarily the lattices that gave them structure. *If that's that the chains are, how did they ever make links? If they had any power when cut, I imagine the lattice of crystals might not only collapse, but do it destructively. Is that what happens when chains explode?*

She reached into the bag of chains and bits sitting open on the corner of the table and fished out a broken link, and then a pair still joined. Closing her eyes, she laid her hand on them and tried to focus as much of her power as possible on seeing the internal structures, the very small.

She could do it for a power-stone—that's how you tell good ones from bad. Wouldn't it be the same, here?

There were layers in the unbroken links—she could feel them. They resonated to her probe in that way that made her think they were almost alive. *If you made a bar like this, unpowered, and somehow cut it, bent links, and welded them together...* She couldn't feel any seams in these links.

*If you forced the cut ends together, could you make them join, crystal to crystal? How would you do that? Could you make the crystal patterns force their shape across the cut, as if they formed that way to begin with?*

If you could, you'd have links like the pair she held in her hand.

When she probed the broken fragment, she felt how the lattices slid over each other wherever it was damaged, their planes no longer absolutely parallel, like a collapsed stack of books. It didn't resonate at all.

She pursed her lips and thought about it. This was a possible theory for the chains themselves, but there could be dozens of things wrong with it. She needed to talk to an expert. But then, there weren't any, once Gialfinnur was exiled.

*And I don't have the skills to do the experimental work myself, even if I had a workroom. You can't do this with a forge. This is an area where you have to make the tools first, and then the materials you're interested in. Where would I even start?*

And what did any of this have to do with the physical manifestations of the chained wizards—the loss of memory, the ears, the various body additions.

She stood up and moved closer to her narrow bed for the extra space. Then she invoked her wings. The brown and bronze-feathered mass changed her balance as always, like wearing a heavy pack, but the weight was evenly distributed from shoulder to hip, if you counted the tail. She could feel with them, as if they were arms, and if you cut them, they bled, briefly. But they touched her body directly nowhere, beginning outside of her clothing with a gap through which clothing and other objects passed.

What were they? The only model she could think of was devices—they had to be devices of some kind. But if so, this was so far beyond anything she had ever heard described that she couldn't credit it.

If they needed extraordinary power, well, there was her chain to draw upon. That was the easiest part to dismiss. But how did they work? How could they align themselves to her body? How was the gap produced? How could she fly with them? And where did they go when she didn't need them?

That was a class of wizardry more impressive than the chains themselves. She'd looked for books on artificial limbs, and those had made interesting reading, but nothing came near these artificial wings on her back.

Penrys wished she'd studied the other chained wizards in Kigali more methodically. From the manifestations she'd seen, they all seemed to be additions to the basic human form, rather than changes to it. Even the most extreme ones, like the wizard who'd died partway through the process of a full body change might only have been adding an outer layer, like a bearskin, rather than modifying his ordinary body beneath it.

Impossible to tell, now. She'd have to write a long letter to her colleagues in Yenit Ping to find out more, once she knew where she would be months from now, so someone would know where to send a reply.

And there were still the animal ears and memory loss to explain. Not to mention, where did the wizards who were chained come from, and how were they sent forth again? Her own attempts at a device detector of magic had gotten her into trouble a year ago when it sent her to the source of what it found. Maybe some much more sophisticated version of that principle? Hers was practically a student piece. What could you do along those lines if you really tried?

*Too much work for one woman like me. Or any one man.* Her hand froze in consideration before she could toss the links back into the bag. *But we're talking about a man who was exiled, what, almost sixty years ago? That's a long time to work on the problem, especially if he had help.*

Her stomach rumbled again, and she spent a moment considering the nearest place that could sell her something to eat in her room. She wanted to sketch out some more of this theory while it was still fresh, before her evening visit to the Collegium.

"Do you have to go do your work now, at night? We were just having fun."

The plaintive, teasing voice dogged Munraz and he tried to think of a way of escaping down the corridor.

Liemma swirled along beside him in her yellows, the informal robes a shade darker than her hair. She'd abandoned her friends to follow him and, in truth, he suspected she was bored with them.

The senior class of what he thought of as apprentices were intrigued by his wearing of green robes instead of student yellows, despite his youthful, unbearded appearance, and his ignorance of physical magic, of devices. He hadn't attended their classes, but they'd sought him out and tonight they'd invited him to their own table in the noisy dining hall and then, once they were kicked out, to one of the students' rooms where they crowded in, full of curiosity and probing questions, now that they'd captured him.

*They must find me exotic.* He felt like a hunted animal at the moment, pursued to his lair in the library. He was on duty tonight, Vylkar told him, and he had to get there in time for Penrys to find him.

*They're so confident, as if nothing had ever hurt them, or ever could. What they want of me is harmless, I suppose—a few interesting stories, a splash of color.* He glanced down at his sleeves. *Green color. They must be longing to leave their yellows behind.*

*They know a lot about wizardry that I don't. But what do they know about its dangers?*

"I'm sorry, Liemma, but I have an appointment to meet someone tonight and no way to make contact. You should go back to your friends. Maybe I can come back afterward, if you're all still there."

She pouted and he panicked. "Would you like that? I know I would." He gave her his finest smile.

"Who are you meeting? Why?"

Munraz swallowed and put on his best dignified airs. "I can't tell you—wish I could."

"Is it that Vylkar? I don't understand what all this council secrecy's about."

He didn't answer and let her draw her own conclusions. He liked her well enough, but she seemed so young to him, and he couldn't just tell her everything.

He cocked his head and smiled uncertainly at her, and that seemed to mollify her. "Come back afterward, then. Think you can find Innurgol's room again? His gatherings go on for hours."

"I'll find it." *Easier to locate a student's room than to hunt for your food. What do they know of my life?*

She sighed and turned back, and he paused to watch her walk away. *How can she know of my life? That's not her fault. I could tell her some of it, maybe. The good parts.*

He hastened on through the stone corridor, ruminating in the sudden silence she left behind. *Another place I don't fit in. They don't think I deserve the greens of an adult visiting wizard, and they're right. Vylkar's coaching and Najud's teaching makes me their equal or better for the mental magics, but devices…*

His hands twitched involuntarily. *Do I really want to learn? Najud knows about Vylkar's private lessons, but he hasn't said anything. What does he think about that?*

Not all young people who could be wizards chose to be—he knew this. A *dirum*, a herd-mistress, in *sarq*-Zannib could make a different choice, and he thought that might be why there were so few Zannib *bikrajti* like Penrys, women who choose to be wizards instead.

Some of these students here were like that—learning to control their talent but not much else. Lots of the others talked about taking up the commercial arts, like the ones he met in the signals tower in Stokemmi, or that goldsmith, or the ship's wizard with the broken device.

Munraz knew that most of the staff at the Collegium had been students here, once. They stayed on to do research, or just to keep the place going. That was one option.

And then there are the ones who ended up in charge of the place. His nose wrinkled. He recognized the types, first from the elders in his own family, and then from several of the Kigaliwen he'd met in Yenit Ping. And he didn't trust these specimens any more than the people they resembled.

He wished there were someone he could talk to about this— Najud, by choice. He would understand. But his master had abandoned him here to do his own work, finding books and, more importantly, people who could help him with his goal of founding another library and school.

*I can never truly go home. I can't rejoin my clan, after their rejection, and I wouldn't if I could. But I can't just tag along with Najud and Penrys forever. Oh, they'd let me, I think, but it's not right.*

*Vylkar's taken an interest, but for how long?*

He chuckled out loud, glad there was no one to hear him. *Maybe Vylkar can teach me to swim, when the weather gets warmer. If it ever gets warmer, here. Wouldn't want to become a qahulaj like that Asuthrys in the story about the Drosentaech, and be drowned in the pool of a waterfall.*

The double doors to the library ahead were wide open, as they should be at this hour, and Munraz quickened his pace. This would be the first time he'd served as contact for Penrys, and they'd never spoken together this way much before.

He found a comfortable chair in an unoccupied corner and picked up the nearest book, trying to look as if he were concentrating on the pages. *What's it like, flying over the river every night to look at this place and not come in? It was her home, wasn't it? She's as much an exile as I am.*

That was a troubling thought. He tried to banish it before she saw it.

*Munraz—are you on duty tonight?*

There she was. He could hear the surprise in her thoughts.

*Najud said to tell you he's still… what did he say? …making himself popular. He promises to be here tomorrow.*

He felt her disappointment before she buried it away.

*And Vylkar?*

*He came to me at dinner and said an emergency council meeting had been called and he was summoned to it.*

That conjured up a different emotion from her, a sort of frustration.

*Can I help?*

Some of his own chagrin at being a poor substitute must have made it through.

*I'm glad to speak with you, too, Munraz, it's just that there are some things I need to talk to Vylkar about. How are you finding the Collegium? I'd really hoped to be there to give you the tour, show you where I lived, and all that.*

He pictured for her all the senior students in the various yellow robes, like so many birds singing in a bush without a care in the world, and he felt her laughter.

*You know that's not fair. They have their own problems, it's just that you can't see them. We all do.*

*It seems like such an easy life.*

*Only from the outside. Everyone's life has joys and sorrows, triumphs and tragedies. Get to know some of them better, if you can. I'm sure Najud can help—I'll bet he's using his Zannib exoticism and charm on the people he wants.*

She pictured for him a snake with a Zannib turban, its body raised and swaying back and forth in front of a whole flock of little birds in wizard colors that were frozen in place on the ground, fascinated.

Munraz laughed out loud and choked it back as heads turned to glare at him.

*Was that what it was like for you?* Greatly daring, he returned her image with the addition of a great eagle in brown and bronze standing amidst the brightly colored songbirds.

This time the laughter was on her side. *Very much that way. Never underestimate the value of charm and humor.*

Munraz thought he heard a faint *and kindness* at the end, but that wasn't for him. He could feel her yearning for Najud, regardless, and it was disquieting. Couldn't Najud go visit her in town? Or Vylkar? *Or maybe I should…*

*I forgot—I have a message from Vylkar. He said he had an answer for you. He said, I found the workroom.*

Her excitement was obvious. *Which one?*

*Yours.*

He felt the shock first, and then the shifting of puzzle pieces to accommodate new information. It was a very disconcerting feeling. He'd never watched her do that before, from the inside.

It was in a completely different mood that she returned to him. *I need to speak to Vylkar tonight. Can you get him the message? Whenever he can. I'll wait.*

As soon as Munraz left to go find Vylkar, she hauled out the little *tennendaer* from her pocket, the fragment of metal slag from the sweepings of her workroom when she cleaned it up the first time. Could it possibly have been lingering there almost sixty years?

Workrooms were often filthy, their corners best left unexamined. Their users liked to carve out a workspace in the middle of them and ignore the rest. It was a rare user who kept a clean workroom—his colleagues thought an unnecessarily tidy space indicated a mind insufficiently occupied with important experiments. If you raised too much of a stink with your work, your neighbors might complain, but otherwise…

She'd been no different, though three years was hardly enough time to truly make a mark. Her workroom had been thoroughly cleaned only the one time, when she claimed it. It was small, far from the best locations and unwanted, but she was low on the list and it was hers, and cleaning it had made it feel more so.

Now she wondered if the older wizards knew about its prior ownership and shunned it for that reason alone. Why tell her, the stranger foist upon them by bizarre circumstance?

All her understanding of her place at the Collegium had shifted with Vylkar's information. First they stripped the place, the other wizards, then they left it unoccupied, even when workrooms were scarce and wanted. Not all them would have known—Vylkar hadn't—but there must have been stories and rumors. At the very least, it was probably spoken of as a place of bad luck, where nothing good could be accomplished.

She held the *tennendaer* in her hand in the darkness under her tree. The starlight couldn't penetrate the young leaves, and the night was chill. She closed her eyes anyway and probed the rough-surfaced metal, worn smooth only slightly where her fingers had rubbed it. Most of it was undifferentiated, chaotic melt, but the flavor of the alloy was similar to the links she'd looked at in the same way.

Was there any structure to it? There! A layer of crystalline lattice perhaps an inch long, and a different lattice, misaligned, below it. Leftover from a partial remelt? Traces only, and meaningless, if she hadn't already seen what they could be, in the link fragments.

Her ears moved back on her head. This was the proof she needed, the tangible connection between something of Gialfinnur's and the chained wizards.

She supposed someone else might have occupied that space between the two of them—that was possible—but she shook her head in denial. Not with that reputation hanging over it. They stole the tools and equipment out of it, but not the dust on the floor or the scraps in the corners.

*I wonder if anyone occupies that workroom even now? My stuff is probably disassembled and gone, but is the space empty? I know where the window is—I could wait a few hours and just go look.*

The action and the knowledge were here, not in Tavnastok, and she was frustrated at being kept away from it. The research would go faster and be more complete if she could use the Collegium resources, and there must be someone who could help her with the metallurgical experiments. Her own work had focused more on wood and power-stones.

If the council let them. If the council let her in.

And were they maybe right? A new material, like a power-stone but man-made and much larger—that would be a tremendous change for all the industries that made use of power-stones. How could you bury that? But they'd managed it, for decades.

Unless they didn't see what she did, didn't understand the potential.

What had Gialfinnur presented to the *hochumranomrethich*, the council of elders? What exactly did they declare *yrmkenrolek*, crooked learning, and why? Was there a record anywhere? Could Vylkar find it?

Would he try?

Penrys shoved the scrap of metal back in her pocket and stood up. Staying within the shadows she paced back and forth, speculating about the possibilities. After a while she paused in mid-step and looked down. She couldn't see it, but she must be wearing a trace of her presence into the ground. Well, no matter—no one would be looking for evidence of someone under a tree near the walls, at the edge of a field.

While she walked she'd been checking for Vylkar periodically in the designated location, without success. *Must be a long council meeting.* She composed herself and sat down in her usual spot, and tried again.

And again.

Finally, an hour later, she reached him. *Vylkar. I got your message.*

*Good. I have much to tell you.*

*One question first. Did anyone else use that workroom between Gialfinnur and me?*

*I don't believe so.*

*Then I know what he was working on, and I have proof of how it connects to the chains.*

She felt his surprise and proceeded to summarize her findings. She waited while his mind chewed on her theories, and gradually his thoughts realigned. *Yes, I find that plausible. It confirms the council's worst fears.*

*But it raises so many more questions. What have you found out about the presentation he made to the holkenramomrethich?*

*Almost nothing. None of my informants were there, and the document he was defending is nowhere. Not even the council notes exist, though the archived schedule confirms there was such a presentation.*

Penrys thought about that. *The thing is, bilappa, he can't have been describing the chains to them. These are a very sophisticated use of the material, and the chained wizards themselves are only four year old, or so. So it must have been something else, maybe just the material itself. Could the discovery of a cheaper and better power-source have been what they suppressed? And why?*

The cynical flavor of Vylkar's response bothered her. *That would be reason enough. Disruption, lack of control…*

*But how would that work? They didn't kill him, we know that—he had children. And the knowledge didn't die—look at the chains. I'm only amazed it's been kept quiet all this time. I found the shadow of it following the same books he did—anyone could have done so.*

*Ah, but you understand the chains, and so you know it's possible. That makes a big difference.*

Penrys mused on that for a moment. *We know he had a family, and that's a logical place for the knowledge to go. What did you find out about them?*

*Again, not much. Elkif listed her home as Glymbeod, but no one has yet tracked that down to see if she or her family are actually there. There hasn't been enough time.*

*Maybe that should be next. I could do that.*

*Not by yourself!*

She supplied the usual expression he wore when he strongly disapproved of something and smiled faintly to herself. It's not like he could stop her.

In a calmer mood, he continued. *He had work partners, possibly. They might also know what he discovered. I'm trying to find out without being obvious about it.*

*What's Najud been doing? It's been two nights now.*

*Drinking with his friends.* The sardonic tone came through clearly. *He's been spreading the tale of your exploits and of the chained wizards in general, very successfully I must concede. Your letter from Neshilik never spread outside the council, and Najud is making up for that beyond any possibility of suppression.*

Her lips curved up. *I can picture it, quite easily.*

*I'll tell him that in the morning, when he's paying the price for his chosen methods.*

*It works for him. He makes friends that way. Other ways, too. He's good at it.*

There was a pause before Vylkar replied. *I hope so, because that's why there was a council meeting tonight. They're outraged that their precious secrecy has been defeated. I nodded gravely when they berated me. Maybe I'll send Najud himself, next time.*

She snorted. *Any chance of him coming to visit me in Tavnastok, bilappa?*

*I'm not sure the council would let him back in. Better to let him stay until he's ready to leave. Or until they throw him out.*

*Who's keeping an eye on Munraz? He sounded a little... lonely this evening.*

The affection in Vylkar's thoughts, suppressed though it was, surprised her. *He's having trouble fitting in. How could he not? Older than his age-mates in some ways, and not confined to the yellows. I'm tutoring him in devices, with Najud's knowledge if not his approval. That will help, I think—make him feel more like he deserves to be here, in the greens.*

Another pause, but he wasn't done. Penrys waited patiently.

*What are Najud's plans for him, do you know?*

She bit her lip guiltily. *You know how he became Najud's apprentice—there was really no other choice. But they're not that far apart in age, which is awkward, and Najud's planning this new caravan route which will be a very odd background for training a wizard, and we all know it.*

She thought about Munraz's despicable family and their incestuous breeding practices to concentrate their wizard talents. *We couldn't abandon him, and he's right to fear his old family and clan. He can stay as long as he wishes—he's welcome and he knows that, too, but it can't be comfortable for him. I want him to find a place he can belong. If that's with us, then fine. If not, we'll do whatever we can to help him.*

Vylkar's emotions were shielded from her. *Thank you, that is most helpful. Now, any message for Najud before I seek my bed?*

*Tell him to save some of that drinking for his wife. I want to find him here, one of these nights.*

# CHAPTER 11

"You don't carry any maps, Lepicher?"

Penrys was her landlord's first customer that morning and got her full attention.

"Nah, too expensive, and most of 'em go to the Collegium. Now, I've heard there're a couple of collectors down in Stokemmi, and some shops that specialize in 'em, but you won't find much of that here."

She eyed Penrys's blue robes. "You could cross the bridge and ask them over there."

The exasperated nod of her head to the bridge across the square from her window made it clear she thought Penrys was asking in the wrong place and wasting her time.

"No, I can't." She left it at that, but Lepicher's face took on a more considering expression.

"Well, in that case, you might try Gylvabil. He carries a lot of books on local topics, and I know sometimes he's had an atlas or two. I don't imagine he sells many of them, not if the Collegium already has a copy, but now and then a merchant takes an interest."

*The merchants—of course. They're the ones who would know the region best, especially along the trade routes. Like the Virtaengi Gaer.*

Penrys smiled. "That's very helpful. I'll give that a try."

With a wave of her hand, she was out the door and contemplating breakfast. The fresh air struck her in the face and made her yawn—the penalty for staying awake in bed long after her chat with Vylkar, too excited by the confirmation that she was on the right track to sleep.

Her fingers crept up to the chain around her neck. *I know what you are, I think. Don't know how I tap into you, exactly, but it's a start.*

The inn on the corner served a meal at this hour. The only Collegium students here this early in the day would have spent the night and have no interest in facing food yet, so there would be nothing but locals in it, even here in Bridge Square.

She walked there absentmindedly, speculating about which merchants to talk to. How would Najud go about this? Importers, for whatever was made upriver, or exporters for the general trade? *I wonder if any of the wizard suppliers have upstream customers. Plenty of those I could be talking to.*

The thought had her staring at the footwear of the people she passed by, looking for the laced-instep boots that her server two nights ago had told her were a mark of the Glymbeod folks. They lived up that river, and at least the one she'd met was a wizard. Where there was one, why not more?

*What else should I expect from a shop that boasts of the patronage of the Collegium?*

Penrys waited impatiently for the opportunity to continue with her questions. This particular shop specialized in rather esoteric wizardry supplies that must have had a restricted clientele. Perhaps that's why it was two blocks off the Bridge Square—probably couldn't afford the rent in the best location, unlike the last five she'd visited.

But it was exclusive, and the evidence of it was in the alacrity with which the manager dropped his focus on a young foreign wizard in blue robes to wait attentively on someone in purples when Neinnur stepped through the door.

She knew him, distantly, from before. He hadn't been with the party at the bridge that turned her away, but she assumed he was of the same mind. He stopped and blinked, surprised to see her there—her face and the chain must have made identification easy for him.

"Please," he said, with a wave of his hand, "I've interrupted you. It's no matter, I'm in no hurry."

"I'm sure the young lady can wait a moment," the shopkeeper oozed. "She's just asking about some of my customers. Perhaps you can tell me what you're looking for?"

Penrys seethed at the casual betrayal of her confidence, and tried to keep it from showing in her face.

"Nonsense," she said, "I would be glad to look around while you take care of *Raer* Neinnur. It's not often I see such interesting… things." And indeed the place contained precision instruments that she would have lusted after for her old workroom—high-quality (and expensive) devices.

"I'm surprised you remember me," he said to her, ignoring the manager. "I doubt we spoke two words, before. You were always busy, as I recall, and I had my own duties."

She eyed him doubtfully. He wanted conversation? She couldn't remember if he was a friend of Vylkar, though he seemed to be of a similar age. "Everyone knows who wears the purple at the Collegium."

He must have heard the skepticism in her voice, for he stammered, "Y-yes, of course. What I mean is…"

He drew himself up straight. "I may sit on the *hochumranomrethich* but my opinions matter little there."

He nodded his head stiffly. "There. I've said it. I'll tell Vylkar I've seen you—I'm sure he'll be glad to hear that you're well."

At that, he turned on his heel and left, and the shopkeeper glared at her for driving off business. *What was that all about? Is the council's decision unpopular? How far have Najud's tales spread?*

Penrys's footsteps stirred up a bit of an echo in a quiet cul-de-sac off the River View road. It wasn't a part of Tavnastok that she had ever explored. Most of her errands had taken her to the northern highlands surrounding Bridge Square, with occasional forays downslope east to the warehouses at the fork, or inland to the west some distance, though never as far as the town itself extended.

On the south side, the Virtaengi side, the land fell off more precipitously from the signals tower ridge that paralleled the Lodentaf. Everything there tended to be steeper, and a bit cheaper, and a good deal more noisy. She'd never seen the south side docks, but she heard they ran quite a ragged distance up the river, paired with warehouses that perched somewhat precariously above spring flood levels.

The bookstore that Lepicher had told her about was just below the ridge, on the wrong side, as it were, and west a bit, in one of the districts that had once been wholly residential and was now drifting into odd mixed uses. The street led her into a dead end backed by a solid building which braced itself to retain its dignity despite the decay threatening the neighborhood around it.

The carved door and window frames had been painted in the last year or so, and the sign pegged over the door was in good condition: Gylvabil's Regional Books and Curiosities."

This was the place.

She admired the thickly ornamented and worn door. Narratives of some kind ran across its panels. *I wonder if it's older than the building itself? Looks like it might be.*

Then she knocked and tried the latch, and the door swung open for her.

It caught the light better when it opened, and she paused on the threshold to examine the carving more closely. From the interior, a man's voice said, "That's the smith's tale on the top. You can see the thunderbolt he forged at the end."

She nodded in appreciation. The style of the figures was archaic, their expressiveness more in their postures than in their faces. And, of course, everyone knew the stories. Once she could make out the hammer in the man's hand, she knew what it had to be.

"And the rest of them?" she said.

"The shepherdess is next, with her dog, then the baker and his wife."

"And the wizard on the bottom," Penrys observed.

She could hear the chuckle in the man's reply. "That's one of the ways you can tell its age—the wizard's on the bottom instead of the top."

Penrys laughed out loud, certain that he could see her blue robes. She walked all the way in and closed the door behind her.

"Lepicher sent me, from the Bridge Square. M'name's Penrys— I spent three years at the Collegium."

As her eyes adjusted, she watched a tall, lean man lay down his book and unbend from his seat by the unlit fire. His hair was a faded blond, but his eyebrows and closely-trimmed beard were dark, an uncommon combination. He could have been any age, from forty to sixty.

"Let me turn on some lights for you."

Penrys could tell he was no wizard and wondered what he meant. He picked up a device from a table and moved a lever on it, and power-stone lamps along the walls and ceilings brightened in this room and others until she realized this was just the broad foyer of the building leading into a great hall beyond, filled with freestanding bookcases, its high walls covered with paintings and engravings and other more curious objects. On the left and right, there was a vista of additional rooms, equally crowded. A majestic stairway rose from the back of the hall. She missed the pervasive smell of dust and quiet moldering that almost all book shops carried. Someone must be keeping this place unusually clean.

Gylvabil followed her eyes to the stairs. "I've promised my wife the books will not own anything but the bottom floor, so I must choose my stock carefully or be forsworn."

He watched her with lively, bird-like eyes. "What can I help you with? It's not often a Collegium wizard comes this far."

"I don't understand why not. Just standing here, I can see many titles not in their library."

"And you would know?"

Penrys nodded. "I haunted the place. There might be collections hidden from me, but the general library… yes, I know it."

"Then are you helping them with their acquisitions?"

"No, no… this is for myself." She walked further into the foyer, which was furnished like a sitting room with tables and chairs. When she turned around to look at the outer walls, she spied an old engraving hanging to the side of the doorway.

"That. It's the rivers, isn't it? May I see it?"

Gylvabil wove a path around the furniture, then stretched and lifted it off the wall. He brought it over to a table under one of the lights so that she could see it clearly. It was an old engraving, hand-colored, of the Estirmet region between the rivers, covering the far shores of the rivers as well. The towns and villages were marked, and all the little inlets and streams. It had suffered some damage from water and smoke but overall it looked in good shape behind its glass and frame.

"Would that be for sale?" she asked.

He pursed his lips and scrutinized her. "Is it art you're after or knowledge?"

"Knowledge, though art is always welcome. I need to understand the Virtaengi, in particular. What the people are like, the towns, how they live."

"The stories they tell each other," he continued for her. "The crimes they hide, their strengths and weaknesses. Is that it?"

She nodded along with his recital. "That's it exactly. Pretend I know nothing, that I was a blind bat at the Collegium, heedless of anything outside its walls."

He cocked his head. "Not blind any more, are you, I think."

"About this I am."

He held up his hand to tell her not to move and vanished into the great hall. When he returned, he carried a large thin atlas which he opened wide and flat on another table.

"This is not as old as the engraving, but in some ways it's more sentimental."

He flipped the pages for her. They were full sheets, shaded but not tinted. "If it were the colored edition, now, it would be very rare indeed. It's all of Ellech, it is, but the mapmaker came from Tavnastok, and so there's more on this district than is strictly fair." He smiled briefly.

Penrys carefully turned the pages. Each region of the country alternated map pages at various levels of detail with pages of statistical and economic information, along with illustrations of typical residents and objects to provide cultural flavor. When she turned to the Estirmet region, she saw the different clothing styles of three parts of the Virtaengi, and the laced-instep boots of the Glymbeod men—still unchanged, in an atlas that was at least a hundred and fifty years old.

Gylvabil noticed her pause. "I can show you more about the folk on the Virtaengi," he said.

"Yes, please."

He returned with three small books tucked under his arm—folk story collections. Two were decades old and illustrated, while the other seemed quite recent. In his hands he carried a model of a boat. He dropped the books into Penrys's hands by raising his arm, and she piled them on top of the closed atlas.

"Here's the typical vessel. As you see, it's made for paddles or sail, when the wind cooperates."

Penrys asked, "Do they still make them, now that there are device-driven boats? That's how I came up from Stokemmi."

"Those don't go up the Virtaengi—it's not reliably deep enough for much of the year, though it's free of rapids most of the way. The far upper waters of the Lodentaf and all of the Virtaengi still use boats like these for travel and freight."

When he moved into the light, Penrys glanced at his footwear. He noticed and laughed. "Thinking I must be a *taunnup*? Won't see many of them in here. Either they don't read much, or they already know all this. Or they just don't care." He waved his hand to take in all of his books.

"Where do they go when they come downriver?"

"There are districts they favor, near the docks. D'ya know where they are?"

When she shook her head, he gave her directions to specific parts of the south side, not far from the water. A number of merchants were established there for business—food and clothing, practical goods, and some wholesalers for raw materials.

"The *taunnupar* are more set in their ways than the rest of the Virtaengi folk, and sometimes they bring old things to trade. I get quite a bit of my stock there, between occasional books offered in trade and home-grown curiosities. And now and then I meet a colorful character with an even more colorful story, for my own work."

He nodded at the books accumulating on the table, and Penrys realized he was the author of the most recent of the folk tales books lying there.

"D'ya mind if I come back and ask some more questions in a day or two, once I've digested some of this?" she asked.

"Not if you give me some clue why you want to know in exchange," he said. "Another colorful story, perhaps?"

It had been awkward carrying the wide parcel all that distance back to her room, but the framed engraving and the atlas were not too dissimilar in size, and the three little books weighed nothing. Penrys attracted glances as she struggled with the burden in her too-short arms, but she hadn't wanted to wait for a delivery.

Her mind fairly hummed with excitement all the weary way. Was Elkif really from the Glymbeod district? Was she raised there? Was her father Gialfinnur there, and still alive?

She had questions to put to him, so she did—lots of them.

That Baelnei seemed to be a *taunnup*. Her mind kept tossing up speculations but she needed facts instead. If she couldn't use the Collegium's books, she'd get some more of her own.

The atlas and engraving had been costly, but she thought both would be useful for Najud's library afterward, as examples of the form. It's not the sort of thing he'd bought much of, yet, and his students were unlikely ever to actually visit Ellech, so it was worthwhile to have a good rendering of it for them. She hoped Najud would agree with her, but it didn't really matter—she had to have them, and any justification would do.

After she hauled everything up the stairs, she paused to disable her lock-dog devices on the other side of the door before she unlocked it. Once she'd dropped the package unceremoniously onto her bed, she collapsed into the armchair and waited for her heartbeat and breathing to return to normal, while she worked out the kinks in the hand that had been cramped trying to keep a hold of the edge.

Would she go back there with more questions after she made an orderly list, even if it meant revealing more of her story? Well, why not? Najud was busy telling the tale all over the Collegium, so it was no longer any sort of secret. And who else could she talk to about the best way to verify her suspicions?

Penrys found it reassuring that Gylvabil wasn't a wizard himself. Too many of the people in this affair were. She'd been tempted to recharge all of his many power-stones for him, as a gesture of thanks, but that had seemed like showing off. Maybe when she went back.

*Let's get started.* She bounced out of her seat and untied the string that held the wrapping. It was too awkward to use the bed as a second work table, so she slipped bits of the waste paper into the open books on her table to hold her place and stacked them up on a shelf. Everything else from the table joined them—the small bag of chains in particular—until the table was bare of everything except blank writing paper and her pen and ink.

After carrying the atlas to the cleared table, she considered the engraving. She'd want to look at that while she did her research. The remaining straight chair, a spare for her non-existent visitors, was pressed into service, and she propped the engraving on its seat, positioning the whole ensemble close at hand so she could see it while she worked at the table.

There. All her materials were ready for her, and her chair beckoned. She sat down and began going through the atlas methodically.

Penrys wished she had time to read through the entire thing in detail. Most of her knowledge of the other regions in Ellech was sketchy, and this was a chance to fill in the gap, but she held herself to the more urgent study of the region between the rivers. The high mountains and the far east would have to wait.

She did spare a glance for the detailed map of Stokemmi. The signals towers hadn't existed a hundred fifty years ago, of course, and she was astonished at how much smaller the capital was then. Most of the working districts along the shoreline between the major rivers had not yet been fully linked to the large cities.

Tavnastok, on the other hand, seemed to have hardly changed. The mapmaker devoted a good amount of space to the famous bridge, a relatively recent achievement at the time the atlas was assembled. There were views from several angles, and a brief account of how it was made.

The maps themselves concentrated more on labels and boundaries than on depicting geographical details directly, but the engraving was full of little lines indicating where the terrain was mountainous, and where merely rough. She knew enough to suspect that some of the detail was hear-say, not direct observation. Still, it would have been the best available at the time, and though that time was close to two hundred years ago it would still be good. The villages might have changed since then, but not the mountains.

The atlas described three different terrains in the five hundred or so miles before the Virtaengi reached its headwaters, not in the slopes of the gigantic Dunnarfeol Mountains, but at a spring in a cove at their base, below the foothills. She'd always assumed it started well up in the range that ringed the country, like the Lodentaf Gaer which took its start from glaciers descending a high plateau. It took its name from that, too—the Ice-Wealth River, the long trade route to Stokemmi for the west-center of Ellech.

The Virtaengi Gaer was smaller and shorter. Closest to the fork at Tavnastok, the district was indistinguishable from that of its companion river for more than half its length—agriculture and broad fields with settlements. As far as she could tell from the atlas, it was a pleasant land with a sizable if shallow river. Unremarkable.

Then things changed. Moving upstream, the river flowed through a pass in a range of worn-down hills and entered a valley drawn with almost a washboard appearance on the engraving. The atlas spoke of thin soils and walls of stone picked from the ground in an attempt to create fields, and of low barren hillocks that criss-crossed the valley floor. The parallel hills that enclosed the valley didn't seen very high, especially compared to the mountain giants looming to the west and north, but they were reinforced at their backs with exploratory spurs sent out from the Dunnarfeol as reminders of what lay in that direction.

The villages were small and numerous, each pocket of usable land sprouting its own settlement. The inhabitants were known for handcrafts and sheep, as well as some silver mining in the surrounding hills. The atlas painted a picture of an area not rich in farming, but not entirely poor, either, though somewhat isolated. They could raise their own food, and were proud of their independence.

*A stable place, if backward. Slow to get the news, slow to change.*

That region took up two thirds of the remaining river. The final section, less than a sixth of the whole, started upstream at the valley exit through an upland ridge into a large, rough cove perhaps eighty miles across. At the western edge, the river rose from its spring, and the Dunnarfeol Mountains began their steep-walled ascent. This was the Glymbeod region.

According to the atlas, the only agriculture was in family gardens, wherever soil could be built and improved upon by man. Wild game was plentiful, and hunting formed a significant portion of their livelihood, at least at the time the atlas was written. The families kept a few livestock animals, but no large flocks.

*What do they do for clothing? Leather, certainly, but do they get enough wool from their sheep? Do they trade for fiber or fabric?*

Gold came from the surrounding mountains, in some quantity, and other metals, too, locally smelted into pigs and ingots that could be traded downstream. There was clay, for ceramics, and small family industries for local use and trade. The atlas depicted smiths and woodsmen with their axes, women at their potters wheels, and a scene of small, separate cabins, each with its garden. Penrys recognized this as a stylized image of the simple, rural life, nostalgic even when the atlas was made. *Was it ever really that way? How is it now?* She had difficulty picturing wizards coming from that background.

Like the region downstream of them, they were independent, though their food security for the long winters was more precarious. *I bet they're clannish, and not overfond of their neighbors. Probably hostile to outsiders entirely. Their backs to the mountains.* As it did for each region, the atlas depicted a typical couple—a mountaineer in leathers with the laced-instep boots that were apparently characteristic. The woman accompanying him wore a printed fabric and an embroidered apron. *Too bad this edition can't show me the color. Did they trade for the cloth?*

*I wonder how many of their young folk they lose to the lure of easier living downriver, or in Tavnastok, or even further.*

She peered closely at the engraving that leaned against the back of the chair. *Here's Elkif's village, at the far end of the cove. All the way back in. How did Gialfinnur wind up there? Is it a lie, what she told the Collegium? And where did she go, afterward? Back home, after a few years of Tavnastok?*

She knew most wizards from isolated rural areas tended not to return to them. And it wasn't just wizards—skilled young people who could leave often did. *What holds them in Glymbeod—the promise of the mining? Something else, other than tradition?*

*Time for me to bounce some more ideas off that bookseller. I'll follow up on some of his directions first. See him again today, late in the afternoon? Maybe tomorrow?*

She wiped her pen off and laid it down across her notes. Then she picked up the collection of folk tales Gylvabil had written and slipped it into one of her belt pouches, to keep her company for lunch.

# CHAPTER 12

Najud leaned on his elbows over the Collegium wall where it came closest to the bridge. Tavnastok was visible far below and more than a mile away—he could almost count the buildings in Bridge Square, but it was further than he could reach. When he tried to pick up the minds of Tavnastok—so many, and so tantalizingly close—he found nothing but a few travelers at his end of the bridge, and a chilly breeze carrying the moisture of the river.

He'd hated leaving Penrys standing for two nights in a row, but he'd thought it couldn't be helped. Daerget had introduced him to many of his friends and colleagues, and he'd talked himself hoarse giving them all the details that had been kept from them. Most were like his new friend—young men and women in the blues—but some were older, and a few were visitors from elsewhere, in their greens.

They'd had so many questions—why had Luveri and the council taken such a strong position, how was Penrys so different and why, what could the chained wizards do, and many more. Then the debates started and ran into the small hours of the night, of which the most persistent was "is this an *yrmkenrolek* or not?"

When he'd heard from Vylkar this morning that he could still have talked to Penrys late since she'd waited for Vylkar, he'd regretted staying until the very end, but there was no fixing it afterward.

Now Najud turned over in his mind everything Vylkar had told him about their conversation the night before. He agreed with both of them, that they now had real evidence that there was a connection between Gialfinnur and the chained wizards, though its nature was obscure. It was like looking for an underground seep with only the fresher vegetation on the surface for a clue.

Would Penrys go off looking for more without them? *I know you must be tempted, Pen-sha, but don't do it. I'll talk you out of it tonight, see if I don't.*

With a sudden revulsion of feeling he stared over the river. *What am I doing here, anyway? We should go home. My home, if not hers.* What a sad home-coming it had been for her here, after all the anticipation on the way. *I'll cut this visit short. I've met enough people, I can do the rest with letters.* He surveyed the sleeves of his green robe with distaste. *I'm not one of them. I didn't know what I was doing when I envied the famous Collegium's students from afar.*

Back down the river they'd go, and out across the sea once more, and then the long trek back to western *sarq*-Zannib, on horses again, at last. Maybe they'd stay longer with his family on the way.

He'd had enough of preparation. It was time to start building something. *Rejoining my wife is the first step.* He pursed his lips at the thought of her unfinished business. *If she has to run down this stale track after Gialfinnur first, then fine. I'll do it with her, and then we'll leave. Make ourselves useful somewhere else, and put the past aside, both of us. Build a family, however it comes. And a town, and a school, and a caravan— whatever we can turn our hands to.*

Penrys paused on the corner of one of the small squares near the docks on the south side, where Gylvabil had directed her. Hers was the only blue robe she saw. If there were other wizards here, they were more anonymously dressed, and a brief probe of the people in the open revealed none. It seemed very strange to stand in the middle of a busy part of Tavnastok and yet see no obvious wizard. It made her feel very conspicuous.

Other than that, the people seemed the same as anywhere else in town, except for the handful with a different sound to them, a sort of a lengthening of their speech, the words slower and slurred. They were shorter, too, though just as light-haired and bearded, on the part of the men.

*Maybe they don't eat as well, at home. Maybe they're from far upriver.* Another question for Gylvabil.

She had an eye out for the giveaway boots but didn't spot any.

The store she approached looked like it sold all sorts of useful things, and it had signs in the windows offering to purchase handcrafts.

When she walked inside, she found shovels and pails, nails and spikes, drills, saws, and planes, and shallow pans with corrugated ridges. She recognized the latter from an illustration in the atlas—they were used to find traces of gold in water-soaked soil. *So they can get mining supplies here, whatever they don't make themselves.*

Past the rest of the hardware and tools, she found food preparation goods—salt and spices for preserving and flavoring meats, small ovens, stovepipe, skewers, pots and pans and griddles—even metal canteens. In with these were ceramic plates, bowls, and vases with a sturdy feel. Many showed the use of a free hand with colorful glazes. Penrys wondered if these were part of the "handcrafts bought" referred to in the sign.

Small mirrors, glass panes, and oil-fueled lanterns occupied one corner, with wicks and parts and a variety of fuels, mostly animal-based. *No power-stone lamps. Do they render their own animal fat upriver?*

At the back of the store, with access to a loading door that led directly to the alley alongside the building, she found the seeds. Any crop that could be grown in the soil and climate of Estirmet between the rivers seemed to be represented, both edible and ornamental.

She had a vivid image of a family coming downriver to town once each year to stock up on anything they couldn't build or make. *And what a long journey it would be, along five hundred miles of river. Maybe only one person went, on behalf of several families. Or maybe it was the shopkeepers for the upstream villages, and families traveled to them instead of making the long trip all the way themselves.*

She nodded her head. That was more likely. She could see that the shoppers seemed to know exactly what they wanted. She watched one pay for his purchases with what looked like small nuggets, and the man behind the counter pulled out his scales as if raw gold instead of coins were an everyday occurrence.

An older woman walked up to her. "Can I help you find anything? You look a little lost."

"It's my first time in a store like this. Are most of your customers people or other stores upstream?"

"Bit o' both," she said. "Mostly the stores. And the townspeople here, too. I saw you admiring those plates."

"They're handsome. Where do they come from?"

"That's Glymbeod work, it is. We get that sometimes, though there's no predicting how much and when."

"How do you know what to carry? Do the places upstream send you orders?"

"You mean, like by signals tower?"

At Penrys's nod, she smiled and shook her head. "Bless you, *rerri*, there's no signals towers upriver on the Virtaengi. Who would man them? Not many people way up there, and even fewer wizards. Maybe someday, but Tavnastok's the end of the line on this side. 'Course, the Lodentaf's got a few of them upstream, but that's different."

"No," she continued, "The stores mostly have standing orders, according to the season. If they want something special, they let us know by boat, like everyone else."

"One thing I didn't see was fabric and yarn. I see the ropes coiled over there," Penrys waved her hand, "but not the materials for clothing and such."

The woman nodded as Penrys spoke. "That's a specialty, that is. You'll find a place like that 'cross the square." And she pointed out the direction through the multi-paned window at the front of the store.

As she walked directly across the square, Penrys couldn't shake the feeling of being watched. She still sensed no other wizards, but she missed the scarf she'd been using to wrap around her chain to hide it from sight. Bad enough the blue robes.

*I can fix that while I'm here.* She crossed the threshold of the fabric shop and smilingly compared it to the place in Stokemmi where she'd commissioned her new clothing.

No stuffiness here or long, sober faces. All along one wall stood hard-wearing fabrics in canvas and wool, suitable for work clothes, and more dark woolens for ordinary use toward the back. But up front, the first thing to catch the shopper's eye, were bright bolts in solid colors and glorious prints, mainly floral. *Long winters up river. Everyone wants a touch of color for relief.*

There were more subdued fabrics, too, for the older buyers, and counter after counter of buttons, ribbons, buckles, and other accessories. The practical boots were separated from the low shoes suitable only for indoors.

Her saunter through the shop came to an abrupt stop there. Finally, in front of her, were the boots with the laced-insteps for sale, waiting for customers.

Up on the walls were soft blankets woven in patterns that echoed some of the illustrations in Gylvabil's book, and quilted coverings that reminded her of finer versions of her bed covering from Asuthgrata. More traded-in handcrafts from upriver?

The only shoppers in the store were matching bolts of fabric against each other up on a counter.

An entire corner was given over to tools, much like the hardware store. There were several spinning wheels of different designs, and two assembled looms. *Must be possible to pack them up small enough for one of those boats. That's quite an investment. Still, there must be buyers or this place wouldn't stock them.*

The yarns and threads and needles were here, and wool rovings ready to be spun.

It was so easy to envision women, and maybe some men, looking for something to fill their hands.

A familiar scent turned her head, and she discovered the leathers for clothing use. Large leather items like saddles must be sold somewhere else, but here were belts already made and blank straps, punch tools, and all the materials required to turn out vests and winter coats and gloves—whatever might be needed.

She snagged a woman to help her find a suitable scarf, and ended up with a yard of a soft blue challis with printed white irises and green stems that she could roll diagonally around her neck over the chain. It would need to be hemmed, but that could wait until she got back to her room, and she pocketed the needles and thread that would be needed.

The woman took her coins without commenting on her robes, but Penrys thought she could feel sidelong glances from some of the shoppers, and she hastened out as soon as she had settled the new scarf over her chain.

Just outside the door, her eye was caught by yet another wizard supplier along one of the sides of the square. It was the first one she'd seen since she'd ventured so near the south-side docks, and she remembered the woman at the hardware store who'd commented on how few wizards there were upstream.

So how could it be profitable to set up shop here? A wizard needing supplies would surely be willing to walk across town to all those north-side shops.

Was it too late in the day to stick her head in and check them out? She glanced at the sun. No, there was still plenty of time to do that. Might even have a chance to swing by Gylvabil's shop again on the way back for more questions.

Her hand rose to her neck and checked the scarf covering it. The memory of the shopkeeper back in Stokemmi who had stared at her chain was still vivid, and she was glad it wasn't exposed here.

She took a moment to stretch before setting out across the square again. It had been a busy day with a lot of walking. *There'll be plenty to share with Najud tonight, assuming he shows up. It's good to have something of a trail to pursue.*

*Najud's a better tracker, though. Wish he were here.*

Najud slipped into the main study room at the library well in advance of the usual time. He wasn't taking any chances of missing Penrys tonight—too much to discuss about when they might be able to leave.

The room stretched out like a great hall, without its grandeur. It was not high-ceilinged, and at least half of it was devoted to small nooks furnished with a table and a couple of comfortable chairs as a way of allowing low conversations while keeping them unobtrusive. Najud had heard that the regular researchers claimed their own spots, over the years, and he wondered which one had been Penrys's. *Or maybe she wasn't senior enough and had to study out in the main section on the long tables, or in her room, or her cold workroom.* He recalled some of her descriptions. *Or even standing up reading at the shelves inside, when they wouldn't let the book out.*

He nodded at the librarian on duty near the entrance and slipped into an unoccupied cranny at the far end of the room. *I wonder whose spot this is. Hope it's not Luveri's.*

Vylkar reported bits of the council maneuvering to him and he was beginning to loathe the woman, especially since she was the voice of the council that had denied Penrys entrance to her old home. But he never saw her himself, except distantly sometimes when they all dined, and she never spoke to him. What business did she have with a lowly visiting Zannib *bikraj*?

He snorted quietly. *Probably thinks I'm quaint.* He pulled out the book he'd borrowed and opened it to where he'd left off. Daerget had gotten him to wondering about just how the Zannib were portrayed in Ellech books. He was reading the standard book on the subject for the senior students, and itched to write corrections all over the margins.

The kindest thing you could say about it was that it was out of date. The author demonstrated a decent understanding of life in central *sarq*-Zannib, the traditional seasonal migration of the clans and their livestock. The *kazrab* were depicted in detail, no doubt because the notion of a round, felt-covered, portable house would be so strange to wood-building Ellechen *taurath*. But nowhere did he find a discussion of the limited availability of timber that made such structures necessary, nomadic or not.

The far west of *sarq*-Zannib barely merited a mention, just a listing of major geographical features. There was but a single page on the Wandat Sea, with its complicated shoreline settlements and trade ties to the rest of the country. He shook his head in disbelief. And the southern shore of the continent with its bandits was ignored altogether.

But he thought the worst was probably the depiction of the eastern third of the nation. The author didn't understand the tribal and clan structures of the traditional culture and how they manifested in the government in Ussha. The economic foundation of the small settled farms and industries of the east that lured people away from the nomadic life were an ongoing source of tension in *sarq*-Zannib, but that seemed to be invisible to this Ellechen author, for whom the eastern towns felt so deceptively familiar and civilized.

He seemed to believe that everything that was good came from the influence of the Kigali, and the flow was all in a single direction. He missed the importance of the eastern caravans into Kigali, and how the Kigalino were dependent on the Zannib to move many of their trade goods, how important the mutual trade was to both nations.

Najud could feel his exasperation rising and took a deep breath. *They really need some better books on these topics.* He looked up from his book and out at the room, partially filled even in the evening with other scholars, and all of them surrounded by the famous library, as if the weight of knowledge in the world anchored them in place with the things that they know.

*And that's how I thought of it, only a year or two ago, when I gazed north and wished I could visit the great Collegium.*

But some books were just wrong, like this one. And none of them had given Penrys a clue about where her home might have been before the chain, based on her appearance. Whoever her people were, they were apparently unknown here.

*There's a lot they don't know. And even more that they think they know, but they don't.* He knew his disappointment should be blamed on his unrealistic expectations, but he couldn't help feeling as if the Collegium's library were somehow a fraud. *Penrys warned me it might not be what I expected.*

His reverie was broken by the appearance of Daerget, peering around the edge of his refuge.

"Found you!" Daerget managed to convey his pleasure while keeping his voice barely above a whisper, clearly a convention learned by every student here. "I was looking for you. I ran into Vylkar and he suggested trying here."

Najud flourished the book in his hand. "This is junk, at best only half-right. I can't imagine what they say about Rasesdad here. Even Kigali is probably suspect."

"That's what I supposed." Daerget plumped down in the other chair with a poof of air from the well-padded seat and made himself comfortable.

"I thought you were meeting someone?" He made a show of looking around.

*Well, does it matter if I tell him? What would happen if it became known—Luveri can't keep Penrys out of the entire eastern bank of the Lodentaf.*

"This is a secret, not for sharing," he said, and Daerget's face assumed a more serious expression as he acknowledged the warning.

"How far can you mind-speak?" Najud said. "For me, it's about a mile."

Daerget shrugged. "I've never really tested it, but that sounds about right."

"So I'm out of range for Tavnastok. Vylkar, too. But Penrys with that chain of hers—she can reach much further, about five miles. So she can find me, but there're too many wizards here, which makes it hard for her."

He glanced sidelong at Daerget. "And I told you about the wings, yes?"

"So you mean she flies here?" Habit kept his excited voice low. "Isn't she worried about someone seeing her?"

"It's only at night, and she doesn't come inside the walls, just out in one of the fields, close enough for mind-speech. One of us sets up here, and all she has to search is this one place—after all, she knows where it is." His gesture took in the entire room.

"You mean, she's there right now?"

"No, not yet. I'm a little early."

"But you missed the last couple of nights."

"Vylkar and Munraz covered for me. It was important, what we were talking about, and the meeting with your friends."

"Then I must be in the way. You'll want to talk with your wife." Daerget began to push himself out of his seat, and Najud waved him back.

"No, stay and keep me company until then, if you will. Why were you looking for me?"

"I'm not sure this is the right time…" Daerget pursed his lips and took the plunge. "I was wondering, and I'll understand if you refuse, but I wonder if you'd consider taking me with you when you return to *sarq*-Zannib. I'd like to see it and I thought… I thought I might do a serious book about it."

When Najud stared at him in silence, Daerget nervously continued. "I can feel the dust settling on my shoulders here, and I don't really want to settle into the cold stone walls and let it entomb me. There's nothing much for me at home. If I'm going to be out of place, why not embrace it? Go somewhere completely exotic.

"I've always liked the idea of the Zannib—that image of the noble nomads, you know, that we all learn as children. And then you show up here, turban and all, and it's as if my wish had been granted. I know the reality will be very different, but then that's what interests me, too—the substance of a thing beneath its appearance."

Najud blinked and raised his hand. "Give me a moment." He cast his eyes down and considered. He liked Daerget well enough—there was a spark of friendship between them—and he sensed no treachery in him.

"It's a very long journey—what if you tire of it before you even get there? The close quarters, when we barely know each other… And of course Penrys would need to approve, and Munraz."

A brief hopeful smile flickered across Daerget's face. "I'm not a child. If I undertake something, I'll see it through. The long journey is part of the adventure, not just a tedious interlude."

He looked intently at Najud. "You told me something of your years of wandering as a journeyman, yes? You must understand the feeling."

"Well, but I'm a nomadic Zan. It's a piece of my heritage, not yours."

"And how many of your countrymen did the same?"

That silenced Najud. He was notorious for his fondness for foreign travel—only the caravans did as much, and they brought *sarq*-Zannib with them, with their clusters of *kazrab* and their families.

He could feel the hope that Daerget was trying conscientiously to smother. A man of his own age, another *bikraj*. *Think how much I could learn from him.*

"You would be a foreigner in a foreign land, your nationality unmistakable."

Daerget chuckled softly. "I could shave my beard or dye my hair. But I won't. People tell outsiders things sometimes that they wouldn't reveal to their friends."

"Don't underestimate the loneliness of it," Najud said.

"I'm lonely now. Can it be worse? Penrys can joke with me about Ellech customs, if she will. And besides, I can always come back, once I know the way."

Daerget took a deep breath. "I can't pay you, but I can take on the responsibilities of stocking this library of yours, once you're ready. I know everyone…"

Najud held up his hand to stop him. "I don't want payment. If we do this, we become a miniature clan, and that has its own assumptions. We can manage all that."

He didn't think Penrys would object, and Daerget had at least known her when she was here—they weren't complete strangers to each other.

He mused out loud. "It would be an interesting challenge, teaching you to fight with only the one eye."

Daerget's face lit up. "You mean you'll consider it? That's all I ask." His hands slapped his thighs as if they were dancing. "I'll wait for you to let me know, once you decide."

Then he pushed himself out of the chair. "I'll leave you now, so you can have privacy for your wife." He bowed briefly and slipped away.

*My wife! What's the time? She's late.* Najud reached beyond the walls to the east, but Penrys wasn't there yet.

*Must have been detained by something. She'll be along.* He picked up the book on *sarq*-Zannib again, to pass the time.

# CHAPTER 13

Najud took his seat in the study room of the library again on the following night. Penrys hadn't come, the night before, and he'd dozed off in his comfortable chair before finally giving up after midnight. *Three nights in a row I haven't talked with her—that's too long.*

Vylkar had shrugged off her non-appearance this morning. "A hundred things could have prevented her coming for one night," he'd said, and it was true. And it was his own fault he'd been absent the two nights previous himself.

*We've been too careless with this line of communication, leaving her to do all the work and swapping the three of us around at our convenience. We have to think of a better way, or maybe I should just move out now and join her.*

Munraz could stay with Vylkar for a while, until they were all done. He didn't think Vylkar would object, for just a few days.

He ran over in his mind what he would need to pack. *Take it all. Maybe I won't be coming back.* He'd talk it over with Penrys, but he knew what he wanted to do.

*And what about Daerget's request?*

Months of journeying just to reach *sarq*-Zannib. Najud assumed the man could ride, but had he ever been at sea? Unlikely. Trapped in close quarters with the same people for long periods? That's when the habits of privacy and manners really matter. The Zannib understood how to live like that, but Daerget would have to learn the same lessons. How would he feel about sharing a *kazr* with Munraz? How would Munraz react? They hadn't even met yet.

Daerget seemed well-balanced, but Najud knew there would come a moment when all his notions of romantic foreign nations would crash into the reality of a strange culture, and not everyone did well with that shock, the overload of wrong food, wrong smells, wrong language, wrong assumptions. It could be paralyzing to a rigid mind.

Maybe Penrys knew him a little better and would have some useful advice.

And then, whatever his family relationships were, would they be improved by adding thousands of mile of distance? *I really need to talk to him about that, before he just throws it all away, perhaps never to return.*

He checked the time device that hung over the desk of the librarian near the entrance. He could just make it out from where he sat at the far end of the hall—this was about the time Penrys usually came. He scanned, outside the walls to the east, but no one was there.

Opening a different book on *sarq*-Zannib, Najud tried to read while he waited, but he couldn't concentrate. *She's not even overdue yet. She'll come.* His stomach knotted. *And if she doesn't? If she was prevented last night, too, and we're already a day late in reacting?*

*I was a fool to let us be separated.*

Movement across the room caught his eye, and he spotted Vylkar in his purples making his dignified way over. He pointed him to a chair when he arrived, and the careful smoothing of the robes before Vylkar took his seat contrasted memorably with Daerget's casual collapse of the night before.

"Have you spoken to Penrys?"

Najud did his best to seem undisturbed. "No, not yet."

"I'll just keep you company, then, until you do."

Najud glanced at him in surprise. *He's worried, too, whatever he says.*

"Tell me, do you know Daerget? I was wondering what you thought about him."

"Is he the one with the eye-patch? One of the younger scholars?"

"Yes, that's him."

"From the east, I think." Vylkar's voice trailed off. "Don't know much about him, good or ill. Seems to be on good terms with a lot of people—I come across him in odd places, chatting to, oh, cooks and stablemen, some of the retired residents. That sort of thing." Vylkar raised an eyebrow. "May I ask why?"

"He wants to write a book about *sarq*-Zannib. Or to run away and have an adventure. Or, perhaps, both."

"Ah. I'm afraid I can't advise you, but I don't see any barriers to it. Some of our better writers were travelers."

He made a show of running his eye up and down Najud, bare-headed in his greens. "I've always thought it was the turbans."

"What?"

"That made boys in Ellech want to grow up and become nomads, that and the sword you wear at your belt in all the pictures. What do they call it?"

"A *khash*." Najud had rarely carried the curved sword of the traditional nomads. It got in the way of managing a string of horses.

He suppressed a grin. "Me, I always wanted to be a pirate, with an eye-patch, like Daerget. The notion of all that water… Later, it was a *zarawinnaj*, the leader of the annual migration. That was before I heard the voices that told me I would be a *bikraj*."

Vylkar smiled. "Pirates are popular with us, too. There are worse reasons to want to travel and see the world."

There was a pause, and both pairs of eyes checked the time. Definitely late, now.

Najud cleared his throat. "I'm going to town first thing tomorrow if…" *If she doesn't show up.*

"They may not let you back in," Vylkar cautioned.

"I don't care. Will you go with me?"

Vylkar nodded, then he stood up. "She'll be here tonight, you'll see."

Najud just shook his head and stared down at the ground. She wasn't coming, not last night and not tonight. Something was very wrong.

*So this was the building?*

Najud tilted his head back—four stories high, like most of its neighbors, with an alley alongside it to provide air and light to the sides. All the windows were dark, this early in the morning. He'd lingered until the pre-dawn began to lighten the sky before he rose from his sleepless bed and stalked through the corridors to roust Vylkar. He hadn't waited for the day's first meal—his churning stomach wouldn't have accepted it anyway.

It had taken Vylkar's authority to make them open the gates that early, and then the walk down the hill and over the bridge took most of an hour. They saw no one the whole time before they reached the Bridge Square—it was as though they were alone in the world when they passed suspended through the chill mists rising from the river.

As they crossed the square, Najud glanced at his companion. Vylkar hadn't complained about the missed meal. In fact, he'd said little at all. They'd both saved their breath for the brisk walk.

All across the wide bridge and in the square itself Najud had been scanning for Penrys, and finding nothing. He knew from Vylkar's face and tight lips that he'd been doing the same.

"Here?" Najud asked, gesturing at the darkened bookshop windows.

"That's what she said."

Without ceremony, Najud pounded on the door and waited for a response, then hammered it again, until Vylkar behind him laid a restraining hand on his arm. "She's coming."

The steady shine of a hand-held device light moved behind the glass and approached the door. A woman older than Vylkar opened the door and glared out at them. She'd thrown a robe over her bed-clothes, and held the light high to see their faces, recoiling at Najud's beardlessness and foreign features.

"What do you want, at this hour? Come back at a civilized time."

"My wife. Penrys. Is she here?" He already knew from his mind-scan that she wasn't, but was this at least where she was staying?

Her mouth made a soundless circle, and she stepped back. She took in Najud's green robes, and then, at the sight of Vylkar's purples, she backed up several more steps.

"Come in, out of the square, *raerra*. Yes, I've rented her a room. I… I haven't seen her for a couple of days. Your wife, you say?"

Vylkar closed the door behind them and bowed. "I'm Vylkar, Lepicher, and this is my friend Najud, from *sarq*-Zannib. We haven't heard from Penrys for two nights now, and we're worried. She's my *byrindyrri*."

"Why're you just showing up now? She's been here for days." She paused to work it out. "Ten days, today." Najud could see hear the accusation in her voice and winced.

"It's a long story, *rerri*—we've been up at the Collegium and…"

Vylkar overrode him. "She decided to wait for us here in town. Show us her room, please."

She glanced at the purple robes again and took that for adequate authority, though not without residual suspicion.

"Last time I laid eyes on her was two mornings ago. Mind you, I don't see her every day, just when she drops in for a question or two." She led them up an internal staircase to the second floor, and paused by the flung-open door of her own apartment. "Now you just stay here a moment while I throw something on." She went in and closed her door.

Najud fidgeted, but Vylkar clucked an admonishment and he tried to wait patiently. In just a few minutes she came back out, with her room keys, and took them up the next flight of stairs which were blocked by a locked door. Her keys disposed of that, and gained them access to the upper floors.

"I rent rooms on the third and fourth floors," she told them, "but they use an entrance out back and a separate external staircase to bypass the first two floors." Najud followed her gesture to the far end of the building where he could make out a large, solid door in the dim light. "Be quiet, now—good folk are sleeping."

They climbed to the top floor and turned toward the front of the building. "I offered her a room on the third floor, but she said she liked having access to the roof, for the view. The nice one in front up here was vacant, so…"

Najud estimated there were eight rooms on each floor. The ones that looked out on the square would have better views but less quiet. They must cost more, too.

He reached for the door, but she grabbed at him. "No, don't touch it. She had them—what did she call 'em?—lock-dogs, I think it was. She showed me. Things she set up to make a lot of noise if anyone came in."

Vylkar held up his hand. "No one's in there, and I don't feel any activated power-stones."

"You sure? You could hear 'em all the way outside when they went off a few days ago. I don't want to be waking everyone up."

Vylkar stared down at her. "She told me about it. Yes, I'm sure. Unlock it, please, Lepicher."

*That was the first night I stayed away. Now I can see what that must have been like, coming home and hearing her alarms, and trying to deactivate them with a crowd standing around.*

The woman bent down with her keys and turned the lock, but she didn't open the door. She took a few steps back and waited for them to go in first, to set off what ever might be waiting.

*Must've been quite a noise.* The humor soothed his tension for a moment.

Vylkar pushed the door open and leaned down to pick up a device that was leaning against the doorframe on the floor. He casually powered the devices on the wall to shed some more light and examined what was in his hand.

Najud shoved past him into the room.

It was small and sparsely furnished, but it wasn't as bad as he'd feared. The bed was as narrow as the one he'd been given in the Collegium, but there was a soft chair positioned to catch the light from the one window, and another device on the floor below the opening.

"Vylkar, I think this is another one over here."

Vylkar joined him at the window and picked it up. "I'd like to study these—haven't seen anything quite like this before. They're not powered, though. Completely drained."

Lepicher had followed them in, carefully. "I asked her how I could turn 'em off if she wasn't around, after that one time, y'understand. She said she charged 'em whenever she went out, and it wore off after a few hours."

Vylkar looked at Najud. "So that tells us nothing useful, then."

They surveyed the room from their place at the window. The bed was neatly made—hard to say when it was last used. Her clothes hung from pegs, and the strong blue of the new formal robe added color to the walls. "She didn't tell me about buying all these rugs and things," Najud said.

Vylkar shook his head. "They're from her old room at the Collegium. I found it all in storage and sent it to the warehouse we're using, and she must have taken some of it from there to use."

"Looks cozy." Najud had been picturing bare floors and no color. He took a deep breath and turned to Lepicher. "*Rerri*, I'm sorry we had to disturb you so early." He ran his fingers through his hair. "We're worried."

She waved it off. "I can see that. No matter. You'll be wanting to know what we talked about last, I'm thinking."

Vylkar looked at her gravely. "Please. Come, sit here and be comfortable." He directed her to the soft armchair by the window, and sat down himself in the chair in front of the table.

*Doesn't want to loom over her.* Since the only other chair was supporting a framed engraving of some kind, Najud took a seat on the bed and tried not to distract her.

"She was in the shop, first thing, two mornings ago, asking about maps. Me, I don't carry much in that line, so I directed her to Gylvabil. Don't know if she went there, but…" She pointed at the table with its wide-open atlas and the propped-up engraving which Najud could see was some sort of map. "Looks to me like maybe she did, or he sent her somewhere else. Those weren't here the last time I was, and nothing that size came by delivery, neither, so she must've carried them herself."

Vylkar's voice was patient. "Where could we find him, this bookseller?"

She gave him directions which were meaningless to Najud but Vylkar nodded his head as she spoke. "He's a strange one, he is, but he has good stock in his own field. I've sent folk there before."

"No one's come by looking for her, before or since? No messages?"

"Only that one time the alarm went off. And packages— packages come all the time." She tilted her head in the direction of the two bookcases. "She's a serious buyer, anyone can see that. Made a practice of coming to me first, which I appreciate, and I sent her on to others as necessary."

Her face went blank. "Oh. There's the book list—that's recent."

Vylkar raised an eyebrow.

"She was making some sort of list of books she wanted but couldn't find. I told her to go to the Collegium, her in her blue robes and all, but she wouldn't. So she gave me the list to see if maybe some of my customers might have 'em, the collectors, y'know, and might maybe want to sell. She said she'd be making several copies of the lists for all the bookshops, but I don't know if she did." Her lips twitched. "That's a lot of lists."

And it was. "Like the trees in the forest" went the familiar proverb that Najud knew, "or the pebbles on the shore, or the booksellers in Tavnastok."

"Can you think of anything else, *rerri?*" Vylkar asked encouragingly, but she shook her head. "Then we'll not keep you. May we stay here a few moments to talk things over? Maybe I could copy that book list she gave you?"

"You won't take anything? I'm sorry, *raerra*, but I have only your word that you're friends of hers."

Najud stood up. "When does the rent run out?"

"She's been paying weekly, in advance, but it still has a few days."

He reached into his pouch and pulled out some coins blindly. "Here, take this and hold the room for her. Get a message to Vylkar there, if it runs out."

She glanced down at her hand where he'd shoved the coins and rose from her comfortable seat. "That's too much, *raer*," she said, and she looked bewilderedly at Vylkar.

He reassured her. "Penrys is family, and something's happened to her. We have to find her, *rerri*. I'll stand behind any arrangement Najud makes with you, and a message to me at the Collegium will always find me."

"Now, please, we have to look over the room carefully and make some plans. We'll come speak to you again before we leave." He eased her skillfully out of the room and closed the door behind her.

Najud returned to his seat on the bed and held his head in his hands. "Two days, Vylkar. Two days."

"Not quite," Vylkar replied. You forget, my colleague Neinnur saw her in one of the wizard supplier shops that morning. She was asking the manager some questions."

"Think he ran off to the signals tower afterward, like the fellow in Stokemmi?"

"Actually not," Vylkar's voice carried an irritating precision. "Particularly since it was to here that the message from Stokemmi was sent. No more signals towers upstream on the Virtaengi, and I agree with her that it's a likely place to be looking."

He waved a hand at the open atlas on the table in front of him and the engraving propped on the chair, so Najud stood up to get a better view of them both.

"This is the Estirmet," Vylkar explained. "I've never seen this engraving before, but the atlas is famous. The Collegium has three of them in the tinted edition, I believe. I'm surprised she found a copy of any kind."

He bent over and peered at the engraving. "See, here's that village Elkif mentioned, when she arrived as a student. How very strange, so far up into the Glymbeod. Didn't anyone question that? How would Gialfinnur have ended up there to raise a family?"

"I don't care about then," Najud grated out. "I care about now. Where has Penrys gotten to?"

Vylkar just looked at him. "Your wife cares about then, and so you must as well."

He relaxed the sternness of his features. "However, I do not believe that even our Penrys would just rush off into some solitary expedition upstream without telling anyone. Or taking her maps."

He glanced around the room speculatively. "The alarm devices have run down, but apparently they only last a few hours on a charge, so that tells us little. The bed's been made, and she clearly went to the shop that sold her the atlas and the engraving and brought them back, if Lepicher received no delivery. That was probably after my colleague saw her. Which brings us to, perhaps, mid-day, the day before yesterday."

"Then what?" Najud said. He had visions of Penrys floating face-down somewhere.

As if he'd read his mind, Vylkar said, "If she were injured or dead here in Tavnastok, word would have been taken to the Collegium. She was a foreigner, in wizard robes. It would not have gone unnoticed. Even without the robes, as a foreigner alone…" He lifted a hand in a half shrug.

Najud walked over to the bookcase that still had a few open shelves. He passed by the small wooden case that held the goldsmith's work from Stokemmi and picked up the half-filled bag of power-stones. Though it filled his hand, it didn't weigh that much, and the smell of the Rasesni-tanned leather was still detectable when he leaned close.

Carefully, he put it onto the open atlas.

"And then, there's this." He grabbed the heavier bag of chains off of dead wizards and chain fragments, and tossed that more casually next to the other one with a clink.

Vylkar, his face impassive, plucked a small ivory piece off another shelf and added it. "One of the *tennendaer* she liked to carry. Must've come out of her stored goods. She probably has the metal one on her, the one she thinks comes from Gialfinnur's discarded work."

He put his hands on his thighs and pushed himself up. "Yes, I take your point, Najud. She would not leave all of this behind, not willingly."

"Come," he said, looking at Najud. "You can't help her by worry, only by action. We must trace her steps that day, beginning with the bookseller Lepicher told her about, whom she clearly visited."

"But she came back from there," Najud said.

"Ah, but where did he tell her to go next?"

Najud let Vylkar carry the conversation with Gylvabil while he listened to the man's mind and pretended to scan the shelves at the same time.

*He seems no odder than any other bookseller I've met. More cheerful than some of them, though. There's this underlying, what, glee? As if he's delighted with the world. What's that about?*

"I'm sorry to hear that the young woman's gone missing," he was saying, in a tone that suggested he was surprised at all the fuss that brought two more wizards to his door, one in purples, and neither apparently interested in his stock.

"She wanted to know about the suppliers on the south side, so I gave her some names. But I don't imagine she went there—it was all she could do to carry her purchases away. I offered to send them, but she said she didn't want to wait." He shrugged at the vagaries of his customers.

"Asked if she could come back later to ask more questions. You'll see—I'm sure she'll turn up."

He ushered them both out, and Vylkar raised his hand to keep Najud from speaking until they were back on the main road.

"What did you think of him?" he asked Najud, quietly, as they walked.

"I couldn't read him. Felt the same the whole time, except for a sort of laughter inside."

Vylkar nodded. "He wasn't surprised. More... pleased I thought."

"We going to go through his list of places?"

Vylkar looked down from his greater height. "No reason to. They're a lie."

Najud stopped and stared.

"Najud, Penrys may not know the south side of Tavnastok, but I do. He left the most important supplier square off the list entirely. Stupid thing to do—better to have buried it halfway down and hope we'd stop before we got that far."

"Maybe we should go back and speak to him a little more physically this time?" Najud suggested, with a glance over his shoulder.

"No point confirming his suspicions. No, what I want you to do is return to her room and go through all her notes. Get that book list from Lepicher, too, and copy it."

"We can go through the shops in that square faster with the two of us," Najud said. His fists clenched.

Vylkar held his hand up to stop him. "It's too conspicuous, a Zan rooting through the seamy side of town looking for another foreigner."

"As opposed to a wizard in purples?"

"We shop there, sometimes. And the kind of attention I would draw is different. No one's going to want to bother a man who might be able to bring them business with the Collegium. We're the biggest buyer in Tavnastok. Besides, no one there will know I'm associated with Penrys."

"Except the man we just left," Najud pointed out.

"And wouldn't it be interesting to find out if that news has spread."

Vylkar let his face uncharacteristically mirror his own worry. "Trust me, Najud—this is something I can do better than you. I'll meet you back at Lepicher's."

Najud stepped into Lepicher's shop to borrow the book list, and she laid two keys in his hand. "Got 'em made for you, you having paid the rent and all. This one's the outer door in back, and the other is the room."

His face must not have been as controlled as he hoped, because she continued. "Haven't found her, then? What about that Gylvabil—he of any use?"

"What do you know about him, *rerr*? What sort of reputation does he have?"

"Keeps to himself. Can't say as I know much, 'cept he's always got good books in his specialty. Guess I only know him professionally."

She looked him over. "Why do you ask? Is there something wrong?"

"No," Najud said, "Just a puzzle. Might be nothing to it."

He shook himself. "I'll just go in the back way then. When Vylkar comes by later, will you tell him I'm up there?"

He waved his thanks and walked out the door again before she could ask any more questions. Before he ducked into the alley entrance, he glanced over the bridge at the distant Collegium on its hill, gleaming in the mid-morning light. *As if any of you care about the results of your arbitrary decision to keep her out of your precious sanctuary.* Munraz was over there somewhere, following his daily schedule, but that was about as much of a tie as he felt for the place now.

He opened the door to the outer stairway and took the steps two at a time all the way to the second floor, and then again for the final two stories on the inner staircase, until he stood before Penrys's door, breathing hard.

Inside, it was still empty. The little decorative touches pleased him. Automatically he tried to evaluate which would do well within a *kazr*, so she could have something of hers there, something not of *sarq*-Zannib. The rugs would work, and that bed covering which looked so warm. The small things on the shelves wouldn't take up much space.

But not the books. No, research projects would have to be weeded out carefully for each journey, with the remainder stored in a *zudiqazd*, a winter camp.

Or in a new library in a new city. *I can build that for her.*

He sat down on the edge of her bed and picked up her pillow. He hugged it against his chest and inhaled the scent of her deeply. *Where are you, Pen-sha? What's happened to you?*

# CHAPTER 14

The slight movement beneath Penrys was soothing, almost like drowsing in a hammock on a summer day in Asuthgrata at Vylkar's lodge. But there was a creak of wood above her and an occasional sound of water that puzzled her. It also brought her bodily needs to her attention.

*What am I doing here? Why is my head pounding?*

She kept herself still and reached out with her mind, but there was nothing, as if she'd been dosed with the Rasesni drug *sedchabke*. When she twitched a hidden finger it moved, so that couldn't be it—no paralysis. Conversations nearby fed an impression of several people, and then she heard the splash of water again as the surface beneath her tilted. *A boat—I'm on some sort of boat, with a sail.*

Her hands were tied in front of her, and her feet bound together. *I was speaking with the manager of that wizard supply place, and a surly woman she was. I didn't sense anyone else in the shop, but it's all a blank after that.*

*I must be on the river. Great. Bait running around without a hook and line to reel in my target. What an idiot I was to have worked alone.*

She turned away from berating herself and tried to concentrate on what was suppressing her power. There was nothing from her chain, as if it were dead, and nothing from her native gifts, whatever they were. She had no memory of herself without the chain, so she didn't even know what to expect.

The chain was still there—she could feel it. Was it… drained somehow? By what?

*What's my situation? Can I get close enough to the edge to reach the river before someone stops me?*

A small voice niggled at her. *Can you keep your head above water, bound hand and foot? How far away is the shore?*

*Can I even invoke my wings, without power?*

None of this made her head any better or the needs of her bladder less urgent.

*It's a shallow boat. I can sense the movement of the water directly through whatever I'm lying on. But it doesn't feel small enough to paddle. What do they do if the wind's against them?*

She cracked her eyes as cautiously as she could. Without moving her head, she could make out several men, all bearded. She heard higher voices but couldn't see the women. The men closest to her were focused on the sail over her head. *I must be leaning against the mast. Am I tied to it?*

She tried to make out if anything led away from her bound hands or feet to tie her to something else, but it was hard to be sure without movement they might spot. She listened carefully but couldn't tell if there was anyone behind her, toward the prow of the boat.

*It's a river. How wide can it be? If my pockets are empty, I can find a sharp rock somewhere to cut the ropes, once I reach the shore.*

She flexed her muscles against each other to warm them up, then lurched abruptly upright, hopped a few steps, and grabbed the gunnel with her tied hands. She pushed off with her feet to tumble herself over and into the water. The icy cold shocked her all the way awake.

Hands snatched at her and missed, but then she had problems enough to occupy her trying to swim with bound hands. She rolled with the current and concentrated on using her legs to beat the water like a whale's tail, and her arms to pull her head up. The wet robe dragged against her.

When she finally broke the surface she gasped for air and coughed on the spray that came with it. The boat behind her had dropped its sail, and the shore beyond it was more than a hundred yards away, the terrain around it flat and open. Nowhere to hide.

The other bank was rockier and not as distant, so she turned that way for what little difference it could make to the outcome. She could already tell her pockets were empty, so cutting the ropes was not going to happen soon. With a gulp of air, she ducked back down and swam underwater as best her constraints permitted, until she was forced to surface again to breathe. At some point a momentary warmth along her leg told her the bladder problem had been resolved, not that it mattered in the freezing water.

Without looking behind her, she snatched a breath and submerged again, but as she neared the shore she could find no rocks in the water to conceal herself behind, and a quick glance back showed that the boat had anchored in the stream and launched a canoe with two paddlers.

They were faster than she was, and would reach her before she could hop-crawl ashore, so she changed her tactics and waited for them to approach, letting her face take on a look of hopeless submission and shivering expressively. Her legs kicked in unison back and forth to keep her upright, since the bottom was out of her depth.

The rear paddler was Baelnei. *Of course.* He looked furious. *Closer, come closer. Here I am.*

The canoe slowed as it reached her, and Baelnei held it in place against the current with a back-paddle stroke.

Penrys let herself sink under the surface, and the front paddler stretched down to grab her clothing. She kicked hard and grabbed his hand with her bound ones, and pulled him over and into the water, almost upsetting the canoe in the process.

While the man in the water floundered to recover, she rocked the canoe harder, hoping to overturn it, but Baelnei kept his balance. He picked up a metal rod with a leather handhold that lay along the bottom of the canoe and waited for a predictable moment in her movements, then he leaned forward and pressed the end of the rod against her bare hands where they clung to the boat.

With a sensation of darkness flooding her mind, her hands lost their grip and she sank motionlessly below the surface.

Penrys woke to a throat sore from retching up water and an infuriated Baelnei straddling her chest and slapping her cheeks back and forth while he shouted at her.

"I…did not take…all this…trouble…just to…have you…die on…me."

She tried unsuccessfully to roll him off with her shoulder, but he stopped and sat back until his weight was on her hips and she could breathe.

Her ribs felt as if some of them were cracked.

"There'll be no more of that, *staka.*"

She panted, trying to fill her lungs. "Best way…to keep me alive… is to let me go."

That earned her another vicious slap. "Put it out of your mind. There are people who want to see you, and I'm going to deliver you, breathing if I can, but I imagine they'll understand if that doesn't turn out to be possible. Big, strong wizard like you—what else could I do when you tried to escape?"

He leaned forward and grabbed the chain at her throat in its sodden rag, lifting her head up by it and letting it drop hard on the rocks before she could muster enough strength to do more than push at him with her bound hands.

Then he levered himself upright on the rocky strand and stepped over her body. The canoe had been pulled into the quiet water outside the current and the other paddler, soaking wet, stood alongside it in the shallows and glowered at her.

"They've been waiting for you since you set foot in Ellech. Thought you might know something, they did, but me, I don't think so. I don't think you know anything." He shook his head is disdain. "Still what do you expect when you poke your nose into the wrong places and ask the wrong questions—a welcome celebration?"

Penrys lay on her back and tried to catch her breath. Her body was ice-cold and she shivered uncontrollably. The deadness of her chain scared her, and she couldn't read anything of their minds— she had no sense of their moods. It wasn't that they were so well-shielded, it was that she had nothing. Mind-deaf. *Is it permanent?*

*What was that metal rod?*

"Get up. Get in." Baelnei pointed at the canoe a few yards away and walked away.

Penrys didn't move.

He turned and stomped back and kicked her hard in the side. She screamed breathlessly as she felt something give way, and turned on her side to curl herself up protectively.

"You want another one?" he said.

*Got to stay alive.* She shook her head and clumsily rolled to her hands and knees. She pushed herself upright until she was balanced, swaying on her feet.

"Can't walk," she spat out.

"You'll figure it out or I'll kick you all the way there."

She tried a crow-hop but it made the cracked ribs flare up viciously. After that she resorted to shuffling, a few inches at a time, while Baelnei waited at the canoe, floating in a foot of water except where the prow touched the shore.

Penrys couldn't move actively enough to warm herself up, and she lost her balance shivering, and tried to protect her side as she hit the ground. The two men watched her impassively as she pushed herself up again and kept on shuffling.

She stopped at the water's edge, next to the canoe.

"Turn around," Baelnei said.

Penrys knew what was coming but couldn't make her muscles work well enough to duck. He knocked her into the boat, and the last thing she saw as she went over backwards was the smile of satisfaction as he did it.

He pulled the canoe past him in the shallows and leaned in to haul her further back toward the middle, then he stepped over her and took his seat in back, pulling the metal rod with him, out of her reach. The other man got in and pushed away from the shore with the blade of his paddle.

Penrys started at the wooden planking a new inches in front of her face and shivered. She tried not to dwell on the nearness of his feet to her face.

Najud looked around Penrys's room to take stock of things. *There's no more I can do here.*

Vylkar had turned up nothing but dead ends. He'd found two shops she'd visited, but after that the trail went cold. Najud had sent him back to the Collegium with a request to send him everything he'd brought with him, and to watch over Munraz for a while. He couldn't take his *nal-jarghal* into this.

He expected a wagon with his packs to arrive before the afternoon was over—that's what he was waiting for. Then he'd need to make a trip to their warehouse down at the fork to drop off surplus gear and to pick up empty packs for a horse. With that, and the materials he'd already purchased lying in heaps in this room, he'd be ready to buy horses and tack in the morning and set off, as early as he could.

His fingers twitched with urgency. That would put him three days behind her, and he had only a supposition about where to look for her.

Vylkar had looked over the notes he summarized from her workbooks, and agreed that Glymbeod was the right place to try. "She's stirred something up. And she's not here, and not by choice—that's obvious."

Najud had just nodded tightly. "I'll be gone by morning."

"What, by river boat?"

"What do I know of boats? No, I'm going by land, through Estirmet. That village of Elkif's on the northern bank of the river."

"It's very rough terrain once you get halfway there." Vylkar had not been encouraging.

"I know. I looked at those maps. I'll manage."

After Vylkar left, Najud had disassembled the frame that held the engraved map and rolled the paper up to take with him. The atlas would be awkward, but he wasn't going to leave it behind. A horse pack could accommodate it. Might get a little... bent. All he cared about was that it remain usable.

He couldn't sit around here just waiting, not with all these reminders of Penrys. It would be bad enough sleeping for the night in a bed that smelled of her, and she absent.

*Better to wait out in the square. That way I'll be able to see when the wagon arrives.*

He pocketed the door key and headed downstairs and out to pass the time. *If it doesn't get here soon, I won't be able to get into the warehouse. And I bet I can't buy a decent horse pack in Tavnastok if I can't retrieve my own.*

He paced for a while in front of Lepicher's shop until he spied a lightly-loaded wagon cutting directly across the square from the bridge. As it got closer, he realized what he'd taken for a second wagoner was actually Daerget, dressed in rough clothing.

They pulled up at Najud's feet, and Daerget climbed down. "Come on, help me out," he said, avoiding Najud's eyes. Between them they lifted three large packs over the sideboards, and Najud paid the fee.

The wagon rolled off and Daerget was left standing on the stone paving, with the packs at his feet while Najud stared at him.

"Not here," he said, finally. He picked up two of the packs and led Daerget around to the back entrance and up to Penrys's room.

"What are you doing here?"

Najud fumed until the door was closed behind them and the packs on the floor before erupting.

"Did Vylkar send you? What was he thinking?"

"I found him in your room, with Munraz, stripping it of all your gear. So I asked."

He jutted his chin out. "And he told me what had happened."

He took a breath. "So I said I'd finish the job, and I got my own things together and decided to come and help."

"This isn't your fight," Najud said.

"Penrys never did me any harm. She's one of ours. I wanted to come."

Najud could feel his face harden, and Daerget hastened on. "I'm a young man, Najud. Don't leave me behind to molder here. At least let me help you with this, even if you don't take me to *sarq*-Zannib afterward."

"There may be nothing left to send to *sarq*-Zannib when this is over," Najud muttered.

Daerget shrugged.

"Look," Najud said, "I'm headed all the way to Glymbeod, by land. That's more than four hundred miles, a week or more. The river route is longer, closer to five hundred, but they have a head start. They're moving upstream so the current'll slow 'em down, but they'll still get there before I do, even if they camp at night."

He stared up at the man. *All these irritatingly tall Ellechen taurath. You need a stool to stand on to yell at them properly.*

"And all of that is based on a bunch of 'supposes.' As in, we suppose the Gialfinnur connection is real, and that his daughter's home really was in Glymbeod, and someone who is somehow carrying on his legacy is still there, and that's where they're taking Penrys. And we're supposing she's still alive."

He closed his eyes after he said that and held himself still. *She has to be alive. Has to be. I won't allow anything else.*

Daerget waited him out. "You done? Whether it's the right thing or not, it's better than no action at all. And it's better with two of us, not just one."

He pointed his chin at his pack. "This isn't my first time on a hunting trip. You were going to have a pack horse anyway, and he can carry for both of us as easily as one. One more riding horse, and we're done, and I can show you the best place to buy them on the west side, so we won't waste any time getting out of town in the morning."

He bristled. "I can fight, same as you. I wasn't always a dull scholar on the hill."

Najud noticed for the first time the curved sword strapped to the pack that Daerget had taken charge of, sheathed in a scabbard with what looked like saddle fixings dangling off of it.

Najud rubbed his hands across his face and gave up. "As you wish, Daerget, and thank you. Now, I've got to do a quick sort of the gear and get down to the warehouse so I can bring back the empty horse packs. You'll need to lay in food for yourself and anything else you're missing before the shops close tonight. You can see what I've got already." He waved his hand at the corner of the room where he'd stashed his purchases.

"I managed to buy a simple tent to ward off the rain. Maybe more canvas covers? A bedroll?"

"You go on down to the warehouse, Najud, and I'll take care of the rest."

A thought struck Najud. "Better come downstairs with me first, so I can introduce you to our landlady. And don't forget—you're sleeping on the floor in here tonight."

# CHAPTER 15

The hands of strangers hauled Penrys back aboard the larger boat and dumped her against the mast again. Baelnei stood over her and kicked her one more time in the thigh, then he found a short rope and ran it through her chain, like a leash on a collar. He tied it off, and hitched the end to a cleat on the mast, high, above her reach.

"Stay where I put you, like a good dog."

She lay there in her sodden clothing and shivered. Her muscles ached from the effort of swimming, and she could feel each separate bruise and cracked rib.

For some reason it was hard to catch her breath, and she concentrated on that for a while. When she looked outside herself again, she saw faces bending over her, wavering in her sight. They seemed to be quarreling.

"They want her alive, Baelnei," one woman said. "You'll have to let her heal herself."

Baelnei's voice drifted down. "See that chain?" A hand reached down and tore the rag away and dropped it on the deck. Penrys could hear the splat as it landed.

"Think what she could do to us. I'm not taking any chances. They can want what they want."

Sometime later, she realized she was still shivering, but she wasn't cold anymore. Her clothes seemed to be steaming off her body, and she shifted around, looking for a cooler position, one that that hurt less.

Another voice commented, "Must've swallowed something in the river water."

A rough hand held her head up and offered her a cup of water which she gulped down thankfully.

The day wore on endlessly, hazy and disconnected. Sometimes she thought Najud was talking to her and then he vanished. *Of course he's not here. I didn't tell him where I was going, did I?*

Most of the time she wondered why she was shivering on a boat, and concentrated on taking her next breath.

She stirred when they stopped to camp for the evening. A man she didn't know untied her legs and hauled her up, but she staggered and almost pulled him down again. He swore, and another man joined him. Together they half-supported, half-dragged her down a rough gangplank to the shore.

They walked her up to the campsite and handed her over to two women. Penrys stared at them blearily. One of them took a knife to the wet lashings around her hands while the other took charge of the leash. "Over here," that one said. "Better take care of your business."

They pulled her off into the bushes and helped, then they dragged her back to the fire. There they bound her feet together again and left her in the sand. She couldn't sit upright and crosslegged with her feet bound, and she couldn't get comfortable any other way, so she laid down again. The heat of the fire felt good, and she curled up to face it, hoping the fire without could fight the fire within.

The faces flickered in and out of her sight. One of them offered her food, and she shook her head, but she was grateful for the water. She dozed a while until the voices woke her up again, and she coughed, trying to get a deep breath. "It's the drowning sickness. Look at her shaking."

Another said, "Leave her be, Baelnei—she'll never last the distance else."

Penrys wondered what they were talking about, and then something touched her, and all her thoughts shrank and vanished.

"Four days of good ground, eh, before you have to choose?"

Daerget's voice roused Najud from his thoughts. *Restful to have a companion who doesn't need to talk all the time.*

They'd been going since shortly after dawn. Daerget's suggestion on where to get horses and tack had proved fruitful, and now each of them had a sturdy mount, well-shod for the rocky ground further west, and led two others—a horse with lightly loaded packs, and a spare.

Six horses instead of three was overkill, but Najud had the funds and the capacity to carry extra grain, and it provided a margin in case of disaster. Small dirt roads wound through the farm settlements, and they stuck with the ones headed west, taking note of every sizable stream they crossed to calculate their position along the route.

"The maps say it should be about four days. I'm planning on doing a full sixty miles or better while we can, dawn to dusk, so it's going to be hard riding. But if we swap out the horses under burden each day, they should stand up to it."

"The horses, yes," Daerget said. "When do we get to swap out the riders?"

Najud laughed. "You'll toughen up. You just won't care for the process."

"Well, I commend you at least on your deep pockets. They may not be flashy, but I like the build of these horses you bought. Easy-gaited, sturdy, and calm."

"If you can't trust a Zan to buy a horse, I should give up all hope of building a new caravan."

Daerget smiled into his beard. "Are all Zannib so wealthy?"

"Hardly. We more commonly breed the horses we want than pay for them."

He glanced at Daerget on his dun gelding.

"No, the last year or so has done well for me. Met Penrys and talked her into marriage. Completed my journeyman period and became a full *jarghal*—that's as high as we go, in *sarq*-Zannib. The Kigali gifted us in Neshilik, that first time, and then again in Yenit Ping. And in between there was the matter of the Kurighdunaq clan..." His voice roughened and he paused. He hadn't told Daerget yet about that disaster, but he supposed that several days travel together and nights in a common camp would draw many of his stories out of him.

"So we're unusually well-funded at the moment. Most of it's intended for the work building the caravan and its base, of course, and this side trip to Ellech, for books and for Penrys's sake..." His voice trailed off, and he clucked up his horse and trotted ahead of Daerget for a while, using a narrowing of the path as an excuse.

When Daerget caught up and pulled abreast again, he had questions ready.

"Najud, why does Penrys care so much about this? Why take that crazy risk of stirring up trouble by poking into Gialfinnur's work?"

Najud thought about how to put it. "Who are your parents, and theirs? What country do you come from? Why don't you remember? Could someone somewhere pull a string and have you come running, willing or not? How would you live with that?"

In a lower voice he added, "Is she a monster?"

"There's something else, Najud—I can hear it in your mind."

Najud took a deep breath. It wasn't a topic he liked discussing, but Daerget was perhaps risking his life coming with him, and he should know all of it.

"Penrys thinks the unusual healing she has comes from the chain. She suspects it'll keep her from having children, that her body will just eliminate pregnancies. It's been a year for us... she might be right.

"She thinks that's unfair to me—we Zannib have large families. I... I can't convince her it doesn't matter. Sure, I want children, but I want her more. There are other ways to build families."

Daerget nodded in companionable silence.

Najud cleared his throat. "I worry that she'll always feel... loosely attached to me, for my own good, as she would say."

He snorted. "It's both infuriating and terrifying—that she won't believe me when I say it doesn't matter, and that she might vanish because of it."

He glanced sideways at his companion. "You're not married, I can't expect you to understand. And besides, none of this matters now. We have to find out where she's been taken, and then get her back."

He kicked his horse back into a trot and pulled out in front through the fresh green of the spring growth.

Penrys had lost track of the days long ago. She sat leaning against the mast and shook. They no longer bound her hands or feet, just leashed her to the mast and left her alone, or tethered her between sleepers in camp at night.

She hadn't slept lying down for a long time—it was too much like drowning. Every breath was a wheeze, and trying to breathe more deeply invoked coughing fits which left her exhausted.

The occasional cups of water were welcome, since breathing through her mouth dried it out, but she couldn't remember when she last ate.

Every now and then someone would drop her blue robe on top of her, and she would shake it off when her fever ran high. Baelnei had almost kicked the sorry garment into the river before someone rescued it. "Not such a pretty thing, any more, is it?" he'd sneered.

She couldn't remember ever being sick before. *Is this the kind of thing people die from? What a stupid, stupid way to go. Naj-sha, I wish I could tell you what happened to me.*

Long since, she'd concluded that her chain wasn't dead, just drained—that the metal rod Baelnei tapped her with each morning and evening was what drained it and whatever internal core of power she had. *Gialfinnur's work, or something related.* She'd seen how everyone else was careful to stay away from it when he brought it out. She thought they were probably all wizards, though Baelnei was the only one with a robe and he wasn't wearing it now. Couldn't tell directly of course, drained as she was.

*I've been drifting here forever, and for what? Maybe I should just lie down and finish drowning. It would be so easy. They'd never notice in time to stop me.*

She thought about that for a moment with longing. She was very tired.

From somewhere else, deep inside, a voice said, *No. No, you can't do that. You want answers and they're taking you where the answers are. Find out, before you die. Don't let it all be a waste.*

Her breath bubbled in her throat, but she chuckled anyway. *Stubborn, that's what I am, underneath it all. Maybe that can keep me alive long enough.*

In camp a few nights later, Najud discussed the options with Daerget.

"You could see, before the sun faded, how we're coming up on the point of the ridge, this one here, on the engraving."

Daerget had focused a light device onto the paper to augment the firelight. "We can go into the valley of the upper half of the river, if we stay to the left of the ridge as it rises. The river will finally veer north again to meet us before turning west with the valley."

"But everyone would hear about us," Najud said. "It's a narrow valley, well-settled."

He rotated his head until the neck bones cracked. "On the other hand, we could maybe get news of Penrys—whether she's already come this way or not." He couldn't shake the fear that he was on the wrong trail.

"If you veer to the right of the ridge," Daerget said, "you can bypass that valley altogether, and rejoin the river when it enters Glymbeod, from the back. Wouldn't think anyone would expect you from there."

He looked over at the pile of horse packs lying on the ground. "What does the atlas say about that region?"

Najud shook his head. "Nothing at all. Maybe it's relatively unoccupied, or maybe it was just omitted."

*And maybe Penrys didn't get that far, or isn't on the river at all.*

He glanced at his companion who waited patiently for his response.

*Daerget's proving to be useful on the road. A traveler newly met either becomes someone you get to know, or someone you end up killing because he drives you crazy. It's the test of the trail.*

*The sparring of an evening helps me judge his other strengths, in case we get into some sort of fight.*

Even the device knowledge that Daerget casually displayed wasn't bothering Najud. It reminded him of Penrys.

"We'll decide in the morning," Najud finally said. "What would your family think about what we're doing?"

Daerget shut down the device so that Najud only had the firelight to see him by, that and the shadow of the emotions in his mind.

"I'm the oldest of the lot, and so my folks didn't want me going so far west for the Collegium. I guess I understand that better now, but at the time, where else would a young wizard want to be?"

He pursed his lips. "I miss my younger brothers and sisters, I do, but now they have a life without me. They won't suffer if I don't return—it would be more disruptive if I did come back."

With a shrug, he said, "I'll write them a very long letter when all this is over with, and an even longer one if I end up going to *sarq-Zannib*."

He cast a pointed look at Najud, who let it slide off without comment.

"You're that *byrindur* of Vylkar's, aren't you?"

Munraz just nodded politely while muttering under his breath, "No, I'm Najud's *nal-jarghal*, much good it's doing me at the moment. Not Vylkar's."

He delivered the summons from Vylkar to this wizard and bowed himself out of the room. Then he stalked down the corridor and calculated the best route to his next stop.

*If Najud had taken me along with him… If Vylkar hadn't made me help that Daerget pack up, I'd be on a horse now, going after Penrys, instead of stuck here running errands.*

*Won't even tell me what the meetings he's setting up are all about.*

He had a good idea, anyway. You couldn't do as much digging in the archives as Vylkar had assigned him and not draw a pretty good conclusion about what he was thinking. It was all who was where for what meetings and where were the notes, but the interesting part was the chart Vylkar had him working on that showed those events very clearly, and who read the notes afterward, and what notes existed but could no longer be found.

Munraz wasn't sure what conclusions Vylkar was drawing from this, but he could tell something about his suspicions—these documents went all the way back to Gialfinnur's time. People had died, since then, or retired, but they had students, and you could trace the actions of some of them.

*What sort of case is he putting together, and for whom? It's boring stuff, but I bet it gives him an outline of the problem—the people to trust, and the people not to trust.*

*But to what end?*

That's what had Munraz puzzled.

*I should be with Najud. I'm his apprentice. If he returns. If I don't lose them both.*

*If I don't find myself abandoned, far, far from sarq-Zannib.*

*What was I thinking when I agreed to go along with them to Kigali?*

He remembered that *bikraj* Khizuwi telling him to stick with Penrys and Najud, that it would be interesting.

*Hah! What did he know? He never got stuck in Ellech.*

*Seriously, what would happen to me if… if they don't come back?*

Vylkar had told him they left a will with the Zannib ambassador when they were in Yenit Ping. Vylkar showed him his copy.

*I can get back to sarq-Zannib, to Najud's own family, if I have to, funded by something Penrys was leaving to Vylkar.*

Vylkar had told him it was important for him to know that. *Of course, that was after Najud went chasing off after her.*

But despite his resentment at being left behind, it did warm him that they'd thought about him and made provisions for him, just as if he were kin. Even if they took him all the way to Ellech.

*And, really, it's not so bad, between the lessons with Vylkar and my new friends among the senior students. Vylkar says if I'm still here for the next holiday, I can come to Asuthgrata and invite some of them along. Wouldn't that be something to look forward to?*

# CHAPTER 16

The boat had stopped again and Penrys stared at the planks in front of her and concentrated on breathing. The light was fading from the sky. *Must be time for camp.*

Familiar feet in laced-instep boots stomped into her field of view and she saw the tip of the metal rod. She tried not to cringe, but she could hear the involuntary whine from her throat. *Stop it. Don't give him the satisfaction.*

Baelnei ran the tip of the rod across her cheek and she felt the dullness of the deadened chain and the vanishing of the least flicker of her awareness of other minds. It didn't last long enough to completely black her out, and she blinked in surprise.

*He usually waits until the campfire. Why now? Maybe we'll camp right here on the boat and build a fire on the water.*

She giggled at the silliness of the image. Hands tugged at her, but she couldn't seem to gather her feet underneath her. *They don't belong to me any more. Let someone else have 'em.*

They lowered her down again and she ignored them all. She looked down into her lap—those hands were too skinny to be hers, but they twitched when she told them to. Whose were they? The fingertips left trails in the air when they moved.

Then a hitch in her throat grabbed her attention.

*No, don't cough. No more coughing.* She concentrated all her effort on suppressing the tickle. *Feels like my throat will tear apart.*

The hands came back and picked her up again, but not very far. They laid her down on canvas, and then lifted it all up. *A litter. And isn't that nice—someone draped my poor wizard robe on top. Such a pretty color.*

*Whoops! Don't drop me now. Feet first down the plank and onto the shore.*

*Big wooden buildings. That's a funny smell, like a forge that's been sick.* She smiled at the image.

*And up the steps and into a big room.*

*Down we go, with a thump. Gotta sit up or I'll drown! That's right, pull me up against the wall.*

All the loud voices made her ears hurt.

She stared at these people. They looked clean. Indoors and off the river, she could smell her own reek. There was a bearded man Vylkar's age, with a chain. He was yelling at Baelnei about something, and Baelnei didn't look happy.

She giggled to herself. *Poor old bully. Someone doesn't approve.*

Then two women, same kind of age, with quieter voices. The taller one said, "We'll have to throw her in with the children until she's well enough to talk."

Penrys looked away and ignored them until people picked her up again and carried her back outside. When she was paying attention again, they were fumbling at a gate, and then at a second gate, and they dumped her there, in the dirt, litter and all. She heard the gates closing behind her and tried to breathe.

When she looked up, there were little faces looking down, all around, like goblins come to eat her. She offered them an arm to taste in friendly greeting.

One of them said, "Look, she has a chain."

Another one, the dark one, said, "That's Taikvali. She's come back."

Penrys lay on a cloth on the floor of a building, and someone was trying to clean her up. She had a wall to lean against and her clothing was being stripped off, rag by rag. She couldn't track the faces—there were too many of them—but they didn't seem to mean her any harm. They all seemed to be children.

She shivered when the cold water touched her sweat-soaked skin, but she wanted to be clean. When the chill hit her chest, she started to cough and she could feel the panic waiting to seize her.

A young boy sat next to her shoulder and said "Breathe, don't cough. Breathe." Small hands rubbed her and the tickle gradually worked its way lower down on her body where it mattered less.

"Roll her on her side." A sturdy voice commanded them, and Penrys found herself tilted back and forth, until the voice declared satisfaction.

"We're going to put you on that pallet there." The voice attached itself to a Ndant girl's face that moved into Penrys's line of sight. "Can you help?"

Penrys slowly turned her head and looked at the blanket covered pad on the ground. She rolled in that direction, and tried to prop herself up on her elbows to crawl onto it. Hands helped her, and shoved padding under her back so that she was semi-recumbent when they added more blankets to the top.

She still shivered under the blankets, but it was good to be clean.

The Ndant girl came back and told her, "We can't do anything for you but keep you warm. I'm going to make you hot soup, and you should drink it."

"Thank you," Penrys whispered.

"You don't remember us, do you?"

Penrys shook her head.

"You were here, too, four years ago, with us. We never left."

Penrys flashed on the memory of the *qahulajti* in *sarq*-Zannib, barely older than this girl, who died a monster with her throat slashed.

The girl must have seen her confusion. "Never mind. Just get better first. Soup and then sleep."

The same young boy who had told her to keep breathing sat crosslegged on the floor beside her. He looked familiar to Penrys, and then she realized, *he's the same as me. We're from the same place.*

He stared at her intently, almost possessively.

When the soup appeared, the Ndant girl took charge of spooning it into Penrys, who did her best to oblige her. Between spoonfuls, she asked "Why are all of you still here?"

"Too young for the last batch. Too few for the next one, I think."

"Who lives here with you?" Penrys asked.

"No one," the Ndant girl said. "Just us, since the last of the older ones left."

The oldest one, a Kigalino boy added, "Sometimes Tiessi checks up on us."

Penrys could make no sense of that. She dutifully opened her mouth for the next spoonful of soup and never noticed fading out between one mouthful and the next.

Penrys's sleep was interrupted with coughing fits, but they were milder. Whenever she woke, she saw the young boy who was like her, sometimes seated on the ground, and sometimes curled up by her side on the pallet.

By morning she felt a little better, not so much like drowning. She heard the boy awaken, and then she realized that came from his mind—her chain was beginning to recharge, and her core power was starting to restore itself, in the absence of that *dre'ski* metal rod.

She had little power for a mind-scan, but she tried it anyway, for the entire set of buildings that made up this one compound now haunted by a few children. She couldn't reach beyond it.

Nine children were here, in this room or the next, all wizards. And no one else.

They gathered around her again, now that they could feel she was awake.

"What's your name?" she asked the boy.

"Tarroak. You were my momma here. Why don't you know me?"

Penrys felt the blood drain from her face. He looked about nine years old. Was he hers? Was that possible? Surely she wasn't old enough.

The Ndant girl shook her head. "You know they lose everything once they're chained, Tarroak. Don't you remember Bilget?"

She turned and spoke to Penrys. "Many of the women who came took charge of the youngest. He was yours. You're not really his mother, of course."

Penrys stared at her.

"The leaders in here wrote down everyone's names, and where they were from, and who their family was, in case someone died."

Her mouth worked, and then she continued. "They didn't know they could still be alive and then lose all that."

She glanced off into the next room. "They had schools and everything, for a few months—I'll show you when you're better. And we tried to keep it up, after they were gone. Made sure everyone could read and write, taught them their numbers. Didn't have any books, but we did what we could."

Penrys could hear the voice seeking approval from an adult.

"How long ago?" she whispered.

"Almost four years, now," the girl said.

"What are your names?" Penrys asked.

They apparently decided to do it in order of seniority. The Kigalino boy stepped forward and nodded his head. "Chon Janwit, and I'm fourteen. I take care of them."

The dark Ndant girl gave him a fond look, and Penrys suspected she knew who the real leader here was. "I'm Ashiwe, thirteen, and this is Ichorke who's my age—we call her Iko— and Hakkur, who's twelve." She indicated a girl from Rasesdad and a boy from Ellech.

"Then there's Amatka and Iramqawj— they're ten, and these three are nine—that's Nimiz, Ju Ochim, and Tarroak."

Penrys tried to keep them straight—Ellech and Zannib for the ten-year-olds, girl and boy, and the Zannib boy, the Kigali girl, and Penrys's compatriot, for the nine-year-olds. The group of them would have been aged five to ten, four years ago.

"More soup," Ashiwe said, "and then back to sleep again."

"I'm getting better," Penrys objected.

"Not fast enough. We have a lot to show you, and you have to tell us what happened when you left."

The very thought of so much talking seemed exhausting to Penrys, and she acquiesced to Ashiwe's orders. "Soup and sleep for now," she agreed. "But wake me if they come for me."

Penrys dozed much of the day, but for the first time in a long while she didn't wake herself up coughing. Her skin was still warm and her lungs clogged, but her head was clearer.

Her chain was partway to recovery, too, and she had no difficulty placing everyone within the compound. She sat all the way up without help and looked for clothes, but there was nothing to hand. A silent call went out that included her by default. *She's awake!*

Ashiwe popped in and smiled at her. "You're better. That's faster than we expected."

"I think the chain helps," Penrys told her. "Now that it can."

"Is that what it does?"

"Well, it does lots of things." Penrys was reluctant to get into a long discussion about what she suspected about the technology around her neck.

"We washed your clothes last night and it's been a sunny day—they should be dry enough."

Penrys sat on the bed enwrapped in a blanket and watched her clothing parade in. No boots, though—those were missing. She spared a glance for the room she was in—raw planking and pallets stacked three high on the floor, with blankets. *The kids must sleep here.* There were more pallets rolled up along one wall. The room was big enough for dozens of people, and an unlit iron stove occupied the corner.

She shooed them out of the room while she dressed. Everything hung loosely on her—she'd seen her ribs, looking down, and wasn't surprised. At least they weren't as tender anymore. *More healing from the chain?* The torn blue robe was welcome for its warmth, but without shoes she left off the socks and went barefoot.

Chon Janwit, the Kigalino boy, was the tallest of them, though skinny in his adolescent growth, so she leaned on him as she picked her way over the stony ground to the outhouse. The dim memory of the leash around her collar at the camps along the river turned her stomach.

When she came out again, she looked west and was stunned by the view of the foothills of the Dunnarfeol, rising like impenetrable walls. The high snow-covered peaks weren't visible—blocked by these nearby hills which were mountain-high in their own right.

She'd seen part of the northern section of the range from Asuthgrata where there was a more balanced view from further away. Here, she'd have to climb the foothills to see the giants beyond them, but she knew they were there. She could practically feel the chill in the air radiating outward.

Ashiwe claimed her now and led her, with the boy in support, into one of the empty buildings around the stockaded perimeter. All the other children trailed behind. It was easier walking on the rough plank floors, and Penrys followed her to the schoolroom.

On one of the narrow walls, someone had engraved a large map. *Did they get to keep whatever was in their pockets, like knives, or did they arrive nude, the way they were sent out, once chained? Sharpened flints, maybe?*

Individual countries were labeled, in Kigali *yat*.

She remembered Najud's long ago description of the known world as a recumbent desert hound facing east. Ellech was the upper jaw, and far-away *sarq*-Zannib was the belly. There, on the wall, was the puff at the end of the upraised tail, an island continent in the north. Two countries were marked there, and the rest blank.

She walked over to the long wall without windows. Writing in Kigali *yat* had been carved into it, in large clumsy signs. She stepped back, and saw it was a list, filling most of the wall. Each column was headed by a country name at head height, and the name was repeated further down after each column had been filled down to knee-level. "Kigali" as a label headed several columns, but Ndant and Fastar and some of the other larger countries were also numerous, and even far away *sarq*-Zannib and Rasesdad were well-represented.

Ashiwe pulled Penrys to a short column with two countries, one over the other and space left between them. The one on top had five names, and the country below just the one. Ashiwe pointed at the solitary. "She was the youngest one they took, in the last batch."

Penrys choked and asked what she looked like, and Ashiwe described the light brown hair and freckles of the *qahulajti* she'd encountered in the west of *sarq*-Zannib.

Ashiwe watched her face. "You saw her, afterward?"

Penrys nodded.

"Is she all right? She was my friend."

Penrys shook her head mutely and started to shiver again.

Ashiwe shared a look with Chon Janwit. Then she pointed at a name on the short list under the other country. "This one is you."

Penrys read it. It meant nothing to her, nothing at all, and she began shaking her head in denial and couldn't stop.

"We're going to leave you alone here for a little while."

The two kids walked out and Penrys leaned against the wall and shook.

Eventually she pushed back and looked over the wall more carefully. She counted the names twice—almost five hundred people. Less these nine and anyone who died before the preparatory work was done, that implied almost that many had been launched haphazardly into the world.

How many died the moment they arrived, or soon thereafter? Half? A third?

How many had yet to be found?

Her face was wooden when she walked slowly out of the building, and Chon Janwit came up to her silently to lend his support. Methodically, she examined every building in the compound. There weren't many. No beds, just pallets on the floors, rolled up, now mostly eaten by rodents. Maybe enough room for one or two hundred people. If they came and went in batches, that would make sense. The enclosed compound held five long barrack-like buildings, three in back, and two on either side in front, framing an open space between them. Each building had a stove but no insulation, and she thought how cold they must be in the winter.

The children followed her but didn't interfere.

And then she entered the building that was used for eating and any other indoor activity. Alone among the buildings she'd seen, it had long benches and plank tables.

Along the walls of its main room, all the way around, interrupted by windows, she found the personal lists. First in Kigali *yat*, and then in the person's native language, if different.

> *Kep Tsugo, son of Kep Junchat and Gen Jipka from Jonggep. Married to Wan Tsufai. Father of Kep Hajing and Kep Hapo. Tell my wife I think of her always.*

Penrys stared at it. *Until you no longer think of your wife because you can't remember her existence.*

She sought her own name, though everything inside her screamed "don't look."

There it was. She couldn't read the native version—couldn't read her own original language any more. If Tarroak couldn't read it, so she could borrow the knowledge, then neither could she, and he was five years old when he came.

That's why they all had Kigali *yat* versions, she realized, so that whoever found them could read them all.

Her own entry was brief.

> *Taikvali, from Noskatoa in Aitzikoa. Daughter of Bizkoak and Deikzi, sister of Irrepi, wife of Eidiz.*

No children, thank all the Kigali gods. Parents and a sibling. I can't even tell which names are male or female. Do I have a brother or is that a sister? And a husband whose name means nothing.

She sank down onto a bench at one of the tables and laid her head on her arms.

After a bit, Tarroak came up to her and said, "Come look at mine." He tugged at her until she got up and showed her the entry.

She scanned him for the language, but it was fading through disuse. The biggest group of adults must have been Kigaliwen and they chose that as the language of record, but here, forced to survive alone with their captors, the children spoke Ellech, relying on the two Ellech children as sources for the language.

He couldn't parse the native entry, so she read him the Kigali *yat* version. When she'd named them all, using her finger to indicate the words, he pointed at one name.

"That's my mother." He looked up at her and his face screwed up. "I can't remember what she looks like any more." He refused to cry.

Penrys knelt down and pulled him to her. "I came back. I'll take care of you."

"Even though you don't remember me?"

"I'll learn you all over again—how will that be?"

Penrys sat on the bench in the old eating room, surrounded by the children, and tried to control herself. She needed to be the adult for them, the person who could make things better.

"Tell me about this. Did they come in batches or all at once, do you know?"

Ashiwe said, "I was in the first group, like Iramqawj and Iko, when these buildings were newly built. They'd bring in a hundred or more wizards from all over the world, then after a while they'd take them all away, a few at a time—all but the youngest—and we never saw them again."

She looked around at the others. "The first ones set up classes for us and started the list in the schoolroom, and these notes in here. A few weeks passed after they were all gone, and then another batch arrived."

There was a pause. "We kids explained things to each group that came. The ones of us who were here the longest ended up with three different groups of adults trying to look out for us. And each time, a couple more kids would join us and be left behind."

Penrys thought her eyes looked much, much older than her years.

"You were in the last batch, Taikvali," Ashiwe said. "All of it happened in less than a year."

Penrys flinched. "That's not my name. Not any more. Not if I can't remember it. It's 'Penrys' now." She fairly spat it out. These children knew more about her past than she did, and it made her stomach roil.

Tarroak looked at her. "Where did you go? What happened to all of you?"

Their eyes burned at her, and she tried to organize her thoughts. *A sanitized tale—don't tell them the full horror.*

"I… I don't know everything. My memory starts here, in Ellech. Naked in the snow a few hundred miles that way." She pointed to the northeast, to Asuthgrata. "I was lucky—someone found me, a wizard. I studied in the Collegium for three years and then there was an accident and I ended up in the west of Kigali."

She had their full attention. "We came across another chained wizard there. He was with the Rasesni," she nodded at the silent Iko standing next to Ashiwe, "but he wasn't from Rasesdad. I don't know where he was from."

*How to put this for them?* "I don't know what he was like before, but with the chain he was a maker of war. He had to be stopped, and… um… I stopped him. It was very complicated, but that's basically what happened. He died."

She licked her lips. "Afterward, I met a Zan and traveled with him to visit *sarq*-Zannib. And we found another chained wizard there. Your friend, Ashiwe. She had no memory either, and she had some very bad luck. A lot of people died."

Ashiwe whispered. "And she died, too. Was she bad? She wasn't bad when she was here."

Penrys's heart ached. "She couldn't help it. Unlucky, like I said. I don't think it was really her fault."

She sighed. "And so people now knew about the existence of chained wizards. Najud and I—that's my Zannib husband… We were summoned to Kigali, to Yenit Ping. They thought there were no wizards in Kigali." She raised an eyebrow at the two Kigalino children and they nodded.

"Suddenly they started finding chained wizards, dead and alive, and their own wizards that they thought banished by an old Emperor came out into the open." She lifted her gaze to the Chon Janwit. "Wizards are now living and working in public, with the approval of the Emperor."

The boy looked at her skeptically, and she told him, "A lot has changed in the last year."

"At the instigation of the Emperor, a meeting of several nations was held in Yenit Ping, and reports were heard about chained wizards appearing everywhere, sometimes dead, and sometimes managing to stay hidden."

Her voice slowed in reminiscence. "I met lots of the ones that ended up in Kigali, though they came from all over. None of them remembered anything before the chain."

"That's like Bilget," Ashiwe said. "He gave his memories to his sister Tiessi before his father gave him a chain."

*Willingly? He deliberately put a chain around his neck for the power, knowing he would lose his memory?*

"Why? Why would he do that?"

No one answered her.

"Gialfinnur was alive?" They looked at her without understanding.

"Their father," she explained.

Chon Janwit said, "Tiessi told us about it. He was already dead when we got here."

"Where are we?" Nimiz asked. Both the Zan boys were particularly attentive since she'd mentioned Najud.

"This is western Ellech, a few hundred miles from the Drosenrolkentham, the Collegium of Wizards. If you could travel down that river outside there, you'd eventually reach Tavnastok, at the fork with the Lodentaf Gaer, and that's where the Collegium is."

Penrys looked up through the ceiling of the eating room. *What was keeping them in?* Her chain wasn't strong yet, but when she probed she found a powerful barrier surrounding them on all sides. She'd never felt anything with quite that flavor before. *More of the power-metal technology?*

"Do they ever visit you?"

Ashiwe shrugged. "They deliver food and firewood and sometimes clothing through the double gates. They've always got these metal rods…"

Penrys winced and nodded.

"Sometimes Tiessi comes. She doesn't say much, just looks around. Once when Iko broke her arm, she brought a doctor in, and he saw her in-between the two gates, but mostly we just take care of ourselves."

Chon Janwit spoke up. "We're strong. Stronger than that Tiessi. I bet you can't break our shields. I dare you."

She could hear the pride in his voice and leaned against his shield lightly to gratify him, then more strongly as she realized he had reason to boast. The other children joined him, and the unified shield was a challenge to her partially recovered chain.

"I'm impressed," she told them, honestly.

The effort tired her, and she yawned. "I should go back and lie down—can't do anything useful until I'm better."

She staggered getting to her feet, and it was with a slow shuffle and Chon Janwit's arm that she made it barefoot across the open yard between the front buildings and back to her pallet.

All evening her temperature spiked again, and the fever gave her horrid dreams, of people flowing into this place, dropping off a few children, then flowing out again to their deaths, like the river. Each embalmed corpse she'd seen in the prisons of Imperial Security at Yenit Ping came back to life, and she wondered which name it would claim, carved into the walls here.

She thought she heard Iko talking about her. "Why is she the only one who came back? How'd she find us? Maybe she can get us out."

"Nah, she's a prisoner again, too, like us, and sick."

"But she's got a chain now, like Bilget."

She drifted into sleep with their hopes and doubts.

When she woke, the next morning, she felt better, and more of her power was back.

And that's when they came for her.

# CHAPTER 17

The chained wizard that the kids named Bilget was at the gate in the morning, waiting while the men he sent in grabbed Penrys and hustled her out. She dragged her feet and pretended to be worse than she was. Her chain felt almost depleted, but her native power was slowly recovering, as slowly as her health. The children were kept at bay by the rods that the guards flourished.

They walked her back up the path to the main building, and she tried to spare her bruised bare feet. She snuck a peek at her surroundings, now that she could make them out better—a complex series of buildings, and about three dozen people tucked away out of sight, all wizards to her mind-scan, like the men surrounding her. She thought there was only the one with a chain. The sounds of cattle and chickens carried from somewhere nearby.

This time they hauled her around behind the main structure, into a workroom in a different building. On the outside, these work buildings were log-built and rustic, but the interiors were comfortable enough. The materials inside that Penrys caught a glimpse of were new to her, as were some of the tools. The guards dumped her into a carved chair with arms. They held their metal rods close the whole time, and she tried not to give them an excuse to use one.

Bilget had them drag four chairs into place in a semicircle in front of her. He caught her watching, and smiled. "We have a few questions for you."

She coughed dramatically, and he turned his back on her and ignored it.

One of the women came in. "Where are her shoes?"

"Ask your son," Bilget told her.

She turned to look at Baelnei who had just walked in, and he shrugged. "How should I know?"

The other woman entered and took a seat, watching the exchange with Baelnei in distaste. "Can't you control him any better than that?"

"You try it, Elkif, if you think it's so easy," the woman retorted.

*Elkif! This was Gialfinnur's daughter, and the other two look like they must be siblings.*

"Let's get started," Bilget said. "You, Penrys—which one are you? What've you got that's special?"

Penrys pretended to have trouble following him.

"Show me her ears." Baelnei strode over and grabbed her head, then pulled the hair away from the furry fox-like ears.

Bilget smiled. "That's the last batch. I can tell by the differences," he told his siblings.

Then he glanced at Penrys. "My mark, like a good craftsman. I'll come up with something else for the next set."

With an air of sharing a secret, he added, "It's all in how you direct the re-growth."

*Regrowth? He carved off my ears and grew the furry ones in their place?*

She tried to mask her involuntary shudder as a fever reaction.

*How is that even possible? Contamination by some animal form?*

He turned to shelves along the walls and pulled down a notebook, and paged through it. "There was only one woman from Aitzikoa in that last batch, so that has to be you." He flipped through his records. "Ah, wings. I gave you wings."

He peered over at her. "How do you like them?"

Penrys kept her face expressionless and tried to mask her emotions with subtlety rather than a full shield which they might have noticed. *Sick, you're sick. Weak. Insignificant. Make them believe it.*

A glance at Baelnei told her not everyone was taken in.

Bilget looked at his sisters. "I told you a top barrier for the compound was a good idea. Flying into that would be like a moth reaching the flame."

"Are you sure she's harmless over there?" Elkif asked.

"We've held as many as two hundred wizards at a time without any problems. I think we can manage one sick foreigner and a few kids."

He turned his attention to Penrys again. "We knew you were at the Collegium, of course—how we smiled at that! Purely random chance, you know, that one of you ended up not only in Ellech but nearby.

"But you were such a studious mouse—there was nothing to learn from you. Nothing happened. It was like one of those Kigali fireworks that fail to explode. Very disappointing. We kept waiting…"

He leaned forward avidly. "Imagine how surprised we were when we discovered what you'd been up to in the south. Tell us all about it."

*They've seen the letter I sent Vylkar, or heard about it. Or maybe the report about that dinner in Stokemmi.*

Penrys smiled at him weakly and cleared her throat. "I have questions, too. Can we share?"

*Make them believe you're willing to cooperate. They'll keep you alive as long as they think they can learn something from you. They can't let you go, whatever they tell you. They can't let anyone find them.*

Bilget cocked his head at her, speculatively.

"Well, now, that's an interesting proposition. I'd like to talk to you about working with the chain, what you've found out. But me first."

He leaned toward her. "What do you remember?" His eyes were avid.

"Nothing," she told him, honestly. "Nothing at all from before I woke up in Ellech and was picked up."

"Not your name? Language?"

"No, nothing." She tried not to think about the freezing snow on her bare skin, and the shock of the torches when Vylkar's riders found her, alerted by her mind-shout when she materialized.

Bilget cast a glance of satisfaction at his sister. "See, Tiessi, that's why I made you the custodian of my memories, so that wouldn't happen to me."

The shorter woman looked haunted, but she nodded, reluctantly.

"So I still have my childhood," Bilget told Penrys, companionably. "I just look for it in her mind instead of mine. And of course I've gotten most of it back that way, so it's mine again."

*Time to share another tidbit and appeal to his vanity.*

"I've met many other chained wizards, out in the world, and I saw some of the things they had, like my wings." She tried to put professional curiosity into her voice. "I've never seen anything like that—are they devices? How do they work?"

"That was our father's doing, most of it. Making devices that could integrate into a person. But it wasn't useful until we found a better power source for them."

*Be suitably impressed, like a good student.*

"What, the chains?"

He smiled approvingly. "That's right. That was my idea. I put it all together. My father's power-metal to hold the charge, with its attachment to the mind that trades memory for other purposes, and the body devices that required the extra power to integrate properly.

"The healing's some sort of by-product. We tried a few chains without the body devices, and there was no special healing."

He leaned forward confidingly. "I think the chain makes a place in the memory space it occupies to teach the body how to heal and works with the body devices to accommodate them."

Penrys thought of what those experiments might have been like for the victims.

Bilget continued his lecture. "My father needed someone to help him, and I was proud to take on that task, to wear the chain he'd perfected. He knew he could trust me, unlike his first trials."

*And I imagine he was tempted by the notion of longevity implied by the healing.*

"Where'd you get your wizards from?" she asked. "For the… experiments, I mean, not your helpers."

"You should know. You were working on a magic detector of some kind yourself, a *ryskymmer*, and it sent you to Kigali. We had someone take it apart and report back on it, and it used similar principles—find the source, then bring the source here. Though you had a new wrinkle on it— thank you for that. Well done, for someone with your handicaps."

He gifted her with a condescending nod.

"That's how we filled the compound—found wizards and brought them there. 'Course we couldn't control exactly where they come from, or where they go, not yet. But *you* know all about that, don't you? I've read the reports."

He smiled. "You're the first one to come back. I'm so glad you're here so I can question you in person. Tell me everything."

All afternoon Bilget questioned Penrys until her voice hoarsened. He particularly wanted to know what she'd seen of the other chained wizards.

He interrupted her constantly, trying to identify each one from his records, and barely masked, his frustration when he didn't succeed.

There were chained wizards who had never found their "special addition" and others who died without revealing it, and that made them particularly difficult to match to his notes.

She spoke openly, trying to drown him in meaningless detail while concealing from him everything she could about actually using the power of the chain against other wizards—its ability to drain power directly, what happened when it was cut, how to invoke it deliberately.

This man used his power-metal rods to drain a wizard—maybe he hadn't thought about how to do it in any other way.

Maybe he'd never been powerless, himself, and forced to improvise.

His sisters seemed to have no control over him, and there was little evidence that their father was still alive, though she was careful not to ask. Their mother was never mentioned. She wanted them to think of her own questions as self-interested, looking for a way to join them, as if she thought they might let her.

It was a tricky thing to balance, all the indirection and subtle concealments with a fawning enthusiasm for what they'd accomplished, and she let the afternoon fever show in her shivering hands and her slumped posture, until Bilget stopped in mid-sentence.

"Still not well, I see. I'm surprised the healing works on injuries but not illness."

She shrugged at him. "It's the only time I've ever been sick."

Baelnei sneered from his corner. "It's all an act, you know, what she's doing. You should drain her again and keep the *staka* drained."

Bilget rounded on him. "If you ever want a chain yourself, nephew, you'll need to demonstrate a bit more courage. Where do you think she's going, eh? How many of our experiments can we evaluate like this?"

Elkif winced, but Penrys smiled inside. *That was a little show of fangs. I'm not supposed to notice that.*

"I just want to learn more about how it all works," Penrys said. "Do you still have what was in my pockets?"

Bilget walked over to a table and poked his finger through the contents of a shallow basket.

"Look for my *tennendaer*," she said. "The bit of metal."

He plucked that out, and then brought it into the light for a closer look. "Where did you get this?"

*They don't know everything inside the Collegium, at least not the recent news.*

"My workroom. It's the same one your father had. That came out of the sweepings when I took it over. For some reason, no one wanted the room until I came along. No one told me the story."

She monitored their minds as lightly as she could. Surprise, and then outrage at the reminder of their family's failure. She'd expected Bilget and Baelnei to react the most, but it was Elkif, which surprised her. Nothing showed on Elkif's face.

*Did the other two ever attend the Collegium, or only Elkif? How much older is she? Who are these other wizards?*

She shivered again and produced a hacking cough.

Bilget held the *tennendaer* as if he'd forgotten it and cocked his head at her. "I think this is enough for one day. Wouldn't want to tire our guest before she's fully recovered."

Penrys stood up on unsteady legs, and he bared his teeth at her in a grin. "Just one more thing before you go," he said. "Show me the wings."

There was no point in resisting. She invoked them, and turned so that he could look, but let them droop suggestively. She felt Baelnei poking at them, showing them off to Bilget. "Better than the earlier models," Bilget commented.

She contradicted him, over her shoulder. "Not so efficient for long flight—the legs get in the way and have to be supported." All this in the tone of a lab assistant commenting on a bit of disappointing data.

She put them away and turned to face him before the surprise vanished from his face. "Thought you ought to know. You'll do better next time." Just as though she believed she would see a next time.

"Hmm. Back to your birdcage now, and I'll see you again in the morning."

Bilget dismissed her, and Tiessi left the room. Baelnei and the guards surrounded her with their metal rods at the ready, and she started the slow walk back to the prisoner compound trying not to bruise her feet further.

From the outside, it did indeed look like a very odd cage—a series of long power-metal arrays organized like petals along the walls, with an entrance at one of the gaps between the petals.

Before they reached the first gate, Tiessi walked up and thrust an old pair of laced-instep boots and socks into her arms. "Your feet look about my size, and you need something."

She turned and walked off, while Penrys called after her, "Thank you for your kindness."

Baelnei snorted but said nothing.

She was marched through the second gate, and then left alone, and all the children came running. She let them surround her and support her back to her pallet, where she was grateful to sink down, and lean her back against the wall.

"What did they want? Are you all right?"

She raised her hand against the bombardment of questions. There'd been enough questions for one day.

"They wanted to know what I'd seen of the other chained wizards. Bilget asked the questions. They didn't hurt me." *Yet. That would change, but no sense scaring the kids.* "See, Tiessi gave me her old shoes. That was nice of her." *Considering it was her son who lost me my originals and almost killed me.*

Ashiwe looked at her soberly. *I'm not fooling that one, am I?* She nodded at her slightly in acknowledgment, and the moment passed.

"It's almost time for supper," Ashiwe said. "We'll bring you something."

She turned to the others and added. "Let's leave her alone for a while, let her take a nap." She herded them out of the room, and Penrys could drop her mask.

*These gentle tactics from Bilget aren't going to last forever, only while they think I might be at risk of dying. Bilget wants his data first, but one of them's going to want to find out who else knows where I am, who might have followed me. And that's more important than Bilget's experiments. That's what'll get me killed, unless I give them some sort of answer.*

*Is anyone following me? Where would they start?*

*I can't let them kill me. It's not just me—if they're convinced someone's coming, they'll go into hiding or brazen it out, but either way they'll never let these kids live. They'll bury that evidence. And they'd burn these buildings this minute if they knew about the records carved into the walls. How did the kids keep Tiessi from seeing that? Maybe she didn't want to go in and see what this prison camp was really like. Why should she care, after all—the prisoners won't remember what happened to them, so why would it matter?*

*Does Bilget have a special addition, like my wings? Did his father give it to him? He couldn't do it to himself, surely, unless it was something very small, just to invoke the healing.*

*Who's really in charge here? Bilget, with his chain? He acts that way. But Elkif's the eldest. Tiessi seems cowed by her brother, but she has moments of kindness that they seem to allow her.*

*Why do the other wizards help him? What's in it for them? Are they kin of some kind, or is that just the general look of people here in Glymbeod?*

*Bilget's demonstrated that you can have both the chain and your memories, sort of. Is that what Baelnei's so eager for?*

*Why did they take it this far? Wasn't the power-metal invention enough?*

*I could take my chances of breaking away from the guards long enough to fly.* She didn't like the odds of doing it without getting touched by the metal rods, but it was at least possible. But she couldn't leave without the kids. She'd have to find a way to get them out of the compound.

*And then what? Steal a boat, only to have a better boat and crew follow and recapture them?*

She'd seen a couple of horses, but the children had been here four years. *How many could ride, much less bareback in an emergency? And how many horses were there?* She could control the horses, even ten of them, but she couldn't keep the kids on them. And where would they go?

Her looks at the map had told her there were only short local roads. All the longer traffic was by water. But there was only one river. Maybe you could take two canoes and hide up a tributary creek somewhere, but eventually you'd be found.

And west of them were the steep foothills of the Dunnarfeol.

Gialfinnur had picked a tough place—easy to defend, and hard to escape.

If it weren't for the metal rods in everyone's hand, she could contemplate a direct attack, once she was better, and once her chain was more fully charged. When she was out of the shielded compound she'd sensed maybe thirty-five wizards and Bilget was the only chained one.

*I'm the only one who's fought with a chain. I could take Bilget, and maybe the rest of them. Maybe—that's a lot of people. But I couldn't control them—*

*I'd have to kill them, there wouldn't be any other choice. Some of those wizards are young. Are they all monsters? If I just kill Gialfinnur's descendants, will the rest let me leave? Why would they let an accuser get away?*

*And if I fail, the children here will die, and no one will ever know what happened.*

*There has to be a way…*

Najud mentally reviewed the contents of his pack as he walked. It was slow work clambering over rock spurs when there was no obvious way around, but at least Daerget and he encountered no one else in this barren upland on the back side of the water divide for the Virtaengi Gaer.

The horses had been left in last night's camp—a meadow almost surrounded by bare rock, with a small stream. Najud thought they'd linger there for a while, but they had a way out if the two of them didn't return. They'd loaded whatever they couldn't carry with them into one of the horse packs in the place of vanished grain and stashed all the packs and tack under the rock ledges of the southwest corner.

It was impossible to tell how many miles they still had left to cover but if they reached the lower foothills, the start of the real mountains, they would know they'd gone too far and needed to turn south, down into Glymbeod. Najud planned to cross the divide to the south anyway, whenever a feasible route presented itself. He wanted a good view of Glymbeod from the height as soon as he could get one.

Daerget intercepted Najud's glance and grinned at him. "Told you I wanted adventure, didn't I? Like the old *drepfarar* in the story, you've just given me what I asked for, eh? I'm not complaining."

Najud half-smiled in appreciation, but all the time he kept chewing on the same thoughts. *You better be there somewhere, Pen-sha. Because I don't know where else to look.*

By mid-day, they'd crossed over into Glymbeod and stopped to eat at a good vantage point. The pocket valley spread out below them with the glint of a thin thread of river in the far distance.

Najud glanced over at his companion. "One mile, I can reach. Even Penrys can only scan about five miles out. Look at all that space—we could crisscross it and never find her, and she has no reason to be looking, either."

Daerget said, "That village of Elkif's is down there, on this side of the river. Gotta get there first. And we need a story—you know what these *taunnupar* are like, probably serve us up for dinner if they think there're no consequences."

He said it with a grin, but Najud wondered how much of that was actually a joke. There was no reason for two wizards to fear the locals, but the longer they could travel unnoticed, the better.

"Explorers," he suggested. "We've been mapping the foothills here for the Collegium, and I'm helping because…"

"Because of your experience in the Mratsanag Mountains," Daerget supplied.

Najud stared at him. "But those are in Rasesdad, not *sarq*-Zannib."

"It's thousands of miles away. Think the locals will know the difference?"

The shrug that accompanied the comment left Najud speechless, and then he snorted. "If you say so. But we're coming up the valley from the east, so that still won't work."

Daerget pointed to his right. "So let's swing around up-vale and come down from the northwest. Easy to fix."

A slow smile spread across Najud's face. "We could do that. Where's our climbing gear?"

"In the house of our guide, of course. We're just the scholars returning home, looking for a ride downstream, in the clothes we saved for when the expedition was over, robes and all. We burned the rest of them. And naturally the Collegium knows where we are and is expecting us. They didn't hear about us before because… because we started by going up the Lodentaf and coming down from the north."

Najud nodded. "I can see I'm in the hands of a master here. Must've learned all this cunning while you were being a pirate, eh? And our maps, should anyone ask?"

Daerget waved a hand airily at him. "I'll whip up something plausible tonight. I've seen enough of the real thing—shouldn't be hard. Just add a few stains to make them illegible and they'll never know the difference. Probably can't read, anyway."

Munraz turned to close the door of Vylkar's room and planted his feet firmly in front of his desk, until the man stopped reading the document he'd just received and looked up.

"Stop treating me like they aren't my family and my responsibility, too. Tell me what you're planning."

Vylkar put the paper down and pursed his hands together. "What do you think is happening?"

"How would I know? All I have for evidence is the questions you've been asking."

Munraz began ticking points off of his fingers until he ran out of fingers. "Where did Gialfinnur go and where does Elkif come from? And were those other two her siblings or not? Do others come from there, and where did they go, when they left? Did all of them leave, or are they still here?"

He was just warming up. "Who else has been lost track of, since Elkif's time? Who used to go around together? Are any of *them* still here? What's missing from the archives?"

He grabbed his simmering temper with both hands and glowered down at Penrys's mentor. He'd shared a cabin on the ship with the man for two months—he knew when he was hiding things. "Who knew what and when, either then or now?"

Vylkar nodded when he wound down. "An excellent summary of my interests in this matter. You've been paying attention. What does it show?"

The man looked… *pleased* with him, not irritated. Munraz realized he'd been leaning over his desk at him and pulled himself back.

"It outlines your thinking." Munraz slowed down and began to present what he'd been mulling over instead of sleeping for the last few nights.

Vylkar waved him to a chair with an invitation to proceed.

"You have a theory. You know that Gialfinnur and his eventual family went unobserved. Is Elkif the only child, or were those other two siblings, as they claimed, or just kinsmen? And where is she now? Are others with her, who knew her or her father then, and are they continuing her father's work?"

He swallowed. "Did some of them stay here, unrecognized? Are they still here, spies?"

Vylkar raised an eyebrow, and Munraz summarized. "In other words, are the people involved both plausible as candidates in the past and possibly still lingering in the present?"

Vylkar nodded.

"Then, is the connection to the chained wizards possible—that's the next part of the… proof you're building. Was Gialfinnur's work sufficient to be the prototype for the chains, if not then, then perhaps now? Penrys's pocket piece, that metal fragment, well that's evidence, isn't it? Real, tangible evidence. The chained wizards are recent, so the threat must be recent, too."

He'd been staring off into space gathering his points, and his eyes swung back in time to catch Vylkar's smile as he leaned back in his chair and gave Munraz all his attention.

"And now you want more evidence. You want to know who knew what when, and who might still be here, watching. That's why all the archive searches and the old meetings with their notes."

He looked carefully at Vylkar's face. "You need proof of it, for someone besides yourself. You—you're already sure."

Vylkar finally replied. "You have a good mind, when you concentrate on using it."

"Easier to concentrate when I'm far from my own problems in *sarq*-Zannib." Munraz surprised himself with that bit of candor and shook it off.

"There's something very wrong here, *raer*," he said.

Vylkar held his gaze steadily. "Yes, there is."

Munraz nodded his head in satisfaction. "So, tell me what you know." He settled back in his chair, gratified to be taken seriously.

Vylkar's eyes flicked to the door as if to verify that it was closed, and Munraz could feel him checking his shields around the room.

"Penrys was surely right about Glymbeod, Munraz. There are little hints about it everywhere. The most obvious one was the error someone made listing Elkif's origin accurately. Those other two *were* her siblings, but their home was given as somewhere else, and I don't believe it. I think that was the first clear mistake.

"And then I've been looking at the sorts of things sold in the wizard shops on the south side of town, where the *taunnupar* shop. The owners tell me one thing, but I followed the metallurgical trail. I looked at the records for the supplies Gialfinnur requisitioned when he was here, especially some of the unusual ores and refined metals. I talked to the people who supply such things for the demand locally, and they sell quite a bit to those same wizard shops. The ones who never mentioned it to me, when I asked."

Munraz smiled appreciatively. He would never of thought of that himself.

Vylkar raised an admonishing finger. "I can't be sure that Glymbeod's where Penrys is. And she might have been killed, Munraz, not just taken—I'm sorry. If someone captured her, I'm surprised she hasn't broken free and returned. And troubled. I was beginning to think nothing could stop her."

The knot of worry in Munraz's stomach clenched, but he kept his face still. Vylkar expected him to take the speculation in stride.

"There are more than a dozen other wizards I know of that might be up there in Glymbeod, too—trained right here. And any one of them, or several, could have trained colleagues locally, and we would never know about it."

Vylkar tilted his head as he watched Munraz. "Something like this has happened before, you know—more than once. We're smarter than we used to be about intervening as soon as we're sure, but others can read the same historical accounts and they've taken good care not to draw our attention, so they've had years and years to bury themselves and do… whatever they're doing.

"The biggest problem is the person I think is still here. There may be more than one, but I know who the big one is, I'm almost sure."

He expelled his breath in exasperation. "I need definitive proof. If I'm right, he's close to Luveri, the head of our senior council, so it needs evidence."

"What kind of proof?"

Vylkar snorted. "A confession would be good."

"We could dangle him by his heels over one of the outer walls."

That earned him a stare, and then Vylkar's expression turned to consideration.

*He's remembering that I'm the one who killed the qahulajti when it had to be done, before she could be turned into a captive for breeding.* The thought still had the power to hurt, but Munraz decided he could live with that. He still believed it was the only choice he'd had.

A stray thought hit him. He knew from Najud that Penrys thought her chain's healing prevented pregnancy. If she was right, that *qahulajti* would never have had children, and her mind-subdued captivity would have been fruitless. *My family poisoned everything it touched.*

A voice in his head murmured, *even me?*

*No, I won't let it. They are no longer my family. They made sure of that and… and I'm all right with that, aren't I?*

Something had healed inside, or at least scarred over, and Munraz wondered when that had happened.

Vylkar raised an eyebrow at him, but Munraz just shook his head dismissively. "About that dangling… If you're right, will the others forgive you? If you're wrong about him, are you sure about the rest of it? 'Cause if you are, that seems like a really good reason to do it."

He could see Vylkar considering it.

Munraz smiled to himself. "And if you *are* right, what then?"

"If I have proof, if I can convince the council, we'll clean out this nest."

"Penrys might be dead by then." Munraz tried to keep his voice steady.

"Maybe. And they might escape before we get there. But Najud's out there somewhere, too, with Daerget. Don't discount him."

The image of his smiling and cunning *jarghal* flashed into Munraz's mind, endlessly resourceful, and lucky, like his name. "I'd never do that," he said.

# CHAPTER 18

No one came for Penrys early in the morning, and she spent the time grilling Ashiwe about possibilities in the eating room with the mute evidence all along the walls.

"What about warm clothing, and shoes?" The kids weren't in rags, but the clothes were overlarge and ill-assorted.

"They brought the clothing back, after…" Ashiwe said, looking away. "Sometimes the adults would cry when they got it back. They'd argue about whether their friends had been killed or not, though they tried to keep us from listening. Some thought not…"

She met Penrys's eyes. "That's what they decided to believe. It made living easier for them. Not all of them agreed. Five of them… they found their own ends."

Her eyes closed as she spoke. "It was peaceful for the two women from Fastar, I heard. They held hands and stopped each other's hearts. The others…"

Penrys reached out along the table they shared and gripped her forearm, and Ashiwe opened her eyes and and took a breath. "An Ellech woman found a way to climb the stockade in back and tried to jump out through the gaps in the metal framework. Her scream woke us."

She shuddered.

"Then two of the Rasesni men, from different groups… one tried to break out when there was a delivery. The guards all went after him with those metal rods. One of my friends, the one you met in *sarq*-Zannib, she told me it was like watching an animal get stung to death by angry wasps."

Her breath came more quickly now. "The other Rasesni, the last one who died in here, he stood by the inner gate and waited for it to be opened on schedule. I saw him. When it swung open, the guards prepared for another fight, but he ignored them and walked straight over to the exposed framework of our… cage. He spread his arms wide and grabbed two struts at once, and just… smiled… as his body shook, until he dropped."

Penrys let her recover herself while she turned it all over in her mind. *All those wizards, and no one found a way out. Let's say they're right, and I shouldn't waste my time with it. That means either I have to find a way for the kids to be released first, or I have to, what, destroy the cage? Yrmur! How would I do that?*

"Anyway," Ashiwe said, "We have plenty of clothing, from what was left. No way to sew, though, so the fit's not good. Enough of the adults were small that we can all use some of the shoes."

"What about packs and extra food?"

The girl's head swiveled and she turned all her attention on Penrys. "You think we can get out."

"Don't know. But why not be prepared?"

Ashiwe grinned wolfishly. "We have knives. They searched everyone when they arrived but a few managed to conceal things. We can cut things apart and tie them back together, even lace them with leather thongs, though there's not a lot of leather in the clothing. I can get packs made for all of us." She nodded enthusiastically.

"And food—we can manage some. They don't like to come in here too often, so it runs to things that'll keep. Root vegetables, flatbreads, dried fish and meat. Oil and salt. Even apples and cabbages, sometimes, and dried fruit. Grain for porridge, honey for sweetener. Could be a lot worse. More than we need. Enough to last a while."

"And all of it good for camping with, given a few cooking tools." Penrys smiled. "That's good news. Don't forget something to carry water, for everyone, plus spares."

She glanced at the walls surrounding them. "Something else."

Ashiwe waited.

"Do you have paper and ink? Any way to write?"

"Sure. They let the adults keep a school for us. There's still lots of paper and we can grind more ink. Why?"

Penrys took a deep breath. "I want the best writers to copy *everything* on the walls in this room, and the other one, with the map. They have to get it all, and they have to be careful, very careful—very accurate. Has to be someone who can read Kigalino."

Ashiwe interrupted. "We can all read everything any of us knows from our own countries, except for Tarroak who doesn't remember his own very well. Some of the writing's from countries we don't know, of course."

"I understand. Get both languages anyway, even if you can't read the second one. It's very important—don't make any mistakes. Do you know how to make a copy with a piece of paper and charcoal, rubbing it over the spot? You can use that for the unknown languages, as an extra step. If there's time, make a second copy from the first."

She tried to frame her emphasis with both her raised hands. "Hide each copy away when you're done and wrap them carefully in something waterproof. If you get out, take them with you, in separate packs. D'ya understand?"

Ashiwe nodded. "Their families will want to know what happened."

"And *your* families, and the whole world. And many of them are still alive, and want to know." She waved a hand at the lists along the walls. "Like me."

"This will take a couple of days—how long do we have?"

Penrys leaned back and tried to gauge the girl's maturity. Her mind was steady—all of the children had been hardened by their experience and forced out of childhood for survival.

"Listen, Ashiwe… Any time they take me, I might not come back, you know. I'll do my best but who can tell? I want you to be prepared for an escape whether I can come back or not. You see, if they're convinced someone's following me they might…"

"Get rid of all the evidence. Like us." The girl tilted her head. "*Is* someone following you?"

"I don't know. It wouldn't be easy—I was taken back in Tavnastok. If you get me paper and pen, I can draw you a map of where you are and where you might want to go, if you end up… on your own."

Penrys tried mind-speech on her. *Can you hear me?*

Ashiwe echoed it back. *Not all of us can do this yet. Just the oldest ones.*

*Then make sure everyone understands. I won't leave without you, but if you get the chance, you should escape and not worry about waiting for me. I'll find you.*

*Not if you're… dead.*

*I fully intend to stay alive. But you kids and that documentation—that's the important thing. Don't forget that. Get it and all of you to the Collegium, to a man named Vylkar. I'll write the name down for you, on the map.*

By mid-morning, three scribes were busy, led by Chon Janwit who proofread everyone's Kigali *yat*. Iramqawj helped, but his work was confined to the Zannib texts, so his less tidy writing was restricted in scope. Ashiwe would double-check the Ndant transcription, once she was done with overseeing the other preparations Penrys had outlined.

All hands were busy, and Penrys stayed out of the buildings after she'd drawn a map for Ashiwe. She was sure that someone would come for her and wanted to give them no excuse to come all the way in and notice the activity. She'd look over the transcriptions from the walls herself, when she came back.

Assuming she came back.

If the children got out and she didn't, could they get to the Collegium? She'd recommended a route through Estirmet, getting as close to the Lodentaf Gaer as they could until they reached Tavnastok, then straight across at the bridge before anyone could stop them.

But that was four hundred miles. That would be almost a month of walking under packs, looking for a water source every night. Could they bring enough food? More than a pound per person per day was a lot for a nine-year-old to carry. Accidents would slow them down. People might find them, especially as they got closer to Tavnastok, and anyone seeing such an exotic mix of youngsters would spread the word, where the wrong people might hear about it.

It was a desperate long shot, and she didn't want to play it, but better any plan than no plan at all. And better than just sending them west into the mountains, away from any help. At the very least, if there were some sort of fight here, they had a chance.

Anything was better than being at the dubious mercy of Bilget and his sisters, if they could get away.

When her escort showed up at the gates, she went with them willingly, walking more easily now in Tiessi's abused and discarded boots. She hacked a coughing fit worse than before whenever the clearing scum in her lungs irritated her throat, but the fever seemed to be in abeyance.

They walked her past the forge, and the rotten-egg smell clutched at her throat. The logs of that building seemed newer than the others, and she wondered if it had burned, once before. She'd have liked to see how the metal was refined and forged, but they passed the building by. Instead, they turned in at a smaller log building. The tink of metal on metal carried to the outside.

Bilget was waiting inside, without the rest of his family. There were wooden bins of materials at different stages along the wall, and three men and a woman looked up from their benches when Penrys was escorted in.

She scanned the device lights—power sources were everywhere, but they weren't power-stones. *These must be bits of the power-metal.* She glanced sideways at the waiting Bilget.

"So, how do you keep them powered up?" She cocked her head at the nearest device hanging from the wall. "Like power-stones?"

He smiled. "That's right, except it's much more efficient. Power-stones are made by nature—some have good crystals, most don't. We make our power-metal to order. Doesn't take much of a charge at all to top them up."

He waved a hand casually. "One wizard can keep that whole compound cage going on a few minutes of attention each day."

"Impressive," Penrys replied, and meant it.

The artisans had gone back to work. "Aren't you worried about people finding out what you're working on?"

"Kin are kin—we don't betray each other, and we don't interfere in someone else's business. We gave our wizards an education, locally under Elkif or off at the Collegium. We brought work to our clan-kin in the area and down in Tavnastok, and everyone's prospering."

He drew her along by one arm toward the nearest occupied workbench.

"I wanted you to see what it's like to build one of the chains. We've gotten quite expert at it—all that practice." They watched the man bend a link with a special vise and lever, lining up the cut ends until they were perfect before using some sort of device to weld the ends together.

To Penrys's scan, the length of chain was as dead as any of the cut chains she had in the bag, back in her room in Tavnastok, but she felt the focus of the man's inspection while he worked. When he was done, the link seemed well-made, if unpowered.

"As you might imagine," Bilget commented, "It's a lot harder to do the final link when it's on someone's neck. Not as much room to work with, and hard to force it shut for the weld."

He walked away with her casually and headed for the door, explaining as they went along. "There had to be experiments, of course. We tried it on a goat, first—put the chain on over her head and took it off again, but there was no effect. No, we really had to use wizards."

They'd reached the door, and the guards with their metal rods fell into place behind them as they walked across the cleared space to the same building they'd been in the day before.

"Not our own kin, of course. Lost a few at the beginning, naturally, but we eventually got the hang of it. I wanted to try it for myself, but we learned about the memory loss. It was my father's idea to put my memories somewhere else."

He smiled at Penrys, as if she could appreciate the joke. "Such a clever old man. My twin was the obvious choice."

"What did she have to say about it?" Penrys murmured.

"What could she say? We convinced her, and she hasn't complained. That was… let me see… eight years ago.

"That's when we started planning. A way out of here, and a reward for my father's discoveries. There's no scope for us here, no justice. He should've been famous, and wealthy—the power-metal alone is the most important invention in generations. There are places in Stokemmi… Well, never mind.

"The first step needs to be the Collegium. Once we're ready, and all our wizard kin have learned to use their chains, that will become our new home. And all Ellech comes to the Collegium for technology. We can make them pay for it."

"But then why did you fill the world with other chained wizards? Aren't you worried about creating others strong enough to oppose you?"

He smiled. "You may have noticed how few ended up in Ellech. No, that's our back door, our escape route if something goes wrong. My father died before he could see our first draft of specimens but he helped to plan it.

"You see, they weren't only necessary for us to perfect the techniques. They depart from us chained but blank, and prepare the world for us by their dispersed presence. They have no memory of us, any more than you do. If we were to join them, chained but not blank, fully aware, no one will be able to tell we're any different. A perfect way to hide, if we must. No need for us to travel unclothed and unequipped, like the others."

*Didn't he understand Vylkar's report in Yenit Ping, about chained wizards appearing in underground caves and a tomb, and dying there, unable to get out? Did he never see a copy?*

He opened the door to his own workroom and Penrys followed him in, with her guards, and took the same seat as before. "So, all the wizards you chained and released, that was just… camouflage, in case you needed to escape?"

"They should be grateful—all that power, and the special additions I gave so many of them." He loomed over her and she tried not to react. "Isn't it splendid that the additions had a practical effect on the chain's capabilities? That healing ability… who knows, maybe I've made them immortal. It's hard to be sure—I've only had my chain eight years—but I feel younger than my twin sister, and maybe I am. Maybe I'm not aging as rapidly."

*Or maybe she's been beaten down by serving as you and your father's… experimental memory repository.*

As he settled himself at his desk, her eye was caught by the spines of some of the books on the shelf behind him. Several she recognized, from a similar position on the shelves of her rented room in Tavnastok. Then she spotted the folk tale book that Gylvabil had written, the one he sold her. He was no wizard, but was he possibly clan-kin to these people?

Bilget looked over his shoulder to see what had grabbed her attention and pulled the book out. "This? You've seen this before? He's a cousin—my father gave him several of his stories. Did you know?"

*No wonder they picked me up like a little lost lamb. Everyone on that side of town must have been on the lookout for me.*

"We've been preparing to leave ever since your report got back to the Collegium. Figured it was just a matter of time before people started looking into my father's work. One more run down to Tavnastok to collect the rest of our wizard kin and a call 'round the hollows, and then we'll visit the Collegium."

"Isn't all this expensive?" she asked.

"Mining ore and refining metal, ordinary metal, pays well enough. We have operations all over Glymbeod.

"Elkif, she wants to raise a second Collegium here, make them open their minds to the possibilities of the power-metal, or specialize in it here for ourselves. I've told her they'll never allow it, never allow something outside their supervision, and we should just take over the existing institution."

He impaled Penrys with his glance. "Guess we'll find out soon enough now, eh? When they come looking for you."

"How would they find me?" She tried to put the right note of despair into it, and was appalled at how easy that was, how close to the truth.

Bilget just laughed at her.

"I've thought of a way to avoid the memory issue for the next generation. Just add a chain to a newborn, and start from the beginning. I don't think you can change chains—we've never gotten one off successfully—so it would have to be adult-sized and tied together so it would stay on, but I don't see why that wouldn't work. And it would be so much easier—wouldn't have to weld that final link in place, you could just drop it on."

Penrys worked on keeping her face expressionless as she contemplated an eight-pound baby with a one-pound chain. *Do they know that pregnancy might be a problem for the chained women?*

"It ought to work," Bilget continued. "Of course, we'll have to test it first. I've been trying to come up with a special addition for something that tiny, so we can activate the healing part of the chain."

Penrys used her hacking cough to conceal the disgust in her voice. "So, how would you test it? On an infant?"

"No, that would be like using a goat. How would I tell? I'll just make a larger chain and drop it on an adult. Or maybe on one of those leftovers, since they're here."

Penrys blanched as she realized he meant one of the children. She tried to make her voice enticing.

"Have you thought about taking non-kin with you?" she asked. "After all, I'm already equipped." She touched the chain around her neck.

He tilted his head speculatively and probed against her shield. "It would take a lot of convincing."

In the late afternoon, after she returned, Penrys paced the compound while the children worked.

Her attempts to ingratiate herself with Bilget had amused him but she was sure he still had no thought of leaving her alive, whatever he might say to coax information from her.

She focused on understanding the structure that kept the wizards confined in this enclosure. The stockade blocked her view, so she found a way to climb the outer corner of one of the buildings where the log ends provided a framework until she could scramble onto the roof. That brought her uncomfortably close to the shield overhead projected by the cage, but it let her see over the outer wall well enough that she could study the design.

Initially she'd thought of petals placed around the compound's stockade, but now she realized they were more like hands. She held up her left arm and looked at her hand sideways, with her fingers lightly bent at the knuckles. The wrist, that was where the structures entered the ground. The much longer fingers bent again slightly at the finger tips, so that the lines drawn from them didn't just project upward, but met each other in a sort of invisible ceiling. She held up her right hand in a matching posture to see what sort of space the geometry enclosed.

Even the count of metal struts matched, and she wondered if a hand had indeed been the original model. She spread the fingers in her left hand, keeping them bent at the knuckles. There were five long struts in each "hand"—the middle one vertical, the ones on either side slanted but upright, and the little finger and thumb bent to the side and pointed at the corresponding "fingers" of the "hands" next to them.

The compound was a rectangle, and the "hands" marched along the outside, eight feet high and some distance into the ground. Ashiwe had told her of a tunnel attempt by the first group. The leading man who reached the underground floor of the shield had died.

It was a sketchy framework, parsimonious of material, and it differed only in the area of the double gates. There, an additional "hand" stood on one side at the outer gate, mounted on a hinge-pole of ordinary metal. Swinging it open from the outside with a long pole made a gap in the field it projected, enough to allow a wizard passage to the inner gate.

The whole thing hummed with power to her scan. Deadly power, to judge by Ashiwe's stories. Was it a unit, or was each strut separate?

The long struts were supported by a metal framework not made of power-metal. It looked to Penrys like common iron or something similar. Even the projecting "fingers" on either side approached but did not meet. She couldn't find any place where power-metal touched power-metal.

She climbed back down and walked over to the gates to get a closer look at the "knuckles." Even there, the struts were gently bent, not joined—all in one piece.

Leaning on the last log of the stockade at the gate entrance, she pictured the invisible barriers sketched in the air above her and underground. She could almost see it. Unwillingly, she admired the design. *Bilget's or his father? You could never do something like this with power-stones and, besides, it would be absurdly expensive. This must be the largest structure they ever made with power-metal, I suppose, and look what they're using it for.*

*But it works.*

*How do they power it? It hums like a single thing, not dozens of separate pieces. Maybe you just load a little more power into one piece each day and it diffuses and balances itself, like water. The alignments must have a lot to do with it—so close and no closer. Why isn't the whole thing power-metal—saving money, or is there a reason the pieces shouldn't touch?*

*Versatile stuff, this power-metal. Charged, it's like a power-stone. Empty, it can suck power, like those dre'ski metal rods. Power-stones can't do that.*

*What's its weakness? What happens if the pieces touch each other?*

"It's a pleasant enough place," Najud said. "If you can ignore the sensation of eyes everywhere."

Daerget grunted in response. Their most recent encounter with a surly woman who looked them over with a sniff and pointed the way to a footpath to take them south along the river still rankled.

"All that work making up a story—and it's a *good* story—and no one seems to care."

"All the same," Najud said, "Keep using it. I can practically hear the word spreading ahead of us already."

They had gone west far enough to lend plausibility to their imposture and then turned south on the first good path they found. The few houses they'd seen since were isolated, log-built, with gardens rather than fields and split-rail fences to hold their livestock. The maps had shown no villages away from the river, and they were eager to work their way down to it, now that they were upstream from the one named by Elkif.

Daerget raised his head and pointed uphill to their left. A silent man in the distance watched their progress.

Najud lifted his hand to him in friendly greeting, but the man made no gesture in return.

"Welcoming folk, aren't they?" he said.

Daerget turned his head so that his good eye was visible. "Maybe they don't like wizards, and us in our blues and greens. The *taunnupar* have their reputation for a reason."

"I thought wood mice were shy," Najud said.

"You wouldn't say that if you ever saw them devour the inside of a cabin over a long winter. Can't say what would happen to you if you were sleeping there drunk enough at the same time."

The eyepatch twitched with what Najud took for a piratical grin.

"Let's just keep moving," he added. "Don't let them get too good a fix on us. The longer we stick to the higher ground off the river, the fewer people we'll find."

"Won't they find that suspicious, if we don't head right for the river to look for transport home?"

Daerget laughed. "They're suspicious anyway. We can hardly make it worse."

# CHAPTER 19

Penrys joined the scribes on the next day. She felt driven to get the job finished, and she couldn't shake the feeling of time running out.

Through the gates she could see an increase in activity, and the fact that Bilget left her alone all day worried her. It meant he had more urgent things to see to, and that couldn't be good. If they decided that now was the time to put their plan into motion, they'd never leave the witnesses behind alive.

Bilget had spoken of more wizards to fetch home from Tavnastok and elsewhere, first, but he didn't strike her as someone who would wait for that, if he felt sufficiently threatened.

The first copy of all the wall carvings was complete and she proofread it while they started the second version. Chon Janwit had done a good job with the Kigalino *yat*, and the rest of the languages she could read seemed all right.

The youngest ones made the charcoal rubbings for the languages none of them knew, as backup in case they failed to write down the exotic shapes correctly. Waterproofing was a challenge, but Ashiwe had concocted a waxed paper which she lined on the inside with leather and more blank paper to wrap around the documents, once they were ready.

When the summons came for her, late in the afternoon, she was almost relieved. *We have another day, at least. They won't leave at night, surely. Not while they have me to entertain them.*

The guards brought her back to Bilget's workroom, and this time the whole family was there.

She took the chair, and this time the guards stooped and tied her arms and legs to it. *Baelnei looks far too happy.* She ran her tongue around her dry lips and watched Bilget warily.

"No, I'm afraid I won't be taking non-kin along, as you asked," he said. "It's time for some answers from you."

He nodded at Baelnei who sauntered over and chucked her under the chin before backhanding her cheek with a will.

"Well, *staka*, who knew you were wandering all over town looking for us, eh? You didn't sneak off without telling anyone."

Penrys could barely hear him over the explosion in her head. Her shields were already up, and that was all that saved her from Bilget's coordinated attack.

He grinned wolfishly. "Good. Defend yourself. Show us what you can do."

With the full force of his chain he flung his mind at her again, while Baelnei added his own punch in the gut to distract her.

Penrys throttled her impulse to suck Bilget dry before he realized it was possible. *I'd still be tied to this chair, and then they'll know they can't leave me alive. Those rods are right behind me. The kids are still trapped.*

Another slap to the face interrupted her thoughts.

*I'm just going to have to take it. Keep Bilget out but let him win, so he can learn his strength by fighting mine—that's what he wants. Shield and silence, that's all I've got. They can't kill me yet, if they don't know for sure.*

*I hope.*

She shut everything else down, just the blows in her mind echoed by the blows on her body. Every now and then she heard a giggle from Baelnei, and was glad she had nothing to spare to see his mind's pleasure in his work.

Eventually a woman's voice intruded. "Enough."

One more blow followed, and then she heard Baelnei's breathing. Exertion and… lust. She was stunned as much as injured, but the real pain was already starting to follow. She tried to crack a swollen eye open far enough to peer at Bilget.

He looked pleased with himself. "I told you she couldn't fight," he told Elkif. "All she could do was wrap a shield around herself. I can do better than that. That report she sent was all boasting, like I said it was."

Baelnei's quiet, intense voice drifted past her. "That was just a taste, *staka*. They wanted me to keep it light, for starters. I've got lots of ideas."

He reached out and gave both her breasts a vicious twist, and smiled when she gasped at the pain.

"Yeah, lots of ideas. You'll like them."

Elkif spoke, and Penrys strained to listen over Baelnei's breathy, intimate threats.

"We have our answer. She wouldn't be defending so hard if there weren't something to hide. The question is, who's coming and should we wait?"

"No warning from the Collegium, so I think they must still be oblivious. It's like you said, sister, they've grown stodgy and complacent."

Baelnei's mutterings continued close to her ear and she tried to ignore them. "You like pain, don't you? I can see that you do. You'll be amazed to discover what you can find enjoyable. It'll be fun teaching you."

"We should drain her now," Elkif said to her brother.

"No. Not yet. I can't learn from her that way. You can see she's no threat. Besides, I wouldn't hand anything over to my nephew defenseless."

That shut up the commentary from her tormentor. Baelnei lifted his head. "You promised her to me."

"And you'll get her, suitably prepared. But not until we're done with her."

"Can they take her back now?" That was Tiessi's voice, uneven and wavering.

Bilget waved a hand. "Yes, go ahead. I'm ready for dinner."

The dim shapes stood and walked out, and only the guards remained to untie the ropes and haul her ungently to her feet.

*One foot in front of the other. Don't fall.*

Penrys shuffled between the guards with her arms wrapped around her body and her shoulders hunched. She couldn't lift her head, couldn't take her eyes off the dry ground as she scuffed up dust from the path.

They stopped short of the compound's gates, and one of the guards lifted his metal rod. "Elkif's orders," he told her, and tapped her lightly with it.

She dropped to her knees, cursing herself for not acting earlier, while she still could. He hauled her back up to her feet and held her by her upper arm.

The other guard pulled the pole attached to the metal "hand" to open the outer gate and let her pass through with the first guard.

He opened the inner gate and shoved her in, then shut it behind her.

She stumbled but caught her balance and stood there, swaying from side to side. The running footsteps and gasps made her try to raise her head, but everything had stiffened up and it was too hard.

Chon Janwit's arm came into her field of view. "Lean on me."

Ashiwe's voice barking out orders accompanied them as they shuffled at her best pace toward the central building across the yard. It seemed to take hours.

When she next paid attention, she was staring at her pallet and Ashiwe was asking her, not for the first time, where she was hurt.

"I don't see much blood. What did they do?"

Penrys's mouth ached from where her teeth had damaged it when Baelnei knocked her head around, and her stomach roiled. *It's all in front. It was a beating.*

She was clumsy. She could feel that some of the pain had leaked in with the words, and she wrapped up her mind to keep it from happening again and shut everything out. Her native power was slowly recovering, but the chain was drained.

She couldn't remember being lowered onto the pallet. When she noticed her surroundings again, she found her upper body bare, and Ashiwe wiping a wet cloth down her left arm. When she started to raise her head to look at the damage, Iko pushed it back down and held her there firmly. "No need. We're taking care of it."

There were no other voices. It was just the two older girls tending to her. She moistened her lips. "It's not as bad as it probably looks. I'll heal."

She could hear the skepticism in their minds.

"If they wanted me dead, I'd be dead. Bilget doesn't want to kill me, he wants to test me, so he can learn about himself. He's had no one else to test himself against all these years—he won't give that up lightly."

She swallowed. "He thinks I can tell him things." It was too hard to explain to the girls that this was part of a plan, that she was doing this deliberately.

*I have to stay alive.*

She shivered from the touch of the cold water and tried to forget Baelnei's promises.

Hours later, Penrys opened her eyes in the dark and found Tarroak curled against her side, breathing softly and regularly.

Iko spoke quietly. "Good, you're awake. Careful how you move. I want to know if we missed anything."

Penrys took a cautious inventory. Her clothing had protected her from most abrasions, but her bare flesh felt almost overripe to the touch, like bruised fruit, wherever she pressed it. The bruising was bone-deep in places, and her gut ached from internal damage. Baelnei hadn't hit her as hard as he could have, he'd said, and she believed it, but the pain was unrelenting, a dull ache punctuated with sharp flashes, and all of it throbbing in time with her headache. Almost as bad was the strain in all her muscles from trying to find a position that didn't make it worse.

"Can you tell if anything's broken?" Iko asked.

Penrys's mouth was dry but the cuts inside from her teeth had started to heal. "Water," she mouthed, and heard the scrape as Iko picked up a cup from the floor and held her head up to sip at it.

It soothed her throat and she wanted to gulp at it, but she held herself to little sips, until she'd drained about half of it.

Then she licked her lips and tried to talk. "Ribs are cracked but not broken all the way. Not sure about m'cheekbones."

She swallowed. "Bet it's pretty colorful in daylight."

There was something wrong with her right eye and she lifted a hand to it, but Iko stopped her. "Let me," she said.

A damp cloth was lifted away from her face, and Penrys tried again to open the eye. The dim starlight that showed her Iko's silhouette was hard to discern, but she thought there was a bit of a glimmer there.

"Is it... damaged?"

"I think it's just swollen shut. You've got to give it time for the swelling to go down." She paused a moment. "My mother worked in the temple, with the sick, and I helped her."

The movement and the voices had finally roused Tarroak, and he sat up. "Are you going to die?"

"Not today, my boy." Penrys put as much conviction into her quiet voice as she could.

"But they beat you up. Couldn't you fight back?"

"This was just another way of fighting. It's hard to explain."

Their voices had woken the rest of the children. Penrys had no idea of the time, but she thought it was probably well after the middle of the night.

Chon Janwit spoke out of the darkness. "Tell us what to do. We don't know how to fight them."

She closed her eyes, as if they could see much anyway. *I have to make it possible for them to get away.*

"Iko, help me sit up, will you?"

Together, they managed to get her propped against a wall without making things too much worse.

Once she'd caught her breath, she picked up her duties again.

"I'm sorry I scared you today. Don't worry about that part—I'll be a lot better tomorrow. I've got a plan for all of us."

She scanned their minds and felt their fear, their apprehension, their shame at their weakness. That would never do. They would have to become warriors, not children. They needed strength and confidence, not self-doubt.

"First of all, Chon Janwit—where do we stand with the copy of the engravings?"

He spoke firmly, ignoring the occasional lapse of the adult timbre of his voice not yet fully under his control. "We have both sets of writing, ready for your final look. The wrappings are ready, too, and all the charcoal rubbings."

"Well done, all of you. You hold the lives of many people in your hands, and hundreds will bless you for it."

She felt pride leaven their heavy thoughts.

"Ashiwe, what of the packs and food?"

The Ndant girl's voice was calm. "We made packs for everyone and they've put them on so we can check the fit. We made you one, too, and you can try yours out tomorrow.

"Clothing was easy—Amatka helped me go through the leftover things to make sure everyone had enough, and we put the bundles in the packs before hiding them. We've got clothes for you, too."

Penrys felt the Ellechen girl's satisfaction in being singled out.

"That's great. What about food?"

Amatka spoke up. "We made ten piles in the kitchen and wrapped them in bundles."

"All the same size?"

"The bigger kids can carry bigger packs," Ashiwe said. "Everyone carries food and clothing, but the bigger kids carry more food."

"How did you decide how much?"

"It was easy," Hakkur said. "We loaded everyone up until they couldn't hold anymore. Then we took a little bit off, 'cause they'd have to carry water, too." She could hear his hesitation, then he added, "How much can *you* carry?"

"Good question. We'll find out tomorrow. What about the water? Did you figure out how to carry it?"

"That was Hakkur, too," Ashiwe said. "It was his idea."

"Chon Janwit did all the work," Hakkur protested.

Penrys waited. "Well, someone tell me."

Finally Chon Janwit spoke. "We removed one of the stovepipes. There are two stoves in the kitchen—we can manage with just one."

Hakkur interrupted him. "See, we figured it was already nicely welded in a tube, so if we cut it into a dozen sections and then crimped the ends shut, we could plug a small opening with a bit of wood. Used our biggest knife as a punch, he did, and we scrubbed out the insides, and then we rolled the ends over to bury any sharp bits. We left a little corner open, and whittled wood to fit it. And it worked!"

"After we melted a bit of wax inside to plug a few leaks," Ashiwe added. "Iko and I added a net bag to carry them with. They look strange, but they do hold water."

Penrys smiled in the darkness. "I'm sincerely impressed. Very well done."

The younger Zan boy, Nimiz, spoke into the satisfied silence. "But what can *we* do, me and Tarroak and Ju Ochim?"

"And me," Iramqawj added. "We want to fight. But how?"

Penrys listened to the feelings of the youngest of them. She wanted to protect them, but that's not what they needed. They needed to feel strong. They all did, even the oldest.

"Let me tell you a story," she said. "It's a true story, and I was there. I imagine Nimiz and Iramqawj probably know how a traditional Zannib clan handles its annual migration, but maybe the rest of you don't, so I'll have to explain a little bit.

"You see, every year, almost everyone in the clan gets together in the spring. A few of them decide to stay in the winter camp—

mothers with young children, people too old to travel, and a few others—but everyone else packs up their herds and their families and their *kazrab*—those are sort of like fancy round tents—and goes on a long walk in a big loop that returns in the autumn. They appoint a leader for the migration, the *zarawinnaj*, and he's in charge of everything and responsible for everyone.

"Now, when a boy or girl turns nine, they're considered old enough to go on the migration, and this story is about two such boys on their first trip. Their names were Birssahr and Zabrash, and the *zarawinnaj* was Umzakhilin. Like many young clan members on the migration, they were assigned as herd boys, helping to keep the animals moving and stop them from wandering off.

"In mid-summer, a disaster happened to the clan in their summer pastures. That's a tale for another night." Penrys wondered if Ashiwe realized this was related to her vanished friend who died, but now was not the time to go into it.

"For Birssahr and Zabrash, it was just another day, far from the camp out in the plains with their portion of the herds of their clan. They returned to the summer camp in the evening, but no one was there. Only the *zarawinnaj* was left, trampled and collapsed on the ground, unable to speak."

The intake of breaths in front of her told her they were listening.

"They were a hundred miles from the winter camp, and there were no adults anywhere, just Umzakhilin, horribly injured, who didn't seem aware of anything around him.

"And the wealth of all the clan was there, in the summer camp. All the possessions of a couple of hundred people, much of their herds, the cheeses and other foods—everything the clan would need to face the coming winter."

"What did they do?" Ju Ochim asked in her light piping voice.

"What, indeed? They wanted to find out what had happened to their own families, to pursue the clear trail of people and livestock, but it seemed foolish to think they could do something that all those adults could not. Their families would never have just left them there, and abandoned all the food and supplies they would need, not if they'd had any choice. Though much of the livestock was gone, many animals remained. And then there was their *zarawinnaj*, not dead. They couldn't leave him behind.

"They sat down like seasoned counselors and thought it through. The *zarawinnaj* would know what to do, and they had a duty to keep him alive in any case, so they took that as their first priority. They set his legs and made him as comfortable as they could, but he was unresponsive and couldn't guide them. The missing adults would have to look after themselves.

"Then they thought, we could wait for him to recover, and he might not, or we could do what we can to bring him home, and as much of the clan's wealth as possible. We can't carry their goods, but we can round up their herds and bring them home, so our clan can eat, come winter. And if we get back soon enough, others can come out from the winter camp to bring back everything else."

She could feel their attention.

"So that's what they did. They couldn't take a *kazr* for themselves—they weren't big enough to erect one—so they found a couple of small tents, and they rigged a travois for Umzakhilin—that's a webbing across two poles, where you tie one end to a horse, and it can drag a person behind him. And they set off across the plains straight for the winter camp, and tried to bring dozens and dozens of animals with them—horses, cattle, sheep, and goats. Just the two of them."

"Did it work?" Nimiz wanted to know.

"By and large," Penrys said. "They kept Umzakhilin alive for many days until he could be healed, and he would have died otherwise. He's now the clan leader.

"The herds were much harder to manage with just two riders than they expected, but they'd come a long way by the time I met them. It was the right thing to do, and they'd made the right choices, and were well honored for it by their clan-kin."

"And *that's* what a couple of nine-year-olds can do."

The audible sighs from several of them raised a smile on her face.

"Now," she said, briskly. "I want you to be ready to leave in a moment, if you get the opportunity. Chon Janwit, you're the war-leader of this band. Do you accept the responsibility?"

"I do," shot out of the darkness, without a trace of adolescent squeak.

"And you, Ashiwe, I appoint you the overall leader. You will direct when you should fight and when flee, where to go, and how to get there. Chon Janwit will be your strong right arm. Will you accept?"

"Yes."

Penrys could feel spines stiffening all around as they settled into a heroic framework.

"I want everyone to be paired with a buddy. If you have to scramble in a hurry, you watch out for your buddy first. Understand? Chon Janwit will be the only one without one, since he might have to act separately. Ashiwe, with Tarroak, Iko with Ju Ochim, Hakkur and Amatka, Iramqawj and Nimiz."

She thought that keeping the two Ellechen children and the Zannib children together would work best, and otherwise it was eldest with youngest.

"Now get some sleep. We'll finish preparations in the morning and then it's just a matter of finding the best opportunity." She'd have to make sure that Ashiwe's map was copied, too, in case they were separated.

She listened to them settle down and drift back into sleep and thought about doing the same, but when she tried to shift her position, she hissed with the pain and decided not to wake them and make them worry about her all over again.

# CHAPTER 20

"You didn't sleep."

Iko's accusing whisper penetrated the gray light of a new day.

"You should have asked me to help you lie down."

"I dozed just fine the way I was," Penrys lied. She'd watched with her one good eye as the dim light gradually revealed the children bundled under their blankets. Tarroak had wriggled against her like a puppy. Hakkur was a restless sleeper, but Ju Ochim was decorous and unmoving. They'd looked so small to her, so vulnerable.

She could smell rain on the way, as she'd waited for dawn, and she thought of them, on the run with their heavy packs and their ill-assorted clothing. They'd find no friends in Glymbeod, if Bilget was right about his clan-kin, and most of them had foreign faces. What would become of them?

*I can't leave them for Bilget's experiments, no matter the risk. And then there's Baelnei... I wonder if it's just me, or all women he abuses? What about children no one cares about?*

She couldn't tell Iko these things—it wasn't suitable to put those fears in her head.

"You can help me get up instead," she told Iko. "Quietly. Let them sleep."

Her muscles had stiffened like rawhide, but the swelling had diminished. No more sharp pains, but deep aches everywhere, and each movement needed careful thought. At least she could make out blurred objects with her right eye.

Iko helped her on with her clothing and shoes, and then she hobbled like an old woman, leaning on the girl, and picked her way around the occupied pallets. "Outhouse first," she said, once they made it outside under an overcast sky, "and then I need to do something to loosen up my muscles before they freeze solid like this." She struck an awkward pose to illustrate her potential fate.

A smile flickered over Iko's face and her mood lightened. "Then what?" she asked.

"Then we wait." Nothing could happen until they opened the cage again.

Penrys paced the perimeter of the compound all morning, wearing a fresh path into the dirt next to the stockade. She walked away the stiffness of her body and gradually it obeyed her orders to move untwisted and upright.

Her right eye was improving but she found it a distraction and had Ashiwe find her a scarf to bind over it while it healed. Every now and then she noticed her bare arms, black with bruises, and wondered what her face looked like.

She knew they would come for her today, probably for the last time, and she tried not to think about it directly—too many things she couldn't control.

Instead she probed at the cage itself, the shield created by the power-metal "hands"—seamless, strong, and unbreakable. The only gap in the design was at the gate, and as long as they had wizard guards with those power-metal rods, she couldn't see a way to break past that, much less get the children out.

What if this cage were maintained by power-stones? How would it be different?

*You can overload a power-stone. They melt or, sometimes, just crack. I can't overload something this size. And the struts are well-made, beautifully made. Flawless. Balanced. What a waste, Gialfinnur and his family. The Collegium could have had this by now, the whole world would have benefited. Instead of this... horror.*

She shook her head. Useless thoughts.

Chon Janwit intercepted her to show her the wrapped bundles of transcriptions and get her approval. They were each the size of a thick book, tied neatly with rolled grass twine around waxed paper. *It'll have to do.*

"Who's going to carry them?" she asked.

"I'll have one, and Hakkur will take the other one."

"Why Hakkur?"

Chon Janwit hesitated. "If something goes wrong, I thought one of the Ellech kids would have the best chance of getting through."

Penrys gripped his shoulder. "Good thinking. Agreed."

He walked off to help the others, and she continued walking, and chewing on her problem.

*What about the spacers? There must be some reason to keep the struts separated. I can't break iron spacers.*

She paused in her perambulations when she reached the gate, the only place where there was no stockade to block her view. *When the gate swings open, the "hand" embedded in it opens, too. Look how close the "thumbs" are—only about a foot and a half apart. Could the gate somehow be forced back on its hinges so that the "thumbs" touched? Everywhere else, there's a spacer to keep the "thumbs" from touching if the array gets misaligned.*

The pole the gate was hung on was thick and sturdy, and there was no way for a wizard to get close enough to it to weaken it. Maybe you could toss firewood at the base and then throw a torch, but it couldn't be hidden. And it would take time to burn, even if it worked, and even then it might not collapse the right way.

Penrys thought about just tapping the power humming all around her with her chain, but she suspected it would be like trying to fill a cup from a waterfall—the current would just sweep her away. Her chain could only hold so much, she'd discovered, and when she compared the quantity of power-metal it used to the struts that made up the outer cage, she just shook her head silently.

Was there anything in the kitchen? A piece of metal long enough, like the stovepipe or a large pot that could bridge the gap between the thumbs? Ah, but what use would that be, no different from the iron bars already used as spacers.

*Ah! This is why chained wizards can't get very close to each other. The chains heat up and keep them apart. Not loose chains, unpowered. Chains worn by wizards, powered chains, like these struts are powered. The links themselves must be able to touch, but not chain to chain, once powered.*

*No wonder Bilget had Baelnei do his dirty work. He can't get that close to me, himself. And he'd know that. Bilget's the only man who's met more chained wizards than I have—he made them all.*

She remembered the fight in front of the emperor of Kigali, where she defeated the chained wizard champion and used his power to thwart an assassination. A smile crept over her face as she mulled what might work. *They're devices. What do devices help you do? Raunarys—the physical magics. Bind, move, destroy. I wonder…*

The gathering clouds overhead with their promise of rain worried her, but it couldn't be helped. It had to be today, when the guards came for her.

She turned her steps to find the kids, to warn them to be ready. She wanted them out of the way when it started.

The rain started early in the afternoon, darkening the sky with a spring torrent that soaked the ground and turned everything to mud.

Penrys stood just inside the open doorway of the building that had been used as a school, with her eye fixed on the gate. The shields kept her from feeling any of the minds outside the compound, but she could hear the milk cows lowing as they grazed in their split-rail paddock, not far up the slope from her. The rain mattered little to them, except for the lusher grass it promised once it had passed.

It meant a miserable night for the kids, if they got away. And worse, if they didn't. *Better wet than dead.* The rain had no impact on her own plans, unless it made the guards more careless. *No one wants to stay out in the rain if they don't need to.*

Ashiwe and Iko came up behind her, each with her assigned buddy. Penrys had insisted they all travel in pairs together the whole day. Tarroak and Ju Ochim were subdued, but she could feel the suppressed excitement from the older children. And the hope.

"Remember, don't do anything until I can do something about the shield and the guards are down. If that works, people are going to come running, and you'll only have a few seconds to get out before they'll catch you again."

She turned to quiz the young ones. "Where are you going to go, Ju Ochim?"

"We're going to run up slope and away from the river, into the trees, and hide with our buddy. Once everything is quiet, we'll wait for the older ones to find us."

Penrys raised her eyes to Iko. *You sure you can find the ones who can't mind-speak yet?*

The Rasesni girl nodded. *We've been practicing all morning.*

Ju Ochim's eyes followed their silent conversation with frustration. "I wish I could hear you," she said.

"It'll come. It's like growing up—everyone does it at a different speed."

"How will you deal with the guards?" Chon Janwit asked.

"Don't know yet. They drained my chain so I might need to borrow a little power." Penrys stared at the boy until he understood, and nodded in agreement.

Ashiwe said, "If you can get rid of the guards, you don't need to take down the shield, do you? Can't we just get out through the gate?"

"Maybe. But I want a big distraction, and that's the biggest thing I can think of. There are lots of wizards out there—I want them looking at me and what I've done, not chasing after you. I can get away on my own, you've seen the wings."

Penrys didn't tell them that she couldn't just fly after them. She'd have to stop the pursuit here, not leave a bunch of them free to recapture the kids and maybe kill them. And she could only think of one way to stop these wizards.

"I wish it weren't raining," Tarroak said, as he peered out the doorway at the steady, soaking shower.

"This rain's a good thing. Better than darkness. You'll still have enough light to see, but it'll make it harder for them to find you. Night will come soon and hide your tracks, and then the rain will wash them away."

"What if they don't come for you today?" Ashiwe asked, quietly.

"It'll be today," Penrys muttered. "Baelnei can't wait to get his hands on me."

"There they are—they're coming. Wait for the guards to go down, remember, then don't make a noise. Maybe no one will see you."

Penrys stuffed the scarf she was wearing over her right eye into her pocket and walked out to meet the two guards, the same ones who'd been escorting her all along. She limped haltingly, as if still incapacitated, and staggered slowly up to the gate on the inside.

*I never did learn their names, and now I guess I never will.*

A quick glance revealed no one else outside, though she'd need to be on the other side of the cage to feel their minds and be sure. She waited patiently, like a leopard in the tall grass, and tried to look damaged and helpless. Defeated.

The taller one hauled the outer "hand" on its gate open by its pole and waited outside holding the end of the pole to keep the outer gate open, while the other one passed through and released the inner gate. His shoulders were hunched, trying to keep the trickles of rain from his hat brim from running down his neck. He beckoned her through impatiently and, as he reached for the inner gate to close it behind her, she tapped the children for as much power as they could spare and added it to her chain. And then she struck.

She needed his power, not just his life, so she held his heart in her *raunarys* grip and let him feel it, and while he panicked, unable to scream, she wrapped his mind and sucked down what power he had into her chain before she stopped his heart and let him drop. His companion wasn't watching and heard nothing and she had enough time to do the same to him before he knew it.

The children ran through the rain in pairs, lumpy with their packs. Ashiwe and Tarroak led, and Chon Janwit brought up the rear, as they'd arranged.

Penrys had her eye on the open gate—if it swung shut now, before she finished, she'd be trapped inside. The pole had dropped into the mud when the second guard fell, and it dragged a few feet with the gate as it rotated inward, but the mud was sticky and held it from swinging back very far.

*Now, let's see what happens.*

She leaned over the body at her feet and picked up the metal rod that had fallen from his hands, by its leather handle.

*Two feet of uncharged power-metal, for draining wizards. I don't need it— I can do that with my chain. I wonder if Bilget realizes that? But what would happen if I power it up, like this, and then...*

She powered it from her chain and used the chain like a *raunarys* device to push the powered rod through the air the few feet from where she stood to the almost-junction of the two power-metal "hands," the one on the gate and the static one on the perimeter, and she jammed it across the two "thumbs" as hard as she could, bare metal to bare metal.

The explosion knocked her into the air and through the outer gate passage where she landed on her shoulders with her head in the mud and her ears ringing. Lightning lit up the sky and cascaded around the perimeter. There was something wrong with her when she tried to get up. Her right arm and leg weren't working and she could smell burning meat.

*Why was it so quiet? Shouldn't there be thunder?*

She rolled to her right and got up on her left knee, but standing didn't seem to be an option.

*Oh, well. I didn't really think I'd be flying out of here anyway.*

She waited, since there was nothing else she could do, and reached out to see where everyone was.

Behind her, the sky was spitting sparks, but it was beginning to settle down.

*Still raining?* She lifted her face to check.

*Why can't I hear it? Must've deafened me.*

She shook her head to clear it, and almost keeled over. *Don't do that again! Stay alive and take as many of them with you as you can.*

*Where are they?*

*Ah. Here they come.*

The first one on the scene was Baelnei. He was shouting something she couldn't hear.

*Good. Perfect.* Her cheeks ached, and she realized she was smiling.

She drained him despite his shield and killed him, and he dropped with a look of pure astonishment on his face.

Behind him were plenty more, but they slowed to a stop when he fell.

*Bilget. Where is he? Gotta get him or the kids'll never be safe. No one will.*

She searched but he must be hanging back somewhere. Others were trying to circle behind her. If they got close enough for weapons, she was done and they'd go after the children.

Tiessi dropped to her knees by Baelnei's body and and tried a mind attack, but Penrys was far too strong for that. She'd been draining every wizard who got close first, before killing them, with the chain as her reservoir, and it took almost no effort to sweep Tiessi's grieving attack aside and do the same to her.

When the woman collapsed on top of her son's body, a mental shout finally penetrated. **You've killed my memory!**

She couldn't see Bilget, couldn't hear anything, but she searched for the source of the cry and felt him, felt his chain, and focused on draining it. He'd had a chain twice as many years, but she knew more about how to use it. Much more—after all, he'd sent her out into the world to learn. It was a losing battle for him, but she had to keep herself from being surrounded and killed before she won, and she realized he was counting on that.

A flung rock knocked her sideways, and she broke her standoff with Bilget to shout to all the wizards. *If you fight me you will die. If you want to live, go to the compound and wait.*

Bilget was shouting something—she could see his mouth moving, but people were starting to move away. She made a lethal example of the rock thrower and two more stubborn ones, and the people moved faster. Finally she could only feel Bilget alive outside the compound, no weapon in his hand.

He hadn't thought he needed one. Not with his chain.

*I gave you this power. You ungrateful child.*

Penrys felt for that hard, unforgiving place inside her. *I didn't ask for it. You'll never do this again.*

She reached out her mental hand and grasped his chain, and he staggered. *Mine, now. I took your past, and I take your future.*

She sucked his power down until her own chain was nearly full, and then she stopped his heart as she'd done for the others.

The rain fell as if it would never stop, and the dead silence in her ears was oppressive. She sensed only animals in the immediate vicinity—all the living people were in the compound. She could hold them there by threat as long as she could stay awake. But she couldn't even get up to see if the stockade was intact. The gate was still open.

If she started to fall asleep, either they would escape and kill her, or she would have to kill them first. Her lip wrinkled. *Yrmur! Hell of a choice. Do I want to be a dead hero or a living demon? Too bloody to keep alive, myself.*

In the twilight, she could make out a dozen bodies or so. She knew the names of three of them. Where was Elkif?

*Ah, there she is—in the compound with the others.*

Some of them had helped keep her alive while she was sick, on the trip upriver.

*What am I going to do about them?*

*At least the kids got away. I can delay the pursuit, if nothing else. Or kill them all, if they force me to it.*

# CHAPTER 21

"Wouldn't you rather find shelter now, before it gets too dark? Bad enough to hike in the rain, but setting up a wet camp is no fun at all."

Daerget's complaint faded into the background for Najud. He hadn't quite realized how much more valley there was in Glymbeod upstream from Elkif's village, the last significant mark on the map. He'd hoped to stumble onto something useful west of there, but what if everything he was looking for was to the east instead? They would have wasted all that time with the detour in support of their story.

"Are you this absent-minded with Penrys, my friend? Because if you are, I tell you that can be dangerous. Things used to go 'boom' in her workroom, sometimes. Best to be paying attention."

"Sorry, just the usual worry. You're right, we should look for a spot soon."

The path was grassy rather than dusty so at least they were spared most of the mud, but Najud hated walking with wet feet. He could smell the exhalation of the plants as they soaked up the water.

*If it rains like this a lot, no wonder they have all these rivers.*

Before the rain started, the Virtaengi had been in view, downslope from them and about a mile distant. The path they were on took a slowly converging course eastward to the river. Najud had expected to reach it tonight but there was no real hurry.

He dipped his head down again, trying to keep the rain off his face under the fold of canvas he'd tied on for an impromptu hood. The trail turned left to bypass a boulder and he lifted his face to navigate it without losing his footing on the slick surface.

And then the sky lit up, below him and to the east. He couldn't see what it was, but the glow was reflected off the bottom of the clouds, like a lightning strike or a forest fire.

"Did you see that?" Daerget said, and Najud waved him to silence as he started counting. After ten seconds, a rolling thunder passed over them.

Daerget stared at him and they said, simultaneously, "Penrys!"

"About two miles away," Najud added. He scanned for her, but it was too far.

"Let's go." He set off at a rapid walk downhill, aiming for the river at a slant.

Behind him, Daerget said, "We could drop the packs and come back for them."

Najud shook his head and settled into the pace. "We'll need them."

It was pleasant sitting in the rain, though a bit chilly for it. There were lights down in the compound now, people moving around. Penrys wondered it they'd found her pack yet, or made themselves a meal. Maybe they'd noticed the writing on the walls.

Maybe they'd seen it all before and didn't care.

It was surprising how a soft rain wouldn't clear the dirt off a person. You'd think it would, but it took scrubbing, and she couldn't do that one-handed.

The crawl through the mud lying on her dead right side and pushing with her left arm and leg had won her this nice stump to lean against with a decent view of the compound gate. She'd had to detour around a couple of the bodies, but she couldn't complain. A porch with a roof and a view would have been better, but she'd doubted her ability to get that far.

She thought the stockade must still be standing, since the count of people inside hadn't changed, but she'd have been happier if there'd been some way to shut the gate and lock it.

She could watch it like a cat at a mousehole for a while, until she got too tired, and then she'd have to decide whether or not she could keep them alive. She knew what the answer would be, balancing their lives against those of the children, and she wasn't sure she could manage more than twenty at the same time, before they realized what was happening and swarmed against her.

A pebble landed at her feet with a little splash, and then another one. She reached out and found Chon Janwit behind her. She turned her head, and his mouth was moving, and she raised her left hand to stop him.

*Can't hear you. What are you doing here? You and the rest of them should be far away by now!*

He stopped, and she felt his tentative mind-speech. *We're all safe, all together. Amatka took a spill, but she'll be all right. Ashiwe's got them half a mile from here, well hidden, and I came back to scout.*

He hesitated. *We all heard the explosion and wanted to know what had happened. See if you were all right.*

She grinned at him and wondered at the look on his face. *Not so much. But they won't be making any more chained wizards, and that's the important thing.*

His glance at the bodies in the rain and mud prompted her to elaborate. *Most of them are down in the compound. For now.*

She drifted for a moment and yawned. *I can't afford to let them get away. Can't keep them without the cage. You don't want to be here when that time comes—you should all be far away by then.*

*But what about you?*

*Oh, well, I'm not moving so great right at the moment. It was worth it, though. Answers to some of my questions. You just get everyone to the Collegium with the documents. They'll know what to do.*

A mulish look come over his face, dimly visible on the twilight. *You're coming with us if I have to drag you there.*

*Don't think so. After I'm done with them, I'll just go have a little lie-down. Sure wish I could hear the rain, though.*

She tuned him out and counted the people in the compound again. Still the same. All the rats in a single sack.

Najud careened down the path through the trees in what was becoming pitch darkness and Daerget was hard-pressed to keep up. As he went he scanned ahead for Penrys or, indeed for any wizards, without success, but he didn't let that slow him down.

*I can't be this close just to find her gone. Life couldn't be that unfair.*

Nonsense. He knew just how little the world cared about the sentiments of its inhabitants.

Behind him Daerget was saving his breath and not talking.

Najud called out. *Pen-sha. Can you hear me?*

He thought there was a faint response, and he tried again. *Where are you?*

There was a whisper of surprise, and then her greater strength reached him. *Are you here? How strange. Just in time, too.*

He didn't like the feel of that at all. It didn't taste quite like her.

*You stay put and don't do anything stupid. I'm coming as fast as I can.*

Her giggle resonated through the link. *Well, I'll try, but I don't think I can really keep all the rats alive. Too many of them. All or none, or no one'll be safe. Sorry 'bout that, but that's what you get when you set out to build monsters.*

What was she talking about?

"I've found her," he told Daerget. "We've got to hurry."

"What do you think we're doing already?"

Najud pounded down the trail, mindful of his footing, and felt his way along where he couldn't see. The ground opened up ahead of him and he discovered that the woods cut off at the edge of a small settlement where no one was stirring. There were no smells of cooking, and few lights. He stumbled as he ran out into the open, and realized he'd tripped over someone in the dirt, not moving. *Pen-sha?*

Movement caught his eye in the dim light, and he saw her sitting on the ground with her back against a stump. The teenage boy with her looked like a Kigalino, with his long hair in a thin braid. *What was he doing here, in the back of Ellech?* The boy grabbed a rock and stepped defensively between them, and Najud held up his hands. "I'm with her," he panted.

He could hear Daerget behind him sliding to a stop.

The boy looked back at Penrys uncertainly.

"Tell him," Najud called.

"She can't hear you," the boy said.

*Pen-sha, tell him we're friends. He doesn't believe us.*

He saw the relief in the boy's face that marked Penrys's silent confirmation, and the boy dropped the rock and stepped back.

"Help me get her out of the rain," he pleaded, "Up onto that porch. We have to keep an eye on the gate." He waved at a compound with a stockade and some sort of ruined metal work around it. The gate was wide open.

Najud scanned inside and realized there were a couple of dozen people there, all wizards.

"Shouldn't that be closed?"

"She couldn't do it. I just got here myself."

Najud shrugged off his pack and set it on the stump. Then he leaned down and picked Penrys up, mud and all. She didn't weigh enough. *What have you gotten yourself into, Pen-sha? Besides a bit of dirt.*

*Oh, it's a long, long story. Don't let those wizards out, whatever you do. And there are some kids around here, too. Ask Chon Janwit about them.*

He carried her up to a wooden chair on a porch that overlooked the gate and settled her down in it. Even in that little trip, he could tell she was hurt. *What's wrong with you?*

*Business first, Naj-sha—I'll keep. Dead wizards out there in the dirt, important ones. The one with a chain is Bilget, Elkif's brother. Elkif's in the compound with the rest of them. Twenty-two, I counted. They're all complicit, but probably not all equally guilty.*

He felt her urgency, the panic in her mental voice. *I can't keep them there indefinitely—I told them if they stopped fighting I'd let them live but…*

*I'll get the gate closed. I can keep the count as well as you, and we'll keep watch all night. You need to let us take care of it now.*

*The children. Don't let them get the children.*

*I won't Pen-sha. Now settle down and do as you're told.*

He broke off to tell Daerget. "I've seen her fight to exhaustion before, and she's done it again. Here's what we'll do. And you—Chon Janwit, is it? You can help. You know that compound?"

"We lived there for more than four years."

That stopped Najud cold for a moment. "Then you can help Daerget see if it's sound enough to hold those wizards until the morning, with the gate shut. Daerget, get a good count of who's inside, will you? From out here—don't go in. I've got a count, too, and we're going to have to trade off sentry duty all night to make sure they stay put."

"What do we do if they don't?"

Najud looked at him. "If Penrys recovers a bit, she can probably keep them imprisoned. But we have to buy her that time."

He cleared his throat. "She was threatening to kill them otherwise. So if they want to live, they'll be well-behaved. You might want to tell them that, if they ask."

By midnight, things were in better shape.

Chon Janwit reappeared with eight children younger than himself who emerged from the woods like forest wraiths. Each carried a pack, and what a varied lot they seemed to Najud. Chon Janwit and another braided Kigalino, a little girl of about nine. A dark girl from Ndant and another from Rasesdad, a boy and girl from Ellech, and two Zan boys. And a young boy that looked like Penrys.

Daerget and the boys built a bonfire near the now-closed gate which successfully fought off what was left of the rain and shed some light on the danger zone, and Daerget had pronounced the stockade sound enough for now, as long as they monitored the count of wizards within. He'd passed the warning about Penrys inside to a receptive silence. A woman's voice promised a peaceful evening.

After Daerget reported on all of this in the front room of the building they'd commandeered, and offered to take the first watch, Najud and the two older girls dealt with Penrys in a small room next to the kitchen. All the device lights were ablaze, courtesy of Daerget.

The Ndant girl, Ashiwe, seemed to be in charge, and Najud was grateful for her help. The Ellech and Kigalino girls built up a fire and heated water, while Iko and Ashiwe sat Penrys in a wooden chair, stripped the filthy clothes off of her and wiped her down. Najud was relegated to helping with the heavy lifting, and he complied without comment until enough of the mud came off to reveal the bruises and other injuries clearly, as well as her too-visible ribs.

"Look at the black burns down her right side," Najud told them. "This is what lightning does. What happened?"

"We didn't see her do it," Ashiwe said, "but she was looking for some way to destroy the cage around the compound. We heard the explosion."

"And these bruises, and her eye?"

"That was yesterday," Iko said. "She didn't tell us a lot about it."

Najud hoped very much that the man who did that was still alive. He wanted to meet him.

He put a rein on his anger. That wasn't what she needed right now.

*There's a substantial bump on her head, with who knows what effect, and she seems to be starving. Deafened by the explosion, no doubt. Will all of it heal, especially the lightning strike or whatever it was, and the burns?*

He took a deep breath. *Probably. Being who she was, with the chain.*

Najud bowed his head and gave thanks to anything that might be listening.

*Pen-sha... you awake?*

Only a tired murmur came back.

*We're doing fine, everything's under control. Go to sleep now.*

He picked her up and carried her to the nearest bed and drew the blanket over her, careful with the wrappings around the various injuries, and then shooed the hovering girls ahead of him out of the room.

"I know it's late, young ladies, but please—tell me all about it."

Najud sat in the front room of the cabin and the children gathered around him on the floor. They were a somber lot, far too grave for their years. The Ellech girl held her arm as if it pained her, but it didn't seem serious.

Ashiwe began the tale, and the others let her do most of the telling. "She was very sick when they brought her to us. Couldn't breathe. You could hear the water in her lungs. We recognized her, of course—Taikvali, from the last batch—but she didn't know us."

The boy who looked like her whispered. "She was my momma from before."

Najud blinked, but Ashiwe explained how the women among the wizards looked out for the children in their temporary care.

She went on in quiet tones to outline the history of the wizards who'd been stolen, in three separate groups, and the children deemed too young who were left behind with each... harvest. She described the school wall with its lists, and the personal notes engraved on the walls of the eating room.

Najud was horrified, as if hearing some ancient terror tale come to life, and then Chon Janwit pressed a carefully wrapped ream of paper into his hands that made it all real. "She had us copy it all down, twice. Told us to take it to the Collegium."

Iko's quiet voice continued. "They questioned her, but she wouldn't talk to us about that. She made us pair up and get packs ready, and then she... she did something to the guards, and they died. We ran into the woods and hid, like she told us to. I don't know how she destroyed the cage, but we heard it."

"So did I," Najud assured her. "Saw the flash, too. And then we ran as fast as we could."

"She told us not to come back," Ashiwe said, "But when Chon Janwit saw you had the wizards shut into the compound, he decided we should return and help."

"Daerget and I'll take care of you," Najud said, "And Penrys, too, once she's better. We'll figure it all out in the morning. Go along to bed now, all of you. Find some place while there's still some of the night left. The two of us will keep watch on the prisoners until the morning."

The children gathered their belongings together with drooping shoulders and flagging energy, and shuffled off under Ashiwe's general supervision to find a room or two to settle in. Najud let them go—they'd been looking after themselves for four years and he supposed they could manage another night of it.

He let his mind touch on Daerget's briefly, to make sure he was awake, and then his eyes were drawn to the tidy ream in front of him, covered with waxed paper and tied with twisted grass. He moved over to a table with a chair under a device light and opened it there, and then began turning over the pages one by one until he could make sense of the order. Someone had started each section with a miniature drawing of the wall in question and an arrow pointing to the starting point of what followed, column by column.

So many people. He held this bare record of their lives in his hand, in this quiet ordinary room with the darkness and the rain outside. The men and women who'd seized them from their lives were dead in the dirt outside, or trying to get some sleep in the bare compound that their victims had used. But at least most of them were still alive.

How many of the chained wizards had died on arrival, once they were sent out? Vylkar had estimated it might be as many as a third of them.

He came to Penrys's entry, from Ashiwe's story. Taikvali. An unknown name from an almost unknown land. Parents, a sibling. And a husband, just as she'd feared. *She's known this for days, now. What does she think about her husband, and her name? Are you regretting our marriage, Pen-sha? Or should it be Taik-sha?*

It was a cold and uncomfortable name in the mouth, not the endearment he was used to.

He reassembled the ream and retied the cover around it loosely, then went out to relieve Daerget on the porch.

"Surely you're early," Daerget said.

"I'll never sleep anyway, not for a while. Listen to this."

Najud relayed the story from the children and described the document.

Daerget bristled indignantly. "And to think she let any of them live. One of those bodies was right in front of the gate, you know, and now I'm glad I left him there where they can see him, all night long. They'll be digging the graves in the morning, I can tell you—not us."

"And they'll name the dead, too," Najud promised. "I want good records of that."

He patted Daerget on the shoulder. "Why don't you go to bed? I'll get you up again in a couple of hours. Let's just get through the night and then we'll see what's to do."

Daerget relinquished his chair to Najud and paused in the doorway into the cabin. "Is this what it's like, after a battle? Bodies lying around, wounded to tend to, prisoners to manage?"

*He's my age. Why ask me?* Then Najud thought of the aftermath of the fight in Neshilik when they'd struggled against the chained wizard known only as the Voice.

"Yes, I think it's just like this."

The quiet rain was soporific, but Najud's thoughts kept him awake. *This obsession with the past almost got Penrys killed. Again. And here I am chasing her around in far Ellech instead of building my caravan. What am I doing?*

The answer came to him from the deepest part of him. *These are my responsibilities—my family, my plans for the future. Like any man. And these children—someone should see them home to their families.*

A nagging afterthought followed. *And see Penrys home to hers?*

# CHAPTER 22

Penrys opened her eyes, unable to account for her whereabouts. *Clean—what happened to all the mud?*

The rain had stopped but everything was dripping. *I can hear it! The eye's better, too.* She lay stretched out on her back and on a bed, and her groping left hand felt a blanket in the dim gray light before the dawn.

When she searched with her mind, she found Najud sleeping below her on the floor, and the kids in the same building, all of them, heavily asleep. That Daerget fellow was awake and on watch. *I remember the eyepatch, of course, but I never knew him very well. What's he doing here?*

She reached out further and counted the wizards in the compound. No change. *Wonder what the cage looks like, after the explosion?*

*So much to do. The prisoners, the workrooms and all their papers and materials. The kids. How can we manage it?*

When she tried to see if she could move anything on her right, the faint noise woke Najud—she could sense it.

*Naj-sha, don't wake anyone.*

*Feeling any better?*

Except for the dead side and its burns, she did feel better, and her chain was humming with power from Bilget and the rest of them. *Much. Maybe not quite up to dancing yet, but it'll do. How'd you find me?*

Najud's mental tone was offhand, but she detected the worry that underlaid it. *Plenty of clues, all those things you left in your room. The maps were handy—we came up through Estirmet. And we were close enough to see the explosion, at a distance.*

His emotions roiled silently through him until he controlled himself so that he could add some lightness. *Nothing's safe in your hands, is it? Always blowing up or falling down or something.*

She smiled in the dimness. He couldn't see her face, but he'd feel it. *Well, you know how clumsy I am. Couldn't think of anything else to do. Didn't know how much of a mess it would make.*

Najud hesitated. *The kids told me some of the story last night before we put them to bed. The part they know, anyway.*

*I sent them away at the end. Had to get them out, no matter what.*

*I know.* He paused. *What about the parts they don't know?*

Now it was Penrys's turn for silence.

Najud persisted. *Tell me how you were captured. What happened?*

With an audible sigh, Penrys gave him the story. Her suspicion of the bookseller, Gylvabil, after the fact. The ambush in the *rystet*, the wizards' shop, and the journey upriver. The dreadful feel of the power-metal rods they used to keep her drained.

She winced at his reaction when she described the drowning and the illness which followed.

*Baelnei, that was his name?* His mind was grim and angry. *You've been beaten recently. Was that Baelnei, too?*

*Yes, Baelnei.* She let him feel the satisfaction in her thoughts. *I killed him first, after I destroyed the cage.*

*Too bad.* His frustration leaked out.

*I'd have saved him for you if I'd known you were coming. Maybe. Maybe not, too.*

She savored that death, and let him share in the sensation.

Then the mountain of things they still needed to do swept over her. *What're we going to do now?*

*What do you want to do?*

Penrys didn't hesitate. *Get the kids home. I'd like to turn the wizards over to the Collegium for judgment, but I just don't trust them any more. If they can't or won't handle it, well, I suppose… I suppose I'll have to deal out rough justice myself and then take the consequences.*

She dreaded Najud's reaction to that bloodthirsty thought, but he was focused on something else.

*And then, what? Go home, yourself?*

He shielded his emotions away as best he could, and then Penrys realized what it was he feared.

*No, Naj-sha, no. You're my home now.* His relief spilled over into her and left her babbling to reassure him. *I'll send them a letter or something, or at least I would, but I don't even know the language—Tarroak has forgotten most of it. Someone in the Collegium might, I suppose. Maybe there are books. Do they understand other languages? I've never met anyone who knew much about the place.*

She made herself calm down, now that Najud felt more like his normal self again.

*The kids never lost their memories, you see. They want their families, of course they do. But me—I'm not Taikvali. I don't even know if that Irrepi is a brother or a sister. And my husband… That life is lost to me, as much as if I'd died. I'll find a way to tell them, so they'll know, but I can't go back.*

Something else struck her. *We've got to get this word out to all the chained wizards we can find—they'll have to make their own decisions, once they know.*

Then she thought of a difficulty. *Only the kids could have told me which one I was, given me my old name, because they recognized me. We're going to have to find a way for them to draw or describe everyone they can, by name, before they go home, or we won't be able to match people up with their families.*

Najud kept his thoughts to himself for a moment, then he ventured in a different direction. *These children… what will the Collegium do?*

*It's not the Collegium's business! It's mine! I'll take them home myself. Someone who understands will need to explain to the families, not one of those… those nothings from the Collegium.*

She felt him trying to be patient with her. *You can't keep them. They're not puppies, and you're not their mother.*

Penrys sighed. *I know. They have their own families. But I've promised to be their guardian, and I will be.* She swallowed. *Don't know what to do about Tarroak, though. How does one even get to Aitzikoa, all the way around the world?*

*The Rasesni might have an answer to that. Their ships have probably been there. He'll just have to stay with us for a while until we can work it out.*

She froze. *Us?*

*We'll take them home together, on our way back, if that's what you want.*

*Nine children?*

Najud chuckled. *It's no burden. I'm in the business of building futures.*

Penrys was stunned. He believed this, in the very core of him, and he had the strength for it. And it was true—new caravan, new city for it, and the children. *Yes, you are, aren't you?*

Her heart warmed, and all her residual tension about the two of them being pulled in separate directions dissolved away. *That's a good business to be in. Better than worrying stupidly about the past. Want some help?* She dropped her left hand over the edge of the bed and he reached up to grasp it.

She could feel his deep satisfaction at her response. *Go back to sleep. That Daerget's coming back with us, too, unless all this has changed his mind. Wants to see sarq-Zannib. Someone you can talk to about devices.*

Penrys yawned and reclaimed her hand so she could tuck it back under the blanket. *How soon can we start?*

The next time Penrys woke up, alone in the room, the morning was well underway and the smell of ham frying tugged at her nose.

Ashiwe stuck her head through the doorway and saw her blinking. "Good. You're awake. Come get breakfast."

She helped Penrys dress in clothing they'd found, and then called Najud off the porch so that he could carry her out to the outhouse. When he brought her back, he dumped her unceremoniously on a chair in the kitchen. The two tables were fully occupied. "See that you fatten her up," he told Iko, who was manning the stove, before he returned to watch duty on the porch with his own plate.

Iko smiled and filled a dish for her—ham, eggs, and flatcakes with butter. "Go slowly," Ashiwe warned her.

Penrys attacked the eggs, the fork awkward in her left hand, but was stumped by the slices of ham until Daerget noticed her difficulty and whipped out a knife to cut things up for her.

"So," she said, around mouthfuls. "What brings *you* here?"

He considered his answer and she had time to swallow. "Adventure."

She choked, and a hot cup of *bunnas* was passed her way. She wrinkled her nose and shook her head at the smell of it. "Anything else to drink?"

The mug of cider Ashiwe handed her was an improvement, and she recovered enough to respond to Daerget, who'd watched the whole performance with a grin that traveled up under his eyepatch. "All the way to *sarq*-Zannib?"

He shrugged. "*You* went, didn't you? Don't hear you complaining."

"Hmmph."

All the children were watching them silently. *Four years since they've seen adults, bantering as if they hadn't a care in the world. No wonder they're looking at us. They've forgotten what that's like.*

Nimiz broke the spell. "Is he really a pirate?"

She caught a flicker of guilt from Hakkur and asked, "Now where would anyone get that idea?"

Amatka said, "We told each other stories…"

Iramqawj butted in. "Hakkur's were the best. Pirates and warriors and rescues and fights!"

Daerget shrugged. "I've denied it, but they don't believe me."

Chon Janwit looked with scorn at his younger companions. "He's not a pirate. He's a wizard, like us. From the Collegium."

At this voice of mundane reality, Daerget assumed a pained expression. "Who says there's no such thing as a wizardly pirate? Or maybe a piratical wizard?" He was rewarded with a grin from the younger boys, and a shy smile from Ju Ochim.

Penrys returned to her meal, and then leaned back to let it settle for a moment. When she reached out to count the wizards, the number was wrong. She counted again and pushed back from the table in alarm—one was missing.

Daerget gripped her arm and held her in place.

"Let me go! One's gone."

He kept his grip and nodded, "That's right. One of them thought he'd sneak out early while you were unavailable, right through the gate. We caught him, Najud and me."

Penrys looked again and didn't find him. "But where is he?"

Daerget glanced at the listening children and paused. "Well, when I say 'caught,' I really meant something a bit more permanent."

She stared at him.

"We *did* warn them," he added. "Not our fault if they didn't believe us."

Najud stuck his head in the room and broke into the moment. "There's a woman standing in the compound's gateway, waving to us."

Penrys scanned. "It's Elkif. She must want to talk."

Najud picked her up, and she found it disconcerting to be hauled around like a package that weighed nothing. As if he'd heard a protest, he mind-spoke her. **Just until you put some more weight* *back on, mind. Then you can carry yourself. A few more meals like that should do it.**

Daerget picked up two hunting spears as they left the porch, and she had a better idea of what might have happened to the morning's escape attempt.

The children followed, too, and Penrys craned her head over Najud's shoulder to tell them not to, but Ashiwe forestalled her. "We want to see them. We want to see what they look like, so we'll know, when we remember them." Chon Janwit nodded in agreement, his face grim and set.

They walked in pairs, with their assigned partners, and Penrys wondered if that was deliberate or just an unconscious grasp at reassurance in the face of danger.

Najud held to the shortest distance through the clearing, except for the brief detours around bodies. Penrys tried to count the dead but couldn't see them all, and Najud shook her when he realized what she was doing.

They stopped outside the gates, where the body of the second guard lay in the mud, his wet clothing beginning to steam in the sunlight. There was another man lying on his back near the first guard. His clothing was dry where exposed, and a hole glistened redly in his abdomen.

Najud whispered into Penrys's ear. "Do you want to speak with her?"

She shook her head faintly. *I killed her brother, her sister, and her sister's child as well as all of these around us. I don't think she's going to want to talk to me.**

Out loud, she said, "Put me down."

Chon Janwit walked up and helped her balance on her one good leg. Once she was set, she took a long look at the dripping ruin of the cage. The outer stockade had taken most of the damage, and was deeply scored and scorched, and the power-metal struts she could see were twisted and blackened. All of it was dead and unpowered to her sight.

Daerget trotted over to open the outer gate. It was just wood and metal now, and he didn't bother with the pole to keep it at a distance. He left the inner gate closed, and the prisoners stepped up to it. Both parties got a good look at each other.

The captives seemed uninjured, but tired and dirty. And frightened.

Penrys smiled grimly. *Well they should be. I'm surprised no one's hurt, but I guess they either died or they lived—nothing in-between.*

The count held steady at twenty-one, all of them on their feet behind Elkif. It was the first time Penrys had seen many of them. None seemed young—forties or older. *Bilget said he'd sent for more of them from Tavnastok—are they younger? And how many—no more than will fit on a single boat, like the one I was on? When will they get here?*

Najud stepped forward as their spokesman, and Penrys could see the surprise on some faces at encountering a Zan in Ellechen clothing.

"I'm Najud, a *jarghal* of *sarq*-Zannib, son of Ilsahr and Kazrsulj of clan Zamjilah. With me is Daerget of the Collegium. You've met my wife, Penrys. On more than one occasion, I believe." He glanced backward. "And, of course, you remember the children."

Elkif nodded her head. "Elkif, daughter of Gialfinnur."

Najud waited for her to continue.

"What are you going to do with us?"

"We haven't decided yet." He tipped his head at Penrys. "She's not in favor of wasting resources holding you at all." He grinned wolfishly and let that sink in. "Some of us think the Collegium's senior council would like to talk to you, and would prefer to keep you alive."

He glanced down at the fresh body. "If we can."

Najud let the silence draw out for a moment. "Do you have enough food and water for a while?" he asked.

"The water from the creek's still coming in from the pipes, but we'll need more food soon. And we need fire, for cooking and for heating water." Elkif had refused to look down at the body when Najud did.

Penrys spoke for the first time. "Can you be trusted with it?"

Elkif closed her eyes for a moment. "We've seen the writing on the walls. We'll leave it alone."

"And so you'd better," Penrys said. "We have copies of all of it, so destroying it will do nothing except make your case worse. If buildings burn, you'll be sleeping in the rain." *If I let you stay alive to feel the wet.*

Najud read her expression. "We'll provide flints for fire. I imagine some of you have steel knives to strike them against."

Ashiwe whispered in Penrys's ear, and she added, "I suspect you may be short of cooking pots, too. We'll see what we can do about that."

She felt for intact power-metal in the ruined framework and found none. *The power blowout must have jumped all gaps.* But there were bits of the metal in the pockets of some of the prisoners, like power-stones. That would have to go.

"I want every bit of working power-metal out of there," she called to them. "No point hiding it—I can find it when I look."

Someone behind Elkif cried out, "But that'll mean no lights."

"Get up early, go to bed at dark," Najud told them. "Or learn to make torches. That's the best offer you'll get."

"Either hand it all in, or I'll drain you all every day. I assure you—you won't like it." Penrys pointed to the metal rod by the outer guard's body, and Iko went to fetch it. "By the handle, Iko! Don't touch anyone."

The girl looked down impassively at the dead man and then stooped to pick up the weapon. She walked back and stood stoutly next to Ashiwe, with the rod grasped firmly in her hand.

A man in the back of the crowd of wizards passed a cap forward, and Penrys could hear the chink of metal as the wizards emptied their pockets. It finally made it up to Elkif who laid it down at her feet. Penrys checked that they'd dumped it all.

Someone else called out. "What about our friends? You can't just leave them out there."

Daerget said, "We need graves for thirteen. No, fourteen now." He glanced pointedly at the fresh body. "You'll do the digging, under our watch."

He considered the raw material in front of him. "We'll take two of you at a time and switch off when you get tired. Deal?"

Elkif nodded. "I want to see my family."

Penrys denied her. "No. There's nothing to see, anyway—it was quick for all of them."

Daerget added, "The diggers will help lay them out with dignity."

Suddenly Penrys was repelled by all of this, and her leg hurt, supporting all her weight. She slashed her left hand through the air in an abbreviated gesture. "*Sennevi.* It's done. They'll come back in a while and get started. Meanwhile, leave the cap and back away."

Once they'd retreated a few paces, Daerget walked up to the cap on the ground and cracked the gate to slip it out, while Penrys monitored them all.

Najud scooped her up again and she turned her face to his chest.

She muttered, "If you find me a stick to lean on, I'll start practicing." She held up her right forearm with her left hand and wiggled its fingers at him. "See, I can move my fingers already. Toes, too."

He bent his head and whispered into his ear. "I'm in no hurry. You can't run off anywhere like this, and that's just how I like it."

Daerget and Chon Janwit consulted with Najud and Penrys from the porch. Najud was to keep watch on the wizards in the compound, and Penrys on the two loose ones that would be grave-digging, under Daerget and Chon Janwit's eye.

"Empty their pockets," Penrys told Daerget, "and get their names. Make sure the diggers aren't lying about it."

Najud added, "If they want to put up a piece of wood for a temporary marker, let them. They can even borrow a knife for the job."

"But don't stand too close, either of you." Penrys could hear the worry infecting her voice and tried to calm down. It was going to take hours to bury her... kills, and she'd never last at this rate.

She'd identified Baelnei for them by his mother lying on top of him, and Bilget's body with the chain was obvious. They'd be buried next to each other first, and then the others. Najud insisted on burying the ones nearest the compound last. "Makes the lesson take a little better," he explained, "the longer they can see them. You don't want prisoners to become desperate, to feel they have nothing to lose. But you want them to believe you, when you issue a threat, or else there's no controlling them."

She watched from her chair on the porch, a blanket wrapped around her to keep warm, since the rags of her blue robe were off dripping somewhere. Najud paced restlessly. He'd found her a stout stick, but her right hand couldn't hold anything yet. At least there was improvement there, feeling coming back into her hand and foot. Control and the larger muscles would take longer. *How long?* She pumped her fingers again. *As long as it takes. Nothing I can do will hurry it up.* She massaged her defective hand with her left one, as if that would make any difference. Something to do.

Najud leaned on the back of her chair. "So. Now what?"

Penrys cleared her throat. "I was going to send the kids out through Estirmet until they reached the bridge at Tavnastok."

"All the way, on foot? Nine-year-olds?"

"I know, I know. It was all I could come up with. I couldn't send them down the river—who else in the area is clan-kin to Gialfinnur? A bunch of foreign children, with me or without me— they'd stand out like torches in the snow. No way for them to hide on the river, not ultimately.

"And besides… Bilget said another load of his people was coming up from Tavnastok."

"When?" Najud asked.

"Don't know. Don't know how many, either."

"You're right, that wouldn't have worked."

"So what other choice is there?" she asked. "Northwest into the Dunnarfeol? Where they can freeze to death in summertime? Southwest across the river's no better than Estirmet, and further from the Collegium."

"We have horses," he suggested. "There are a few here, and Daerget and I left six behind before we crossed the divide. I bet they're still there—it was a little pocket of grazing and water. We could go get them, look for a path they could take. Or you could find one, from the air, once you're strong enough again."

She was shaking her head before he was halfway done.

"First of all, none of these kids have been on a horse in years, if ever. And secondly, I can't leave to scout a route for you. If I go off to do that, who's left who can drain the prisoners remotely in case of a threat? You'd have to wade in there with that metal rod to do it any other way, and eventually you'd make a mistake.

"I can't let them go. As long as they're still alive and prisoners, then so am I."

Najud shoved off from the chair and resumed pacing.

"So. We can't send the kids off on their own. Even if Daerget went along with them, there aren't enough horses." He rubbed his hands together. "We'll shelter here, then, for a while at least. We've got everything we need. Vylkar knows where we were headed. When we don't return, that'll tell him something."

He stared off at the compound, and Penrys kept her eyes on the gravediggers.

"We'll give it a couple of weeks to settle in to a routine. If the next load arrives, we'll just have to deal with it. Or rather, you will and we'll just watch."

Penrys glared at him.

"Otherwise, if nothing suggests itself by then, we'll send messengers to the Collegium to fetch them. Daerget and Chon Janwit, perhaps, on horseback. There's no one else who has the resources to handle prisoners like this."

Penrys sighed. "If they believe us when they hear the story."

# CHAPTER 23

"Look at them," Penrys said, and Najud turned his gaze to the children, seated on the ground not far from the gates and watching the prisoners go about their business inside.

More than a week had passed, and he worried each day about the anticipated arrival of more of Bilget's wizards. They all counted on Penrys's greater range to give them some warning.

*We're counting on her for too many things. For security whenever anyone approaches the wizards in the compound. For alerting us about visitors. She has to sleep sometimes. This isn't stable—too many ways for it to blow up on us.*

The children had taken to coming out each afternoon, like this, once their chores were done in the house and the garden and the byre, and after their riding lessons with Najud, turn and turnabout on the three plow-horses. Penrys had wanted them to learn a normal life again, to prepare them for their families.

Whenever the children sat and stared like this, Najud could feel the discomfort of the prisoners who noticed. Inevitably, the traffic moving across the area visible from the outside would diminish to nothing. Just to avoid the eyes of children.

When he'd asked them why they wanted to do this every day, Iramqawj had told him, "We don't want to forget what evil looks like," and Nimiz had nodded, too, with the same contemplative expression on his face.

*Countrymen of mine, no matter how young they were when they were stolen away.*

Penrys always came with him when the children walked out. She was hardly stumbling at all now, and the long burns down her right side were fading quickly. She was obsessive about checking the count. As far as she was concerned, the kids were still in reach. If these wizards could kill them and the kids, they might even evade discovery or punishment. It kept her in a constant state of frustrated anxiety.

It worried him that she refused to interact with the prisoners. "They make me too angry," she'd told him. "If you want to keep them alive, I need to stay away from them."

It was a side of her he hadn't seen before, forced to the front by the unresolved danger of their situation. He didn't fancy the prisoners' chances of survival if they threatened those children in any way.

"What are they doing in there, all day long?" he asked her.

"Writing, most of them. They're not… optimistic about what's going to happen, and I think they're constructing their own versions of the events here and the part they played. Justifications and excuses for when they stand before the Collegium's *hochumranomrethich*. Glad it's not my problem to deal with."

She grinned at him coldly. "You know my preferred solution."

"I imagine they'll all blame Gialfinnur, if they're old enough, or Bilget."

"No doubt, but the records Daerget and I are reading say otherwise. It's a funny thing—everyone signs his own notebooks. That's what'll condemn them now."

She sighed. "Oh, Najud, I just want to get out of here. Get out of Ellech altogether, after we get Hakkur and Amatka home."

"We'll send our messengers in a few days, if nothing happens. We'll be gone before mid-summer."

"I hope so," she said.

"Daerget, you've missed your calling," Penrys said. "You make an excellent schoolmaster."

The morning session had just broken up in the front room, and the older children were in the kitchen setting out a meal with the help of the younger ones.

The geography lessons were popular. No one wanted to leave their friends of four years, and it helped for them to see just where each of them lived, more or less.

Najud described what it was like to travel from country to country, to prepare them for what was to come. There was a general consensus that Iko was most to be envied, since she'd get to see where everyone else lived on her way to Rasesdad, but some held out for Tarroak, who'd be going all the way home with Najud and Penrys.

"Until we figure out how to get you to Aitzikoa," Penrys reassured him. "The Rasesni might have some ideas."

Daerget made sure they were all fluent in Ellechen *guma* and had them work on their writing. Najud's promise of getting them an address for everyone so they could write letters had all of them diligently working away at it. None were old enough to just learn another's language with the mind-speech, but they'd had four years of practice with their captors, learning from Hakkur and Amatka, and Daerget passed over most of the inevitable spelling errors—as long as they could understand each other, the niceties could come later.

He'd made up packets for them, in Ellechen *guma*, that listed the names of all their families, so they wouldn't forget. Each day he'd handed out another set, until every child had one, a treasured possession.

Penrys stood to join the children in the kitchen, but Daerget held her back a moment, and then laid a packet like all the others in her own hand. "Yours, and theirs," he said. "So you can remember."

It took effort to keep her hand from clenching it and wrinkling his careful work. *What use to me is that Aitzikoa family?*

She froze, and Najud plucked it from her hand. "I'll take care of that for you. I already have a pack, and you don't, yet."

They could hear excited voices from the kitchen. "D'ya think they'll remember me, my little sisters?" That was Amatka.

Chon Janwit's deeper voice wondered, "I hope my grandfather's alive. He wasn't very well when I... when I left."

"What about my dog? Where's she been sleeping while I was away?" Ju Ochim worried.

Iko stuck her head into the front room to see what was keeping them. She looked at Penrys a bit shyly. "I've decided what I want to do, when I get back. I want to dedicate myself as a temple healer of Ksheri, like my mother. She'll like that, I think."

Najud bowed to her with a smile. "A fine calling, and I'm sure you will serve it well, Ichorke."

The use of her full name startled her for a moment, and then she smiled back at him. "You understand, don't you?"

She ducked back out of the room, embarrassed.

"You're going to have her half in love with you before she's home, Najud," Penrys muttered.

"And why not? She's just the right age for it." Daerget laughed at Penrys's glare.

Najud shrugged it off. "Alas, I am already claimed."

"What about the rest of them? What'll they become?"

"Too early to tell," Daerget said. "But that Hakkur's destined for device work or I know nothing about youngsters."

"And Ju Ochim for drawing," Penrys said, and both the men nodded.

That had been a revelation. Part of each school session was spent trying to remember the faces that went with the names on the lists. Penrys had explained to them that the people they knew wouldn't know their own names, just like her, and so they set to the task with a will.

Daerget had a fair hand, and he was adept at seeing an image in someone's mind and putting it on paper, but Ju Ochim was very fine at drawing the adults in her own batch, the last one. She couldn't remember all the names, but she seemed to have all the faces, and they poured out of her, while the older children looked on and called out the names to match. Even Penrys's face had appeared, and Ju Ochim bowed and gave it to her, when she realized what she'd done.

That was one paper Penrys treasured, even though Ju Ochim named it as "Taikvali."

The older batches were still missing at least fifty faces, mostly in the first group, who'd been witnessed by fewer of the children, but it was a much better result overall than any of them had anticipated. Once the first group was gone and the second bunch arrived, the older children had realized it could happen again, and paid more attention to meeting everyone.

There were also a handful of faces now on paper to which no one could assign names.

It had been a shock to Penrys and Najud when people they'd met in Kigali acquired names. They'd offered their own memory of faces to Daerget—the Voice, in Neshilik, and the chained wizards they'd met in Yenit Ping, living and dead. Ashiwe's memory had already supplied her young friend, the one they knew as the *qahulajti*.

Hakkur was revealed as an unexpected contributor. He remembered the odd things about people—the way they moved, their ticks, their posture. He recalled the scars and marks he'd seen, too, but no one was quite sure if scars were erased as part of the chain's healing process. His additions helped them link at least a dozen faces to names by jogging the memory of the others, and Daerget took note of all the other details he described, in case they should be helpful for identification.

When Penrys had asked Ju Ochim how she could draw the adults so well, she'd said, "I thought of them carefully every night, so someone would remember them. Then I practiced." That simple declaration from the delicate little girl with her long thin braid had stopped all conversation, and she sank back into her next drawing while they all looked at her in astonishment.

"That's not how it works."

Najud looked up from his work in the front room of the commandeered cabin to cast a somewhat jaundiced eye on the nightly technical disputes between Daerget and Penrys. "I can't speak to the metal-forging—that's beyond my expertise," she was saying. "But you can use the chains like power-stones, only better, since they're not just passive receptacles."

She pulled a piece of the power-metal from her pocket, one of the bits scavenged from the prisoners. "This works just like a power-stone. It can power a device, or you can use it directly for *raunarys*—I have. I've used the chain that way."

"But a power-stone can't do those things—moving people, charging other power-stones." Daerget was insistent.

"Sure it can, it's just not very strong, and it's easy to destroy one. You can move a piece of paper with one, maybe, by itself, with no device or array to amplify it. But this stuff—this is much stronger. All the crystals align, or many more of them, anyway, so each piece is like dozens or hundreds of power-stones. Imagine what that would cost!

"And you can make it in much larger sizes. Think of those struts that made up the cage. That barrier held one or two hundred wizards, and it only needed a bit of topping up each day, like one of those."

She waved her hand at the nearest device light.

"Quiet, both of you," Najud said. "You'll wake the kids."

Daerget shook his head, but let himself be hushed. "Nothing wakes them once they're asleep. Don't you remember what it's like at that age?"

"You could always go ask one of *them* to settle your debate," Najud suggested, tipping his head toward the compound. Everyone paused, and Najud thought they were checking the count, like he was.

Penrys snorted. "This is as close as I want to get to them." Her gesture encompassed the piles of notebooks and records stacked high on the floor around the table.

They'd raided every building and opened every cupboard. Najud had flipped through every book, and brought along the ones where anyone had scribbled notes. Daerget was convinced they'd found all the documentation.

They knew who'd worked in each place, and had drawn charts of the individual wizards and their specialties which they'd gleaned from their own test results and records.

Najud knew that it would take a team of people months to sort through it all, but they had a preliminary outline and, more importantly, they had the names to match.

His own task was matching up the names, since the technical notes meant little to a wizard who used no device magic. He'd gotten a list of names from Elkif and matched it up with the names of the dead and all the names in the documents.

Everyone alive and dead had appeared somewhere in the records, even if they worked in a minor capacity. There were no servants here, only wizards who did whatever work was necessary to keep the settlement running. He'd been surprised that no false name seemed to have been claimed, but then everyone alive was being monitored so perhaps they despaired of maintaining a hidden identity.

But Najud had a second list—names from the records, that matched none of the living or the dead. Wizards who had worked here, but weren't here now. That was the list that worried him. Where were they? Were some of them no longer alive? Were these the ones coming from Tavnastok?

Daerget was still debating with Penrys about how to make the power-metal and what it could do, and Najud interrupted him.

"You're not planning on using this, are you?"

Daerget exchanged glances with Penrys. "Not to make chains, certainly. But it's absolutely revolutionary for power design. It'll change everything. Devices made with it will last a long time between charges, and can be made very powerful. Big machines. Wonderful things.

"These *drepfarar*, they got sidetracked with a… a sick ambition and charismatic leaders. There's no defending what they did with the chains. But the power-metal itself—it's not guilty. It's a tool. You don't condemn a knife that kills, you condemn the hand that wields it. Knives are useful."

Najud grunted but held his tongue. This was at the root of the device prohibition among the *bikrajab* of *sarq*-Zannib. They thought the physical magic corrupted, and he could understand why, though most accepted that as simple wisdom with no matching experience of their own.

His personal view had broadened now that he'd seen so many wizards comfortable with devices, not least his own wife. He knew Munraz was fascinated and talked about these matters with Vylkar since he couldn't discuss them with Najud comfortably. *Not a good situation for a nal-jarghal, is it, to have forbidden topics in the way of his education? I'm going to have to do something about that, when I see him again. But what?*

He changed the topic. "It's been well over a week. Don't they have neighbors? Don't they go down to that village of Elkif's for things they don't grow here? Why aren't there any visitors?"

Penrys shrugged. "If you kept prisoners like they did, would you encourage visits? If someone shows up, so much the worse for them—we'll have to add them to our little jail. Maybe they'd be happy by now to have some new faces in there."

# CHAPTER 24

These smaller river boats on the Virtaengi were more exciting than the big one that had brought him to Tavnastok, Munraz decided. *Closer to the water, shallower—less stable.* But he liked the creak of the sails, and the tilt as the boat bit into the current, propelled against it by the wind. *Like riding a horse and leaning into the curves.*

The three vessels spread out during the day, but they camped together at night. *How did they keep those robes clean around the fires?* Even in their less formal robes, this wizard… troop impressed him with their seriousness. No more effete scholars. From somewhere they'd managed to dig up almost fifty men and women with a militant air who looked like they were eager to come along on this expedition.

Munraz remembered the story about the rogue wizard Asuthrys, drowned in the falls on the Baegyl Gaer. *I guess it took people like this to do that.*

Vylkar leaned on the rail next to him. "We've been lucky with the weather. The current's against us, but the winds blow toward the mountains, this time of year. I'd hate to see all of them sitting on the lower deck pulling oars."

Munraz snorted at the image. This was no galley—he'd encountered one in the harbor at Kwattu in Kigali, so he knew the difference—and the only paddles he'd seen were reserved for the hired crew. They used poles instead, when they had to.

Most of the boats at the piers on Tavnastok's south side were small things that could be rowed or paddled, whether or not they had a mast, but the Collegium had commandeered three of the two-masted freight carriers, the boats that could only advance when the wind countered the current and the river ran deep and relatively placid. There were too many people for a flotilla of smaller boats.

"Won't we run out of river soon? You said it got too shallow halfway up Glymbeod."

"Soon, yes, but not quite yet. We should pass Elkif's village today—that's usually the turnaround point, the highest upstream spot for the larger boats."

"Do we have to walk from there?" Munraz asked.

They both turned at the sound of footsteps, and Vylkar bowed his head to Luveri. Munraz thought her broad face suited the shorter purple robes. He still resented her for shutting Penrys out of the Collegium, but he admired her competence once she'd been spurred into action.

"You think we'll find them there?" she asked Vylkar.

"That would be too easy," he said. "Where would be the challenge in that?"

She grunted, and watched the river banks go by, broken every now and then by a landing and a small settlement. "If I'd known there were this many wizards lingering along here, I'd have been more suspicious years ago."

Vylkar nodded. "The density is surprising. Everyone says there are few wizards along the Virtaengi, but that's clearly a lie. I don't think I've been out of range of one, on one shore or the other, the whole trip. Why is that so, and we ignorant of it?"

"You'd never know it from the attendance records. We get fewer students from the upper Virtaengi than any other district I can think of."

She eyed Munraz, and then decided to ignore him. "I owe you an apology, Vylkar, for being taken in by my steward all these years. I should set aside the purple and let someone else run the *hochumranomrethich*. I'm only staying on now because this… foray can't wait."

"Nonsense, *raegar*, how could you know? He fooled your predecessors, too, after all."

"Yes, but I *trusted* him. What kind of judgment does that reflect?"

Munraz thought she was angry, more at herself than anyone else. *That's what drives her now, isn't it?*

She didn't mention Penrys, he noticed, or the missing Daerget. Or Najud. She was hunting for the nest of rogue wizards she now believed existed, somewhere upriver—that was the focus of this expedition. He thought she probably considered the missing dead already, or they would've been heard from by now. It'd been almost four weeks since Penrys had disappeared. He felt the familiar shortening of breath and chilling of his skin, whenever he thought about it. *Are they dead, and me abandoned in a foreign land?*

Theirs was the lead boat, and as it curved around a bend in the river, the ship's owner-captain shouted something. When they turned, he pointed to the northern bank where three piers jutted out from a small settlement.

"Doesn't look like much," Munraz commented.

"They're not there," Vylkar said. "None of the three."

Munraz envied his easy skill at sorting through the minds in his range so quickly, but Luveri nodded in agreement.

"Now what?" she asked the air, and stalked off to speak with the captain.

"Can we sail upstream from here?" Munraz asked.

Vylkar pushed off the rail and straightened up, and for once Munraz could see the worry on his face as well as in his mind. "I don't know, *byrindur.*"

He walked off to join Luveri, arguing with the captain, and Munraz stared after him. *He called me his protegé. What does he mean by that? Does he think they're dead, too, and he's responsible for me? Is that all? Or does he actually recognize me as an apprentice, a nal-jarghal? Here, in Ellech?*

"Sit deep and drive her forward with your buttocks," Najud called to Amatka, slapping his own rear in emphasis. The girl's serious expression deepened, and she tried to put the instruction into practice, but he wasn't sure the horse even noticed, light as she was. Her friends waiting their turn contributed catcalls or advice, variously, while Chon Janwit and Nimiz coped with their own difficulties on the other two horses.

Penrys appeared unexpectedly around the corner of the cabin that blocked the enclosure where Najud held his riding lessons from a view of the clearing.

"Visitors coming, up the river," she called to him, and vanished again.

*Not mind-speech? Oh, of course—they could be wizards and might notice.*

The children froze and looked to him. "Dismount, and untack the horses. You can drape the saddles over the fence, with everything else, for now."

He waited for them impatiently, his mind turned outward to the river, but Penrys's range was much greater than his, and he felt nothing. He shut the gate to keep the horses penned. *Wouldn't take but a moment to tack them up again, but where would they go with three plodding work horses and nine youngsters?*

When he finally brought everyone to the clearing, he found Penrys pacing by the pier and Daerget keeping an eye on the compound. When Penrys turned at the noise of the children, he was surprised to see a broad smile on her face.

"Wizards. Ours. Lots of them. I recognize Vylkar and Munraz, but not the others. It's hard to count them—they keep shifting around. Must be more than one boat."

"You could always…" Najud thrust an arm into the air as if loosing a falcon.

She shook her head. "Not until the prisoners are truly secure. I can wait."

Daerget called back to him, "We should get our robes."

Penrys wrinkled her nose, but Najud agreed. "I'll fetch them," he said.

He ducked into the main cabin and found Daerget's and his own, easily enough, but he had to search harder for Penrys's. He half-expected to discover it wadded up in a ball on the floor, but Iko had taken pains to clean and repair the worst of it, and Penrys had left it lying under other discards along the back of a chair.

When he came back out, already robed in green, he tossed Daerget's robe to him, and then held Penrys's out for her until she reluctantly shrugged herself into it.

All the robes had seen better days. Penrys's blue was fresher than Daerget's, but the garment itself was more abused. They weren't meant for rough travel and rougher handling, and they looked it now, but the children seemed to be suitably impressed.

*Perhaps it'll prevent mistakes, since none of the prisoners were so equipped. How many were entitled to them? Elkif, surely, would still have her student robes. Did she ever pull them out and look at them, during her life here, and wonder at the turn it took?*

They hadn't searched the personal items of their captives yet, not systematically. Hadn't seemed necessary. Documents and books, yes—but not clothing.

It wasn't long before both Daerget and Najud could feel the approaching wizards, too. Iramqawj shimmied up a tree to get a higher view. "I can see them! Three big boats, with sails!"

"Don't lose track of the prisoners in the distraction," Penrys said, and all three of the adults ran through the ritual of the count.

Najud turned his head to see them crowded at the compound gate watching their activity. "Visitors," he called to them. "From the Collegium."

Their hope that it was the arrival of their missing colleagues soured, and they backed away, though he saw Elkif holding her position to watch. *She would know some of them, wouldn't she?*

Finally the first boat passed the bend in the river. They saw the sail first, and then a second mast, and then two more boats behind it. Penrys looked back uncertainly at Najud, and he waved her onto the rough stone pier.

She stood there unmoving, as the boats tacked once away, and then back for the last time. The hem of her robe fluttered in the breeze that was driving the boats upriver. Najud and Daerget took their positions where the pier met the bank, and a glance back at the youngsters found them finger-combing their hair and twitching at their ill-fitting clothes.

"Manners, now," he warned them.

The first boat lowered its sails and swung in close to the shore to let momentum carry its prow through the turn and forward to dock alongside the pier. Penrys caught the rope that was flung to her and hauled it in. A small man not in a robe jumped down from the boat deck to take it from her and attach it to something like a rough stone cleat, and another man did the same at mid-ship with another rope, once the boat touched lightly there.

Najud wondered what the other two boats would do, and then he saw the next one repeat the same maneuver to tie itself off to the side of the first boat.

Penrys stepped back, after a smile at Vylkar and Munraz, and waited.

A gangplank was shoved into place to link the boat deck with the pier, and Luveri in her informal purples was the first to come down the ramp. She spared a glance for Najud and the others, but then fixed her gaze on Penrys.

"*Hakkengenni,*" she said, and Penrys nodded, her face expressionless.

"Chancellor," she replied.

Najud tried to rein in his exasperation at this unnatural restraint. *Say something, one of you!* Then he realized, the head of the senior council had just given Penrys her old title—*Adept.* It was recognition, in a single word, of her standing, and an admission that Luveri had been wrong.

The two women walked to the shore to leave room for everyone else and joined Najud and Daerget there. Luveri's eyes missed nothing—not the fresh graves at the edge of the clearing, not Elkif and the unseen others waiting behind the closed gate of the compound, and certainly not the unexpected children of several nations lined up in front of her.

"And these are?" she asked Penrys.

"*Rerri,* let me introduce to you the survivors of Bilget's experiments. I have taken on the task of guardian to see them all home."

Najud lifted his eyebrows, and she added, "*We* have, Najud and I."

She went down the line, naming them, and Luveri gave each child her full attention.

Then she walked off, waving away accompaniment, and planted herself before the compound gates. She stood there unmoving, staring silently inside. From Najud's position, no one else was visible in there.

Penrys looked back at Najud and shrugged.

Vylkar with Munraz in tow joined them, and behind them a surge of men and women carrying bundles and packs emptied from the ships. Vylkar spared an arms-length embrace for Penrys. "I had feared for you, *byrindyrri,* I will admit it."

Munraz smiled shyly at Najud and Daerget, and Najud could feel an undignified grin on his own face.

They were interrupted by a stout woman in purple who marched up to Vylkar. "Right. Now, who's going to tell me how things are set up here?"

Vylkar introduced her as Istacher. "She's the… the captain when the wizards at the Collegium go on expedition. Would that be the right way to describe it, *rerri?*"

"Good enough," she said. "Now, someone needs to tell me what I can use for shelters, a tent ground, water, and so forth."

Daerget volunteered, and the two of them went off for a tour of the settlement, followed by three of her subordinates.

The stream of wizards seemed to be coming to an end. Najud wondered why so many wore green robes. "Vylkar, a third of them must be in greens. Didn't the Collegium have enough of their own to spare?"

"You've got it wrong. First of all, many had to stay behind to deal with that batch of wizards we dug out and picked up in Tavnastok. Luveri left Aergon and Neinnur in charge of that, for the council. That slowed us all down while we were sorting it out. That and chartering these boats, once we were sure of where to go."

He glanced at Najud's own green robes. "And then, you know, it's been a long time since the Collegium's forces have sallied forth. A generation or more. Every visiting wizard wanted the opportunity to come along and witness it, with suggestions for how they were uniquely suited to help out. To restore order, Luveri set aside a number of slots and we made the volunteers draw lots for them. But, of course, there were a few who were just too important to turn away, and so it added up."

A smile flickered over his face. "I remember, Najud, your interest in how wizards could be organized."

He waved his hand at the busy scene of activity before them. "Not many ever get to see this. You should find it instructive, just like the other green robes."

By the middle of the afternoon, the scene had been transformed. Most of the clearing had been turned into a tidy encampment, and Penrys could smell the start of something savory in the cooking area, nearest to the creek where it exited the woods. By some arcane rating system, the more important of the visiting wizards had been allocated the abandoned rooms in the buildings, though the workrooms were left unoccupied for the present. The remainder had set up tents of waxed canvas in tidy rows, like so many soldiers.

The ships' crews had their own encampment and fires, down by the shore, and maintained a scrupulous distance from the goings-on of wizards.

Penrys was at a loss for something to do. It was as though an invading army had occupied the space, and she stood and watched with Najud and Munraz from the porch of the cabin they'd commandeered, with all of the children, trying to stay out from underfoot. Daerget joined them when he could escape from errands laid upon him by his elders, and Vylkar checked in from time to time with updates.

"They practice this as a whole, every two or three years," Vylkar told them now. "The permanent officers, like Istacher, run their own exercises at their discretion. So the backbone of what you see is planned for that once-in-a-generation call that can't be handled by a dozen wizards by themselves. But for all the rest of them?"

He snorted. "It's a holiday and a military exercise, all at the same time. Not to mention getting to tell all their family and colleagues, afterward. They're enjoying it."

He eyed the somewhat subdued children. "All this, and they don't even have to fight. You've done all that for them already. It could hardly be better."

"Well, that's a good thing, isn't it?" Munraz suggested, puzzled by his tone.

Penrys muttered. "They're not taking it seriously."

Vylkar looked at her steadily. "No, they're not. It's up to you to change that. We may be the rescue, but you're the host. Make them understand."

His words struck a chord with her deep uneasiness and she nodded Then she walked off the porch past him to intercept Luveri, passing by in discussion with two of her staff. She waited in her path, until Luveri stopped and paused in her instructions.

"I think it's time I show you a few things. All of you."

Before Luveri could do more than raise a considering eyebrow, Penrys continued. "The only place big enough for all of us to meet together is in there." She hooked a thumb to the compound with the prisoners.

"What I want to show you first is in there, too. You need to see it. You all do."

Luveri lifted her eyes in Vylkar's direction, and whatever she saw there had her pursing her lips.

"Then let's set that up. We'll meet you at the gates in ten minutes, yes?"

Penrys nodded. "Thank you, *rerri*."

She waited for the head of the council to start her arrangements, then she turned to Daerget. "Quick—We're going to need lights—lots of them. They may have brought their own devices with power-stones, but I want to take as many of the power-metal ones as I can with me. Grab them from the walls wherever you can."

He pivoted to the door of the cabin and started raiding the interior.

Next she looked at the children. "I want you to be ready to tell them what you told me, but it means going back into the compound, into the schoolroom and the eating room. You don't have to go."

Nimiz was the first. "I want to!"

Iko added, "Everyone should know." Heads nodded all around.

"What about the prisoners?" Amatka asked.

Vylkar told them, "We'll confine them to one of the other buildings in there, if they're large enough." He glanced to Penrys for confirmation and she shrugged. "There're plenty of wizards here to keep them from doing you any harm now."

"Najud, can you grab Chon Janwit's copy of all the writing, and bring that?"

She thought a moment. "Anything else?"

"Someone should take notes," Vylkar suggested. "Pen, ink, paper."

Ashiwe volunteered to get that.

"I'll ask Daerget to do it," Penrys said. "What else?"

"You'll be glad of a flask of water, if you're planning a long meeting." Vylkar's diffidence failed to mask the voice of experience.

Najud smiled. "Spoken like a man who's done this before."

# CHAPTER 25

Penrys was waiting in front of the compound with her entire party when Luveri arrived, with almost all the wizards crowding behind her.

She motioned Luveri to stay where she was, then she opened the ruined outer gate and stood at the inner one. "Elkif!" she called, and the woman stalked out of the schoolroom, and surveyed the mob outside with a bleak expression.

"We're going to use the front two buildings. I want all of you to pick one of the other buildings while we do it, and wait there."

Elkif nodded silently and headed for the one nearest the river, and Luveri sent three men in blue robes, armed with spears, in through the gate to go with her. Guards, Penrys assumed.

It took a few moments for the building to fill with the twenty-one wizards Penrys was so used to counting, but the doors were eventually closed, and the guards posted.

She turned to face the wizards and wished she were taller. She tried to pitch her voice to carry. "The wizards here worked on many things. One of these was power-metal, Gialfinnur's discovery." She waved at the destroyed "hands" that framed the stockade. "And one project was chained wizards, like me. This compound used the one to hold the people stolen from all over the world to make the other."

"Follow me." She led them to the schoolroom building on the left first and held them outside while Daerget gave all but one of his armful of device lights to Ashiwe and Chon Janwit to hang everywhere they could inside. He handed the leftover one to Penrys.

After Chon Janwit stuck his head out the door when they were done and gave Penrys a nod, she stepped into the building and pulled all the residual power from the device lights into her chain. Daylight still filtered through the windows, but the walls were dim.

"Come in," she invited, and held her own people to the front before the engraved wall. She made sure Luveri stood in the first rows in the shadowed space.

Once everyone was inside, she began to speak, intoning the words like a traditional storyteller. "This was a room used by the three groups of wizards—altogether almost five hundred people whisked away from their homes in many countries and trapped here. Old and young, they were, and there were children, too.

"This was the schoolroom they set up to keep the children focused on learning. Then they were taken away, a few at a time, all but the ones deemed too young, and another batch appeared, with its own children, and they left, too. Finally there was one last batch, and when they were gone, only the children of all three groups were left behind. By themselves. For four years."

She powered all the devices at once, including the one she held in her hand, and the room blazed with light. There were startled breaths—none of them except her old companions had ever seen her do that before. It needed the chain to do it.

She shone her light on the rough world map, carved into the wooden wall. "This is the tally by country that they made, and each group extended it. They must've decided that Kigali *yat* would be the best common language to use. As they filled up each column, they started a new one."

She cleared her throat. "Chon Janwit, would you show us your name?"

There was no need for him to search for it. He walked directly to the spot and laid his hand on it. Ashiwe did the same, without waiting to be asked, and then the rest of them, until all nine were ranged along the wall, claiming their tiny fraction of the list.

Not a sound could be heard from Luveri's people.

Penrys walked to the truncated column for Aitzikoa and its neighbor where Tarroak stood and claimed her own name. "This is me. Was me. 'Taikvali' of Aitzikoa." She aimed her light at the island continent on the world map. "I was in the third batch, so the children tell me."

"Munraz? This was the *qahulajti*." She moved her hand downward to the single name in the country below hers on the list. "Ashiwe's friend." She glanced at Najud. "We haven't identified the Voice yet."

She tried to keep the emotion out of her voice. "All the rest of these names… Some may have died in experiments—we're still trying to sort that out and we haven't questioned the prisoners yet. Six killed themselves or were killed attempting to escape.

"But all the rest of them were chained, like me." She grabbed her own chain and tried to stay cold-blooded. "The process overrides our memory, permanently. Some of us, possibly all, received what Bilget liked to call 'special additions,' biological devices that triggered a strong healing capability, powered by the chain."

Penrys swallowed. "My special addition was wings." She invoked the wings and tail and turned the light on herself so they could all get a good look. Neither Daerget nor the contingent from the Collegium had seen this before, and there were gasps on all sides of her, before she let them vanish again.

"And then we were scattered back into the world, stripped of clothing and language and history, to live or die as chance would have it. Many, a great many, died. And none of their families know what happened."

She pulled the power out of the device lights again and led the way out of the building while Ashiwe and Chon Janwit gathered up the devices again.

She waited across the yard at the entrance to the eating room, and again sent the two oldest children in to arrange for lighting. When Chon Janwit opened the door for her, she led them in and let everyone find seats at the tables on the benches scattered around the room.

When they were all in place, she powered all the device-lights again. She could feel the attention of several wizards as they watched her and tried to figure out how she did it.

This time, the carved writing extended to more than one wall, the individual family names of each wizard, first in Kigali *yat* and then in their native language.

"Ashiwe tells me that each wizard chose to list his family here, in hope that the record would someday be found. They assumed they might die here, but they never thought that they might survive without any memory of that family.

"Not every name from the tally in the other building is listed here. I don't know why—perhaps some despaired. This one is mine." She walked over and claimed it, and the children followed her and stood by their own.

She took a deep breath but could still feel her voice thicken. "These are my parents. I can read the names, in Kigali *yat*, but Tarroak here can't read our native speech well enough to read that part and, of course, I don't know it at all." She paused to get control of herself. "I was married, in that other life." She stroked the name with a finger, and then walked over and grasped Najud's hand and intertwined her fingers with his. "That other life is gone, for me, but not for my family who will want to know what became of me."

She raised her voice. "And it's not gone for these children who never lost their memories and have been longing for their families for four years, all by themselves, waiting as they grew older for the time when they would vanish, too.

"I wanted you to see all this before you begin your discussions, here in this room, the best location in the settlement for your work. We made a copy of the walls in these two buildings, the children did—two copies. And Daerget, Najud, and I have started to identify faces with names—we'll show you that later. And we've got the notebooks and records from the workrooms.

"You'll want to get a history of events here from us, I know, and from the children, and there's a great deal to talk about. But you needed to see this, first."

She stared at Luveri and thumped the side of her fist hard against her name, and the wooden wall boomed. "*This* is the crime. This is almost five hundred people from many countries, stolen and changed and killed. That's what I put a stop to. That really was an *yrmkenrolek*, Luveri, a crooked path."

She lifted the device in her hand into the air. "But the technology, the power-metal, some of the other items… Those are just things, tools. That's not where the evil lies. Don't confuse the one with the other."

She could feel the attention of their minds. Many had monitored her as she spoke.

"*Sennevi*," she said, with the customary slash of her hand, the one that had pounded the wall a moment ago. "It's done. That's what I had to say, before you get started."

Luveri stood silent for a moment, and then bowed to her. "Find seats," she called out. "We have two hours before dinner, and I intend to use them."

Late that night, Penrys curled against Najud in the little room off the kitchen. Her back was tucked into his chest.

He could feel her exhaustion. They'd worked until well into the evening in the compound's eating room, with a break to fetch dinner, and then they ate in place to continue. Penrys had described her tests on the remnant chains in Yenit Ping with Vylkar as a witness, and then Vylkar explained why he'd suggested Gialfinnur as a possibility.

She'd laid out her research and actions, once the Collegium had refused her entrance. Najud interrupted once to tell them about the wizard shop keeper in Stokemmi who'd reacted to Penrys's chain, and what Munraz had discovered from the signals tower.

Even Vylkar had been called upon to explain the dinner he'd held in Stokemmi, and why. He'd given his testimony with an easy air, calm and unconcerned.

Then they took Penrys through her abduction and questioning, and that's when her voice began to give out. The flask she carried at Vylkar's original recommendation helped, and she kept sipping at it to soothe the hoarseness of her voice as she recounted the deaths of the guards, the destruction of the power-metal cage, and the one-sided fighting that followed.

Even for his own testimony, Najud had felt the minds touching his and monitoring his statements. *What must it have been like for Penrys, under scrutiny for hours, her words being tested for truth?*

Najud and Daerget had brought them up to date on their pursuit and the cleanup and research since then, but the testimony of the children had been reserved for the next day.

In fact, a few had protested letting the children stay to listen at all, and Luveri had cut them short. "What say you?" she'd asked them directly, and first Chon Janwit, and then each of the others had stood up. The Kigalino boy spoke for them all. "We want to stay. We want to hear it."

Penrys had hoisted herself to her weary feet and added. "They have the right, if anyone does," and Luveri supported her.

Penrys's voice muttered now, somewhere below Najud's chin. "Did it do any good, d'ya think?"

"What, your… dramatic preamble?" He could feel the smile in her thoughts. "That was a fine setup, and making the eating room the place to hold the meetings was inspired."

"It would be good to leave this place," she murmured.

"You don't want to delve into all the notes, learn about this new metal, design devices?" His tone was joking, but he did wonder.

"Let others do it. There are masters of the device arts here—couldn't you feel them? It'll take years to digest what Gialfinnur and his family accomplished, if they don't just bury the whole thing. That's not my job now."

He leaned down to nibble on her ear. "What's your job now?"

"Getting those kids home. And us, too. Never thought I'd say it, but I miss the *kazr*, all warm and private. I want to see the new caravan get started."

Najud hesitated but he didn't want there to be forbidden topics between them. "And the family you hope to have?"

"What, nine's not enough for you?" He smiled at her in the dark, and she continued more seriously. "We'll probably have Tarroak for a while till we can figure out how to get him all the way home, and then we'll just have to find some more. I'll bet you're good at that. You have a way with strays."

Three weeks later, Penrys was back in Tavnastok.

A research party of a dozen device specialists had been left behind in the settlement with the smallest of the boats to conduct a final search of the workrooms and to gather up all the possessions, tools, and materials they could find to bring back to the Collegium. They planned to leave nothing behind, not even the animals which would be sold to the nearest buyers.

Within the first couple days of the council's arrival, a small boat, detached from the largest one, bore Vylkar, Munraz, and two messengers back downstream to the Collegium to make initial preparations for the return of the larger party. They carried preliminary summary reports and some of the papers, including one of the transcriptions of the walls of the two buildings. Penrys missed them, but Vylkar had volunteered and she assumed he had his reasons.

At the end of the intensive questioning on site, all the rest, prisoners included, crowded into the two remaining boats, and a tense journey with guards and false alarms in the nightly riverbank encampments strained tempers all the way back.

Once docked at the south-side piers on the Virtaengi, there was no help for it but to march them all to the bridge on the Lodentaf side, through the busy districts where people gaped at the mass of wizards with their *taunnupar* prisoners and the carts of baggage that trailed behind them.

The children walked with Penrys and Najud, well back from the leaders, and Daerget tried to distract them by pointing out the sights. He turned the competitive counting of bookshops into a game.

Word traveled ahead of them, and the crowds thickened, if anything, as they approached the north shore and the Bridge Square. Penrys looked for Lepicher as they passed by her shop, but there were too many people to spot her.

The younger children were flagging, and Penrys waited for the carts to roll by. She and Najud perched a couple of them on each one, where they clung to the sides and gave their necks a workout looking at all the people and the buildings. Chon Janwit, Ashiwe, and Iko stuck close, and Daerget took charge of Hakkur who poked like a puppy into everything that interested him, with no thought of getting lost.

Penrys breathed a sigh of relief once they all set foot on the bridge. "Harder for them to go astray now, I hope. I feel like a mother hen."

"It's easier when there's a whole clan looking out for them," Najud told her.

Up ahead she could see the prisoners drooping in their bonds, shoulders sagging from the long walk. "I'll be glad to have them completely off my hands," she said. "I'm tired of counting to twenty."

It was no longer twenty-one. A man had managed to kill himself, in the compound, after Luveri's arrival.

"Now you'll only have to worry about Luveri and the entire senior council, eh?"

Her mouth tightened. There'd been initial disputes about what would happen with the children, and Penrys didn't look forward to more of it. She was determined to fulfill her promise of guardianship and here in the Collegium would come the first real tests of that.

As the procession entered the main gates of the Collegium itself, she hung back until the carts rolled by and rescued her charges, until all nine stood there with her. Najud and Daerget had retrieved their packs, but Penrys and the others had little but their clothing. She had no idea where Vylkar had arranged her room, or anyone else's, but someone must know. The stone arch of the great entrance across the courtyard loomed above her as they passed through, but she was too distracted looking for a familiar face to feel any twinge of home-coming. *Hardly a year and a quarter gone—where is everyone I used to know?*

"Over here." Munraz's waving hand caught her eye and they crossed the flagstones to greet him.

"What news, *nal-jarghal?*" Najud asked. Penrys noticed a fleeting expression cross Munraz's face but was too distracted to seek the cause. Daerget kept a firm hand on Hakkur's shoulder.

"Vylkar says I'm to take you up to your rooms, and you're to stay there until he can come get you."

"I'm not leaving the kids," Penrys said.

"No need. That's why I'm here instead of him. You'll see."

The children were awestruck by all the wizards in red and yellow robes, some not much older than Chon Janwit, who filled the staircases and stared at them unabashed. Najud pushed them along up the stairs after Munraz and down a warren of hallways until they reached a region unfamiliar to Penrys. Halfway down their current hall stood an open doorway, and Vylkar waited inside to greet them. There was a common room with chairs and tables— one of which supported a stack of folded red robes—a small kitchen visible through an archway, and three doors leading to other rooms.

"Boys at the end," Vylkar pointed, "and girls in the next room." The children rushed off to see what was inside.

"You two get the remaining room," he told Penrys and Najud. "Sorry, Daerget, I'm afraid you're stuck with your old room for now. Munraz, too. It was the best I could do."

"And lucky to get it," Munraz muttered for Penrys's ear. "It was a fight—wasn't settled until early this morning."

Vylkar ignored Munraz and lowered his voice. "Three things you need to know. All the children get red robes, like junior students. It'll help remind people that they aren't just captive witnesses to a crime, but children as well, and wizard children. There should be enough choices there to fit even the smallest, I hope."

"Good idea," she said. "Very good idea. What else?"

"Signals went out as soon as we got back. You'll find delegations from all the embassies involved set up in visitors' suites, like this one."

Penrys nodded thoughtfully, but she could see there was more. "And?"

"And the families of Hakkur and Amatka were notified. Amatka's got here more than ten days ago, and Hakkur's arrived yesterday. All the way overland from the Baegyl Gaer, Daerget—not so very far from your own family, I believe."

A knot formed in Penrys's stomach, but this is what she'd wanted. Just not so soon.

Vylkar continued, "I don't think Luveri will let them leave right away, but I can't keep the parents away from their children for long, and she hasn't told me not to let them come. Yet. I'll bring them here before lunch, if you think you can prepare them."

She swallowed. "All right. Get those robes for them as quickly as you can. "Daerget, could you…"

"Bring them to you in your room, Penrys?"

"Thanks, yes." She rubbed the base of her palm across a stinging eye, and pulled Najud into the room they'd been given. There was just time to notice all the little things from her old room which she'd last seen in the place she'd rented at Lepicher's, and then both of the Ellechen children came in, puzzled, with their new robes over their arms.

"Daerget said you wanted us?" Hakkur said.

Penrys glanced around the room. *Not enough chairs.* "Sit down on the bed, both of you. I have good news."

"Our families," Amatka whispered. "They're here already?"

Najud nodded. "Vylkar sent word when he got back. They'll be coming right here in about an hour. I want you to clean up, quickly now—put on your new robes."

Amatka said, "They gave us other clothes, too."

"Then wear those, too, under the robes. Penrys and I will show you how, if you need help."

"I'll braid your hair for you, Amatka. Maybe even give it a little trim. You, too, Hakkur," Penrys had never done that for a child, but how hard could it be?

"Are we going home right away?" Hakkur said, as quiet as Penrys had ever seen him. "What if I don't remember what they look like?"

"Nonsense," Najud said, briskly. "It'll be fine. I don't think you'll be going home immediately—Luveri will probably want to talk to you some more—but that's a matter between the council and your parents. Nothing for you to worry about."

Penrys walked over to the door and stuck her head out. "Daerget, can you find me a comb and scissors?"

When she looked at the children again, she could see the war on their faces between hope and anxiety. "Hurry up now," she said. "Get a good wash, and I'll be along to take care of your hair when you're done. Off with you! Munraz'll show you where."

She shooed them out of the room, thinking activity would be the best thing for them, and then looked at Najud who opened his arms to her. "Too soon?" he muttered, down at her head.

"Just unprepared. Better for them, after all."

An excited uproar from outside their doorway testified that the news had spread.

At the mid-day meal in the large dining hall, the seven remaining children divided their time between staring at the other wizards, especially the younger ones, in red robes like theirs, and enviously watching Amatka and Hakkur with their families at nearby tables.

Penrys and Najud had spoken to the parents apart from the children and added a few details to what Vylkar had already told them. Najud warned them that their children would miss their companions of four years badly.

"They kept each other alive—those bonds are strong," Penrys told them. "The others will want to write to them, and I hope you'll let them."

Hakkur's father had nodded. "I can't tell you how grateful we are, truly. To you, to their friends, to…" He broke off at the sight of the tears on his wife's face. "My father wanted to come, too, but he's not as young as he used to be. He'll be so happy."

Amatka was shadowed by the younger sisters she thought might have forgotten her, and two older brothers, too, all envious of her red robe. Her mother wanted to know why they couldn't just go home now.

"I know Vylkar told me there's to be more questions, and I'm sure I want those criminals punished, but she should be home, away from all of this. We have a lot of catching up to do."

Penrys nodded."I agree, *rerri*, and I'd like to hurry them along. We'll find out, soon, what Luveri's intentions are, so I urge patience for a day or two. Most of the senior council has only just returned."

At the end of the meal, a Zan in turban and robes bore down upon them and bowed to Najud. "You are Najud of the Zamjilah, and Penrys?"

Najud stood and bowed in return, and Penrys nodded. Daerget gave the man a once over. "How about I take the children back to the rooms while you deal with this?" he asked Penrys, and she gave him a grateful look.

"Thanks. We'll try not to be long."

The children went away obediently with Daerget, satiated with excitement for one morning, and the Zan bowed again.

"Please, I am Ashtirqa of clan Hadjark, of the Yawdhad tribe. I represent the ambassador of *sarq*-Zannib in Stokemmi. May I sit?"

Najud waved him to a seat, and Penrys spied two more coming their way—a woman from Ndant, and a Kigalino man.

"Might as well wait for your colleagues to join us," she said, and he twisted in his seat to watch them, with a small smile on his face.

"We traveled together upriver, and see—we are still of a common mind."

Once introductions had been made, and everyone seated, Ashtirqa continued.

"You have children of ours that should be reunited with their families. I'm sure we all feel the same way." Heads nodded all round.

"Can you get to *sarq*-Zannib any faster than we can, or Ndant, or Yenit Ping?" Najud said. "My wife and I have pledged guardianship for these children, to see them home to their families. And more—one is from Rasesdad, for whom we crave your assistance, Ashtirqa, since Rasesdad maintains no embassy in

Ellech. And one is from Aitzikoa, at the ends of the earth—perhaps Rasesdad can give us some assistance there."

"It would be better for each child to come home under the care of his or her countrymen." This was the contribution from the Ndant woman.

"No, it wouldn't." Penrys was adamant. "They've been a family of their own for four years, and they want to travel together as long as they can. The two Ellech children were just reunited with their families this morning, and as soon as the senior council will let all of us go, we'll get to Stokemmi and find a ship for Ndant. And since our home is in the west of *sarq*-Zannib, we won't be far from Rasesdad, at the end."

The Kigalino held his own council.

"Why not let us help you do it faster?" Ashtirqa asked reasonably. "Why should the Zan children wait for the Ndant one?"

"We promised them," she said. "We want to talk to their parents about what it was like, so that they'll understand and make it easier for them. And the kids know me, from before this." She clutched the chain around their neck. "I'm someone they trust. We've explained, shown them maps—they're prepared."

He tried another tack. "What of these lists of Zannib *bikrajab*, stolen from our land? What has become of them?"

"We know who was taken, because they carved their names into a wall of a prison compound, up the Virtaengi river. We know the names of their immediate family. What we don't know is what became of them, whether they're chained wizards somewhere with no knowledge of their past, like me, or whether they're dead. Any chained wizard of Zannib appearance is a candidate, and we've managed to get drawings of most of them.

"It'll take teamwork and time for all the countries involved to find their chained wizards, in their various nationalities, and match them up with a picture or, if necessary, with their potential relatives in other countries. Meanwhile, at least the families can be notified so they know what happened. Maybe they can supply their own pictures, to make identification easier."

"It's a nightmare you're describing," Ashtirqa said.

"No one knows that better than my wife," Najud said.

The Kigalino man raised his head and said, quietly. "Trouble coming."

Penrys twisted around and saw Luveri headed their way. "Indeed. No doubt we'll speak on these subjects again." She folded her hands demurely as the ambassadorial delegates rose and departed.

Luveri watched their backs, and then pinned Penrys with a glare. "I'd like to see you both in front of the full *hochumranomrethich* in one hour. Vylkar can show you the way."

She waited for a nod then took her leave.

"Back to our room?" Najud asked.

"Yes… except…" *Munraz, how do we find our rooms again?*

# CHAPTER 26

"I'll hold them to it if I have to fly the children out of here, one by one."

Penrys sputtered as she hiked back to her room with Najud after a long and irritating session with the senior council, kicking her long formal blue robe out of the way as she marched along. "I mean it," she said, looking up into Najud's face when there was no reply.

The smile he was struggling to contain set her off. "What're you laughing at?"

"I'm laughing at the bear defending her temporary cubs, the one I was foolish enough to marry. Will it be safe in my bed tonight, do you think?"

She chuckled involuntarily. "Try it and find out."

They reached their rooms, without Munraz's help this time, and she stomped in. All seven of the remaining children were there as well as Daerget and Munraz.

"Five days," she told them, "and then we can go. That's what they told me. All of us together, like we planned. I told them if it was any longer, I'd sic the ambassadors on 'em."

She turned to Munraz. "I don't know about you, but I'll be glad to cross the ocean, if it means I get to stay in my *kazr* at the end of it. I've had enough of stone walls and Ellechen bureaucrats." She was peeling off the long robe even as she spoke, and draped it over her arm as she made for her own room.

Something in Munraz's face caught Najud's eye, and he paused before following her. "Something the matter, *nal-jarghal?*"

Munraz drew himself up straight. "Could we go somewhere, *jarghal?*"

They walked back out together, and Munraz found an outer battlement wall to lean over. He was silent all the way there, and Najud respected his choice.

Once they were settled, Najud prompted, "What's troubling you, Munraz?"

The young man visibly swallowed. "Vylkar has offered to sponsor me, to be my *bilappa*."

"To stay here, in Ellech? Not to come home to *sarq*-Zannib?"

"What home in *sarq*-Zannib? I can never rejoin my clan, and if I could I wouldn't. And I can't tag along with you and Penrys, not forever. I am very grateful, *jarghal*, but…"

Najud waved that part away. "All we want is for you to grow into a future worthy of you, to find a family and work to turn your hand to."

"That's just it. We've been making families out of fragments. Look at Penrys, with those kids. How am I any different?"

He lowered his face while he spoke. "I have to choose for myself. There are others here I can learn from, that I can be friends with. Maybe I can find someone to love. Maybe *my* children, someday, can escape my past, my blood. Why not?"

Najud was unsettled, but he could feel the earnest intent behind the choked-out words.

"There's a whole world out there," he told his apprentice. "Vylkar, the Collegium, the study of devices, which I know intrigues you. You could do worse than to stay, it's true.

"But are you ready to give up on *sarq*-Zannib? To never travel with the herds? Live life outside the stone walls?"

"No herds, perhaps, but maybe a real wife someday, not some hollow shell of one, like my one-time family." Munraz's voice lowered. "No one to scorn me for my origins. I'll be on my own if I stay, but then we all are, aren't we? We have to make our own homes. Maybe Ellech will be mine."

Najud stepped back from the battlement and bowed low. "Well-spoken, Munraz, and I release you from your apprenticeship. May you find happiness and hard work and a good life."

"I still say it's not fair."

Penrys eyed the Ellechen clothing laid out over a chair in the room she shared with Najud. The new informal robe from Tavnastok was untouched, its blue just a shade less subtle and the fabric just a touch less elegant than the one it had replaced from Stokemmi.

Najud in his Zannib turban made no reply, but she thought she detected the trace of a smile on his face. They'd argued about this, the night before. She'd wanted to discard the remnants of her Ellechen garb for travel and return to the Zannib clothes she'd worn when they arrived in Stokemmi, a match to her husband.

"You're the representative of Ellech while these children are in our care," he'd insisted. "You're going to have to dress that way. Medals and all."

He was patient but as immovable as a boulder, and eventually they'd used the lock on their door and their last bit of privacy to reconcile.

*Medals, is it?* There were two new ones, more standardized than the exotic Kigali specimens. One was the Commendation of Excellence from the Collegium, something that they awarded when a wizard took the purple. Penrys was emphatically not so qualified, but it was the closest thing to a "well done" that they could grant. She thought it looked strange against the blue—all the ones she'd ever seen were worn on purple robes by people twice her age. It was different from the three small silver badges Vylkar had pressed upon her in Stokemmi—all wizards more advanced than students had some of those. This one was no larger, but it was gold.

The other medal had been arranged by one of the official Ellechen government representatives who were working with the council. Just like the foreign embassies, the Ellechen embassies in the other countries would be involved in the same paperwork and tracking for their own chained wizards, with an added dollop of guilt for the crime having occurred in their own nation. This award was in the shape of a pine tree and marked "For meritorious service."

"You don't suppose they just carry these around, do you?" she asked Najud.

He shrugged. "Perhaps the local goldsmiths keep the pattern on record."

The papers for both of them were in her personal pack, with the Kigali honors. "If I'm going to be wearing all this hardware a lot of the time, with my formal robe, I'll have to get some sort of rack made in Stokemmi to pin them to, so I can make fastening them easier and keep them from clanking together like so many hammers."

For her informal robes, only the small silver badges and new gold one from the Collegium were appropriate, and the three larger ones went into their carrying pouches.

She pawed through her pack and yanked out a different pouch. "Meanwhile, I have an idea for how to balance them."

Her fingers caressed her wedding brooch, and then she pulled it out and handed it to Najud.

"Perhaps you could fasten this for me?"

He hesitated a moment. "That goldsmith in Stokemmi said they don't wear jewelry with the medals."

She glared at him. "Much I care." She softened. *Put it on, please, Naj-sha. On the other side. If I can't wear the clothes, at least I can make this much of a claim on you.*

It was large and silver, and almost balanced the miscellaneous silver and gold bits on her right breast, and Najud pinned it carefully in place, running his fingers across the spread-winged eagle.

"What else is in that pack of yours?" he asked.

"I still have most of the power-stones," she said. "You know, if they start making power-metal here, the value of the natural stones will greatly diminish."

Deadpan, Najud said, "Maybe we better sell them while they still have their value."

"Maybe." Privately, she thought it would take years for the market impact to be felt, and there was no guarantee the Collegium would allow it, much as she'd argued in its favor. "We'll have plenty of warning."

She cast one last look around the room. All the personal bits of her life had already been packed away, and nothing was left. "Let's go get the kids."

Out in the common room Daerget had the children prepared and ready. There were grins on all the faces outweighing the anxiety Penrys could sense inside them, as they looked each other over in their unfamiliar clothing.

The representatives of their various embassies had provided suitable garments. The two Kigaliwen were transformed by their robes. Ju Ochim kept running her hand up and down the side to feel the silk, and Chon Janwit had taken on a sudden maturity, now that his upright demeanor was encased in the appropriate clothing. The lengths and styles were suitable for their ages and the travel they would be doing, but all of it was new and that alone was enough to overwhelm them after four years of castoffs and rags.

The blue-green garment the color of ocean foam that was draped diagonally on Ashiwe under a short jacket was stunning, and Penrys could feel how transformed she felt, her maturing figure suddenly on display.

She was startled by the apparent sight of four Zannib children, instead of two. Iko explained, "I asked the Zannib delegate for this. They weren't prepared for Rasesni clothing, and I would rather travel with you like this, if you don't mind."

"Not at all," Najud declared. "It suits you well, *lijti*."

She blushed at the address, more suitable to a young woman than a child.

Penrys sighed silently. She'd have to keep Iko from dwelling too much on him, for everyone's comfort. It made her long for Najud's lively young sister Rubti as a travel distraction.

Tarroak was watching her face. "Do you mind? No one knew what to give me, and they all said I should dress like the Zannib." He looked at her Ellechen robes doubtfully.

She smiled at him warmly. "Very suitable." Two small boys' heads with dark curls, and one with straight brown hair. No turbans at that age, and they all looked at Najud's enviously. "I wish I could wear the same clothes, like Iko, but they tell me I need to represent Ellech in an official capacity."

With a conspiratorial whisper she leaned down. "But when I'm not being official, well… that's a different matter."

She straightened up. "Everyone ready?" Heads at various heights nodded. "Let's get going, then."

The courtyard before the main gate of the Collegium was controlled chaos. All the stored goods from the warehouse near the docks were already on the pier waiting to be loaded, and an agent from the warehouse had it in charge. But all of Daerget's worldly goods, Penrys's books, and Najud's gleanings in trade had to be loaded up, with room left for the youngest of the children to ride all the way across the bridge, and then east along the bluff at Tavnastok and down to the waiting boat at the fork of the rivers.

*Plenty of time before the boat leaves, assuming we ever get out of here.* Penrys had a vision of waiting another day and facing this scene a second time.

Daerget was bidding his friends and colleagues farewell off along one side of the courtyard. He'd already sent goods and letters home with Hakkur's family, since they were also on the Baegyl Gaer, within reach of his own family. His well-wishers were many, Penrys noticed.

*Where are my own colleagues? Did I make so few friends, or is it just that so many are no longer here, after the passage of more than a year? What was I hiding from?*

But there was Vylkar. She looked at him with fresh eyes, without his observing it. *Unchanged from four years ago.*

She walked over and forced a hug upon him. *"Bilappa."*

He received it awkwardly, not given to such demonstrations.

"You're the only father I will ever know," she told him. "I can never repay my debt to you." She bowed deeply. "Tell your mother I will miss her, and wish her a long life."

He tapped the Collegium's gold badge over her heart. "Close this chapter of your life, *byrindyrri*, and get on with this one." He accompanied that with a tap on her wedding brooch. "And let me hear about it."

"I will, *bilappa*."

Najud and Munraz walked up to join them. "Take care of my apprentice, Vylkar. I've already warned him to behave himself."

"If you'll take care of mine," Vylkar said, with a wink at Penrys.

"I want you to have my *kazr* to remember me by," Munraz told them.

"As if that were necessary." Penrys surprised him by hugging him strongly. "You've gotten taller. Again."

She swallowed. "Prosper here, Munraz. Make this place your own." She bowed to him as she had to Vylkar. This was as far as they could take the young man they'd rescued from his family, and the rest would be up to him.

With a quick scan, she checked for the special trunk holding the watertight metal boxes with all the correspondence and documents they would need for their travels. At Daerget's suggestion, she'd tossed a little packet of three power-stones into the trunk, and one each into the boxes to make it easier to keep track of them. *Might as well do something useful with them.*

Now both of them could check the location of the paperwork easily. It was Daerget's responsibility as an emissary of the Collegium, as the children were hers and Najud's.

*At least there's no shortage of money. Letters of credit for the children as recompense from the Ellechen government, travel expenses, and the funding of deposits for the chained wizards, as they're found and identified. That'll take years, surely. There can be no adequate compensation for lost lives, but travel expenses to reunite them with their families—that's another matter.*

*Not my problem. Not anymore.*

Daerget left his friends and strolled across the courtyard. His eyepatch was new, and so were his clothes. He tossed a purse to Najud. "Your expenses for the horses and supplies, from the pursuit."

Then he surprised Penrys with a smaller purse, but one heavy with gold instead of silver. When she stared at him, he told her, "That's a bounty, for tracking down this *yrmkenrolek* and bringing the people involved to justice."

Penrys looked at Najud. "We should hire out as adventurers. Clearly there's money in it."

"I can promise you adventure with the new caravan," he replied with a grin. "It'll have to do."

She looked around them at the excited children in their mix of exotic clothing, from the almost-grown Chon Janwit and the responsible Ashiwe to lost Tarroak, so much like herself. "This is the adventure—life and its chaos. You build what you can, but only a fool thinks it can be controlled."

"And this?" Najud reached out and tapped her chain.

Penrys shrugged. "The past is the past—you can't live there, and why would you want to?"

She glanced at the famous Collegium and turned back to her husband. "Let's go home—we have work to do."

# GUIDE TO NAMES & PRONUNCIATIONS

PRINCIPAL CHARACTERS & PLACE NAMES & TERMS

PEOPLE - AITZIKOA

**Bizkoak** (beez-koh-AHK)
The name of Penrys's father.
**Deikzi** (DEYK-zee)
The name of Penrys's mother.
**Eidiz** (AY-deez)
The name of Penrys's husband.
**Irrepi** (eer-REH-pee)
The name of Penrys's sibling.
**Taikvali** (tyke-VAH-lee)
Penrys's original name.
**Tarroak (**tahr-roh-AHK)
A captive boy.

PEOPLE - ELLECH

**Aergon** (AIR-gohn)
Senior wizard at the Collegium of Wizards.
**Amatka** (AH-mat-kah)
A girl left behind in the captive wizard compound in Ellech.
**Asuthrys** (AH-sooth-rewss)
A legendary rogue wizard who came to a bad end by drowning.
**Baelnei** (BAL-nay)
The son of Tiessi.
**Bendondaer** (BEN-don-dair)
The author of a standard reference work on devices.
**Bilget** (BILL-get)
The son of Gialfinnur, twin brother of Tiessi.
**Daerget** (DAIR-get)
A librarian from the Collegium.

**Eldendaer** (EL-dem-dair)

An author of an advanced book on devices.

**Elkif** (EHL-kiff)

The older daughter of Gialfinnur, who carries on her father's studies.

**Feolderri** (FAYOL-dehr-ree)

A member of the Senior Council at the Collegium. She keeps the records.

**Gechendaer** (GEH-kehn-dair)

A signals clerk in Stokemmi.

**Gialfinnur** (GYAHL-fin-noor)

An old scholar who wrote a book on devices and was banned for *yrmkenrolek*, crooked learning. Father of Elkif, Tiessi, and Bilget.

**Gylvabil** (GEWL-vah-bill)

A seller of regional books in Tavnastok.

**Hakkur** (HAHK-koor)

A boy left behind in the captive wizard compound in Ellech.

**Innurgol** (IN-noor-gol)

A senior student at the Collegium.

**Istacher** (ISS-tah-khehr)

The camp captain of the Collegium wizards on expedition.

**Lepicher** (LEE-pee-khehr)

The owner of a bookshop in Tavnastok who also rents rooms.

**Liemma** (LEE-ehm-mah)

A senior student at the Collegium who is intrigued by Munraz.

**Luveri** (LOO-veh-ree)

The Chancellor of the Collegium.

**Neinnur** (NAYN-noor)

A member of the Senior Council at the Collegium.

**Ossadaer** (OHS-sah-dair)

The Steward of the Collegium.

**Penrys (Ryssi)** (PEHN-rewss)

The chained adept. Wizard trained at the Collegium of Wizards.

**Redenchek** (REH-den-khek)

A famous tailor and clothing specialist in Stokemmi.

**Syrlyggi** (SEWR-lyg-gee)

A goldsmith in Stokemmi.

**Tiessi** (TEE-eh-see)
>The younger daughter of Gialfinnur, twin sister of Bilget, mother of Baelnei.

**Varmatau** (VAR-mah-tow)
>Author of an advanced work on devices.

**Vylkar** (VIEWL-kar)
>Senior wizard at the Collegium of Wizards. Patron of Penrys.

## PEOPLE - KIGALI

**Chang Zenju** (CHAHNG ZEHN-joo)
>The *laigomju*, commander, of the cavalry squadron sent from Jonggep to Neshilik.

**Chon Janwit** (CHOHN JAHN-wit)
>The oldest boy left behind at the captive wizard compound in Ellech.

**Ju Ochim** (JOO OH-chihm)
>The youngest girl left behind at the captive wizard compound in Ellech.

**Kep Tsugo** (KEHP TSOO-goh)
>A wizard held captive in Ellech.

**Ki Sechat** (KIH SEH-chaht)
>The personal name of the Emperor of Kigali.

**Sar Luplen** (SAR LOOP-len) - Shining Magic
>The Kigali name given to Penrys.

**Sar Tobek** (SAR TOH-bek) - Fortunate, Lucky
>The Kigali name given to Najud.

**Tun Jeju** (TOON JEH-joo)
>The *notju*, intelligence master, and imperial representative for Chang Zenju's expedition.

## PEOPLE - NDANT

**Ashiwe** (ah-SHEE-weh) - Shelf Cloud of the Approaching Storm
>The oldest girl left behind at the captive wizard compound in Ellech.

**Kalavo** (kah-LAH-voh)
>The nephew of Mpeowake, missing and apparently converted into a chained wizard.

**Mpeowake** (m-peh-oh-WAH-keh) - Sparkling Foam
The leader of a group of wizards, very senior in her temple.

PEOPLE - RASESNI

**Ichorke (Iko)** (EE-chor-keh)
A girl left behind in the captive wizard compound in Ellech.
**Ksheri** (k-SHEH-ree)
A god with special powers in the domain of healing.
**Surdo** (SOOR-doh) - The Voice
The chained wizard-tyrant who wreaked havoc in Rasesdad.
The name was given by the Rasesni—his actual name was
unknown.
**The Voice**
See "Surdo."

PEOPLE - ZANNIB

**Ashtirqa** (ash-TEER-kah)
Part of the Zannib embassy in Ellech.From clan Hadjark of
tribe Yawdhad.
**Birssahr** (beers-SAH-her)
A boy who survived the Kurighdunaq disaster.
**Hadjark** (ash-TEER-kah) - Eagle Rock
A clan in eastern *sarq*-Zannib, part of the Yawdhad tribe.
**Iramqawj** (ee-rahm-KOWJ)
A boy left behind in the captive wizard compound in Ellech.
**Khizuwi** (khee-ZOO-wee)
A senior wizard from clan Umzabul, tribe Maqurrah.
**Kurighdunaq** (koo-REEG-doo-NAHK) - World-bow (Rainbow)
A clan in northwestern central *sarq*-Zannib, part of the
Undullah tribe.
**Munraz** (moon-RAHZ)
An apprentice wizard, nephew of Jiqlaraz, from clan Rashaban,
tribe Dhajtawhaz.
**Najud** (nah-JOOD) - Lucky, Fortunate
A master wizard of the Zamjilah clan, in the Shubzah tribe.
**Nimiz** (nee-MEEZ)
A boy left behind in the captive wizard compound in Ellech.

**Rubti** (ROOB-tee)
Najud's second sister.
**Shubzah** (shoob-ZAH)
A tribe in the northeast central region of *sarq*-Zannib. Zamjilah is one of its clans.
**Umzakhilin** (oom-zah-khee-LEEN)
The *zarawinnaj*, migration leader, of the Kurighdunaq clan.
**Undullah** (oon-dool-LAH)
A tribe in the northwest central region of *sarq*-Zannib. It has three clans—Winnajjinza, Kurighdunaq, and Akshullah.
**Yawdhad** (yow-DHAHD)
A tribe in eastern *sarq*-Zannib. Hadjark is one of its clans.
**Zabrash** (zahb-RAHSH)
A boy who survived the Kurighdunaq disaster.
**Zamjilah** (zahm-jee-LAH) - Eye of Heaven
Najud's clan, part of the Shubzah tribe.


PLACES - AITZIKOA


**Aitzikoa** (ite-zee-KOH-ah)
A country in the northern island continent.
**Noskatoa** (nohs-kah-TOH-ah)
A village or town in Aitzikoa.


PLACES - ELLECH


**Asuthgrata** (AH-sooth-grah-tah) - High Region
Upland district of mixed grazing and woodlands, famed for its hunting.
**Baegyl Gaer** (BA-gewl (GAIR)) - White Milk River
The river which drains the eastern slopes of the Dunnarfeol Mountains and shares the Nachompolek Lappyri outlet with the Lodentaf Gaer, east of the capitol harbor city Stokemmi.
**Drosenrolkentham** (DROH-sen-rohl-kehn-thahm) – Wizard-learningplace
The Collegium of Wizards in Tavnastok.
**Drosentaech** (DROH-sen-takh) - Wizard-falls
The great waterfall on the Baegyl Gaer in the pool of which the rebellious wizard Asuthrys was finally drowned by his colleagues.

**Dunnarfeol** (DOON-nar-fayol) - Winter's House
The highest mountains in the world, forming the north border of Ellech.
**Ellech** (ELL-ekh)
A northern nation tucked along the southern margin of the Dunnarfeol mountains, with precipitous timber- and grass-covered slopes running down to a deep-water port. Famed for industry and research, with a well-armed merchant navy to seek out new markets.
**Estirmet** (ES-teer-met)
Land between the Virtaengi and Lodentaf rivers, beginning with Tavnastok at the fork and ending at the Dunnarfeol foothills.
**Glymbeod** (GLEWM-bayod) - Cold Dell
The enclosed valley in the foothills of the Dunnarfeol where the Virtaengi Gaer has its source. See *taunnup*.
**Lodentaf Gaer** (LOH-den-tahf (GAIR)) - Ice-Wealth River
The river which runs from the Dunnarfeol Mountains past Tavnastok to the capitol harbor city Stokemmi.
**Meirgas** (MAIR-gahs) - Milk-froth
The rapids of the Lodentaf Gaer, just below Tavnastok. They are bypassed by a lock system for navigation.
**Nachompolek (Lappyri)** (NAH-khom-poh-lek LAHP-pew-ree)
The harbor where the Lodentaf and Baegyl rivers meet the sea.
**Stokemmi** (STOH-kem-mee) - Mother of Cities
The capitol city, on the east bank of the Lodentaf Gaer where it meets the Nachompolek harbor.
**Tavnastok** (TAV-nah-stok) - City of Wealth
Inland city based on river commerce and industry, on the forks of the Lodentaf Gaer. Famous as the home of the Collegium of Wizards.
**Virtaengi Gaer** (VEER-tang-ghee) - Ladle
The western river that joins the Lodentaf Gaer at the fork below Tavnastok and stirs the Meirgas rapids there. It originates in the lowest foothills of the Dunnarfeol, at Glymbeod.


PLACES - KIGALI


**Gentu Hanjong** (GEHN-too HAHN-jong)
The northeast bay for the harbor city Kwattu.

**Jonggep** (JONG-ghep) - The Meeting of Waters
The largest inland city, at the junction of the two main branches of the Junkawa River: The Seguchi and the Neshikame.

**Junkawa** (joon-KAH-wah) - The Mother of Rivers
The longest river in the world, with two main branches: the Seguchi and the Neshikame. It finds its outlet at Pingmen below the walls of Penit Ying.

**Kigali** (kih-GAH-lee) - Land of the Ki Dynasty
Set in the mid-latitudes of the southern continent, Kigali is a wealthy and hard-working nation with a history of political stability and expansion. The Junkawa River and its hundreds of tributaries provide internal communications, and well-placed ports support its strong mercantile interests.

**Kwatka Kote** (KWAHT-kah KOH-teh)
The eastern rift valley running from northeast Gentu Bay to southeast Pingmen harbor.

**Kwatna Jun** (KWAHT-nah joon) - Kwatna River
The river linking the chain of lakes with Gentu Bay in the eastern Kwatka Kote lowlands.

**Kwattu** (KWAHT-too)
The busiest port city, in the northeast on Gentu Bay at the mouth of the Kwatna River in the eastern Kwatka Kote lowlands.

**Neshikame Jun** (neh-shee-KAH-mee joon) - Little Sister Water
The northern branch of the Junkawa River. It is navigable well into the Lomat region.

**Neshilik** (neh-SHEE-lik)
The western district of Kigali, surrounded by mountains and traversed by the Seguchi River. Often disputed with Rasesdad.

**Pingmen Hanjong** (PING-men HAHN-jong) - City View
The bay or series of harbors carved out by the Junkawa River.

**Seguchi Jun** (seh-GOO-chee joon) - Seguchi River
The southern and main branch of the Junkawa. It finds its source in the Mratsanag Mountains in Radesdad above Nagthari, and Gonglik in Neshilik is the site of the last downstream bridge. All crossings are by boat or ferry below that point. It is navigable up to the Steps at Gonglik, and navigable again above the rapids to Dzongphan.

**The Meeting of Waters**
See "Jonggep."

**The Mother of Rivers**
See "Junkawa."
**Yenit Ping** (YEH-nit ping) - Endless City
Capital city, on both sides of the Junkawa River, overlooking
Pingmen harbor.

PLACES - NDANT

**Shokona Hanjong** (SHOH-koh-nah)
The main bay in eastern Ndant.

PLACES - RASESNI

**Damsnag** (DAHMS-nahg) - The Right Horn
The southern encircling range at the eastern end of Mratsanag.
**Dzongphan** (DZONG-fan) - Temple Quarter
The capital city, which includes the mother temples of all the
gods, in Nagthari.
**Garshnag** (GARSH-nahg) - The Left Horn
The northern encircling range at the eastern end of Mratsanag.
**Mratsanag** (m-RAHT-suh-nahg) - The Wild Ram's Horns
The second tallest mountain range in the world.
**Nagthari** (NAHG-ta-ree) - Between the Horns
The region between the eastern mountain pincers, bordering
Neshilik.
**Rasesdad** (RAHS-ess-dahd)
The Rasesni nation includes the Mratsanag Mountains and the
well-watered and fertile plains they support on two coasts. It is
the western neighbor of Kigali, in the southern hemisphere.

PLACES - ZANNIB

**Qawrash im-Dhal** (cow-RAHSH eem-THAHL) - Well in the
Steppe
The city in the eastern region from which the largest caravan to
eastern Kigali originates.
**(Mard) Ussha** (mahrd OOSH-shah)
Capital city, founded by Kigali, on Pago Bay on the east coast
near the Kigali border, at the mouth of the Harin River. Also
known as Zudiqazd mar-Sarq, the Winter Camp of the Nation.

**(Hilj) Wandat** (heelj wahn-DAHT) - Enclosed Sea
Very large almost landlocked sea in the far west, bordered also by Rasesdad.
**Sarq-Zannib** (SAHRK-zahn-NEEB)
The Zannib nation. It occupies the bottom of the southern hemisphere and is neighbored on the north by both Rasesdad and Kigali. The western third concentrates on fishing and small farm agriculture, while the remainder is steppe and grasslands.
**Zudiqazd mar-Sarq** (zoo-dee-KAHZD mar-SAHRK) - Winter Camp of the nation
See Mard Ussha.


WORDS & PHRASES - ELLECH

**Amka** (AHM-ka) - Little room
Elevator cage.
**Bendu** (BEN-doo) - Device
A device for performing *raunarys*, usually made of wood.
**Beolrys** (BAYOL-rewss) - Mind-skill
The wizardly skill of mental-magic, things of the mind such as mind-speech.
**Bilappa** (BILL-ap-pa) - Father of learning
Mentor, patron.
**Byrindur, Byrindyrri** (BEW-rin-door, BEW-rin-dewr-ree) - Protected one (m, f)
The protegé of a wizard.
**Drepfarar** (DREP-fahr-ar) - Lost souls
Spirits, haunts, ghosts.
**Dre'ski,** short for **Dreppaski** (DREP-fahr-ar) - Damnable
Literally "ought to get lost."
**Drosnommystu** (DROH-snom-mews-too) - Wizard grove-roots
The metaphor for the society or collection of all wizards, as intergrown tree roots in a forest.
**Ellechen guma** (ELL-ekh-en GOO-mah) - Ellechen language
The language of Ellech.
**Ellechen taurath** (ELL-ekh-en TOWER-ahth) - Ellechen people
The people of Ellech.
**Emkenrys** (EHM-kehn-rewss) - Moving
One of the aspects of *Raunarys*.

**Felkenrys** (FEHL-kehn-rewss) - Binding
One of the aspects of *Raunarys*.

**Hakkengenni** (HAHK-kehn-gen-nee) - One who knows
An archaic term for a wizard with unusual strength in mind-skill and thing-skill both. Usually translated as "Adept."

**Hochumranomrethich** (HOKH-oom-ran-om-reh-thikh) - Elders' Council
The Senior Council, the governing body of the Drosenrolkentham, the Collegium.

**Hortkendrosi** (HORT-kehn-droh-see) - Working wizards
The term for wizards who work in commerce—building devices, maintaining utilities, etc.

**Ossanutkenbendu** (OHS-sa-noot-kehn-behn-doo) - Man-lifting device
Elevator, powered by a device.

**Ponka** (POHN-ka) - A punchy
Nickname for the data strips that drive the signal towers. See *rekenponkenkiemmenbar*.

**Raegar, Raegrar** (RA-gar, -grar) - Master, Masters
A senior scholar in the teaching/research system, often a teacher of others.

**Raer, Raerra** (RAIR, RAIR-ra) - Sir, Mister, Gentlemen
Polite honorific for men.

**Raunarys** (ROW-na-rewss) - Thing-skill
The wizardly skill of physical-magic, things of the real world, such as moving, binding, and destroying.

**Redenrolek** (REH-den-roh-lek) - Straight learning
Teachings that are considered orthodox or correct.

**Rekenponkenkiemmenbar** (REH-kehn-pohn-kehn-kyehm-mehn-bar) - Punched hole paper strip
Data strips that underlie the signals transmitted from signal towers. See *ponka*.

**Rerri, Rerrinir** (REHR-ree, REHR-rih-neer) - Madam, Miss, Ladies
Polite honorific for women.

**Rysefeol** (REW-seh-fayol) - Device framework
A composite framework, usually made of wood, a level of complexity greater than a *bendu*.

**Ryskymmer** (rewss-KEW-meer) - Magic detector
A specialized *rysefeol*, for smelling out the use of devices and moving to their location.
**Rystet** (REWSS-tet) - Magic shop
A specialized store selling supplies for wizard, especially related to devices.
**Sennevi** (SEHN-neh-vee)
"It is done." The customary final phrase that marks the end of a traditional tale, often accompanied by the slash of a hand.
**Staka** (STAH-ka) - Missie, bitch
Clipped form of the diminutive of *ista* - lady.
**Strekenrys** (STRECK-ehn-rewss) - Destroying
One of the aspects of *Raunarys*.
**Taunnup, Taunnupar** (TOWN-noop(-ar)) - Woods-mouse, Woods-mice
Pejorative name for people from Glymbeod, referring to them as mice hiding in holes.
**Tennendaer** (TEN-en-dair) - Finger-friend
Little objects to fondle in a pocket, randomly acquired.
**Yrmkenrolek** (EWERM-kehn-roh-lek) - Crooked learning
Teachings that are considered corrupt or immoral, sometimes on insufficient grounds.
**Yrmur!** (EWER-moor) - Broken, Wrong!
A curse.

WORDS & PHRASES - RASESNI

**Sedchabke** (SEHD-chahb-keh) - Mind stop
A drug that both paralyzes the body and inhibits all use of magic. A tool of discipline for errant mages.

WORDS & PHRASES - ZANNIB

**Anah im-ghabr** (ah-NAH im-GAHB-er) - Flower of the head
The turban, common but not universal headgear among the Zannib.
**Biziz** (bee-ZEEZ)
A merchant caravan.

**Biziz Rahr** (bee-ZEEZ RAH-er) - Big caravan
The Grand Caravan that runs three seasons of the year from Qawrash im-Dhal through eastern Kigali and *sarq*-Zannib.
**Bunnas** (boon-NAHSS)
A low wild shrub native to *sarq*-Zannib whose berries are collected and dried as part of the *taridiqa*, the annual migration. The infusion of ground, dried, berries in hot water is high in caffeine. Popular throughout the southern countries and a significant trade item for *sarq*-Zannib.
**Ghuzl mar-Tawirqaj** (GOOZ-el mar tah-weer-KAHJ) - Circle of Speakers
The national tribal assembly in Ussha.
**Jarghal, Jarghalti** (jar-GAHL(-tee))
The title for a master wizard (wizardress).
**Kamah, Kamahab** (kah-MAH, kah-mah-HAHB) - Tent, Tents
A small one or two person tent used for rapid travel.
**Kassa** (KAHS-sah)
A bushy plant grown on mountain slopes, the leaves of which are used, dried, for a stimulating infusion.
**Kazr, Kazrab** (KAH-zer, kahz-RAHB) - Yurt, Yurts
A structure similar to a yurt, made of a wooden framework encased in felt.
**Khash** (KHASH)
The curved sword that is the typical weapon of the nomadic Zannib.
**Lij, Lijti** (LEEJ, LEEJ-tee) - Sir, Lady
A term of respect. *Lij-mar-lij*—Master of masters. Derived from Kigali *li* and *ju*—Country-king.
**Lud** (LOOD)
Numinous objects or locations, often referred to as "little gods."
**Nal-Jarghal** (nahl-jar-GHAHL)
The title for an apprentice wizard.
**Qahulaj, qahulajti** (kah-hoo-LAHJ(-tee)) - Taboo (m, f)
Wizard-tyrant, one who does taboo things.
**Sarq-Zannib** (SAHRK-zahn-NEEB)
The Zannib nation.
**Taridiqa** (tah-ree-DEE-kah)
The annual seasonal migration performed by the traditional Zannib of the central region.

**Wirqiqa-Zannib** (weer-KEE-kah-zahn-NEEB)
The Zannib language.

**Zamjilah** (zahm-jee-LAH) - Eye of heaven
The central crown at the top of the *kazr* that holds the rafters together and lets the smoke escape.

**Zan** (ZAHN)
An individual member of the Zannib nation.

**Zannib-hubr** (zahn-NEEB HOOB-er) - Free or Swift Zannib
The Zannib who continue a nomadic tradition of annual migration.

**Zannib-taghr** (zahn-NEEB TAHG-er) - Slow Zannib
The Zannib who live a settled life.

**Zarawinnaj** (zah-rah-wee-NAHJ) - One who rides in front
The leader of the *taridiqa*.

**Zudiqazd** (zoo-dee-KAHZD)
The winter camp, from which the *taridiqa* begins and ends. It houses those who do not go on the migration.

# IF YOU LIKE THIS BOOK…

## MORE GOODIES

You can find **more information** and **maps** at:
KarenMyersAuthor.com/link-on-a-crooked-track/.

Continue reading for an **excerpt** of the first chapter of **To Carry the Horn**, the first book in **The Hounds of Annwn** series, and find out more about it here:
KarenMyersAuthor.com/link-to-carry-the-horn/.

Sign up for the **newsletter** to stay informed of new and upcoming releases and to get occasional bonuses, like free short stories:
KarenMyersAuthor.com/signup.

Let other readers know what you think by leaving them a review where you bought the book.

## CONTACTING THE AUTHOR

You can contact Karen Myers at KarenMyersAuthor.com or by email at KarenMyers@KarenMyersAuthor.com. You can also follow her on Facebook: Facebook.com/KarenMyersAuthor.

# ALSO BY KAREN MYERS

## The Hounds of Annwn

To Carry the Horn
The Ways of Winter
King of the May
Bound into the Blood

*Story Collections*
Tales of Annwn

*Short Stories*
The Call
Under the Bough
Night Hunt
Cariad
The Empty Hills

## The Chained Adept

The Chained Adept
Mistress of Animals
Broken Devices
On a Crooked Track

## Science Fiction Short Stories

Second Sight
Monsters, And More
The Visitor, And More

See KarenMyersAuthor.com for the latest information.

# EXCERPT FROM TO CARRY THE HORN

## The Hounds of Annwn: 1

## Available from Karen Myers and Perkunas Press

*Prologue*

I did it! He's finally gone, dead, finished. A few snicks and snecks, and there he was on the ground, wasn't he, throat twitching. And they just stood around, didn't they, deluded like fools by the spell, that wonderful spell he gave me, he was right about it, all those hounds and nothing they could do.

The mighty prince. Ha. One less for you. I remember how he helped you hold him down before you cut him open…

Hush, hush, no, don't think about that.

He won't be holding anyone down anymore, will he, no, not him. Not with those hands. I've got them now. I have my own plans for you, don't I.

Time to run all the way home now. They'll never catch me, I'm too clever, I'm too slick.

Such a long time to wait but we're all ready now.

❧

Misplacing a pack of hounds was not on George's "to do" list this morning.

"Come on, Mosby, get moving," he said. "I don't know how they got way over there either, but you can hear 'em. Let's roll."

He leaned forward, using his legs to urge the horse into a canter on the narrow trail. The damp grass muffled the rhythmic pounding and filled the air with a tangy mid-autumn scent. Most of the leaves were still clinging to the trees, and the wild grape vines, draped wherever the sunlight penetrated, obscured his view, but he could clearly hear hounds giving tongue off in the distance. Sounded like the whole pack was on. One voice would lift, then several in chorus, then single voices again. As always, the hairs on

285

the back of his neck rose. They were somewhere on the far side of the woods, and the trail looked like it was headed in that direction.

He turned his head at a flash of white and the sound of twigs breaking to watch a big whitetail bound across the path before him. He sailed over a fallen branch, then spun around to stare at him boldly.

A magnificent buck—what a rack, twelve points at least, George thought, turning to admire him as he rode by. Why's he just standing there looking at me, with his great brown eyes and his flared nostrils? What's he waiting for?

As he cantered past he swung his attention back to the front, startled to find two small trees lying fallen together across the trail just a couple of strides away. He hastily settled himself for the jump, his gaze fixed on the topmost part that his horse would need to clear, and beyond. Not until Mosby rose to spring easily over the barrier did it occur to him that he might better have spared a glance upward, as a high branch materialized from the side and swept him out of the saddle.

❧

The fall knocked the wind out of him when he hit the ground, with a thump to his head. He paused before trying to move, taking stock. Nothing felt broken. He rolled to the side and pushed himself up, his snug knee-high boots making it awkward to bend his legs fully as the calf muscles swelled. This wasn't the first time he'd come off a horse and he felt it in the usual places. The woods had pulled back into a little opening after the fallen trees, and the glare from the sunlight made him blink. Odd. He'd had the impression that the trees were still enclosing the trail after the jump when he looked ahead as Mosby rose.

He tried to clear his head and focused on the sound of a horse grazing. Good, at least Mosby had stayed with him instead of running off in a panic after losing his rider. The reins trailed on the ground and he heard the bit clattering as the horse munched around it.

He limped stiffly over, picked up the reins, and led Mosby forward a few steps, looking for injuries or any evidence of impeded movement, but the horse seemed sound. Well, that's a blessing. Better me sore than him.

He couldn't hear the hounds anymore, nor John's horn. Couldn't hear the foxhunt at all. Maybe catching up wasn't going to be so simple. He could already imagine the lecture he'd be getting from the huntsman for letting this happen.

John needed to know about his delay. He pulled his cellphone out of his hunt coat's inner pocket. No signal, as usual.

Off came the leather riding gloves, and he used his thumbs to type a brief text message describing what had happened and where he was headed. The cellphone would look for a signal every few minutes and would forward the text if it found one. Out of habit he pulled out the pocket watch chained through his vest's buttonhole to check its time against the cellphone. He stood a moment, running his thumb across the engraving of St. George and the dragon on the back of the watch before returning it to his vest. As he shuffled the cellphone to his left hand to put it away, it dropped from his fingers—his old injury kicking in again. He bent stiffly to pick it up.

Standing there with the leather reins in his hand, he put his gloves back on, turning around to see where he'd fallen. He wasn't going to take that jump again, but maybe there was a way past it that rejoined the trail.

The tangle of tall pokeberry bushes on the edge of this little clearing were thick and unbroken. No trail was visible, much less any downed trees.

That can't be right.

He continued turning in a full circle and scanned the woods all around, methodically. There were two openings for paths, but both were on the far side from him and no fallen trees were visible from here. Still holding the reins and bringing Mosby with him, he walked all along the margin, peering past the thickets whose leaves were just starting to turn color.

When he stood at the openings of the two paths, he found he could see some distance along them. They were true rides, larger and better defined than deer trails, but without droppings or hoof prints to show that any horses had traveled them recently.

A shiver went through him and his stomach tightened. There was no way into this spot, other than the rides he hadn't used.

Well, George, pick a path and worry about it later. You have to get to the hounds.

He'd been headed west when he last had a clear sense of direction. His hand reached back into his other inner pocket for his GPS tracker. Power, no signal. That's strange, he thought, as he put it back. All it has to do is line-of-sight up to a satellite, not find some cell tower on the ground. It's usually reliable.

Good thing I brought backup, he thought. He hauled out a small, well-worn brass compass from his left vest pocket, attached where a fob would have been on his watch chain.

Using his compass he confirmed that the right-hand path started in a westerly direction, toward where he'd last heard the hounds. Alright, he thought, the sensible plan is to just try and get out of the woods directly so that I can orient myself and make contact with the hunt as quickly as possible.

He led his horse back away from the margin a few feet into the clearing. He checked the saddle girth, then tossed the reins over his horse's head. At six foot four George was used to looking over a horse's back from the ground but gray Mosby, a Percheron/Thoroughbred cross, stood 17.2 hands high at the withers, or just two inches short of six feet.

You'd think someone my size would have less trouble mounting but I had to fall for a horse too tall for me, just like everyone else, he thought. He'd been unable to resist the dark smoky dappled gray gelding with his silvery mane. As Mosby aged he would gradually lighten until he became white. Always going to be a problem keeping a white horse clean, but he's worth it. "Aren't you, boy?" The horse cocked his near ear back at the sound of his voice.

George lifted his left foot into the stirrup, careful to keep the toe of his boot away from Mosby's ribs. With his hands on the front and back of the saddle, he bounced on his right toes twice for momentum and hoisted himself up, swinging his right leg over and settling into the saddle with a comforting creak of leather.

He adjusted the fit of his hard hunt cap. Time to get back to where I belong.

⌘

George roughly remembered the layout of this property from his years of adolescent trespass, but it was a big place, several thousand acres, and many of the details had dimmed over time. This wooded covert was new to him, but no private woodland in this part of Virginia was very large. Can't cost me but a few hundred yards to get clear of all this, he thought.

His current trail was clearly intended for horseback, with no tight spots. Even so, he held Mosby to a walk, trotting where he could, since the path was unfamiliar. *Too late cautious, but I'm not going to be surprised a second time.* He watched for the thinning of the trees ahead, eager to get out and see the Blue Ridge to the west.

The woods seemed to extend into dimness indefinitely in this direction, and the mid-October day was turning cooler.

He checked his compass again. *Still going west, not in a circle, so how's it possible I'm not out by now? These woods weren't here twenty years ago, but these trees are older than that.* He thought about retracing his steps and trying the other path from the clearing, but he knew it went in the wrong direction, or at least started that way.

*Alright, then, when in doubt, double down. Let's pick up the pace.* He sent Mosby forward at a stronger trot, using his horse's momentum to rise in the saddle on every other stride to smooth the movement as he'd been doing all his life.

The ground began to fall away to the south, the trees finally opened up a bit, and the path entered another small clearing which was not, he noted with some relief, the one he'd started from.

As he brought Mosby to a halt to recheck his bearings, a nearby rustle on the right caught his attention. George saw two hounds just inside the woods, all by themselves. They ran silently into the clearing, looking for scent.

His years as a whipper-in took hold and he lifted his hand with the furled whip in a warding-off gesture, saying, "Get back to 'im," in an authoritative tone, to send them back to the pack and its huntsman. The hounds glanced up at him in acknowledgment and turned back in the direction they came from, but he hardly noticed, stunned.

*Those aren't our hounds, not white hounds with red ears. I thought those were mythical.* He chuckled uncertainly, remembering the Welsh tales his father had told him when he was a child. He looked around at the trees, the sunlight flickering on the autumn leaves as the breeze caught them. It all seemed very ordinary. *Well, I suppose it can hardly be the Wild Hunt, in broad daylight. Maybe someone's lost dogs?* They looked like working hounds, though.

He glanced down at the hounds on the buttons of his coat. *Maybe they're Talbot hounds,* he grinned. *If I'm wandering dream-*

ing in an endless woods, might as well have the legendary beasts of grandfather's ancient family to keep me company.

Wouldn't he be pleased at my invoking the old lineage, back to the Norman Conquest. He smiled wryly. Better never tell him I think a man should do his own deeds, not lean on those of his ancestors.

Still, he sat up straight like a Talbot of old, and headed after the errant hounds, seeking enlightenment.

The couple of hounds led George to the edge of the trees at last. He picked his way after them with care and paused to take in the view, a welcome relief after the enclosed woods.

He gazed southwest down a gradual slope of upland meadow. Glancing right automatically, he was relieved to see the smoky wall of the Blue Ridge, running north-south like a compass line laid out on the earth. From this angle the ridge line seemed quite high and completely wooded. The air was crisp and clean, with a chill rising despite the cloudless sky.

His eyes followed the two hounds, obediently loping down the slope ahead of him. Before him was a familiar scene of hounds and riders, but this wasn't the Rowanton Hunt. Several hunters were dismounted, gathered around someone on the ground while others held their horses.

He examined the riders more carefully. What's with the clothing, he wondered. They look like reenacters for a Revolutionary War event—tricorns, long coats, and bright colors.

A small group of mounted men near the hounds wore something that seemed to be hunt livery, green frock coats, longer than any he had ever seen in use, with prominent turned-back cuffs, and brown boots that rose over the knee.

The nearest hunt servant glanced up as the two hounds rejoined the pack and looked along their back trail, spotting George sitting his horse at the edge of the woods above him. He called out to one of the men standing over the fallen figure and pointed. The standing man followed his gesture and then dispatched two of the riders next to him up the slope.

George quelled his momentary panic at the strangeness of the scene and stood his ground. That must be the master of this hunt, he thought, by the way he gives orders. Who are these people, and what are they doing on Bellemore land?

As the riders cantered up the slope, he got a closer view of their gear. Swords and long hunting knives? That's eccentric even for a private pack. These clothes look genuine, worn and comfortable, not stiff and unused like costumes.

The hair rose on the back of his neck and for a moment he had to resist the urge to turn and flee. His pride stiffened him, that, and the knowledge that Mosby wasn't built for speed. Whatever this is, it's real, he told himself. Deal with it.

He decided to take them at face value, kicked his rational disbelief firmly into the back of his mind to await a better moment, and rode forward slowly to meet them.

He stopped just before the first rider reached him and looked him over as he approached. The man was tall and dark, wearing a blue frock coat with a long buff inner vest. Must be what they call a weskit, George thought. He nodded to him, and they waited a moment for the second horseman, a brown-haired man on a bay gelding. They eyed his own gear in some puzzlement, though they said nothing about it.

The first rider bowed his head before speaking. "I'm Idris Powell, and this Ifor Moel. My lord Gwyn would speak with you, sir, if you please."

My lord Gwyn? Conscious of the revolver holstered at the small of his back under his coat, George briefly considered resisting, but what would be the point? Instead, he let his well-schooled Virginia manners take charge.

"My name's George Talbot Traherne, whipper-in for the Rowanton Hunt, and I seem to have gotten lost on Bellemore land."

"What's happened here?" he said, pointing with his chin at the fallen man. "I'd be glad to help, if I can."

The three of them cantered down to the group of standing men and the man in charge came forward to meet them. George dismounted to speak with him, not wanting to loom over him on horseback.

He saw a tall man accustomed to authority, lean and fit, with gray eyes in a dark weathered face and black hair starting to silver. He was dressed with dignity and quiet richness, his thigh-length coat of green wool cut away in front, partially covering a long matching waistcoat. The color matched the livery of the hunt staff, but the details were more elaborate and the cloth of higher quality.

His cream breeches were cut full for ease of movement. White sleeve ruffles extended beyond the coat sleeves with their broad turned up cuffs. He wore no stock around his neck, but his shirt collar was closed by a green silk scarf. His high boots were brown and well worn.

He held himself rigid in some strong emotion as George approached, and said stiffly, "I'm Gwyn Annan, and this is my land. What's your business here? What do you know of this?" He pointed behind him.

George was startled to recognize the name but it was impossible to make sense of it—perhaps this was a cousin? He opened his mouth to tell him about the hunt meet today at this fixture, but before he could speak his eyes followed the gesture and he looked down at the fallen rider on the ground.

One motionless outstretched arm ended in an oozing stump. A reek of blood rose in the clear autumn air, more blood than he could see through the tangle of men standing around the body. Why, that fellow's been killed, he thought, shocked. This isn't from a fall.

Where are his hands?

George was speechless for a moment. Into the silence Idris Powell announced from horseback, "My lord, this is George Talbot Traherne. He declares himself a huntsman."

At the name, Gwyn's face froze, and he turned back to George.

"Who is your mother?" he asked, staring at him intensely.

George tore his attention from the dead man to the man before him, puzzled by the question and the focus of his attention. "Léonie Annan Talbot." He stressed the "Annan."

"And hers?"

"Georgia Rice Annan. I was named for them both."

Gwyn Annan closed his eyes briefly, and bowed. "Welcome, kinsman."

## Find out more about this book here:

KarenMyersAuthor.com/link-to-carry-the-horn/

TO CARRY THE HORN

# ABOUT THE AUTHOR

Karen Myers is a fantasy and science fiction author, best known for her heroic fantasy novels.

After a degree in Comparative Mythology from Yale University and a career as an industry pioneer building software companies, she has devoted herself to writing speculative fiction. Her stories feature heroes in real and imagined worlds filled with magic, space travel, and adventure.

When she's not writing, she enjoys hunting, fishing, photography, and playing her fiddle.

Karen lives with her husband, dogs and cats in an old log cabin in the mountains of central Pennsylvania, surrounded by wildlife. Bears, coyotes, deer, and possums visit often, and when she fiddles on her porch, the wild turkeys talk back.

She can be reached at KarenMyers@KarenMyersAuthor.com.